Mongolian Plateau
in the Late 12th Century

KHINGAN MOUNTAINS

Argun River
Jadarats
Jalairs
Tartars

Lake Buyr
Lake Dalai
Onon River
Kerulen River
Argun River

Onguts

Zhongdu
(Beijing)

Chin Empire

The Great Wall

Lake Baikal

Mongols

Taichiuts
Keraits
Tula River

Yellow River

GOBI DESERT

Qori Tumad

Merkids

Selenga River
Orkhon River

Oyirats

Shisha Kingdom
(Tanguts)

KHANGAI MOUNTAINS

Naimans

ALTAI MOUNTAINS

Uighurs

1:14,800,000

D1158633

GENGHIS KHAN

The World Conqueror

VOLUME I

By

Sam Djang

Printed in the United States of America

ISBN-13: 978-0-9846187-0-5 (Volume I, case bind)
ISBN-13: 978-0-9846187-1-2 (Volume I, perfect bind)
ISBN-13: 978-0-9846187-2-9 (Volume II, case bind)
ISBN-13: 978-0-9846187-3-6 (Volume II, perfect bind)

Library of Congress Control Number: 2010932313

Contents

Preface

Human history could be distorted. The intentional, or unintentional, distortion of history has happened in the past, present and, possibly, in the eternal future. The exact reasons for this are varied, but one important explanation is that people tend to try to understand history from their own point of view. A respectable person to one group of people could be a sworn enemy to another; a historical and greatly influential figure to some could be meaningless to others. Someone identified as a hero in a certain era could be perceived as anything other than that in times that follow. Once we accept it as truth that self-protection and selfishness are a basic part of human nature, we will realize how hard it is to accept historical facts that could be detrimental to our own sense of self, community and culture. It is also hard to pass fair judgment on historical facts of which we have no eye witness.

One year, in the 1990s, I had a chance to see the Genghis Khan exhibit on display at the Natural History Museum in Los Angeles. Within this exhibit, I had a chance to see historical relics, remains, photos and records related to Genghis Khan. Observing these historical artifacts and information inspired the writer in me. Immediately following that experience, I began intensive research on Genghis Khan, his history and his lineage, which took me eight years to complete. During my period of research, I took numerous trips to Mongolia, Russia, China and related countries. My research in these countries led me to read hundreds of articles and related books, and to interview numerous people in Mongolia, including scholars and college professors. After all this effort and time, I finally arrived at a conclusion regarding the life of Genghis Khan, which happened to be the exact same conclusion the American historian Owen Lattimore had declared years ago. He proclaimed that, "The greatest conqueror in human history is Genghis Khan."

I think the history of Genghis Khan has been distorted, belittled and depreciated in many ways. Some of the ignorant accusations describe him as "the Scourge of God," "the Destroyer of Civilization" or "the Warmonger." Anyone who looks at his in-depth history will inevitably discover that none of those descriptions are accurate. How could there be such vast and negative misconceptions of this man? One explanation is that most of his recorded history was probably written by his enemies. In many parts of the world it is still taboo to even mention his name, for a variety of false reasons. When we compare all the great conquerors and their empires of the past, Genghis Khan and his Mongol Empire are outstanding. He was the greatest among all Emperors and no other nation, besides his Mongol Empire, has made as great an impact on the world. He was the only successful one and a true victor in the end.

The size of the land he had conquered in his lifetime was 2.2 times bigger than that of Alexander the Great, 6.7 times bigger than that of Napoleon Bonaparte and 4 times bigger than the Roman Empire. Also, the Mongol Empire, which his descendants continued to expand in later times, was the biggest empire in history by the time of A.D. 2010. The actual size of the Mongol Empire was 13,754,663 square miles (the potential conquered land was 14,493,569 square miles) and the 19th-century British Empire comes in second, in size, at 12,788,632 square miles.

The kingdom of Alexander the Great was torn to pieces by his generals after his death, Napoleon had been exiled to the island of St. Helena after losing the battle at Waterloo and Hitler's glory did not last more than three years. The Mongol Empire continued to grow after the rule of Genghis Khan because of the strength of the empire he built.

The greatness of the Mongol Empire is represented by their success in opening trade between the East and the West. The most meaningful and influential items in human civilization, such as paper, gunpowder and the compass had been transferred from the East to the West. Among many other important items are Arabic numerals, the concept of mathematics, astronomy and the manufacturing technique of glasses that went from the West to the East. Marco Polo's visit to the city of Dadu (Beijing), which had marked the turning point of Western history, was made during the Kubilai Khan's time, the golden age of the Mongol Empire. The voyage of Christopher Columbus, which introduced the existence of the American continent to Europeans, after all, was related, directly or indirectly, to Marco Polo's travels.

Before the emergence of the Mongol Empire, it was considered very unsafe to travel from the Italian Peninsula to the city of Dadu (Beijing) in China, in a small group, which Marco Polo, his father and his uncle made frequently.

This book was written in the form of a historical novel, and yet, 90 percent of its contents are based on the sensible, true story. The only elements that have been fictionalized are the areas that recorded history does not tell, mostly in the early part of his life. I sincerely hope the readers of this book do not judge or measure him based on our modern standards. If so, this could lead to further misunderstandings about him. Thank you very much for reading.

CHAPTER ONE

Will of God

On the northeastern part of the Eurasian continent, bordered by Lake Baikal to the north and the Gobi Desert to the south, lies the vast steppe, which endlessly stretches westward all the way to the heart of Europe, Hungary and Poland. Upon this sea of grassland, the scenery is nothing but an endless horizon and low hilly elevations of earth, blown by dry winds all through the year, leaving the land barren and arid.

People had lived there since the dawn of mankind, and, like in other parts of the world, they relied on hunting and animal husbandry for a living. They were herders of cattle, horses, camels, sheep and goats, and they migrated from one place to another with the change of each season. These nomadic people represented a strong contrast to the sedentary settlers who had built houses and stayed in one place.

If a boy saw the age of three, he was already a horse-rider, and when he became big enough to lift weapons, he was a warrior.

Sometimes these nomads grouped themselves into a huge mass and attacked sedentary people like city dwellers; otherwise, they dispersed throughout a large area and lived peacefully.

In the twelfth century, the Mongolian Plateau was rampant with unrest. The massive group of nomads had divided themselves into hundreds of different clans and tribes, resulting in constant conflict, leaving them to battle one another for survival; they killed or were killed, each and every day. They turned to stealing and robbing and a man could not even trust his brothers. Pillaging, plundering, rape and mass murder were part of the daily routine and there was no guarantee of safety, not even for a single day. In this unstable, feudal society, eighty-one strong men were holding and sharing the power and were controlling the plateau. Even in the darkest times of ungodliness and violence, they did not give up hope. They were waiting for the savior who could put an end to all the disorder and chaos and fatefully lead them to a balanced and stable society.

The Onon River, originating from the heart of the Mongolian Plateau, becomes the largest river in eastern Siberia as it flows, joining all other branches, and finally running into the Pacific Ocean. The Onon River was the cradle for many forms of life and all through the seasons, these creatures gathered there and thrived.

On this upper part of the Onon River, spring had arrived as usual. Unlike the steppe, along the river, there were thickened forests inhabited by many different forms of wildlife. Around this forest of big and small shrubs, birches, poplars and larches, roved and prowled the bears, wolves, deer, foxes and gazelles. Over the placid river surface, a variety of winged migratory creatures would flock.

On top of the hill, where they could see the eastern side of the Onon River fading into the horizon, a man on his horse looked around the area. He was wearing a brown sheepskin coat, white fox-fur cap, and long-necked, dark-brown boots called gutul. He seemed to be out for falconry, for one hunting hawk was perched on his left shoulder. He had a broad forehead, thick eyebrows, sparkling eyes and a good-sized straight nose along with his suntanned skin that had been dried by the hot desert wind. With these features, he appeared to be a balanced and good-looking man. He surely seemed to be a steppe aristocrat due to the extraordinary garments he was wearing, and his reason for being there. Falconry was reserved for only the steppe aristocrats.

Though it was late spring, the early morning wind was quite chilly, and you could see his cheeks flushed with red. Yesugei was his name. They called him Yesugei Bagatur, which meant Yesugei the Brave. Bagatur was a title only for the aristocrats.

It was early in the morning and the sun was still hanging on the eastern horizon. Yesugei saw a group of people traveling along the riverbank, with the rising sun on their backs. He could not see them very well because of the glare of the strong morning sun in his eyes, so he approached the group with slow, careful motions to find out who they were. The group was made up of twelve to thirteen men on their horses and they were escorting a two-wheeled carriage pulled by a single horse. On the carriage was a framed structure that resembled a palanquin, with a pointed top and four walls, three of which were covered with a thick, purple silk curtain, with only the front left open. They were driving two to three extra horses that were all loaded with stacks of luggage, creating the impression that they were on a long journey. They were heavily armed with bows, spears and scimitars, the nomadic people's long, curved sword, which were hanging around their waists. They would not be considered a caravan because their luggage was that of the poor and they were over-armed to be simple travelers. Yesugei had reined in, halting his horse on the spot with a safe distance between him and the strangers. The strangers seemed surprised by the sudden appearance of Yesugei, and immediately held their reins while casting looks full of caution and hostility.

"Take it easy! I am unarmed. My name is Yesugei. Who the hell are you to trespass on my territory without my permission? Identify yourselves!"

It was common law at the time that caravans or travelers trying to pass through certain territories without permission from the ruler of that territory could be the target of attacks and plundering.

After these words, Yesugei took a close look at the group. Thirteen was the number of men, plus a woman sitting in the carriage. She appeared to be seventeen or eighteen years old and she was extraordinarily beautiful. She was clad in silk garments, embroidered luxuriously with flowers, but was wearing a man's thick sheepskin coat to cover them. From her head, numerous strands of beads and silver decorations were hanging down, long enough to reach her shoulders.

The woman's hair decorations and garments clearly demonstrated that this group was a newlywed couple and their armed bodyguards heading for the bridegroom's hometown. Yesugei watched her carefully and when she noticed his stare, she moved back quickly to hide herself. One man drove his horse a few steps forward and said, "My name is Chiledu. I am a Merkid. We are on a long journey back home. Allow us to pass through."

The man who introduced himself as Chiledu appeared to have a big and strong body, yet it was a mystery if he also had a strong heart.

He was the second man of the Merkids. The Merkids were a ferocious, forest-dwelling tribe, whose homes were in and around the forests near the Selenga River, south of Lake Baikal. He was lucky to get his second wife from the Olqunuud, the tribe whose base was near Lake Dalai, east of the Mongolian Plateau. The Olqunuud was the sub-clan of the Onggirad, whose territory covered the area between the Gobi Desert and the Great Wall of Cathay. Their women were well-known for their well-trained manner, virtuousness, fair skin and beauty. Chiledu's new and second wife was of noble birth, the daughter of one of the chieftains of that tribe. He and his men were on a fifteen-day journey back home to the Selenga River. Chiledu had handpicked his bodyguards before leaving his hometown. The twelve he chose were believed to be the best.

Chiledu had three options. One way was going straight to his hometown by the Selenga River, taking a direct northwestern route. This was the shortcut. However, high mountains and thick forests blocked it, so it was considered too tough for the newlywed bride, who was carrying many belongings. The second choice was to detour all the way down to the southern part of the mountains and then change course to the north. This route was also considered inappropriate, as it would be a long journey and would take them through an area of frequent conflicts and battles among the local tribes.

The third choice was the only one considered possible. They were to go straight to the west, cross the mountain, and then change course to due north.

"But with this route, don't you think we have to pass through the territory of the Mongols?"

Before his departure, of course Chiledu had a discussion with his men. Chinua, his right-hand man, was against this decision.

"You are right. We have to cross the Onon River at the earliest possible time. If everything goes right, we can cross the river at the farthest point from their ordu. We had better cross it before dawn, and get out of there at the earliest time possible. If not, we could be exposed to them and could be in trouble. Let's leave all of this to God's will."

"Ordu" means the tribal base camp, town or city. They started like this. At the time, a wedding journey could be very dangerous. At any time, by sudden attack from enemies or other unfriendly tribal members, the bride could be abducted and the dowry stolen in a matter of moments. Dangers were everywhere. Chiledu considered two or three hundred bodyguards at first. However, he picked only twelve men for fast mobility and minimum exposure. Twelve was the right number, he believed.

The woman's name was Ouluun. She was a born of Olqunuud's noble blood, a ruling family. She was smart and had extreme beauty. At the time, steppe women were not allowed to choose their own men; their parents did, mostly the father. The protection and security of their tribes were of the utmost importance for the steppe and desert people at this time. It was because of this that the traditions of marriage had been developed. Marriages between the same blood and bone were not allowed among the steppe aristocrats. They could only marry someone of different ancestry, or marry by the principles of exogamy. Nobody knows when this tradition began; however, it seemed to be based on the need for security because two tribes, socially combined by marriage, could be stronger than the individual tribes. By the order of the chieftain of Olqunuud, Ouluun was given to Chiledu, sworn brother of Toktoa Beki, who was one of the strongest men in the northern part of the Plateau.

After a seven-day journey, they arrived at the planned point, somewhere along the upper part of the Onon River. However, the river had risen due to the increased volume of water coming from the melting snow and ice covering the upper mountain area. It was the thaw of springtime and they had not planned on that. They could not cross the river at the point they intended and that led them to moving further upriver. This is how they came across Yesugei.

"If you are on a long journey, what is the purpose? Tell me! If you don't, I have no other choice but to treat you as spies."

Chiledu hesitated; he could not give an answer right away. He did not want Yesugei to know that this was his wedding journey. At this moment, Chinua approached him and whispered in his ear. "Let me get rid of this man! It will be easier and safer."

Chiledu tried to stop him. "No! I think I know him. He is one of the powerful Mongol chieftains. We could be in trouble later if we kill him."

However, it was too late. Before Chiledu could finish speaking, quick-tempered Chinua picked up one of his arrows and shot at Yesugei. Yesugei ducked his head and dodged Chinua's arrow. The next moment, he turned around, spurred strongly on the ribs of his steed and began to run away with lightning speed. A moment later, a second arrow went flying, but it did not hit Yesugei or his horse. Yesugei was very experienced in such situations and knew how to escape.

Yesugei arrived at his ordu with his blood boiling. It was not caused by the attack, but because of the woman he saw on the carriage. *"The woman is mine. Look! My heart is pounding. I will surely take that woman."*

Yesugei called Daritai, his younger brother. "Get thirty armed men ready, immediately! Big brother Nekun, too."

Yesugei began to chase down Chiledu's group with his thirty armed men and his brothers. Chiledu crossed the Onon River and was on the way to making his escape. "Once we get to that hill, we may find woods and rocks where we can hide and protect ourselves."

Chiledu pushed his men, but Ouluun's two-wheeled carriage could not speed up. Before they could reach the hill, the images of the chasers began to show up on the scene. As time went by, it became more and more clear that Chiledu was in trouble.

"Master, go ahead with your bride. We will stop them here."

Chinua neared Chiledu and urged him to go on. Chiledu agreed and continued on his way with his bride. Chinua and the other eleven men remained at that very spot, preparing for one decisive battle. They knew the chances were not in their favor. They began to shoot arrows toward the approaching thirty-three armed men. The two groups of nomads fought for their lives, embodying their loyalties. Though the bright spring sunlight was pouring over the field, the air was cold, as if it were foretelling the massacre that would happen at any moment.

It was a quiet day with no winds. Only the shrieking sounds of neighing horses and the clanging of metallic weapons echoed into space. Chinua, the last man standing on Chiledu's side, fell from his horse, speared in his waist by Nekun. Daritai immediately jumped down from his horse and sliced his jugular with a dagger. A stream of blood blended into the dry, thirsty earth mixed with desert sands. Soon, everything became quiet, which meant no more resistance. Nobody could stop Yesugei and his brothers now.

Chiledu and Ouluun saw three men were coming. They knew that everything was over. Ouluun, looking up at Chiledu, said, "My lord, don't you see those three men? They will surely kill you. Please, leave! Quick! Wherever you go, you will find women. Forget about me. Save your life!" After these words,

Ouluun took off her purple scarf and handed it over to Chiledu. "Go with my scent. When you find a new maiden, you can name her Ouluun. Please, save your life. Go now!"

Chiledu was afraid. He thought Ouluun was quite right. He strongly struck the ribs of his dun and left there hastily. His dun was a swift one. Even after passing over seven hills, Yesugei and his two brothers could not catch him. Chiledu's image diminished and finally faded away into the horizon.

Ouluun was wailing when Yesugei and his two brothers returned to her carriage. Her wailing seemed to stir up the Onon River and shake the woods. "Why has this happened to me? How can this horrible thing happen to me?"

Yesugei and Nekun were leading the carriage and Daritai was riding beside the shaft. Ouluun's wailing and cursing and lamentation never ended. The three men ignored it.

Woman,
The man who had embraced you,
Has gone forever.

Even though you lament,
He will not return.

Even though you cry hard,
It cannot be heard by him.

Even though he looks back,
He cannot even see your shadow.

Even though you run and run after him,
His figure will not be found.

He has gone far, far away,
Over the river, over the hill.

Ouluun, after wailing for so long, suddenly raised her head and began to yell at Yesugei and his two brothers.

"Why has this happened to me? How can this horrible thing happen under the heavens? He did not do anything wrong!"

In response to her words, Yesugei, who was guiding at the front, paused and looked back for a while with mixed feelings of sympathy and disagreement showing on his face. He slowly drove his horse close to Ouluun's carriage and spoke in a low tone.

"He didn't do anything wrong? How silly! He was an intruder. We attack anyone who trespasses on our territory without permission. Furthermore, they tried to kill me first, and I was unarmed. You saw it! Be quiet, please!"

Nobody knows what happened to Chiledu after that. It is like he disappeared into the horizon; he faded away from the stage of history. Nobody knows if he actually named his next woman Ouluun, either.

He was the second man of the Merkids, and yet he couldn't do anything, because at the time, the Mongols were too strong. Even if he wanted to retaliate, Toktoa Beki, the chief of the Merkids, probably would not have allowed him. Retaliating against the Mongols could have created a big disaster for them.

Yesugei was one of the powerful men on the plateau at that time. In addition, he was the anda, or sworn brother, to Toghrul who was the khan of the Kerait, the most powerful tribe. The Mongols were merely one of the many tribes of that time; however, after Genghis Khan's rise and unification of the entire region, the name "Mongol" began to represent all the groups of people on the plateau.

Yesugei was returning to his ordu. When they had reached the hill with the view of the whole city of domed tents, Yesugei stopped and looked down below the hill for a moment. Below his feet lay a vast plain, embraced by the winding Onon River and covered by the eternal blue sky. It was late afternoon and the sun's angled rays were pouring on the plain, and the land was reflecting back a sparkling, dazzling, light-green hue imbued with earthy brown. On the plain, numerous mushroom-shaped felt tents, or yurts, were spread out in every direction in a very orderly way. They were arranged in a radiating pattern around a huge, oval-shaped open ground. High-pitched cries from sheep keepers and herd boys, as they were drawing back their flocks and herds, closing the day, echoed faintly into the space. Golden clouds of dust, stirred up by moving the numerous flocks and herds, were reflecting the dazzling late afternoon sunlight.

Children and dogs were the first groups who came out to see Yesugei and his returning brothers when they arrived near the entrance of the town. Children were shouting and running after the two-wheeled carriage with great curiosity, because the carriage seemed unfamiliar and rather luxurious to them. Behind the children, the dogs were following, barking noisily around it. Yesugei and his brothers ignored the children's and dogs' reactions and trotted along the street lined by yurts. The women and elders of the town stopped working to look at this unusual happening, as others, inside the yurts, did the same thing through half-opened flap doors. They eyed the woman sitting in the carriage being led by Yesugei, the chief of the town, with great curiosity. A number of men and women were waiting for him when he arrived at his yurt, which was located at the northernmost end of the town.

After handing over Ouluun to the group of women, Yesugei asked his men about casualties of the fight.

"Five wounded and no one killed. Excellent result, my lord; the wounded are taking a rest in their yurts after emergency treatment."

Yesugei was satisfied. He issued an order to distribute enough top-quality beef and mutton for a fifteen-day supply, two bottles of Chinese rice wine and a roll of silk to each of the wounded. At that time, in his storage houses, mountains of goods were stacked that had been collected from the caravans as taxes. Yesugei's ordu consisted of fifteen thousand households with twenty thousand yurts.

Those were amazing numbers at that time and they were only increasing. This growth showed clearly that Yesugei was one of the most popular leaders on the steppe. Yesugei announced a feast. The sun had set over the western mountains. The vault of the sky was already turning into deep, darkish blue and crimson, with the evening glow emerging from above the faraway western and southern hills, covering the plain like an aurora. From the eastern sky, the night was gradually coming on like a dark silk curtain and the crescent moon was hanging above the hills. A dry, heated evening wind was beginning to blow from the desert area. Numerous campfires were alight on the huge open ground located at the center of the town. The men and youth from the day's hunting team began to skin their game, such as deer and gazelle, for barbecuing. The women and girls were busy delivering food and lambskin bags filled with kumis, fermented mare's milk. The feast began.

Yesugei appeared before the crowd with his two brothers and the chief priest of the town, Aman. Upon his arrival, the men and young ones gave out great cheers and the elders and women clasped their hands. Some soldiers among them raised their spears and shields highly and waved them. After stepping onto the platform, Yesugei began to speak in a clear, strong tone.

"Brothers and sisters, and all my dear friends! Today we had a small conflict. The Merkids intruded on our territory. They were trespassing on our land without permission. Anyone who tries to pass through our territory needs our permission and must pay the taxes. There can be no exception to this policy. More importantly, they attacked me first, and I was unarmed. We punished them and they were completely destroyed. The damage to our side is slight. This clearly shows that heaven is helping us. We will all rejoice today; greatness for the Mongols!"

When Yesugei finished speaking, he stepped down from the platform while cheers erupted.

"Yesugei! Yesugei! Yesugei!"

Warriors repeatedly hammered their shields with fists and the crowds chanted "Yesugei," pushing their fists energetically into the air. The roaring lasted for some time and the shouting of hundreds, maybe thousands, of people was absorbed into the mysterious, inscrutable, deep blue sky like smoke.

Next to Yesugei, Aman, the chief priest and the prophet, stepped onto the platform. Aman was a shaman and his powers were enormous among the Mongols, who were, traditionally, of a shamanistic nature. He not only held all the ceremonies and rituals related to the good, and bad, things of the townspeople, but also blessed the soldiers heading for war. He was believed to be able to communicate with God and to prophesy. He was tall and thin and had slanted eyes and a crooked nose. His face was covered with numerous fine wrinkles and the color of his skin was deathly pale, because he spent most of his days in his yurt praying and meditating. For all the Mongols, both men and women, military service and labor were legal and moral obligations; yet the shamans were different. They were free from those obligations. Aman was wearing a cone-shaped, white silk hat with the flaps down to his shoulders as well as a white cloak. White was the sacred color for the Mongols and only the chieftains and the chief priests were allowed to wear it. From his neck was dangling a necklace with a shining bronze mirror, and in his hand was a stick made from white birch tree. All these things were believed to have the power to expel evil spirits. He raised both his hands highly and began to shout to the sky in a metallic voice.

Oh! The creator of the world,
The creator of all living things,
And the owner of the universe,
Tenggri,
The eternal god in heaven.
Who dares to stand in front of you?
Who dares to be against your will and deny your order?
The followers,
Shall bloom like an iris on a spring day.
The offenders,
Shall wither like grass on a winter day.
Your voice can reach to the abyss,
And your spirits are engraved in the rock.
Tenggri,
The almighty,
May you bless Yesugei.
Tenggri,
The greatest,
May you bless the Mongols.

As he was stepping down from the platform, the crowd began to chant as if they were awoken from sleep.

"Tenggri! Tenggri! Tenggri!"

The chanting lasted until Yesugei, his brothers and the shaman sat down in their seats, and the shouting echoed into the mysterious blue sky beyond the desert. They toasted with kumis, began to enjoy the barbecued game and steamed mutton. Women laughed openly, children hopped around in joy. The musicians began to play their two-stringed instruments, which made soft, smooth and lovely sounds, although sometimes made a strong, grand style of music. Some of the town's elderly cleared their voices and sang to the tune. The warriors and the young ones then began to dance to the drumbeat. They were tough like wild horses, fierce like boars and agile like stags. Their eyes were shining in the light of campfires, and beads of sweat began to stand out on their foreheads and necks. It seemed that they never tired. The feast continued. The desert night grew deeper and deeper while the women shrieked in mirth and the children shouted in joy.

It was late in the morning when Ouluun awoke. From her bed, she looked around the unfamiliar interior surroundings of the room. She was in a domed felt tent with two large purple pillars. In the center of the vault, there was a big hole for the egress of smoke and around this were numerous long and thick wooden rods placed in a radiating pattern to support the tent. The huge cylindrical inner wall of the tent was framed with thin, slender sticks, and on one side of the wall, there was a rectangular-shaped entrance opened to the south, which was covered with a thick felt flap replacing a wooden door. Between two large pillars was a bronze stove, and from it, a tendril of thin, light-gray smoke was dancing out, up through the center hole. To the north, there were two large, deep, red chests, side by side, and on each one of them was a bronze incense burner. On the floor, two snow-leopard skins were spread on each side of the bronze stove.

A young woman was sitting on a taboret beside Ouluun's bed, watching her quietly with a look of worry. As the woman noticed that Ouluun had woken up, she stood up slowly and asked with a soft and friendly tone of voice, "How do you feel?"

Ouluun gazed at her for a while without answering her question. The woman asked, "Are you hungry?"

Ouluun, still without answering, raised herself up and asked, "Where am I? How long have I been here?"

The woman answered, still with a soft and friendly tone, "My name is Sochigel. I am a companion to the lord Yesugei. You are in his second yurt. You have been in the same bed for two full days. Everyone was worried about you because you fell down when you arrived here."

The woman who introduced herself as Sochigel looked like she was not yet twenty years old, like Ouluun, and was portraying a soft and friendly image. Ouluun closed her eyes with grief as the painful memories came back to her mind. She kept her eyes closed for some time, but she did not weep. After she opened her eyes, Ouluun looked at Sochigel for a moment and then asked, "Are you his wife?"

"No, I am not. I am just his companion. He is not officially married yet."

"Are you a Mongol?"

"No, I am a Merkid. My parents were both Merkids. I lost both of my parents during the war. I have been here since I was sixteen. I am eighteen now and I have a son. His name is Bektor."

Ouluun pondered for a moment. If she was telling the truth, she surely was a prisoner of war or booty from the war between the Mongols and the Merkids. It was not uncommon in the steppe and desert society that a woman taken as a prisoner of war would become a wife to the enemy who killed her parents and would bear the enemy's children. It was the steppe law that the losers became slaves to the victors. Ouluun thought her situation not much different from Sochigel's. Ouluun thought about her fate from that moment forward. The uncertainty of the future turned into uneasiness and it squeezed into her mind like smoke.

"Your son is Yesugei's child, right?"

"Yes, that is correct."

"Then, why are you not his wife?"

"I was not born to a noble family. My parents were just commoners. The lord Yesugei wants his wife to be of noble birth."

Ouluun pondered a while. She knew that, in the steppe society, the aristocrats were ruled by the tradition of exogamy, which did not allow them to marry within their own lineage. Oftentimes they had to solicit from other tribes for their spouses. When this could not be accomplished in a peaceful manner, they had to do it by force. They practiced polygamy, too, which meant a man could have as many wives as he could afford. So, sometimes, conflicts arose among the tribes not because of territory, but because of women.

"Are you happy here?"

Ouluun asked this question of the woman as she was leaning back on a doubled pillow, after she raised the upper part of her body.

"I don't know. I have never asked myself that question. The only thing I know is that the lord Yesugei is quite a reasonable man. He has never given me a hard time and I have managed well, so far."

There was deep silence between the two women for a moment. Ouluun began to feel some kind of warmth from the woman, like camaraderie, due to their similar situations.

"Are you hungry?" Sochigel asked again and began to set out the food she had prepared. After she scooped up the millet soup, made with chopped beef and vegetables, from the iron pot, she gently poured it into a wooden bowl. She arranged it on a large wooden plate, along with a bowl of green tea with a touch of fresh milk. She carefully put the tray on Ouluun's lap.

"Help yourself, please, before it gets cold."

Ouluun realized that she was hungry and thirsty. She picked up the tea bowl and began to quench her thirst slowly. She could hear the faint sounds of children playing, herd boys shouting and the hooves of moving cattle pounding from afar, like in a dream.

CHAPTER TWO

The Man Called
Mamay

The Mongols were busy preparing for their migration to the summer grazing field after the crescent changed into the full moon and again began to wane. The nomads never built houses and settled down; instead, they migrated from one place to another with each season. This was partly to provide fresh grazing fields for their livestock, but mainly for the escape from the choking hot, dry winds coming from the deserts in summertime and from the biting cold coming from northern Siberia in winter. In springtime, they suffered through the gusts of wind creating thick dust and blowing sands from the north. Facing these winds caused choking that was oftentimes painful. This life was cruel and nature was not kind to them. They were forced to live in the constant fear of hunger, poverty and attacks from their enemies. The desert was only for the fire ants, snakes, scorpions and other creatures with special traits that made the desert an inhabitable place for them. God might not have created it for humans, but nobody knows. And yet, in this land with only the horrible emptiness of the plains, choking dry winds, biting cold, thick dusts and sands and hail, people have lived here since the time only God remembers. In this kind of environment, only the strong in mind and body could survive.

One day, in the afternoon, when the Mongols were busy preparing for the migration, a man on a horse was slowly approaching from the southern entrance. He was on a black horse and wearing a black bearskin coat and a cap made of animal fur, with the flaps folded up due to the hot weather. He had a relatively large body and his two big, dark, brown eyes, under the thick straight eyebrows, were sparkling in the reflected sunlight. His large, firmly closed mouth seemed to reveal his stubbornness, yet at the same time it showed that he was a man of conviction. Mainly, he looked wild and tough, and yet it was surprising that he was giving the impression of an intelligent man who had studied in the civilized cities of Cathay below the Great Wall. In his right hand he was holding a spear, firmly gripped, and dangling from either side of his waist were a scimitar and a Chinese dagger. He was also wearing a quiver on his back, in which a few arrows were showing. He looked tired, perhaps from the long journey, and yet, it seemed that his high spirit had not been exhausted. As he slowly passed along the road lined by yurts, he was carefully eyeing both sides. The town children followed him in great curiosity and several dogs barked noisily as they followed behind his horse's back hooves. Some people were surprised by the noise and opened their flap doors halfway to peer out to see what was going on. As he arrived at the center part of the open ground, he began to shout, rotating slowly.

"Yesugei, come out here! I am here to challenge you to a duel! If you are a man, come out and stand in front of me! Yesugei, where are you?"

As he was shouting the same thing again and again, rotating around the open ground, some of the townspeople began to gather, one by one, with great curiosity. At this moment, Yesugei was taking care of his horse equipment in front of his yurt, which was in the northernmost part of town. He was with his two brothers and heard the man's shouting from afar.

"What is that noise? What's going on?"

Frowning, Yesugei asked his men around him, again, what was going on. Since nobody knew what it was, they just shrugged their shoulders in silence. Without delay, Yesugei ordered one of his men to go and find out. The man with Yesugei's order got on the horse and galloped to the area where the noise originated. After a while, he came back and reported, "A man is looking for you, my lord. He wants to see you face to face."

"Face to face? Who is he? Is he alone?"

"I don't know who he is. I never saw him before. He looks like he is all by himself."

"Is he armed?"

"Yes, my lord. He is heavily armed."

Yesugei tried to figure it out who it could be, but failed. Their town was an open community. There was no gate. Sometimes they had uninvited visitors, mainly individuals or very small groups. Could it be a rover from the plain, or a lost hunter?

In either case, a man cannot demand to see Yesugei face to face.

"He must be a crazy one."

In response to this comment, some of the men laughed as if to agree. Yesugei then gave an order to another one of his men.

"Go fetch me a spear and a lasso."

Yesugei galloped to the open ground. He stood face to face with the man, leaving some distance. The two men on their horses were surrounded by hundreds of curious people, anxious to know what would happen next. The sun was sinking in the western sky, casting long shadows from both men. Yesugei spoke first.

"I am Yesugei, the one you are looking for. Who are you and what do you want?"

"My name is Mamay. I am Ouluun's brother. I am here to get my sister back. I know you have kidnapped her."

"Kidnapped? Nonsense! She is my prisoner. I won't let her go!"

"You won't? All right, then I will take your head instead!"

"Fine! Go ahead, if you can!"

The man in the bearskin coat took aim at Yesugei's heart with his spear and ran at him at full speed. At the same time, Yesugei's horse reared high, pushing its front legs strongly from the ground. Just before the tip of the stranger's spear would have penetrated Yesugei's heart, Yesugei dodged the weapon and successfully put the lasso around the neck of the stranger's horse. As a result, the stranger's horse, neighing loudly, stood on its hind legs. The next moment, losing balance, the stranger fell from his horse. The spectators, impressed by Yesugei's swift movement, clapped and cheered. Yesugei turned his horse and slowly approached the man on the ground.

"How was that? Do you have anything to say?"

Yesugei grinned as he was saying this. The stranger looked very embarrassed. He glared at Yesugei as he stood up and dusted himself off. Yesugei continued, "Do you still think you can beat me? If you want, I can give you a second chance. But this time, bare hands only."

Mamay agreed. After they took off their coats, they began a bout of a Mongolian wrestling match. It was one of the Mongolian traditions that when two men have a dispute and cannot come to an agreement, they are to have a wrestling match and the winner will have the right to decide the argument. Mongolian wrestling had strict rules and regulations, and yet, sometimes it was still very cruel. Almost all techniques were allowed except hitting the opponent with fists or elbows, holding their hair or biting. Oftentimes the Mongols used the wrestling match as a legitimate maneuver to remove their political enemies. In those cases, they would strangle their opponent to death in a standing position or would break their neck or spine.

The two men, with their arms lifted, their backs bent, staring into each other's eyes, took steps slowly and carefully, making a circle. This maneuvering was to wait for the moment their opponent would make even the smallest misstep, creating an opportunity to take control. For a while, there were no movements. Suddenly, Mamay's right arm was stretched over to grip Yesugei's neck. However, in a flash, Yesugei grabbed his opponent's wrist with his right hand and began to twist. Mamay turned his body to the side in pain. Yesugei began to constrict Mamay's neck with his left arm. This lasted for a while. However, with his strong left hand, Mamay unfolded Yesugei's arm, little by little, and eventually was able to free himself. Almost at the same time, Mamay turned his body swiftly, pushing off Yesugei's right hand, and grabbed Yesugei from behind.

Now it was Mamay's turn. Mamay began to constrict Yesugei's chest with his two strong arms. Yesugei could not breathe. On the sides of both men's necks, their veins swelled, wriggling like red worms, as beads of sweat ran down. Yesugei lowered himself down slowly to remove himself from the attack and when he reached a certain point, he raised his two arms high, pushing away Mamay's arms, and then swiftly turned around. Being taken aback by this, Mamay stepped back, reeling. The two men returned to their original positions. Hundreds of spectators gathered around, shouting in excitement and encouraging the duel.

The wrestling match continued. The two men's arms and backs, displaying well-developed muscles, were shining with heavy sweat. At that moment, something unexpected happened; Mamay's leather belt broke off and his pants slipped down. As his buttocks became exposed, some men giggled and some women turned their faces away, shrieking. Mamay picked up his pants with great embarrassment, and tried holding them with one of his hands, but the wrestling match could not go on. There was much laughter. Yesugei also laughed. As he was laughing out loud, Yesugei walked up to Mamay and tapped him on his shoulder.

The desert night fell upon the town of tents. The town had fallen into deep silence and terrible loneliness. Only feeble chirpings of insects echoed through the everlasting abyss of loneliness. The hot midday air was rapidly replaced with the cold, heartless air from the northern mountains and forests. Ouluun was sitting face to face with her elder brother, Mamay, in the yurt filled with dim light from an Arabian lamp. Near to them was a red Chinese tea table and on it was a Chinese-style teapot and porcelain cups. Next to this was a large silver plate on which Turkish dried dates and Chinese cookies were piled high. Ouluun was weeping. Tears fell down her cheeks and onto her silk garment, drop by drop. Mamay regarded her for a while without saying anything. At last, Mamay opened his mouth and began to talk in a quiet voice.

"Sister, Father and I decided to attack Yesugei when we heard something had happened to you. But Father gave up; he realized they were much stronger than us. All the elders of the ordu were against our retaliation too. It was not because we are cowards, but because we knew that we had to handle things carefully. Impulsive mobilizations of the troops could bring disaster to our ordu. The Merkids probably had to give up for the same reason. Yesugei is too strong now. He is very close to Toghrul Khan and that adds to the problem."

After speaking those words, Mamay sighed lightly. Mamay then went on to mention that Yesugei was one of the strongest men in that region, with twenty thousand yurts or more, and is the anda, or sworn brother, to Toghrul Khan, the most powerful man on the entire Mongolian Plateau. At that time, according to their customs, the anda relation meant a strong bond between two sworn brothers, not only in the sense of protecting each other when needed, but also having a closer relation than real brothers.

"Then why are you here, my brother, risking your life?"

Ouluun looked up at Mamay as she honestly asked this of him.

Mamay answered in a slow and careful tone, "First, I wanted to see, with my own eye, if you are doing fine. Secondly, I wanted to persuade you."

"Persuade me? To do what?"

"Sister, listen. I am not a reckless daredevil or a fool. Before I came here, I gave this much thought, and even resigned myself to accept death. But I heard that you will be his first wife, and I wanted to make sure of that."

In Mongolian society, the status of the first wife was meaningful. A Mongolian man could have as many wives as he could afford; however, only the descendants from the first wife were allowed to inherit their father's title, position or his properties.

"I remember he promised that. But how can you be sure about that?"

"I think he is a man of his word. I wish to believe that, at least. Today I saw him as a reasonable man, if my judgment is correct. If not, he probably would have killed me. Nobody kills his first wife's brother without any reason or benefit."

After this, Mamay tried to read Ouluun's face, and carefully continued.

"If you are with Chiledu, you are just his second wife."

Ouluun understood it fully. There was a long silence between the two. It seemed that the yurt was filled with warm air loaded with brotherly and sisterly affection.

"Do not try to escape the reality. You don't have much choice."

After these words, Mamay got to his feet slowly. Ouluun did too. They looked at each other with eyes filled with love for their own blood.

"I am going to leave tomorrow. Take care of yourself."

Mamay hugged her and patted her on the back. Before leaving he gave her one last piece of advice.

"Give him as many sons as possible. And raise them in the right and decent way. That is the best possible choice you can make."

CHAPTER THREE

The Descendants of the Bluish Wolf

In the beginning, there was the lake Baikal. God created this huge lake between the areas of the hundreds of thousands of square miles of the big Siberian forests and the endlessly stretching southern steppe. The lake was deep and wide like a sea and her image was of grandeur and magnificence itself. The bluish-green water, with incalculable depth, was awesome and seemed to be embedded with divineness and unknown great power. Sometimes she changed herself moment by moment, like a goddess changes her garments to accentuate her attractiveness. At other times, she refused to reveal herself, remaining veiled behind foggy clouds, adding to her own mysteriousness. She had thousands of faces. The huge waves breaking onto the high, rocky cliffs, making white bubbles, showed the vitality of her spiritual energy, and the scenes of seals resting peacefully on the long, silvery beach, along with the fragrant water plants on the water's placid surface conveyed soft, motherly love. She was the birthplace for all kinds of different life forms, home for living creatures such as the wild beasts and migratory birds, and also the abode of gods and goddesses.

There was a legend in the land of Mongolia. Here is the tale. There was a bluish wolf. He lived with his wife, a fallow doe, in the land north of the lake Baikal. One day, he heard God's voice from the heavens. "Go to the south! I have already prepared a land for you and your children."

He moved to the south, crossing the lake Baikal. They built a nest at the foot of the mountain Burkan, north of the river Onon. His name was Borte Chino and his wife's name was Goa Maral. They bore a son. His name was Batachigan. He had his father's valor, swiftness and keen eyes and his mother's delicacy and alertness. He was the very first Mongolian. The Burkan Mountain where he grew up, which provided him with full spiritual blessings, became the holy mountain for the Mongols in later times.

The first Mongol, Batachigan, married and begot a son. His name was Tamacha. The son of Tamacha was Qoricha Mergen. The son of Qoricha Mergen was Aujam Boroul. The son of Aujam Boroul was Sali Qachau. The son of Sali Qachau was Yeke Nidun. The son of Yeke Nidun was Sem Sochi. The son of Sem Sochi was Qarchu. The son of Qarchu was Borjigidai Mergen. The son of Borjigidai Mergen was Toroqoljin Bayan. And the son of Toroqoljin Bayan was Dobun Mergen.

There was a lady named Alan Goa. She was the legendary holy woman for the Mongols. She was beautiful, noble and renowned. She married Dobun Mergen and begot two sons. Their names were Bugunutei and Belgunutei, respectively.

After Dobun Mergen died, she begot three more sons. Their names were Buku Qadagi, Buqatu Salji and Bodonchar Munqak. Because their mother begot three more sons even after their father passed away, the two brothers, Bugunutei and Belgunutei, conversed in alarm.

"Even after our father has died, our mother continues to have babies. It is clear that she is seeing another man. What shall we do?"

"According to our law, an adulterous woman shall be thrown into the river with her hands and feet tied. However, when that woman is our own mother, what can we do? After our mother dies, let's get rid of them, one by one, and let's take all her property."

One day, Alan Goa was sitting with all five of her sons. She was handing out arrows, one by one, to each of her sons.

"Break it!"

Each one of her five sons broke an arrow easily. Then, she gave each a bundle of five arrows tied together.

"Break it!"

But, this time, nobody could do it.

"That's it! Each one of these arrows represents each one of you; if you are together, nobody can break you."

She paused and then continued.

"Bugunutei and Belgunutei, it is quite right of you to be suspicious of me. Yes, I have had three more sons, even since your father died. But listen carefully."

Alan Goa told her story.

"Every night, a shining golden man slid down from the sky into my tent, through the ventilation hole, on a bright, light bridge. He rubbed my belly and his glaring light became part of me. When he left, he disappeared like sunlight or moonlight, or like wind disappearing through the hole."

Alan Goa continued.

"You two should not talk lightly. My other sons are the children of heaven's spirit. No ordinary man will understand that. Someday, their children's children will rule all the living creatures of this world."

After their mother died, Bodonchar Munqak left his brothers. He couldn't inherit any small bit of his mother's property because he was not considered smart enough to keep property. All he was given was an old gelding. Was he really not smart enough to keep any of his mother's property? Bodonchar, a fifteen-year-old boy who had to start a new life, from nothing, roved around the mountains and plains. It did not take long for him to find a way to survive. He had a strong spiritual power and a resilient life force. If he had inherited his share of his mother's property, he could have then found himself a target of one of his half brothers.

One day, he came across the scene of a falcon attacking a peasant. He was successful in capturing the falcon with a noose that he had made with his horse's hairs. He trained the falcon and it would always bring him food. He was the first man to train a falcon and use it for hunting. He trained other people around him to train falcons.

"Before you go hunting, make them fast for about three days. Be sure to blindfold them. Let them go where there is prey. And after that, it's their job."

Some time later, he gathered the people around him, who were nothing but wild animals, and he became their leader.

"Without a leader, a group of people would be like a snake with no head."

People followed him. He taught them the importance of group consciousness.

"You can catch much more game collectively, when you hunt in a group, than the sum of what you can catch individually."

He became the strongest among his brothers. His half brothers couldn't touch him. Since then, among the Mongols, a new tradition had been established that the youngest child would inherit the father's property. Hundreds of clans branched out from these five brothers, and the Bodonchars were the strongest. Bodonchar was the many-times-removed forefather of Genghis Khan.

CHAPTER FOUR

The Mongol Khans at Earlier Times

As history progressed, the Mongols increased in great numbers. Hunting was their way of living. There was constant conflict among the men over the bountiful hunting grounds due to the consistent shortage of game. It was not until much later that they learned animal husbandry and farming livestock for their own use. They had no central force of unity. They were a fractured society and could not build a powerful organization, a nation. They were easy prey for other, more powerful, groups. These opposing groups used to invade Mongolian territory and loot, plunder and kill whenever they wanted.

In the early part of the twelfth century, the Juchids were an emerging power. Of half nomad blood, they began to gain strength after importing iron for weapons from the neighboring Sung by bargaining with gold, which was abundant in their territory. Akuta, a hero among them, destroyed the Lio Empire of Khitans that ruled over them for centuries, and declared a new empire of their own, called Chin. They kept expanding their territory, and in the end, almost half of China had fallen into their hands. It was at this time that the Jalairs, pushed by the Juchid, arrived in Mongolian territory. They killed the Mongols and looted and plundered. Finally, they took over the land. It was as if the stronger preyed upon the weaker and the weaker preyed upon the weakest.

Kaidu was a direct descendant of Bodonchar. He had eight brothers and his mother's name was Nomolun. His eight brothers and mother were killed by the Jalairs and all their property, including livestock and land, was taken over by the invaders. Kaidu was successful in escaping, with the help of his uncle, Nachin. As he was growing up, he realized that his people needed a concentrated power to be a nation. He began to gather his people and establish the foundation of a nation.

Kabul was the great-grandson of Kaidu. After four generations' efforts, they finally formed an organization similar to a nation. Historians later called this primitive nation the Mengku. Kabul was the first khan of this nation.

It was late fall in 1125 and the Mongolian Plateau was covered with white snow. Winter arrives early in the northern land. The endless plain, the small and large hills, stood in great silence and stillness. A group of people on horseback were approaching from the south, toward the campsite where numerous domed tents were spread out over the plain. They were the envoy from the Chin Empire. Kabul Khan greeted them. They handed over a personal letter from the Chin emperor to Kabul Khan. Kabul asked his aide, Chagan, who could read the Juchid language, what the letter said.

"About sixty days from now, there will be an enthronement ceremony for Chin's new emperor. And you are invited," Chagan explained.

"What's the true meaning of their invitation?" Kabul asked.

"They might want to establish a new relationship with us. They are preparing for full-scale war with the Southern Sung and might think it necessary to have good relations with us, in the north."

Kabul, in his forties, with big eyes, thick beard and mustache, was a man with a strong personality. However, he was also a man with a hot temper and low tolerance. He pondered a while, smoothing his beard. He asked Chagan, "If I refuse to be there, what will happen?"

"They might consider us their enemy and might dispatch troops to destroy us first, before they go to the Sung."

Kabul decided to accept the invitation. He needed security for his nation's further development and he thought he wasn't strong enough yet to go to war with the Juchid.

Kabul arrived at Lioyang, interim capital city of Chin, with forty official visiting members of his entourage. At that time, Chin's new emperor was Wukumai, Akuta's younger brother, who was in his forties, like Kabul. He was an ambitious man and as crafty as the devil. After his brother died, he destroyed Liao completely, which his brother couldn't accomplish. He captured and killed Yelu-yenhsi, the last emperor of Liao, and about 200 members of his royal family. After completing the first phase of his plan, he was ready for the next. Before he disposed of the dead bodies, whose faces had been destroyed beyond recognition, he took the time to plant evidence that would lead to his next phase. He forged a letter and publicly announced that it was written and sealed by the emperor of Sung and found on the dead body of the last emperor of Liao. The letter stated that in the case of a war between Liao and Chin, Sung would take the side of Liao and help them, which they never did. Wukumai declared war with Sung based on this letter. He wanted the Southern Sung while he had strong muscles.

"They are also our enemy! They are worse than Khitans! We have to get rid of them."

That was what the Chin emperor, Wukumai, used to say about his neighboring Southern Sung.

It was about this time when Kabul Khan was invited. Kabul refused the demands to kowtow at the ceremony. Kowtowing was a Chinese greeting to their emperor, kneeling and touching their forehead to the ground, which symbolized complete obedience. After the ceremony, in the middle of the banquet, there was an incident. The two drunken men, Kabul and Wukumai, who were drinking side by side, tweaked each other's beards. This was witnessed by the subjects of Chin and they saw it as humiliation to their emperor. They did not see Kabul as anything more than a barbarian from the northern region. After the banquet, they demanded this barbarian's head. Wukumai stopped them.

"What would be the benefit of getting rid of him? If we do it here, some other will replace him there. We are about to start full-scale war with the Sung. The timing is not right. Let him be until the end of the war with the Sung. And moreover, I promised him his security."

Despite Wukumai's wishes, the hawks in the Chin court dispatched their soldiers to chase down Kabul and his forty aides. Most of them were killed before they reached Mongolian territory, leaving only Kabul and two other men. He survived because he took Chagan's suggestion to switch his white horse with Chagan's black one. In Mongolian customs, white horses were only used by the chieftain or khan. Chagan died in place of Kabul Khan.

After that, Kabul concentrated on gathering his people and building their strength. He did not take any action lightly. When he felt he had accumulated enough strength, he organized the army and launched an attack. He and his army were invincible. He was successful in capturing forty fortresses on the northern boundaries of Chin in 1142. Hsi-Jong, the third emperor of Chin, sent 80,000 soldiers to stop him; however, they were not successful. The Chin court realized it was not going to be easy to rein him in, so they decided to take a different approach. They offered a peace talk. After six months of negotiating, they agreed and signed a peace treaty on the condition that, if Kabul Khan returned thirteen of the fortresses, Chin would pay him a tribute of 50,000 head of cattle, 50,000 sheep, 50,000 barrels of both rice and beans and 300,000 bales each of silk and satin each year. That peace treaty was in good standing and lasted several years until Kabul Khan's death and the replacement of the Chin emperor from Hsi-jong to King Ti-ku-nai.

After Kabul Khan's death, Ambakai became the second khan of the early, primitive Mongol nation. At that time, the Mongols had chosen their leader by election at the meeting of the heads of all tribes. Kabul and Ambakai were both descendants of Kaidu; however, they did not share the same grandfather.

Ambakai turned out to be an unlucky man and was killed before he could take even the very first step of his ambitious plan. The Chin's new emperor, Ti-ku-nai, was Hsi-jong's cousin and staged a coup to take over the throne when Hsi-jong made a political blunder and no longer seemed trustworthy. He was extremely unhappy with the fact that Hsi-jong turned twenty-seven fortresses over to the Mongols that Akuta, the founder of the Chin Empire, had built up with great effort. He was also angered by the enormous amount of the tributes that were being paid to the Mongols each year.

One day, at the imperial meeting, he complained about this.

"If there is anyone who has any ideas as to how to rein in the emerging Mongols and to get the twenty-seven lost fortresses back, do not hesitate to tell me."

In response to his words, one senior officer stood up and spoke.

"Your Majesty, there is a traditional maneuver to handle the northern barbarians. It is called the policy of barbarians for barbarians. They are divided into many different tribes and clans, so if we can get them fighting each other, they would never be a threat to us."

At these words, the Chin emperor asked, "Which tribe can stand against the Mongols?"

"The Tartars, Your Majesty."

The Chin emperor asked, "And, how can we make them fight?"

"It is simple, Your Majesty. If we offer them the tributes that we are paying to the Mongols, they will surely accept. They are the ones who are willing to do anything for their own good. Presently, a man named Ambakai has become the Mongols' khan in place of Kabul, who died months ago. Ask the Tartars for his head, Your Majesty, then a war between two barbarians will automatically follow."

About six months after the secret agreement between the Juchids of the Chin and the Tartars, Ambakai Khan received a proposal from one of the chieftains of the Tartars, whose territory was mainly the eastern part of the Mongolian Plateau. The chieftain of the Buiruud Tartar asked for the hand of Ambakai's first daughter, Noulan, for his second son, Qoricuchu. Cautious, Ambakai demanded one year of labor in his ordu from the would-be son-in-law. At that time, the aristocratic society of the steppe people adhered to the strong customary law of exogamy. Oftentimes, the bride's family would demand that the would-be bridegroom stay in their ordu for some time to show them that he was the right one. It could be one or two years, or sometimes more. For about a year, Qoricuchu had been very successful in proving his worthiness. Ambakai had been pleased, and as promised, he gave a wonderful wedding ceremony for the new couple.

Ambakai left to see his daughter off, leaving his ordu with only about ten men. At this time there were endless conflicts and hostile actions taking place on the Mongolian Plateau, and if the head of a tribe was on a journey without enough guard soldiers, it could be an open invitation for disaster. However, there were exceptions. With a wedding procession or travel, it was considered good manners to travel without heavy guards. The presence of too many guards could bring on an attack based on suspicions about the true purpose of the journey.

They were about halfway to their destination when they found numerous horsemen approaching them with a long tail of gray, dusty clouds following. At first they were believed to be the bridegroom's family members and their guards. As they were nearing, it became clear that they were heavily armed soldiers who had nothing to do with the bridegroom's family. They were Jurkin Tartars. Ambakai's sixth sense told him that he had stepped into a trap.

"Alas, I have been duped!"

He looked around. A man was galloping away from his group at full speed toward the approaching horses and soldiers. It was the bridegroom himself, Qoricuchu. He was the bait to pull Ambakai out to the open ground.

"Bring me a bow and an arrow!"

Enraged, Ambakai raised the bow and aimed at him with all his skill and then let it go. The arrow, loaded with great fury, flew with lightning speed while making a fearful whistling sound and hit Qoricuchu's neck exactly on target. The dull sound of his lifeless body falling down from the horse and hitting the ground arrived at Ambakai Khan's ear through the wind. Moments later, Ambakai and ten of his men, who were barely armed, were captured by 150 heavily armed Tartars. Ambakai and Okin Barak, the son of the late Kabul Khan, were handed over to the Chin as planned.

They were taken to Yenking, the new capital of the Chin. Once there, they were chained and dragged around in the marketplace for humiliation. After the humiliation, they were flayed alive by a skillful butcher and then their skins were used to cover wooden donkeys and finally nailed down. The wooden donkeys wearing human skins were displayed in the busy marketplace for many days.

"The northern traitor."

That was the name of their crime. The reason they used wooden donkeys was, at that time, they believed donkeys were the symbol of the untrustworthy.

Since Ambakai Khan's death, the Mongols' worst enemy were the Tartars. Qutula, the third khan of the Mongols, following Ambakai, fought against both the Chin and the Tartars. He was the fourth son of Kabul Khan, and known to be a giant, and also a great fighter. He was known to eat a large sheep for each meal. He was successful in handling the Chin, but not so with the Tartars. He successfully managed thirteen large and small battles, but at last, was killed in a final, decisive battle, near Buyr Lake, against the coalition forces of the Chin and the Tartars.

The loss of the Buyr Lake battle brought enormous disaster to the Mongols. Their society completely collapsed and became fractured. The people made their way into the desert and the barren lands in units of one or two families. They were forced to live on field mice and wolves' leftovers. They sold their sons and daughters for a mere lump of meat and, in some extreme cases, they ate human flesh. The economic disaster accompanied the moral collapse.

They hated and slaughtered each other. They stole at night instead of sleeping, they killed and were killed for the benefit of a very small profit. Nobody trusted his brother, a son did not listen to his father, and a wife was not loyal to her husband. The seniors did not take care of the youngsters and the inferiors did not obey their superiors. Their mutual respect and confidence had been drained, leaving only enmity and conflict among them. Despair, fear and viciousness became the norm in their society. Robbery, plunder, rape and assault were considered acts of masculinity and valor, instead of vice. The earth had been sunken, the stars had been hidden away and even the sun had turned his face away from this society.

This was the time when Genghis Khan was born.

CHAPTER FIVE

Birth of the
Iron Man

Spring on the plateau comes with hardship and cruelty, not with the warm and soft sunlight or the smooth and silky breeze. It comes with gale, hail and dusty brown clouds covering the entire sky. Even after the horrible winter of bitter cold and heavy snow, the people of the plateau continued to suffer from the painful wind, as did the livestock, including horses, cattle, sheep and camels. The grass on the plains was still dried out and on top of high hills and mountains, the snow and ice still remained. The chilly rains and late snow in the springtime were often regarded as a harbinger of disaster, bringing epidemic outbreaks that threatened the livestock, who were weakened from the long winter of limited grass. However, after this harsh period, in late spring or early summer, life is renewed on this land that was cursed or dead during those harsh earlier times. The sky changes its color to cobalt blue, broadening its depth, and the plants that had been dried out and tweaked, like an old man's beard during wintertime, begin to produce their greenish buds. The earth shakes off its shabby, deathly, grayish clothing, replacing it with a new green cover that is full of life. At this time of year, the nomads became much busier. The men cared for their horse equipment, such as their harnesses and saddles, and they sharpened and made weapons, tasks that had been delayed for quite a long time.

The women had to smooth the leather of the livestock that had been drying all winter. Battle and hunting were for the men and setting up the tents, smoothing the leather, making the felts and blankets, and milking the cows, horses and sheep was for the women. The herdsmen and herd boys took their hungry livestock out to the field and let them move around freely, feeding on the rich, abundant, newly grown green grass. From this moment on, the horses and cattle became strong and began to produce enough milk and give birth to new lives.

The great Onon River basin, the stronghold of the Kyat Mongols, was in the heart of the Mongolian Plateau. It was the home of the Kyat Mongols' strong man, Yesugei, and his fifteen thousand households. The Onon River, running through the basin, had never dried up through the seasons. It was the lifeline for the nomads.

The tent town was in deep sleep. It was late at night, and still far from dawn. The town was in absolute silence. Sometimes wolves howling, feeble-sounding but fearsome, could be heard from a distance.

In the yurt built on the small hill on the northern boundary of the town, several sheep-oil lamps were burning actively in contrast to the town's darkness, and a thin light was coming out through the slightly open thick flap doors. In the yurt, several women were taking care of a young woman on the bed. One of them, an old woman in a traditional Mongolian sheepskin coat, which was long enough to drape to her ankles, with wide, open long sleeves, was murmuring to herself with her two hands in the sleeves and her eyes closed. She seemed to be praying for something repeatedly.

It was late spring, close to summer, but due to the early morning chill, dried horse dung was burning in the bronze stove and from it an orange flame was blazing. Ouluun was lying in the bed covered with smooth animal fur and silky sheets. Her long dark hair was hanging down on her shoulders and on the silk pillow filled with soft bird's feathers. Her dark brown eyes, below her thick and long eyebrows, were mostly closed, but would open abruptly; beautiful, sparkling under the sheep-oil lamp when something would cause her to flinch. Around her neck, a glaring, milk-colored pearl necklace was hanging down to her breasts and it was attractively balanced against her smooth, light skin. The thin, light-pink lips below her symmetrical nose were a little bit parched and sometimes she seemed to be chewing or clenching her teeth. Below the smooth curvature of her shoulders were two full breasts and below, her belly was swollen like a mountain around her navel. She was nineteen and was an expectant mother.

With her eyes closed, she was lost in her thoughts. The baby about to be born was Yesugei's baby. Ouluun did not love him, but did not hate him, either. Anyway, from her perspective, the world belonged to the victors. She was smart enough not to ruin the present because of an irreversible past; she was practical. For some time, Ouluun refused Yesugei. In those moments, Yesugei never forced her. He simply stood there without remark and would then leave.

Her eventual change of heart could largely be due to her brother, Mamay, who persuaded her ardently that she should change her mind.

"Give him as many sons as possible and then you will be the winner. When that moment comes, your mind will be changed, of this I am sure. The human mind changes as the situation changes, always."

Finally, one day when Yesugei approached her, she did not refuse him. Yesugei neared Ouluun's bed, on his knees, held her hand and spoke softly, "Be my wife, please. And let me have a son. Your first son will be the owner of this ordu, I promise. I need a son who will bring unity to this plateau. I will raise him that way and that is my dream."

Ouluun, as she stood up from the bed, held his hands. Yesugei also stood up. Ouluun, after looking into his eyes for a while, held him around his neck. Then, burying her head into his chest, she spoke softly.

"So be it."

They hugged each other tightly and stood like that for a while.

Perhaps due to early labor pains, Ouluun moaned occasionally, making feeble sounds while beads of sweat collected on her forehead. The women in the yurt became busier. A woman near Ouluun's bed repeatedly wiped the sweat with a soft cotton cloth. Badai, the chief midwife of the town, noticed the first signs of childbirth and had the other women prepare for the birth. First, she told them to build a small wood fire outside the yurt and to get melted butter and warm water for cleansing the newborn baby. She double-checked all her supplies for the new baby, including cotton and silk cloth for wrapping, and a cradle. Badai had been preparing for this for many days, since she was given the order from Yesugei. Regardless of Yesugei's orders, she was an excellent midwife and had never disappointed anyone before.

Loud screams began to emanate from Ouluun's half-opened mouth due to the labor pains. Two women, beside her bed, held her hands firmly. The baby's large head began to emerge from her body. Badai carefully held the baby's head. The torso moved out gradually and when the two arms were out, the baby began to cry loudly, swinging its arms powerfully, even before its whole body was out. Then, Ouluun's silk bedsheet became stained with blood and bodily fluids.

"It's a boy!" a woman cried out with excitement. At the same moment, shouts of joy from the other women filled the yurt. They hopped up and down, filled with excitement, hand in hand, as if it were their own baby. Badai cut the umbilical cord with a red-hot knife and began to tend to the baby with skilled hands. She carefully began to clean the baby's body with soft cotton cloths soaked with melted butter. Due to his uncanny strength, two women had to hold the baby from each side while Badai did her job. Ouluun looked tired, but the happy smile on her lips never went away while Badai was cleaning the baby.

A woman covered Ouluun with a silk sheet and wool blanket. Badai suddenly opened her eyes wide in great surprise when she noticed the baby was holding something firmly in his right hand and wouldn't let it go. She had bad experiences before with some babies being born with congenital deformities, such as a claw-hand. She had seen it twice before. Soon she found that an unnecessary fear. She carefully opened the boy's fingers, one by one. When all five fingers were opened, what she found was a rock-hard, dried blood clot, the size of a sheep's knucklebone.

"Look, what I found!" Badai cried out. All the women in the yurt looked at the blood clot with great curiosity. There was silence. No one dared open her mouth and make comments about anything related to the newborn baby of the owner of twenty thousand yurts, even though they were the type of women who enjoy chatting. They wouldn't do it and they couldn't do it. They were the ones picked by Yesugei himself and were believed to be trustworthy and were expected to take good care of his newborn baby and its mother.

Badai wrapped the blood clot with extreme care in a small piece of silk cloth and then put it into a teak jewelry box embellished luxuriously with silver flowers. Then, Badai hung a bow and arrow high on the left and right sides of the entrance to the yurt. This was an old tradition to chase off the evil spirits with the power of a newborn baby's great valor, if it was a boy. Five soldiers were posted as guards around the yurt and only six women, including Badai, were allowed in and out.

The sun had risen from the eastern horizon, radiating its strong, dazzling sunlight all over the land. It was 1167, when the spring was changing into summer.

Yesugei was approaching his tent town on horseback around sunset, when the western sky was changing to purple. He was with about 400 of his men, 200 camels loaded with stacks of war booty, and several captured high-ranking enemy soldiers. He and his warriors were returning victoriously from the campaign. He had attacked the Tartar caravan that left Yenking of Cathay, heading for Chunghing, capital city of the Shisha Kingdom via the southern border of the Gobi Desert. The Tartar caravan was composed of 150 members of their own and 450 heavily armed Tartar soldiers as guards. However, the Tartars could never be a match for Yesugei, the master of surprise attack. The booty was expensive Chinese silk products, high quality tea and perfume, porcelain and silver products, women's ornamental jewelry, daggers decorated with precious stones, ivory products, and many other things. The Tartars were eager to obtain control of the Silk Road, so they sent their top-level warriors, like Temujin Uge and Qory Buka. Nonetheless, it ended in miserable defeat. Their two generals were taken captive and most of their soldiers were dead or had scattered into the desert. Among the captives were some Arabs, Indians and Chinese; however, Yesugei released them before he left. He crossed the Gobi Desert, taking only two high-ranking Tartar captives and about 30 Tartar women and several Chinese women who were with them. As Yesugei's victorious warriors were approaching the entrance of the tent town, many of the townspeople, young and old, came out to see them. The children shouted joyfully, the elders and women cheered as they cast their eyes curiously at the packages on the camels. Soon Yesugei was welcomed by his brother, Daritai, who was in charge of the safety of the town during his absence. Daritai gave him the news of Ouluun's newborn baby.

"Big brother, rejoice. You just got a son."

For a while, without saying a word, Yesugei stared at him intensely, with a huge smile on his face. Yesugei began to feel his own heartbeat. Yesugei's face, though imbued with the toughness of the desert and the wildness of the steppe, began to show mixed expressions of excitement, jubilation and relief. He could feel the fulfillment of a long-cherished desire. Yesugei approached his brother, shaking his shoulders with his strong hands, and said, "What did you say? Tell me again."

"A son."

Yesugei shouted, "Woo-ha!" and then hugged him. Daritai patted his brother's back as he was doing the same. Daritai almost fell from his horse as his gelding stood on his hind legs, surprised by Yesugei's continued loud shouting. Yesugei spurred his stallion to Ouluun's yurt. The crowd parted swiftly and made way for him.

Ouluun was on the bed and several serving women were with her. Next to Ouluun's bed was a cradle with a handle in which a baby was sleeping, wrapped in silken swaddling clothes. Mongolian cradles were designed to be carried easily with one hand, and sometimes they could be carried on horseback, tied with rope to a saddle. This was a need because of their nomadic lifestyle; nobody knew when the enemy would fall upon them. As darkness was creeping into the tent, the serving women began to light the Baghdad lamps and put them on the chest or hung them on the wall. When Yesugei showed up, the serving women greeted him hurriedly, bending one knee, with their heads down. Yesugei signaled off the serving women after he handed his helmet over to one of them. Yesugei neared Ouluun's bed and went down on his knees. After watching the baby carefully for a while, at last he bent his head and gave a light kiss to his forehead. He said excitedly, "My son. My hope."

Yesugei held Ouluun's hand softly and said with a gentle voice, "I thank you, my dear. I am really proud of you."

In return, Ouluun said in a low, soft voice with a look of pride and happiness, "What will be the baby's name, my lord?"

Yesugei pondered a while, looking up as if into space. Ouluun could see Yesugei's handsome profile. Still with the desert's dust on his face, he gave the appearance of a wild, untamed, tough guy; however, in that particular moment, his face was full of a father's love and affection.

"His name will be Temujin."

His voice was full of confidence and pride. The Mongols used to give the name of an enemy, captive or someone they had killed in battle to their newborn baby or descendants, to celebrate the victory and keep it long in their memory. The victorious Yesugei brought two Tartar prisoners on that day, and one of their names was Temujin, which means "iron man."

CHAPTER SIX

Prophecy of Aman

The following morning, Yesugei was visited by Aman, the shaman and the official priest of the ordu. As usual, he was clad in wide, white shamanic robes, long enough to cover his ankles, and on his head was a cone-shaped cap with a long fluttering rim. He had a pale-skinned face with sleepy, slanted eyes that seemed to be imbued with slyness, cruelty and the sharpness to see through other people's minds. No one knew his age, though the numerous wrinkles on his face and his withered hands, like dried-out aspen bark, told that he was quite an old man. He was a lascivious man, with many concubines, and also very greedy; he had amassed countless personal property. He was always with nine little boys, who served him on every occasion. Yesugei didn't like shamans. They were the people who were enjoying the privileges of exemption from labor and military service, which every Mongol man had to endure. They were well off and hadn't done hard labor or risked their lives. However, Yesugei also thought they were a necessary evil.

Nomadic people were shamanistic people. Once you experience standing alone in the middle of the terrible, empty plain, covered only by the endless horizon and sky, you will be struck by some kind of inspiration that can make you believe in some sort of supernatural being. A gusty wind, strong enough to blow a man or a horse down, a choking heavy snow, thunder and a bolt of lightning were irresistible powers of nature to them, and the night sky, with sparkling stars, was a mysterious one. All these powers could influence them to open their religious minds. They believed that holy spirits are everywhere in nature and Tenggri, god of the heaven, was the highest god, the one that rules all other spirits. They believed the shamans could communicate with the spirits, even with Tenggri, depending on their individual abilities. The shamans ruled the spiritual world of the nomads. It is easy to understand how powerful the shamans were, seeing many of the tribal chieftains on the Mongolian Plateau at that time.

"My lord, a strange rumor is going around the town," Aman opened his mouth and said in a high-pitched tone.

At this, Yesugei looked at him and asked, "A strange rumor? What do you mean?"

Moving his chair close to Yesugei's, Aman said in a lowered, whispering voice, "The baby, your newborn baby, my lord, he was born with a blood clot in his hand. Some people are very superstitious and are spooked by this. They believe it could be a bad omen and eventually bring a terrible disaster upon us."

Yesugei recalled what happened yesterday. When Ouluun opened the jewelry box and showed him the blood clot, he didn't take it as anything serious or anything to be considered.

"What is wrong with a newborn baby holding a blood clot in his hand?" Yesugei shouted angrily and gazed at him in profound contempt.

Aman looked around the inside of the tent, as if he wanted to make sure they were alone, and whispered in Yesugei's ear, "It could be a message from the spirits, my lord. Even though it means nothing, it will be a problem as long as the people believe it so. I think you'd better do something about this."

Yesugei pondered for a while. The people of fifteen thousand families in the ordu followed and trusted in his leadership and valor. However, he knew that there was an area he could not reach, their spiritual world. As Yesugei remained silent, Aman continued.

"We need a ritual, my lord. With permission, I can leave for Burkan Mountain tonight and will start an overnight prayer there. Then, we can start a ritual at daybreak the day after tomorrow. I will surely be back by tomorrow evening."

From the ordu, it usually took a half day to get to Burkan Mountain on horseback, at trotting speed. Near Burkan Mountain was a small cave where Aman would stay for overnight prayers before any important rituals.

"I will get ready for everything. However, there's one thing I have to ask you."

"What is it?"

"Two prisoners."

Yesugei asked while staring into his eyes, "What do you need them for?"

Aman narrowed his slanted eyes and said, "They are supposed to die, I presume."

Yesugei answered in a serious manner, "No! You cannot say that! They are highly qualified soldiers. It will be a good thing for us, if I can turn them into my men. That is my plan. That's why I brought them alive. We Mongols need such a policy to unite the whole plateau in the future. However, I will ask my Mongolian brothers before I make any decision."

Aman looked disappointed.

"We need a sacrifice, my lord."

Yesugei answered in a stiff manner.

"If you need a sacrifice, use a horse. I won't allow you to use any humans for sacrifice. And more, I don't want to see blood during the feast. That will be the day the celebration for my son starts. If I have to get rid of them, I will find a different way."

Yesugei had already planned a three-day feast for his son. Aman could not ignore Yesugei, just as Yesugei could not ignore Aman.

"So be it, my lord."

Aman showed respect and agreement, bending his head down slowly. Then, with an obsequious smile, he spoke in low voice, "I wonder if you can allow me some of the booty from the Tartar caravan."

Yesugei understood he was asking for a reward for his service. Yesugei allowed him a portion of the booty, in the amount of ten camels and the opportunity to pick freely three of the thirty women prisoners.

At daybreak, three days after the baby's birth, on top of the hill in the vast area of the upper part of the Onon River, numerous Mongols gathered around a newly built altar. That was the place where the baby was born. It was not a big place, though they had the view of the entire river valley from there, where the very first sunlight arrives. The air was fresh, clear, cool, and imbued with the spirit of the plain. Gradually, all the big and small hills at the eastern end of the horizon, which showed only dark silhouettes minutes ago, began to show their real images and the sky over the hills began to turn to bright orange, from darkish purple. The mighty sun was rising, radiating like an aurora.

Around the altar, several flagpoles were arranged and at the southern side of it, a huge metal burner stood on a tripod. From the burner came a huge plume of gray smoke, with orange flames spiraling up and into the sky, which had just begun to show its daytime blue hue. Mongols believed the spiritual energy was greatest with the rising sun and that fire was holy and could cleanse everything.

The ritual started with sprinkling kumis around the altar. Yesugei, capped with a helmet and covered with lacquered, leather armor, stepped onto the altar and kowtowed nine times toward the eastern sky. Then, holding the baby high with his two hands, he prayed with a strong and resounding voice.

Oh, Tenggri,
God of the heaven,
The owner of the universe!

The mother earth,
The home for all living creatures!
The sun,
The source of power and energy!
The moon,
The basis of all wisdom!

Bless the baby!
Allow him to hold his head high with dignity.
Allow him to have a strong body like iron,
Limitless energy,
And a never-ending fountain of wisdom.

Let him protect himself,
And let him not be ashamed in front of his enemy.
Your enemy shall be his enemy,
And let his enemy be your enemy!

All the souls and spirits of our ancestors,
Bless the baby!
Let him protect his ancestral land,
Which we inherited from heaven to the bluish wolf and
  his descendants.
Let him keep this beautiful land,
From the enemy horses' dirty hoofprints!

Yesugei's resounding voice echoed into the mysterious sky, which only added to the magical deep blue. As Yesugei stepped down from the altar, the crowd, as if awoken from a deep sleep, began to chant in one voice, "Tenggri! Tenggri! Tenggri!"

Their shouts waved into the space filled with desert air and then to the vault of the sky, which looked as if it was filled with holy, spiritual energy. The sun, which just had risen, was pouring its strong, golden sunbeams over the great basin of the upper Onon River.

Aman, the shaman, stepped onto the altar and began to pray. On his head was a copper crown and hanging from his neck was a shining bronze mirror, the size of a human face, connected with leather string. He was wearing a deep purple gown decorated with numerous rings, to which were attached several metal objects, the shape and size of a man's little finger. He was holding a staff in his left hand and a small drum with a handle in his right, on which several beads were dangling from strings. His copper crown made it possible to travel to another world, the bronze mirror was for chasing off the evil spirits and the purple gown with its numerous metal decorations protected his flesh and bone while traveling.

> *Oh!*
> *The great spirit of the eternal blue sky!*
>
> *I am calling you, and I am praying to you.*
> *You allowed us a beautiful new life.*

For mortals,
It is forbidden to peek into the future.

However,
To know your expectation from us,
And not to offend your will,
We need your permission.

If there is any meaning in the baby's blood clot,
Please, let us know.

After this prayer, Aman began to shake the hand drum. It made a loud tinkling sound. As he was repeating the same movements, he stepped down from the altar and began to walk around it slowly. Nine little boys followed him. He continued for a while, murmuring indistinct words. Beads of sweat began to collect on his brow, and later it flowed down his face like rain. After a while, when he reached a certain spot, he suddenly stopped. His face was distorted, and his eyes were staring at the space pointlessly. The staff in his left hand was shaking uncontrollably and, a short time later, it made rapid movements as if on its own. His eyes rolled up, and foam was coming from his mouth. He fell down. As he fell, the nine boys supported him and laid him down on the ground gently. For a while, he did not move.

The crowd began to make noise. Some time later, with the help of two of the boys, he got on his feet and staggered to the burner.

He looked very tired, like someone who had just come back from a long journey or had been wandering over the plain for a long time. After recovering, he grabbed a handful of aromatic bark chips from a wooden bowl that one boy handed over to him, and he began to throw them into the burner. Thick, gray smoke was spiraling up, forming odd images and then, mysteriously dispersing into the sky.

The crowd gazed at this in great silence, as if they had been hypnotized.

Aman mounted the altar and began to shout, "The great god of the heaven, Tenggri, has answered my prayer. I saw the future! God allowed him unlimited power and a new order will be created on this earth. His heart is stronger than wrought iron, his valor will surpass that of the mountain lion and his shrewdness will outshine the snakes. He will be invincible. Nobody will match him! He will destroy our sworn enemy, the Tartars, and unite the whole plateau. All the emperors of Cathay and the grand dukes of Russia will bow to him, and the blue-eyed women from the western land and the fair-skinned women from Baghdad will serve him."

Deep silence remained for some time among the crowd, for the words from Aman's mouth could not convince them. The Mongols were relatively small in numbers and considered a weak tribe compared to others on the plateau, making it difficult for them to believe they could accomplish such things.

Aman opened his mouth and continued, "There will be a sea of blood, mountains of dead bodies and endless war."

These words, suddenly, caused quite a stir in the crowd. People seemed shocked, and sighed deeply with fear. Aman, ignoring this, continued, "The mountains will be leveled and the rivers will change their course for this baby's path."

The stir escalated and the noise grew louder.

"The dead bodies of the Mongols will cover the plain and their families will be dispersed."

At this, Yesugei jumped up from his seat. The crowd was on the verge of explosion. Aman continued, "We need a sacrifice. A sacrifice will replace the Mongols' blood."

Someone cried out from the crowd, which still seemed to be hypnotized, "The Tartars' blood! The Tartar prisoners for sacrifice!"

This sent the crowd into an uproar. They chanted in one voice, thrusting their fists in the air, "Revenge for Ambakai Khan! Death to the Tartar prisoners!"

The uproar lasted for a while. Aman slowly stepped down from the altar and stood in front of the burner again. He threw aromatic bark chips into it. For some time, he watched the thick, gray, spiraling smoke in fascination and then stepped back onto the altar.

"The spirits want a white horse. A white horse will save the Mongols' blood and it will take away all the curses of the evil spirits. This is the will of God and also the will of our great leader, Yesugei. Brothers! Follow!"

The Mongols killed a white horse. It was a three-year-old, untamed mare. Two strong men held the reins from opposite sides and a third man hit the mare on the head with an ax.

The horse fell down with a sharp scream. The axman then cut the horse's neck vein with his well-sharpened short knife. He collected the spouting blood in a big wooden bowl. Aman, after he received the bowl, circled around the altar sprinkling the blood with a bamboo brush. He then ordered the axman to pick up the spleen. The horse's spleen, which was so big that two men had to use their four hands to carry it, was put into a big, purple teak box. Aman added the blood clot from the baby's hand and the umbilical cord to the box. Then, he prayed toward the sky with his arms wide open.

"Oh! All the great spirits of heaven and earth! We are offering you a sacrifice! Protect the baby and the Mongols from the evil spirits and save their blood!"

They dug a large hole, right on the spot of the baby's birth, and buried the box. Later, the Mongols will call the spot Deliun Boldok, meaning "hill of the spleen." At that time, burying the baby's umbilical cord was their usual custom and they buried the blood clot and spleen for protection from the evil spirits. After the ritual, Yesugei ordered his brother, Daritai, to expel the two Tartar prisoners, Temujin Uge and Qori Buka. Though Yesugei was the actual ruler of the fifteen thousand families, he never ignored his Mongol brothers when he made important decisions related to the ordu. The two prisoners were taken to the harshest desert and dropped in the middle of it. That was how the Mongols dealt with criminals. It would be a tough punishment. They were given only one or two days' worth of food and no weapons, horses or camels. Due to lack of transportation, escape was impossible. Eventually, they would

face death from thirst and hunger and their fear would make
it worse.

The Mongols rejoiced during three days of feasts. They
enjoyed whole roasted camel, which had been baked in an
underground charcoal pit for two full days. As night fell, numerous campfires were built on the open ground in the center
of the town. Wrestling matches were everywhere, while children sang a song to the tune of musical instruments played
by elders. Some of the warriors, tipsy with kumis, danced a
sword dance to the drumbeat and the cheering crowd gathered around shrieking. Some young men, going around with
young women, were telling dirty jokes and the women never
stopped giggling. The barking of the dogs chasing the children
scuttling between the campfires, the neighing of the horses
and camels, the husky shouts from the men and the shrieks of
the women's laughter—all were mixed together and scattered
into the desert sky.

CHAPTER SEVEN

The Boy, Temujin

By the time he was seven years old, Temujin was already a skilled horse rider and archer. His dark brown eyes, under his broad forehead and neat, smooth eyebrows, shone like mysterious, precious stones. His eyes, deeply imbued with intelligence, courage and dignity, sometimes instilled fear and respect in his watchers. His well-balanced nose seemed to show his high self-respect and high vision, and his firmly closed mouth showed his well-managed self-control. The boy already had charisma and a clear understanding that he was unique. He was extremely smart, quick in motion and thoughtful.

"A man should be a hunting expert. Hunting is the basic means of life for the Mongols."

Yesugei taught him like this. Temujin had explored a wide area of the hunting grounds with his father and when he caught his first game, a black sable, Yesugei celebrated with a hunting ritual, as was customary after a child's first successful hunt. Usually they put the prey on the altar and prayed to the spirits related to hunting, for their children's safety and future success as good hunters. Sometimes this small ritual became a big party.

The boy, Temujin, from a very early age, learned and trained how to survive in the desert and on the plains from his father. He learned how to make fire, how to find water, how to build a temporary hut to protect himself from the cold weather and how to differentiate between what is edible and what is not. Like other boys, he enjoyed horseback riding, archery and wrestling. In the summertime, he played the game of kicking a ball made of rolled leather and in winter, a game of hitting a puck made of a horse's knee bone on the frozen Onon River.

The best time for Mongol children was after dinner, when it grew dark. They would gather around the lamp and listen to the traditional Mongolian folktales from the town's elderly, eloquent storytellers. Temujin could often listen to his mother's stories or those of the town's elders, and they remained in his memory for a long time. Temujin's mother, Ouluun, was an excellent storyteller. With rare exception, she came into her children's tent after dinner, took care of their beds and never forgot to tell them a story or two until they fell asleep. Temujin used to listen to the stories with his brothers, Kasar, who was two years younger than he, and Kachun, four years younger, under the dim, lighted, sheep-oil lamp. Ouluun was like an actress on a stage, making the voices and facial expression for the characters, which amused her audience, her own children.

Once upon a time, in a small pond, there lived a frog and two geese. They were good friends. At one time, after a long drought, when the water in the pond was drying out, the two geese talked to each other and decided to move to some other place. The frog was stunned upon hearing this and begged them, "My dear friends, please take pity on me. Take me to the place where the water is."

The two geese talked each other and then asked him, "Tell us how we can move you." The frog found a small piece of stick and explained, "I will bite down hard in the middle of this stick and each one of you will bite the other two ends and then fly up to the sky."

The two geese held onto each end of the stick in their mouths, as the frog explained, and then flew away high up into the sky. They passed over mountains and plains. When they had passed over a high hill, a small town appeared. When the town's people saw them, they exclaimed in wonder at the scene.

"Look at that! What an amazing scene! Two geese are carrying a frog, with a stick. What smart and clever geese!"

People down on the ground repeated the same thing again and again with a loud voice. At this, the frog was annoyed and became very unhappy. He shouted in a loud voice down to the people, "This was my idea! These two geese just followed my idea!"

At that moment, when he opened his mouth, the frog lost his grip on the stick. He fell down to the ground and died.

When she was finished telling the story, as she stroked her three sons' hair affectionately, Ouluun asked, "What do you think this story is really about? Even though you have a great idea, it is impossible to try some ideas out without someone else's help. And more importantly, even though you have done a great job, you should not boast or brag. You have to wait until you are recognized by others. You have to train yourself to control your unnecessary self-conceit."

Ouluun heard this type of story from her mother, and her mother heard the same stories from her mother's mother. These were the traditional Mongolian stories handed down from generation to generation.

Some other stories were like this: There once lived a snake with two heads. One body with two heads was a great convenience. With four eyes, it was easy to find prey and while one head was sleeping, the other could be on guard. One day, an eagle found this snake. In the blink of an eye, the eagle attacked the snake. The snake tried to find a place to hide. Under a big rock, there was a hole, but the hole was so small, only one head could fit inside. When the eagle picked up one head, the other head also came out with it. The snake with two heads was eaten by the eagle.

Or this: Once upon a time, there was a hunter who, along with his wife and a small son, lived near the vast Mongol forest. One day, he brought home a baby fox that he had found during his hunting travels. His toddler son and the baby fox grew up together and became good friends. One day the hunter went out hunting and his wife went out to the field to tend the sheep, leaving their son and the fox in the yurt. In the late afternoon, when the hunter came back, he found that the fox was panting in front of the flap door with its muzzle covered with blood.

"Alas! This fox killed my son."

Having no doubt about this truth of this, he took out his sword and cut the fox's head off. What he found, when he opened the flap door and entered the yurt, was his son playing by himself and next to him a big snake lay on the ground, chewed into pieces. The hunter regretted his hasty, thoughtless decision.

One day, the boy, Temujin, was playing with the other boys, as usual. Suddenly, a horrible animal's scream came from the northern side of the hill. The boys froze. It was a scary, blood-chilling scream. The boys looked at each other. Without hesitation, they got on their horses and rushed to the northern hill. They found a big doe lying on the ground and a huge eagle circling around it in the sky. The deer was bleeding heavily from her eyes and seemed to have lost her eyesight. She was repeating the same motions, struggling to stand up with her two shaking front legs, managing a few steps and then falling down again. The boys watched this in silence, chilled. Eventually the deer couldn't get up at all and only pawed with her four legs in the air. She was as big as a small calf.

"Let's take this deer with us," one big boy said as he looked around at the other boys. He was Temujin's half-brother, Bektor, and he was two years older than Temujin. Either everybody thought he was right or maybe they were afraid to protest because of his large size, but nobody was against him. At this moment, one boy stepped forward.

"No! We should not take this. This is not ours, it is the eagle's."

As Temujin was saying this, he stopped Bektor. Bewildered and annoyed, Bektor pushed Temujin away with his shoulder.

"How dare you try to stop me?"

While the two boys were arguing, two of the town's elders arrived on their horses. One of them was Temujin's uncle, Nekun. After hearing both sides, Nekun told Bektor, "Temujin is right. The deer belongs to the eagle. If we take it, the eagle will get angry."

At this, Bektor got on his horse and, glaring and mumbling at Temujin, he galloped away.

That night, Temujin was in deep thought as he watched the flames coming from the sheep-oil lamp, with his chin on his hands, lying on his stomach in bed. The orange flames were dancing gently and sometimes seemed to stand still. Outside, the wind was making noise, flapping the tent.

Why did the eagle attack the deer's eyes?

That was the question on Temujin's mind. The answer came to him in a short time. The eagle doesn't have a weapon to kill the deer in one breath. Later, he learned that eagles, after the initial attack to take away their big prey's eyesight, wait until their prey dies in exhaustion, no matter how many days it takes.

From that point forward, Temujin became very attentive in his observation of nature. Nature was his real-life classroom. He understood that there's an endless struggle for survival and existence in the visible and invisible areas of the land.

One summer afternoon, after the rainfall, the boy Temujin came across a toad in a small stream. Because of the rain, there was more water than before. The toad was sitting on the rock, blinking yet remaining perfectly still. A snake was approaching the toad in complete silence. When the snake arrived within range of attack, it seemed the toad was doomed. The toad suddenly took a defensive stance, with its four legs standing more firmly than before, instead of attempting a hopeless escape. At the same time, the toad's body swelled to twice its usual size, its eyeballs were popping out and horrible protuberances were sticking out from its skin. It even made grotesque noises. But, the truly amazing thing is what came next. The snake gave up its attack plans and slipped out of the scene. After the moment of danger, the toad's body returned to its original shape and size.

Why did the snake give up attacking the toad?

The boy Temujin gave a lot of thought to this issue. Finally he came to his own conclusion: the answer was fear. The toad had scared away the snake by making his body big and horrible, he thought. The boy Temujin stepped forward to find out why frogs didn't have such an ability, like the toad. If you tap the toad with a stick, it swells, but if you do the same thing to the frogs, nothing happens, they just run away. He found out later that the frogs had their own unusual ability that the toads didn't have. Frogs had protective coloration. When the frogs were in the green grass or leaves, they were green. But as soon as they moved onto the ground, their body color changed to the same color as the ground.

One time, the children found a lizard in the field and chased it. As they were chasing it, they tried to hit it with a wooden stick. The lizard tried to scuttle away by changing directions, this way and that, but finally it was hit. At this, the lizard cut off its own tail and continued to run away. The children gathered around the cut-off tail in great curiosity. The tail was wriggling like any another living thing.

Why did the lizard cut off its own tail?

The answer was simple. The lizard earned the time to escape by distracting his enemy.

The boy Temujin learned that in the arena of struggle for survival, even the smallest bugs have effective protective measures or weapons. The porcupine has quills like needles to protect themselves from approaching enemies, the pangolin has thick scales covering their entire body, like armor, and the scorpions have tails that sting with poison.

God created countless numbers of living creatures on this earth and then gave each one of them effective protective measures or weapons, and also the instincts to find food. That is not limited to the animal kingdom, but also includes the plant world. Some plants have poison or spines to protect themselves.

Owls have eyes with which they can find prey, even in the dark night, eagles have strong eyes to detect the tiny movements of a small mouse from high in the sky, spiders have thread stronger than iron, tigers have strong teeth and jaws that can crush the skull of any prey and leopards have instantaneous, reactionary force. The rats or the rabbits, which are considered to lack such efficient protective measures or weapons, instead have the power of fertility to increase their numbers greatly in a very short time. Some creatures thrive and increase in numbers, some others decline and become extinct. Why? Nobody knows.

One day, the coalition army of Tartars and Chin made a surprise attack on Yesugei's ordu. The Mongols had been looted by the Tartars on occasion, and from time to time, were invaded and ravaged by the regular Chin army. The ruling class of the Chin was afraid of the Mongols becoming stronger, so they dispatched their troops on a regular basis to reduce their numbers. They killed anyone they could see in the Mongol territory without any reason. They called it "Operation Thinning" and its aim was to weaken and eliminate future threat. Mongol children, especially boys, were the primary victims.

Since the Chin troops usually hit them by surprise, the biggest question for the Mongols was how to sense their attack beforehand and earn the time to escape or to be ready to defend. On that morning, the Tartars and the Chin army approached silently through the forest area under the mountains, bypassing the open land to minimize their exposure. It was early dawn, so it was still dark. When their vanguard passed a certain point, countless pigeons came out from wooden boxes hanging on the trees. The surprise attackers were surprised. Since the pigeons were carrying bells tied to their legs, Yesugei's ordu heard the loud noise of bells ringing. Yesugei could get ready for the attackers and minimize the loss. The attackers didn't know that between the trees there were many strings tied to each other and the end of the strings were connected to the covers of the boxes. It was early dawn, so they didn't notice that the horses of their vanguard cut the strings as they passed through.

At another time, about a thousand of the Chin and Tartar troops advanced toward Yesugei's ordu. Upon arrival, they first attacked the scores of yurts built on the small and large hills. They destroyed and then set fire to the yurts. But it was a ghost town; nobody lived there. Yesugei's ordu was far from there. The smoke from the burning yurts, or tent houses, was a signal to Yesugei. He knew they were coming, so he could defeat the enemy.

After the critical moment, Yesugei called Temujin. Both ideas, the pigeon's signal and the ghost town, came from Temujin. At first, Yesugei ignored his suggestions because he thought them too childish. However, after hours of thinking, he changed his mind, and decided to give them a try.

"Where did you get all those ideas?"

To his father's question, Temujin just smiled and shrugged. At that moment, Yesugei realized that his son Temujin would grow up to be someone important. He hugged his son firmly and said, "Oh, my son, I am sure you will destroy the Tartars and unite the whole plateau!"

Yesugei's love and attention toward Temujin doubled.

CHAPTER EIGHT

Return of Mamay

The nomads' winter migration begins when the Siberian chilled wind starts blowing from the north and the sea of green grass of the plain changes its color to a light tan and finally into meaningless, vague gray. The earth shrinks and the life force retreats back underground, starting the long winter sleep until next spring. Silvery snow covers the land like a sheet for the dead, making it more isolated and terribly lonely. Yesugei's winter migratory pasture was at the furthermost upper part of the River Onon, close to the mountain Burkan. If they went up further to the upper end of the Onon River, they could reach the point where the river becomes two small streams. It usually took a half day to get there by horse's trot from his summer pasture. The Burkan Mountain and the thick forest of fir trees, larches, and white birches around it were not only natural protective windbreaks, but also the home of many different forms of wildlife, including deer, gazelle, boars, bears, foxes, leopards and wolves. It was a great hunting ground, which was indispensable for the Mongols.

It usually took only half a day to assemble or disassemble a yurt. Sometimes khans used movable yurts, which had floors made of securely tied, half-cut logs with huge wooden wheels underneath. When this was the case, several oxen were needed to pull this structure and the bigger the yurt, the more power they needed. Sometimes, several dozen oxen were needed to move it.

Yesugei's group moved toward winter pasture, making an endless line. Since slow-paced livestock, like cows, sheep, and goats, were accompanying them, they could not speed up. They moved through the endless wilderness, without pause, like ants, along the watercourse of the Onon River. Over their heads, numerous groups of migratory winged creatures moved along with them or away from them. Occasionally, one or two eagles would circle high above and then fly away to the horizon touched with purple. Sometimes, a dim image of other migrating groups, faraway, at the other side of horizon, came into sight. The faint shouting of their herders, driving their livestock, reached their ears like in a dream. In those situations, they became more curious and alert. When one group made a movement, they had to be alert to the possibility of enemy attacks, so usually they would place heavily armed soldiers at the front and back. Yesugei preferred flat land for their course, instead of high or low hills, and when he found another migrating group, he always dispatched a scout to find out who they were. Yesugei's group could reach their destination in two days. They built the yurts, placing them into many folds of an oval arrangement with a huge, circular, open space at the center of it. At due north, the head of the ordu, Yesugei's yurt was built and to the left and right sides of it, his wives and children's yurts were placed.

The first thing Yesugei did after he moved to the winter pasture was go hunting. The hunting expedition was a big group event, joined by all the warriors and select young people in the ordu, numbering several hundred or, sometimes, several thousand. This expedition took them a minimum of several days, and up to, sometimes, more than a month. First, they encircled an area and slowly closed in, driving their game. This maneuver was divided into numerous small units and each unit had its own leader to control it. Each unit leader stayed in contact with the other leaders through messengers and reported to the chieftain or tribal leader on a regular basis. If the game escaped, the unit leader of that location took responsibility and it was considered great dishonor and shame. After careful investigation, if any mistakes were found, the person responsible was punished severely. They slept in the snow or sometimes they did not have the chance to sleep for days. The last day of closing the circle usually became the first day of their celebration or feast. The chieftain used to go into the circle first, where the scared gazelles dash and jump, the boar shrieks and the leopard roars and roams.

Yesugei entered the encirclement armed only with a bow and a few arrows. The first target he encountered was a leopard, crouched, roaring, with his horrible fangs exposed. Yesugei knew by the leopard's posture that it was only a moment before it would attack its prey. When Yesugei's arrow left his hand, at that same moment, the leopard jumped at him with its two strong hind legs pushing off the ground. However, the animal's speed could not surpass the arrow. Yesugei's arrow penetrated the animal's skull between its eyes, lodging deep in the brain tissue. The animal, while making a shrill cry, rolled over a few times on the ground, then became quiet and still. All the warriors watching this sent a roar of applause. They shouted "Yesugei!" rhythmically, as they were hitting their leather shields with their fists or stabbing the air with their spears. Next was Nekun, Yesugei's elder brother. He took aim at a big boar. His arrow was also accurate. His arrow's head passed through the boar's heart. The beast fell down, shrieking, and became stiff. The second roar of applause burst out. After that, one by one, the hunters showed their skill and valor.

Soon, the game was piled up in a great mass. Yesugei broke up the circle when he thought they had enough. The nomads, whose main occupation during the fall and winter was hunting, usually stopped killing after they had enough meat and leather for the winter. Killing baby animals was taboo and strictly prohibited.

Aman performed a ritual in front of the game as an expression of appreciation to the hunting spirits. First, he put a bowl filled with blood from the first animal killed, the leopard, on the altar and prayed. Then, using a bamboo brush, he sprinkled the blood around the altar. After the ritual, the game was distributed based on each household's performance and needs, and the households with pregnant women received double.

Yesugei's tent town began to get busy that afternoon. Even though the sun was still high in the sky, they began to build up the campfire and barbecue game. The cooking smells soon filled the space and hung in the air. Men were busy flaying, removing the claws and horns from the game, and women were dividing the meat for storage for the winter, or for immediate use.

Temujin was looking around the open ground with his brother Kasar. When he was near the southern end of the grounds, he heard a group of people shouting for something and making a loud noise. Temujin glanced at Kasar, and then they both dashed to that area. There, Temujin found a strange boy fighting with his half brother Belgutei. Belgutei was six months older than Temujin and he was bigger and stronger than any other boy in his age group in the ordu. It was a rather chilly afternoon; however, the two boys, with no clothing on their upper bodies, were striking the pose to begin a wrestling match and staring at each other. Several dozen boys and youngsters circled around them, encouraging the bout, shouting, hammering their fists in the air. The Mongolian boys started riding horses at age three and by age ten, they already knew how to use some of the weapons. Therefore, their fights sometimes developed into a life-or-death match. They were a people who rather enjoyed fights, probably because of the harsh environment and the never-ending small and large battles and wars among them. They were born fighters. Physical strength and valor were basic requirements for survival in a harsh land and anyone without them was simply doomed to perish.

The two boys, staring at each other, were moving their feet slowly and carefully, making a circle, waiting for their chance to attack. Suddenly, Belgutei stretched his left hand and grasped his opponent's neck, while at the same time, with his right hand, he held the other boy's right hand and tried to twist it. The other boy escaped swiftly from Belgutei's attack and then he began to attack Belgutei by holding his wrist with his right hand and twisting it. The strange boy began to strangle Belgutei from behind with his left hand. On Belgutei's brow, beads of sweat began to stand out. This position lasted for a while, but Belgutei was able to escape successfully. Belgutei massaged his painful right shoulder for a moment and then took an attacking posture again. This time Belgutei was successful in clinching the other boy's two arms and waist from behind. Gradually he applied more pressure to his arms to tighten his hold. However, the other boy quickly changed his body posture to a squatting position, raising his two arms up. He freed himself from Belgutei's attack. The two boys' torsos were covered with sweat and were shining like fish scales reflecting the afternoon's strong sunlight. Belgutei began to show his impatience and irritability. He had always believed that he was the strongest wrestler in his age group. Many of the town's people agreed with that. The strange boy showed no sign of fear; rather, he was cool and stable, even though he was surrounded by unfamiliar people.

"The outcome of this fight is very clear. The strange boy has already won," thought Temujin. A Mongolian wrestling bout, in many cases, ended up with one contender's death by strangulation or by breaking the other contender's neck or spine, unless one of them surrendered.

The two boys gripped each other's hands again. This time, they wrestled with their arms for an advantageous position. Suddenly, Belgutei began to kick the other boy's groin. The strange boy temporarily dropped down on his knees with a short scream. Without hesitation, Belgutei began to strangle him from behind.

"This is absolutely against the rules. Isn't it?" thought Temujin.

It was against the rules in Mongolian wrestling to hit the opponent with fists or elbow, and especially to kick below the belt. Temujin threw his horsewhip to the strange boy. After picking up the whip, he stabbed Belgutei's eye with the hard tip of the handle, which was made of woven leather string. As he was screaming, Belgutei stepped back, releasing his opponent's arms and then covered his eyes with his hands.

At that moment, Bektor appeared on the scene. Bektor was a full brother to Belgutei and a half brother to Temujin. Bektor and Belgutei's mother was Sochigel, who was the second wife of Yesugei. Bektor was always unhappy with the fact that, even though he was two years older than Temujin, he couldn't be an official heir to his father's ordu because his mother wasn't the first wife. He became a violent, troubled boy. He took the horsewhip from the strange boy and then began to kick his belly. Temujin walked up to him and tried to stop him.

"Bektor! This is not right! You shouldn't do this!"

Bektor was a little surprised by this unexpected new enemy. Soon his eyes were filled with anger and hostility toward

Temujin. Bektor often thought that the main cause of his frustration and unhappiness was Temujin.

"Today will be your last day!"

He spat these words out to Temujin and came up to him. Now it was their turn. The four boys started each of their bouts risking their own lives. The audience was excited for this unusual dual match and cheered, rooting for the side they had chosen. The fights became very furious and it seemed that there would be no end until someone's death.

Yesugei, upon learning of his children fighting, galloped to the site. The crowd quickly opened a path for him. After he passed through the crowd, he began to whip the four boys mercilessly.

"Get off! Stop it!"

Temujin, Bektor and Belgutei, seeing their father, parted and stopped their fighting. Staring at each other, they stepped back.

"Let them continue! A boy cannot grow up without fighting!"

A man on horseback, who had been watching the bouts from the beginning, made this remark with a gentle smile on his lips. All eyes turned to this man. He was wearing a cap made of fox fur and a coat made with an unknown animal hide. On his left and right sides, from his waist, a Turkish half-moon-shaped scimitar and a Chinese dagger were hanging. His face was deeply suntanned due to the strong, wild steppe wind and desert heat, and yet his two eyes were sparkling.

"They don't have enough power or skill to kill their opponents."

He made this short comment to Yesugei. As soon as Yesugei glanced at him, he realized that he was Ouluun's brother, Mamay.

"Mamay! It's been a long time!"

Yesugei welcomed this unexpected visitor with both arms wide open. They kept on shaking hands for a while.

"How can a beast possibly pass by barbecuing smoke?"

Mamay said this as he laughed loudly. He was referring to the barbecue smoke filling the town.

"What is your name?"

Temujin asked the strange boy, as he was handing over his clothing, after he picked it up and shook off the dust.

"My name is Jamuka. I am really grateful for your help."

The two boys shook hands.

"Come with me! My mother is probably waiting for us with barbecued meat."

Temujin led him by his hand. The boy Jamuka belonged to the Jadarats. His father was the chieftain of the Jadarats, but after he lost the war with another tribe, he disappeared. Some said he ran away to a faraway land to live there and some others said he died on the battlefield without being recognized, and was eventually eaten by the wolves and vultures, like every other dead body. His mother left their ordu with Jamuka and wandered around from town to town, giving help to others for food. His mother learned there would be a hunting feast in Yesugei's ordu, so she stopped by with Jamuka to get some meat.

"A boy cannot grow up without fighting. Same thing for the adults; non-fighters will never grow up."

Mamay was talking like this in front of the boys. It was an early winter afternoon full of warm sunlight. Mamay was taking a break on a small hill with the boys after watching their archery contest. The boys' topic was the bouts that had happened on the previous day with Jamuka versus Belgutei, and Temujin against Bektor. It was one day after Mamay and Ouluun had met again after a ten-year gap. It was an emotional moment for both of them. Ouluun was weeping, like the day ten years ago when she said farewell to her brother. Even for a woman like Ouluun, who had grown up in the toughness of the steppe and dryness of the desert, there could be a moment for tears. Her two dark brown eyes, shedding the tears, were filled with beauty. Her body, after carrying and birthing four children, had not lost its original shape and fitness. Mamay was quite relaxed when he found his sister was doing fine and was healthy, except for the fine wrinkles around her eyes.

"I am a vagabond," Mamay answered when Ouluun asked where he had been. "Since I left you, I have been roving around and been to many other places."

After these words, Mamay regarded her as if he were trying to read her face. Mamay worried a bit that his story could mislead her to believe that his recent whereabouts were relevant to her.

"Why don't you settle down? Stay with us."

Ouluun said this wholeheartedly.

"Sister, that is the lifestyle I like; it is probably in my blood. I'd like to share my stories of my travels and experiences with your children. I will stay until I finish."

Mamay was with the boys and among them were Temujin, Jamuka, Temujin's brother Kasar, Jelme of the Uriangkads and his brother Chaulqan and also Temujin's cousins, Quchar and Sacha.

The boys were talking to Mamay on a small hill covered with dried grass, each in his own comfortable position, sitting cross-legged, lying down, or leaning on their arms. Over them, a group of migratory birds were passing by, high in the sky, lined up in an orderly manner.

"Even the adults cannot grow, if they don't fight?"

Kasar asked Mamay this with the look of a child's innocence, recalling what Mamay had said the other day.

"That is right. Even the adult cannot grow without fighting. Fighting is an essential part of life. Through fighting, you can learn something and become stronger. That is nature's law." That was Mamay's answer. His voice was a little bit husky, but strong and heavy. His tone was friendly and quite persuasive. He showed no trace of fatigue or servility, which sometimes could be found in the wanderers who left their hometowns long ago. He was bright, cheerful and full of high spirits. While he was talking, he made facial expressions and gestures to accent the meaning and at other times, he tried to enhance his persuasiveness through body language.

This time, Jelme joined the conversation and gave his comment.

"Belgutei wasn't right. He kicked the opponent, between the legs. That is against the rules."

At this, Mamay thought for a while and then responded.

"Correct. Belgutei wasn't right. However, Jamuka's reaction, poking Belgutei's eye with the horsewhip, was against the rules also. After all, you have to win the fight, especially when you are risking your life."

The boy Belgutei was commonly acknowledged by others as the wrestling champion of his age group. Maybe he couldn't tolerate losing face in front of the group of people.

This time Temujin asked in a quiet voice, looking at his uncle, Mamay, "There are always rules and regulations in fighting, right, Uncle?"

Mamay answered, looking straight in Temujin's eyes, "Of course, there are always rules and regulations in games and fighting. However, in games of life and death, things can be much different. In that case, rules and regulations could be meaningless."

That was it! Looking for the rules and regulations in the fight of life and death would not be considered a smart philosophy or a piece of comedy played by a buffoon. Victors are always right, because they can justify themselves. The losers have to beg for mercy for their existence and have to accept all the rules and regulations that the victors impose. The losers are inferior, below moral standards and against God's will. That is the universal rule in human history for the past, present and future.

At this point, Mamay stopped talking and looked each boy in the eyes. Mamay could sense that Temujin and Jamuka were following him through their eyes. Mamay continued.

"Danger and fights are routines in a man's way. If someone is trying to escape these, he is already a dead man."

This time, Jamuka, who had intelligent eyes, asked a question of Mamay.

"How can you get courage?"

Mamay looked at him and shrugged with a smiling face, yet said in a firm and decisive tone, "The courage comes when you are completely sure that what you are doing is completely right, I think."

After these words, Mamay got to his feet slowly. He smiled as a token of appreciation to the boys who had been attentively listening to his story. He added one more thing.

"The fight should not be started on impulse. A victory is not a victory until it is complete."

They continued the archery contest. The target was a dummy man made of a leather bag filled with dried leaves and grass, posted fifty steps away. They were using junior-sized bows and arrows, which were smaller and shorter than the adult versions. At the final round, only three contestants were left: Temujin, Kasar and Jamuka. They were given five arrows each. Temujin was first. Three of his arrows hit the dummy.

Same with Jamuka. Kasar was the last and he hit the dummy with four of his arrows. Kasar won the applause from the group and became the champion. Mamay, who had been watching this game from the beginning, approached Kasar with a smile and patted him on his back. After checking Kasar's bow, he remarked, "You seem to be a born archer. With hard training, you might be able to become a master."

Mamay asked the boys to retrieve the arrows lodged in the dummy, and to choose five of them. He started shooting. He squinted at the target for a while, controlled his breathing and then let it go. The arrow hit right in the middle of the forehead. Mamay got applause from the boys. The second one hit the same spot. He won a second round of applause. The third through fifth arrows also hit the same area, resulting in five bull's-eyes. The boys' applause rang out five times. Mamay, after retrieving all five arrows, readied himself for the second shootings. He took a piece of black fabric out from his pocket and blindfolded himself. The boys gave a look of curiosity and wonder.

"What is he doing? Is he going to try shooting with his eyes blindfolded?"

That was the common question for all the boys there. Mamay began shooting blindfolded. He aimed at the target, took a deep breath, and then let it go. The arrow hit the exact same spot he hit before, the bull's-eye. The boys exclaimed in amazement. The other four arrows all hit the same spot, as they did before. The boys couldn't believe their eyes and couldn't close their mouths. Mamay, after removing the fabric, let out a loud laugh at the boys who were giving him a look of awe.

"Uncle, how could you hit the bull's-eye while blindfolded?"

Temujin, in great amazement, approached Mamay and asked him this.

Mamay, with a faint smile on his lips, said in a strong tone, "You should shoot not by your body, but by your mind. When your mind is accurate, your body will follow. Everyone has the power inside of them. Obey it!"

After these words, Jamuka neared him and asked, "What is the inner power?"

Mamay also gave a smile to Jamuka and answered, "That will be your homework. When you find your own answer, it will be more meaningful."

CHAPTER NINE

The Road
for the Man

"This is my story of when I was traveling around Cathay across the Great Wall," Mamay started. It was the night of the day the boys had the archery contest. All the boys, Temujin, Jamuka, Kasar, Jelme, Chaulqan, Quchar and others, gathered in Mamay's yurt. They were listening to Mamay, sitting on the floor covered by Persian carpet, or on the wooden taborets, each in their own, comfortable positions. In the metal burner, located in the center of the room, they were burning dried horse dung, and from it, orange flames were dancing up gently, while thin grey smoke was spiraling up into the ventilation hole on the vault of the yurt. The wind occasionally flapped the felt door covering the southern entrance. It was warm inside. The shadow of Mamay with his thick beard, made by the light from the Arabian lamp, was being cast on the inner wall of the yurt.

"One day, I was walking on the mountain road in exhaustion. I was lost and I couldn't eat or drink for three days. I was looking around for houses, and I sometimes shouted for help.

No help came. All I could see was low and high mountains covered with thick forest and I could hear nothing but the sound of the wind. It was getting dark. I couldn't even tell the direction. To make it worse, I was getting sick. I had a high fever and my body was shivering. I fell down. It was very clear that, without a miracle, it would be the last day of my life, and then eventually, I'd be eaten up by wild animals. I was losing consciousness. It was getting darker and darker like thick grey fog was engulfing me."

After this, Mamay picked up the Chinese teapot and poured the hot tea into the porcelain cup and sipped it slowly. The tea was still hot and gently steaming. The boys were waiting for him to go on in deep silence.

"Later, I opened my eyes and noticed somebody was pouring water into my mouth. I tried to collect myself and looked around. One man was repeating the same action, pouring water from a leather bag into my mouth and then shaking my shoulders. It was already completely dark. Several men on their horses were watching me and a couple of them were holding torches. When I regained consciousness, they asked me some questions like who and what I was and also where I was from. After they had my answers, they talked to each other for a while, and then finally, a couple of them lifted me onto one of their horse's backs and carried me to their dwelling place."

Mamay paused a moment and emptied the tea out of the cup, into his mouth.

"Their dwelling place was a big cave in the mountain. The entrance was not so big, but once you stepped inside, it became wider and higher. It looked like at least twenty to thirty people could live there without any problems. I could see wooden beds in there and also a stack of possessions that looked quite valuable. They were using the water coming down from the rock wall as drinking water. They gave me something to eat and drink and also provided me a warm, comfortable bed, so I could recover faster. They saved my life and I really appreciated that. There were seven of them and they really didn't give off a very good impression with their rough manners and harsh language, but I never asked them who they were.

"One day, before dawn, they left for somewhere, leaving me alone in the cave. It was almost the end of the day when they came back. They were carrying a great mass of items on their horse's backs, and to my utter astonishment ..."

Mamay stopped at this point and stared at each one of the boys' eyes as if he were trying to study their reaction.

"... to my utter astonishment, they brought five young Buddhist nuns. No, actually they kidnapped them. They were bandits. My life has been saved by bandits. On that day, they attacked the Buddhist temple, killing all the monks, old nuns and disobedient ones, and then robbed valuable things and kidnapped the young nuns. They raped the nuns one by one and asked me to do the same thing. I refused, telling them a lie that I hadn't fully recovered yet. The Buddhist nuns were wailing in fear, with their faces buried in their curled up arms and bodies. I could see with my own eyes how miserable human suffering can be with that terrible scene. That night, I couldn't sleep at all. I had been suffering emotional conflict, agonizing for a long time about how I can accept this and how I have to react to this. They saved my life and I owe my life to them. However, before dawn, I made up my mind. At early dawn, when they fell into a deep sleep, I set a fire at the entrance. When the thick smoke was coming in, they woke up in surprise, and rushed out from the cave. At the entrance, I killed them all, one by one. After that, I descended the mountain escorting the five Buddhist nuns, who were shaking in fear until that time, and took them to a safer place."

At this point, Mamay stopped talking and regarded the boys one by one. He asked the boys, "What do you think? Have I done right or wrong?"

The boys talked to each other for a while and then Temujin turned to Mamay and said, "I think you were right, Uncle."

Mamay asked, "How come?"

"If you had stayed, you probably would have become one of them. They wouldn't let you go, being that you knew their whereabouts," Temujin answered without hesitation.

Mamay asked, "I could have run away without killing them, right?"

To this question, Temujin also answered without pause.

"No! That might not be a good choice either. It would be a cowardly act if you ran away to protect yourself, leaving five helpless Buddhist nuns behind."

Mamay looked at Temujin's face in deep silence for a while, in an unusual way, with eyes of admiration, wonder and surprise. A boy was clearly understanding a man who's had tremendous experience in life. Temujin's balanced facial outline, well-proportioned forehead, nicely shaped and positioned nose and firmly closed lips were in good harmony and gave the impression of stability and unchallengeable dignity. His two dark brown eyes looked to be imbued with unaccountable mystery, like an abyss of which nobody could see the bottom. His eyes were sparkling, even under the dim light from the lamp. They looked as if they kept the delicacy of the eagle, which can notice even the slightest movements of a small worm on the ground from high in the sky, the sensitivity and sharpness of a wolf, which senses movements of small animals from far away, the smartness of the fox and the dignity of the tiger. Mamay pondered a while.

"What can I teach him? He already knows the answer, even before I tell him. He probably knows that I didn't feel good about killing the seven bandits and if I ran away, even if I succeeded in escaping, I might have suffered from a self-inflicted label that I am a good-for-nothing coward."

Mamay even felt certain fear. He continued, "The concept of good and evil can be dubious. The good in certain cases can be the evil in others. It depends on the direction you are seeing it from."

After these words, Mamay picked up the porcelain kettle from the table and showed it to the boys.

"Look at this. If I hold it like this and if you see from that direction, you can see only the round portion of the kettle. However, if I put the kettle sideways, like this, you will see both the body and nose portion together. That is it. If you judge anything from the point of view only you can see, chances are you will make a mistake. You should see the whole picture, not just one part of it, if you want correct judgment."

The boys talked with each other. Mamay continued, "Men made the law to differentiate the good from the evil and also punish the evil. This is the story of the civilized world."

After this, Mamay picked up the kettle again to fill the cup and sipped slowly. He then took a dried date from the wooden bowl, put it in his mouth and handed the bowl over to the boys. They forgot to talk during the pleasure of the sweetness from the dates. The strong wind was continuously hitting the tent wall, sounding like drumming.

Jelme asked Mamay, "Don't we have the law?"

To answer this question, Mamay took the date seed out from his mouth with his fingers and said, "Of course, we have the law. There are certain rules people agree to; among them, that you should do this or you shouldn't do that. However, we don't have a systemic law. To have systemic law, you need a writing system. We don't, so they call us 'barbarians.'"

Mamay picked up a small piece of a wooden stick from the ground, and put one end of it into the orange flame coming out from the burner. He took out the flaming stick, blew out the flame and waited until it became sooty. Then he began to write something on his palm with the sooty end of the stick.

"This is the Chinese letter meaning 'the law.' In Chinese, each letter has its own meaning. Sometimes, two, three or more letters combined together make up a completely different meaning. This letter meaning 'the law' is made of two different letters. This part, the one on the left, from your direction, means water, and the right side means 'going.' That means the water flows."

At this point, Mamay had to make sure that the boys were following him.

"Chinese thought that 'the law' is like the water flowing. Why is that?" Mamay asked, while continuing to show the Chinese letter on his palm. The boys talked with each other again. This time, nobody gave an answer immediately. Mamay looked at Temujin. That was a kind of message telling Temujin that Mamay was waiting for his answer.

Temujin opened his mouth.

"The water runs downhill, right?"

"So?"

"I think the law is the same thing. The law also runs down."

"Why is that?"

"As the law runs down like water, it influences the downstream people. So, the law is made by upstream people to control and manage the downstream people."

Mamay got excited. It was a wonderful answer. It was the same or very close to the reason why the Chinese made that letter based on their philosophy that the law is like water flowing.

"I think in this way."

This time, Jamuka came forward. Mamay watched him.

"The river winds on its way down, right? It's because the river bypasses the mountains or big rocks. I think that means the law cannot pass over the strong or powerful men, only bypass them."

Mamay was astonished one more time. The two boys gave an answer without difficulty that even adults couldn't think out easily. Mamay regarded Jamuka for a while in great wonder. He had a well-balanced face with a well-built nose, firmly closed lips and his two eyes sparkled with brilliance. However, his overall image was not as strong as Temujin's, Mamay thought, probably because of his light skin.

Mamay felt happiness deep inside. It was like the feeling when you talk to a friend who understands and communicates with you very well. The boys gathered every evening at Mamay's yurt and talked. The boys were thirsty for the stories about the mysteries of life and nature, stories about the curious, faraway countries beyond the horizon. Mamay was the right one to quench their thirst.

"The greatness of the Cathay was in the scale. They had grandeur and delicacy as well. They developed the arts and on top of that, they built up philosophy."

Mamay was talking about the Cathay across the Great Wall, about their civilizations, their riches and power and about all the empires that had emerged and perished.

"They live in cities covered by big walls. The populations of some of their cities was more than a million, they said. The emperors built their palaces inside the city with many more walls. They were living in a city that was built inside the city.

They were supplied everything they needed and their luxurious lifestyle was beyond imagination. They didn't need to go out, because they had everything."

Chinese civilization may have been built by the people living inside the wall; however, because of the wall, they couldn't go out. They became selfish, self-centered and conceited. They put up the wall to protect themselves; however, they actually put the wall up in their minds, too. Those were the points of the story Mamay told.

"They regarded all other people around them as barbarians. I, rather, laughed at them. They had fat bellies and, at the same time, they lost their pure minds. Honesty was considered stupidity and humility was a weakness. It was a sick man's world."

The collapse of the great empire begins not from the outside, but from the inside and the very first sign of it is moral collapse.

"The emperors and the ruling class were seeking only the pleasures of life and their main concerns were delicious foods and beautiful women. Their emperors' tombs were as big as large mountains. Once they became emperor, the first thing they did was build their own tomb. They said it usually took more than twenty years."

Mamay continued, "One time I visited a big city. Its name was Chang-An. The marketplace in that city was crowded with many people, selling and buying rare and luxurious merchandise from many other countries. There were a lot of foreigners there and it was like an international city. I could see many lodging houses

and inns for the foreign merchants and visitors, restaurants selling rare foreign foods, and theaters and opera houses. They had temples for Buddhists and temples for Muslims, which were built in the Chinese style, and even worship-places for Christians."

All these stories were like fantasies for the boys who had been living only in the desert and the grassland.

"There, I could meet the merchants from Baghdad. There was a caravan of merchants traveling to Baghdad from Chang-An and they were looking for temporary employees. They were very cautious about hiring someone, but, after I gained their confidence, I could accompany them all the way to Baghdad. It took one year to get there and another year for me to come back, so in total, it was a two-year journey. They left Chang-An with three hundred horses and camels and also mountains of merchandise on each one of them. The main item they purchased from Cathay was silk. Their members were about 200 in total, yet the combined numbers with temporary employees could reach about 250. They seemed to know the route very well, because they had traveled it many times before. However, in cases when they weren't sure, they would hire local guides. They were tough and tolerant of the hardships coming with the long, dangerous journey. Wherever they went, they had to get permission from the local chiefs and also had to pay taxes."

Mamay was talking about the Silk Road. The Silk Road was the main route not only for trade between the East and the West, but also for the exchange of information, techniques, science, culture and religion. Nobody knew when it had started, or who had started it. On the other hand, the Silk Road was a route paved with blood. Many warlords raised wars to monopolize this route, which could bring them tremendous wealth. The winners could build up their wealth based on the taxes they collected from the caravans.

"I crossed several deserts and many mountains with them. When we were crossing the Pamirs, even the horses fell down from dizziness because of the lack of air. The mountain road to the Hindu Kush was so narrow, only one camel could pass through at a time. One misstep could bring horrible disaster for both men and animals, because next to it was an enormously high cliff of rough rocks. They said once you fall down, your body will be torn into pieces before you even reach the bottom."

Mamay explained to the boys where the Pamirs and the Hindu Kush were located. He also told them about the cultures and lifestyles of the people, and any special products they had, like charcoal or yaks.

"We arrived at Samarqand several months after we left Chang-An. Samarqand was a beautiful city."

Mamay was talking about the oasis city located in the middle of Central Asia. He talked about the mild weather there, Arabic-style buildings, beautiful gardens and their richness.

"They said their population was more than a half million. It was a big city."

Mamay told the boys about the Soghds, the major tribe who was controlling Samarqand and how they could amass riches by collecting taxes from the caravans.

"They have watermelons and pomegranates."

Mamay had to spend a lot of time explaining what watermelons and pomegranates were and what they looked like for the boys, who had never seen them before. He also talked about the cultures and customs of the Tajiks, the Kirghiz, the Cossacks and the Uighurs.

"We headed for Baghdad, passing through Bukhara and Merv. We had to speed up because we stayed too long in Samarqand to reorganize. Before we had arrived at Samarqand, five of our group lost their lives from accidents, diseases and combat with small groups of bandits. They said there is a much better chance of survival in caravanning than in joining the war, and they laughed loudly at saying this. Usually, once we paid the taxes to the rulers in those regions, their soldiers escorted us to a safer place. Sometimes, disagreements with the chiefs about the unreasonable amount of taxes they were demanding delayed us from further negotiations. Some caravans cover only a limited area due to high taxes and safety issues, but usually they were the small groups. While traveling, we encountered many other caravans and on that occasion, we exchanged information about safety and road conditions, such as actual conflicts or the possibility of war in certain areas."

At this moment, among the boys, who were listening with breathless attention, Temujin came up with a question.

"Uncle, if one person or nation holds and controls the whole Silk Road, it would be good for the caravans and for many people, too, right?"

Mamay, as he looked straight into his eyes, answered firmly.

"Right, if someone takes over the whole Silk Road, he will be the conqueror of the world."

Mamay was right. At that time, the two big axes of civilization were the Chinese and the Saracens, based in and around Baghdad, and the bridge that connected these two civilizations was the Silk Road. The one who held the Silk Road would dominate the market and acquire commercial power and, at the same time, get all the valuable information coming from these two civilizations. Later, the knowledge and techniques to make gunpowder and paper transferred from the East to the West and techniques to make glasses, the Arabic numerals and the concept of astronomy were introduced from the West to the East. That was only a part of it.

"I went to Baghdad. And from there, I went further west to Syria and even to the Mediterranean Sea.

"There, I saw endless war between the Islamic world and the Christian kingdom. They were repeatedly taking on and losing the city named Jerusalem, which they declare their own holy place. Many people were dying under the name of the holy war and it seems it will never end until one side perishes."

Mamay's story continued for many days and his invaluable experiences were engraved in the boys' minds and remained there a long, long time.

Mamay left. It was about the time when the new spring began after the northern land's long winter. He had stayed there for about four months. He was wearing the fox-fur cap and the coat made with animal leather just like when he had arrived four months ago. He disappeared into the horizon. Temujin saw his mother's eyes full of tears. Ouluun must have had her heart broken by sending her brother off again. Mamay left one poem. The night before he left, he sang a song for Temujin and all other boys, playing a two-stringed instrument. When his husky, strong voice was drumming the tent wall, the boys were captivated and fascinated.

> *The earth is my cradle.*
> *The whisper of wind is my lullaby.*

> *Where the red sun rises,*
> *And where the silvery moon stays,*
> *That is my homeland.*

> *Who gallops on the dark barren,*
> *Soundlessly?*
> *Who gallops on the red desert,*
> *shadowlessly?*

> *One scimitar, two arrows,*
> *They are my only friends.*

> *Those are the lonely,*
> *Who seek the truth.*

> *My right hand, as tough as ever,*
> *Will guide me through.*

CHAPTER TEN

Betrothal to Borte

One day Temujin was called to his father. He was nine years old at the time. While he was heading for his father's yurt, he had been thinking and wondered why his father wanted to see him. He had a little hint. A couple of days earlier, his mother, Ouluun, hugged him firmly for a while and wouldn't let him go. That was unusual. Ouluun looked directly into his eyes, as she held his shoulders with her two hands, and then said, "Soon you will get engaged. A man needs a woman who will take good care of him. That is the one who will keep your bed warm, be a friend when you feel lonely and eventually become your soul mate. You will leave us for a while. Don't take it hard. You will stay in your future wife's home with her family members until you get married. After the formal marriage, you will be back. Someday, you will take over your father's ordu and become the leader of fifteen thousand households."

The flap door of Yesugei's white yurt was wide open. It was a balmy spring morning. As Temujin stepped into the yurt, he could see his father and mother were sitting on their chairs side by side, and around them were Aman, the shaman, and the other two town elders, including the old man Charaka, sitting next to each other. By the door, Munglik, Yesugei's loyal servant, was standing. Ouluun was looking at Temujin with moist eyes, but still with a smile full of love and pride. The two old men were also wearing gentle smiles around their eyes and lips. Yesugei, who was the only one who looked serious, scanned Temujin from head to toe and then said as if he were making a solemn declaration, "My son, you are old enough to get engaged. Now, you have to leave your parents. Stay there until you get married, for as many years as you need, and then come back to us."

The old man Charaka, who was watching Temujin with a smiling face, said jokingly in a singsong tone, "The woman is an oasis in the desert, a horse in the battlefield and a burner in the cold winter days."

He then laughed openly, looking at the other old man as if asking for agreement.

The old man Charaka was a career war veteran who had trodden on many battlefields when he was young. Temujin liked to listen to his stories of the battlefields and he took care of Temujin very dearly. Ouluun picked up a small purple and gold inlaid wooden box from the table and showed it to Temujin. The box was shining from the enamel and a good polishing.

"In this box, I put a small bronze hand mirror and an ivory comb. These are my gifts for your future wife."

Ouluun carefully wrapped the box with the red silk cloth embroidered with flowers, and handed it over to Temujin. Temujin, as he was receiving the wrapped box, asked, "Who is my fiancée?"

To that question, Ouluun looked at Yesugei, who was sitting next to her, for a moment, maybe for his consent, and then answered with a smiling face.

"Your fiancée is a daughter of an Olqunuud chieftain. We have chosen her among my hometown girls. She is one year older than you, so she is ten now."

Yesugei, after a long silence, opened his mouth and said gravely, as he was getting on his own feet, "Son, we will leave soon. Get ready. Jelme and Chaulqan will accompany you. If you have any other friends in mind, tell me."

Temujin gave Jamuka's name.

They headed for the east. Yesugei and the four boys, Temujin, Jamuka, Jelme and Chaulqan, went across the vast expanse of the steppe. It was springtime. Warm sunlight was pouring over the plain and hills; nevertheless, the air was still chilly. They had to wear the del, the thick Mongolian-style wool coat. The new buds of the plains, which had retreated underground during the wintertime, began to show up and covered the ground, making the hills look like green velvet. The shimmering air at the far distant horizon was like wriggling snakes, and if you watched the horizon for some time, you would fall into the illusion that the earth was dancing. On their way ahead, one or two larks, making short, feeble but pleasant nasal sounds, were repeating the same movement again and again: flying up high in the sky, diving down close to the ground, gliding for a while over it, and then flying up high again. Sometimes, they could see three or four marmots, hurriedly returning to their holes, waddling their fat bodies, surprised by the noises and indication of the group's approach. The boys would yell and shout to make the small plains animals more surprised and to enjoy the scene that the animals made, doubling their speed and then making their waddling motion look much funnier.

The boys, full of curiosity, dreams and ambitions, were very excited by their journey. As they continued on, they chattered and raced each other and sometimes rode up to the top of the hill and looked around seriously at this new land that they had never trodden before.

"You must be excited to get a girl, Temujin."

Jamuka giggled as if he were playing a joke on Temujin. In return, with his whip, Temujin hit the rump of Jamuka's black-spotted, grey horse to frighten it, and then said, "You are one year older than me. How come you don't have one?"

As Jamuka's surprised horse bolted, Temujin followed him and hit it again and again.

Close to sunset, they crossed the plain and arrived at an area like a barren. It was not like the land they just had passed through, which was made of good soil and abundant grasses. This was a land with only short shrubs, with thick dried branches, and the ground was made of half sand and half gravel. Since even the horses refused to eat the dried shrubs, it was impossible to stay in this area too long. They didn't have camels, which were the only animal that could eat and digest this type of plant. As they were moving on, they found a small lake. The lake was covered with a mixture of mud and gravel around the shore area, and some dead, dried water plants were around it. The dark-blue lake was immeasurable in its depth and the water didn't move at all, like ice. A deathly silence covered the lake and caused an unknown chilling; an unpleasant air was hovering around it. A big, unfamiliar water bird suddenly pierced the stillness with a horrible cry, flew over the water and disappeared into the far distant hill.

To the north and northeast, they could see a big mud cliff, seemingly artificially built, that was surrounding the lake like a folding screen. The mud cliff was reflecting the orange color of the setting sun, and as time went by, it changed into blood red.

"I think I know this place. Several years ago, there was a big battle around here. Before the battle, many people lived here and it was quite busy. However, after numerous people and horses had drowned in this lake, it was abandoned and became a dead lake. There are probably still remains of numerous humans and horses at the bottom of the lake."

Yesugei gazed at the lake with deep emotions, his eyes shadowed with dark memories. Nobody knew what was on his mind. Maybe the last cries of his friends and followers who died beside him in this battle were coming back to his memory and making him sad.

"We will camp out here tonight."

Yesugei told the boys his plan. The boys were against his plan because they didn't like the place; however, Yesugei persuaded them that they could not proceed because night already had fallen upon them. They dismounted and began to build a tent. The boys gathered the small and large dried branches and set the fire. Fire was necessary not only for cooking and warming, but also for warding off the dangerous wild animals in such places. They put a small pot on for tea and chewed dried beef.

Yesugei had a nightmare that night. He was strolling along the shore. From underneath the surface of the water, which was still, dead calm and covered with thick fog, rose numerous bodies, making bubbles. They were the dead soldiers from the battle. They were all approaching Yesugei with their faces and bodies covered with blood. Their eyes were unfocused, like dead men's, and some of them were holding their own dismembered arms or legs. Their hair was disheveled and their torn combat uniforms and armor were hanging on their bodies. As they were approaching, they were chanting "Yesugei" in feeble voices, horrible and full of agony and sorrow. Yesugei tried to escape from them, but he couldn't move at all, as if his two feet were locked in thousand-pound shackles. Yesugei tried to shout as he was punching them away, but he couldn't make any sound.

He struggled and writhed to free himself for a while and at last woke up screaming. It was a cold night, but he was wet with sweat on his forehead, face and all over his body. As he was sitting down, he wiped his face with his sleeves. He looked around at Temujin and the three other boys. The moonlight through the open space of the flap showed the dim image of sleeping boys. He sighed. Temujin woke up from his sense of somebody else being awake and sat up. He looked at his father and asked, "Father, are you all right?"

Yesugei hugged Temujin, and whispered in his ear, "Of course, I am all right."

Yesugei kept on hugging him for a while. Temujin felt a little bit uneasy because this was not like him. What's on his father's mind? Temujin would never find out. As he was feeling the warmth of his father's arms and chest, he recalled the words his father had given him many times before.

My son, you are my only hope. You must fulfill our ancestral dream of unifying the plateau, and building up the great image and power of the Mongols.

The moonlight through the half-open flap door was pouring over the father and son, who were hugging each other tightly.

Early in the morning, they left the lake and galloped for half a day. They could see on their left side the branch of the Kerulen River and thick forests of poplars, tall bushes and an occasional willow along the river. They kept moving along the winding river for a while and then they arrived at a spot where they could see a big mountain covered with tall larches and fir trees. Between the mountain slopes and the river was the reed forest, as tall as adults, and when they had passed throught it, a vast plain appeared in front of them. At the far distant end of the plain, a faint image of numerous yurts, like thousands of mushrooms, came into their sight.

"This mountain is called Chekcher and the town you can see there is our destination," Yesugei explained to the boys, waving his hand. The boys were shouting and tried to spur their horses to speed up, but Yesugei stopped them. It had come into Yesugei's sight that a man on a horse was approaching them. They stood still and gazed at the approaching man. The horse was white and the rider was a medium-sized man of middle age. His thin, balanced and light-colored face was covered with numerous wrinkles, and his eyes had a prestigious and dignified look.

He recognized Yesugei. With a smile on his lips, he dismounted his horse and raised his two arms as a welcoming gesture. Yesugei did the same thing in response. They hugged each other and touched their cheeks together, one side after another, three times. That was the nomads' way of greeting, but only between two parties in complete confidence and mutual trust.

His name was Dey Sechen, an Olqunuud tribe chieftain, and he was a leader of about ten thousand households.

"I am giving you my warmest welcome. I came out to look around because I thought this was about the time of your arrival. I might have been worried if you came later than this."

Yesugei introduced Temujin with a smiling face. When Dey Sechen faced Temujin, he stopped his movements for a moment, and took a careful look at Temujin's face and body. Before long, with a big smile on his lips, he hugged Temujin and said, "Oh, you are my son-in-law! I am really happy to see you."

Dey Sechen seemed to be quite happy with Temujin. He may have been thinking something like *Look at this boy! He has sparkling fire in his eyes, and has glaring light in his face.*

Yesugei introduced Jelme and Chaulqan.

"These two boys are called Jelme and Chaulqan. They are brothers. Their father is an Uriangkad and has been helping me for many years now."

Then, Yesugei introduced Jamuka.

"He is my son's friend. He is a Jadarat and I knew his father a long time ago. He is staying in my ordu temporarily with his mother now."

Yesugei and Dey Sechen headed for the town side by side at a slow, relaxed pace. Dey Sechen said, "I had a dream last night. A white falcon perched on my hand with the sun in its one hand and the moon in its other. Thanks to the sun and the moon, it became very bright around me. I was laughing in great joy and then I woke up. I told this story to those around me and they all said it's a good omen. Today, my future son-in-law, Temujin, has arrived and I think it is related to my dream last night, and I am sure he will bring glory to my clan, too." After this, Dey Sechen let out a loud guffaw.

"Is that so?"

Yesugei simply responded like this. However, in his mind, he might have said *What does a dream have to do with the real world? I had a bad dream last night. It has nothing to do with the future.*

Some time later, they arrived at Dey Sechen's ordu. Yesugei's group received a warm and courteous welcome from the town elders and warriors, who came out to see them at the entrance of the town, seemingly notified of their arrival beforehand. In the nomadic society, the connection of marriage between two clans meant a strong political bond.

When they were passing along the wide road between the two lines of yurts, curious women stepped out, watching them coming in, and the town's children and dogs followed them, shouting and barking noisily. As Temujin frowned, Jelme and Chaulqan escorted him on both sides, driving off the dogs with whips.

Temujin didn't dislike the dogs, but sometimes he feared them because of a bad experience he had had years earlier. When Temujin was five years old, one day, one of his favorite big dogs had disappeared. The town's children grouped together to look for him, but they were not successful. Several days later, the dog came back. However, he wasn't like he was before. He was sick. His eyes were aglow with madness, radiating a frenzied, blue light and his mouth was foaming. He became furious, snarling at anybody approaching. He didn't even recognize Temujin, who was his owner. People didn't know he was attacked and bitten by a wolf before he disappeared.

"Watch out! Don't get close to him! He is a crazy dog," the town's adults warned the children. Finally, the crazy dog had bitten a boy's hand, and then ran away. Yesugei ordered his men to chase the dog and kill him. This unhappy memory had caused Temujin to avoid dogs ever since.

Dey Sechen ushered them into his first wife's yurt. It was a huge one with two columns, unlike the others, which had only one, and inside, it was furnished with luxurious furniture and decorative items. First, each one of the guests was served a big silver basin with water and towels to wash their face and hands, which were stained with dust and sweat. They were also given dels, the Mongolian traditional coat, each one of them in their own size. Yesugei was served Chinese rice wine, and for the boys, honey drinks were provided.

"We trade with the Chinese over the Great Wall," Dey Sechen said as he was offering rice wine, which he had just poured into Yesugei's Chinese porcelain cup. They toasted each other.

"I have three wives; however, I have only one daughter and one son. I am probably the one who has problems."

After he said this, he burst into laughter. At this moment, a servant came in and notified him that his first wife and his daughter had arrived. A middle-aged woman in luxurious red silk garments with a bogtaq (a cylindrical headgear only for married women) on her head stepped into the tent with a girl, hand in hand. The woman greeted Yesugei by bowing and putting her palms together.

The girl, standing tall, glanced at each boy, one by one, without any movements. On the girl's head was a pink half-moon-shaped headgear, decorated with numerous milk-colored beads in a flower pattern. Under her flying-seagull-shaped eyebrows were deep-seated eyes shining like black pearls, and under the nicely shaped nose were two red lips, which were nicely balanced and closed. She had a chubby face and quite light skin, unlike desert and grassland women. From her headgear, numerous lines of beads were hanging down, covering her ears and shoulders. She was clad in a light pink silk garment covering her ankles, and over it, a deep red vest that fell to her knees.

Though the girl was ten years old, she looked like she had already begun to develop a woman's body. Her sparkling eyes bespoke her smartness and wit, and her bright face suggested nobility and high self-esteem.

"My daughter's name is Borte."

Dey Sechen introduced his daughter and then proudly praised the girls and women of his clan, Olqunuud, the sub-clan of the well-known Onggirads.

"Our women have beauty, smartness and virtue. Many chieftains and their children want to find their brides among us."

The moment Temujin saw Borte, he felt like he had been struck by a thunderbolt or hit by a big fireball burning his flesh and bones. His heart began to beat uncontrollably and it even became difficult to remain sitting down calmly because of his shaking hands and legs. His mouth became dry, and he could hear his own heart beat and could feel the pulsations of his neck vein. Temujin was dazzled by her beauty and nobility.

"Borte, who will be your fiancé? Tell us!"

For this question, it was not Borte who was frustrated, but Yesugei. Yesugei looked at Dey Sechen, but Dey Sechen gestured him to wait and see how it went by holding his hand lightly. Yesugei was nervous that the girl might make a mistake.

If she were to err, it would be a shame, not only to herself, but to everybody in the room. For a while, the girl, with a smile on her lips, looked at each one of them carefully. Then, she pointed directly at Temujin. Yesugei heaved a sigh of relief and Dey Sechen gave a hearty, loud laugh.

"Borte, how did you know he will be your fiancé?"

Dey Sechen, after the laugh, asked Borte in curiosity. He was always amazed by his daughter's brilliance and wits and he was sure that his daughter would not disappoint him on that day, too.

"Father, that was an easy one."

"How?"

"First of all, he was the one that looked most like his father. Second, he was closely sitting next to his father, and third ..."

"Go on!" Dey Sechen urged.

"He is the only one who is shaking."

With this reply Yesugei burst into laughter. Jamuka, who was sitting next to Temujin, made fun of Temujin, poking his waist with his finger, and whispered in his ear, "Temujin, you got entangled with a difficult one. This lass is too clever. It is better with a none-too-clever one."

CHAPTER ELEVEN

Death of Yesugei

I t was next to impossible to survive on the steppe in a unit of only one or two families. That was because big-game hunting, which was essential for the nomadic lifestyle, was impossible for the small group and they couldn't protect themselves and their livestock efficiently from attacks from their enemies. They developed the clan system for this reason and if one clan was relatively weaker than others, they had to seek unification with others for more power. The smallest possible form of the union of the clans was called an ayil. If two or more ayils merged together, making a bigger group, they called it a kuriyen. Usually a kuriyen consisted of a thousand households or more.

The strong and rich clans were independent. If not, they had to submit themselves to a stronger one, going into serfdom, or had to attack a weaker one to make themselves bigger and stronger. If the head of the independent unit was a soldier, they called him the Bagatur. If it was a shaman or religious chief, they called him the Beki. If he ruled the clan with his wisdom, they called him the Sechen.

When many clans merged together to form a big group, they called the head of the group the noyan. If many clans of the noyans merged together to become big enough to be called a nation, the head of the entity was called the khan.

Yesugei's clan of fifteen thousand households was a comparatively large one at that time and was composed not only of the Kyat Mongols, but also many other clans. Yesugei was one of the eighty-one strong men who were ruling the plateau at that time, and they called him Yesugei the Bagatur.

Yesugei stayed there for two nights and on the third day, early in the morning, he left. Yesugei left Temujin there. Temujin was supposed to stay in his future wife's home until he was married, regardless of how many years it took. That was the long-standing tradition of the steppe people. Basically, the purpose of this was for the boy to build up a close relationship with his future wife's family and let his future wife's family have the chance to see more closely what was in store for their family member's future. Yesugei left three other boys along with Temujin, so that Temujin should not get homesick due to sudden change.

"You boys, stay here five more days. I will send somebody to pick you up."

Many people came out to see Yesugei off.

Yesugei kept on galloping without pause. He took the same route home. Since there was no reason to delay, he spurred on and on. He galloped alone on the endless plain. On his way back home, however, he was unlucky. After a half-day's run, he met a gale with heavy rain. The wind was strong enough to blow down a man and a horse, and the streaks of heavy rain kept hitting his eyes and cheeks. Some bean-sized hail among the raindrops added pain. Even his horse was kicking and screaming.

Knowing that proceeding farther was impossible, he had to find a shelter. He hid himself behind a nearby small hill. The wind was a little weaker there. He remained there for almost another half day. The gale had stopped; however, it was already getting dark. He sped up. Some time later, a dim light from a nearby place came into his sight. Suddenly, he realized he was wearing a coat soaked with rainwater. He headed for the light. On the plain, there were two temporary camps, and around them several men were preparing dinner. They put an iron kettle over the campfire for hot tea and were also barbecuing meat. At the sudden appearance of Yesugei, they seemed to be surprised and they looked at him cautiously. Yesugei tried to relax them.

"I am a traveler. I wonder if I can warm myself at the fire. I am all wet because of the rain."

With permission, Yesugei dismounted his horse and sat by the campfire. Yesugei quickly realized they were the Tartars. However, there were some customs and etiquette among the steppe people. If you encountered someone who was lost or hungry and thirsty on the steppe, you had to help them, even if they were your enemy. At the same time, the recipient should not refuse the favor.

"It seems you didn't have much rain here. But the area I came from had a big storm. It delayed my travels."

After these words, Yesugei looked at the sky. Strangely enough, the sky was clear with the exception of a few small patches of clouds. It was a full moon. Yesugei decided to continue his travel with the help of the bright moonlight. One of the Tartars recognized Yesugei. He signaled with his eyes to the other Tartar to come to the other side of the tent. He whispered, "I know that guy. He is the Kyat Mongol chieftain, Yesugei Bagatur."

After this, he took a small leather bag from his waistband. "Put this into his food and tea!"

It was an extremely poisonous powder made from the wild mushrooms in the forest, which had no smell and no taste and once in the human body it destroyed the nervous system and blood vessels. They secretly put the poisonous powder into the tea and the barbecued meat that they would offer to Yesugei. Yesugei couldn't refuse their favor.

"Now, I feel pretty warm and so I think I have to continue my travels. I really appreciate the favor." Yesugei mounted his horse and left. As he was departing, he waved his hand at them, but there was no response from them. They just gazed at him from their sitting or standing positions.

Yesugei galloped for a while. Soon he found something was going wrong within his body. It became hard to breathe and he began to feel his stomach ache. At first, he ignored it. He thought it was simple food poisoning. However, when he saw blood was coming out of his nose, he realized that he had eaten deadly poison. Yesugei immediately dismounted the horse and began to vomit. He became exhausted. He was the man with an iron body, trained on countless battlefields. But he could not defeat the poison, which was already circulating in his blood. He knew he could make it to his ordu by dawn on horseback.

Yesugei was lying in his deathbed. Around his bedside were standing Ouluun, Yesugei's brothers, Aman the shaman and the town elders, all with sad expressions.

"I have been poisoned by the Tartars. I know my days are over. Go fetch me my sword! It is a shame to die with my hand empty, without a sword."

Yesugei summoned his children. They all gathered, except Temujin. They were Kasar, Kachun, Temuge and a one-year-old daughter, Temulun, who came from Ouluun's womb, and Bektor and Belgutei from his second wife Sochigel.

"My children are still young. Who will take care of them after I die? That makes me heartbroken."

Yesugei said this in short breaths. His face had turned dark-blue from his difficulty in breathing.

"Who is there?" Yesugei shouted toward the door. His loyal servant Munglik was standing by the door and he quickly responded to his master's call.

"Yes, master, Munglik is here."

"Bring Temujin back!"

Yesugei didn't feel comfortable leaving Temujin in somebody else's hands, even though they were his future wife's family, now that he was going to die. By order of his master,

Munglik galloped at full speed a whole day and night. He arrived at Dey Sechen's ordu the next day.

"My master, Yesugei Bagatur misses Temujin very much since he left him. I came here to bring him back to my master temporarily."

Dey Sechen approved without any question.

"If your master misses his son so much, you may take him back to him. But I want him back as soon as possible."

Munglik left there with four boys.

Yesugei could manage three more days after he sent Munglik. But he couldn't remove the veil of death. Ouluun was wiping the sweat from his forehead and cheeks with a soft towel. Yesugei knew his last moment had come. He held Ouluun's hand and said, "Ouluun, I loved you. It's been pain in my heart that, to have you, I had to kidnap you from somebody else, not by an official marriage proposal. Please, forgive me if you still have even a tiny bit of hatred toward me."

Ouluun regarded him in tears for a while and answered, holding his hand tight, "None."

Yesugei died in Ouluun's arms. Ouluun wailed. Temujin arrived after his father had died. Temujin could only see his father's cold, dead body.

The boy Temujin left his ordu for a seven-day camping trip about three months after his father's death. Jamuka was with him. Temujin didn't go back to Dey Sechen's ordu. He wanted to be with his mother. Their destination was the Burkan

Mountain. The Burkan Mountain was the place that Batachi-gan, who was believed to be the first Mongol, had settled on and so it was looked upon as the holy mountain by the Mongols. They galloped together, side by side, on the grassland. Temujin's thick gray stallion and Jamuka's brown mare were swift. Their horses' manes and tails were fluttering in the wind. They galloped, making long tails of golden dust as it reflected the midsummer day's shining, sparkling sunlight. They went up, farther north, along the Onon River branch. They crossed the plain and arrived at the shrubbery zone at the upper end of the Onon River. Now the river was a small stream, flowing over a large area of gravelly field, and alongside it, shrubs and bushes were growing.

The stream was making a clear, pleasant sound. After the shrubbery field, they had to pass the reedy area, where the reeds were as tall as an adult. Later, they arrived at the gently sloped hill, and, at the end of it, there was the great mountain, covered with huge rocks and sky-high pine and fir trees. It was Burkan Mountain.

The mountain was standing in great dignity against the background of the deep, blue sky and it seemed to be covered with mysteriousness and holiness. It was dead silent, except an occasional wind sound passing though the needles of the pine trees. The air was clean, cool, fresh and soaked with the purity of the rocks and greenness of the pine trees.

The Mongol boys used to go on camping trips by themselves or with friends. These were solely for training. They had to test themselves on a regular basis on what they learned from their parents and town elders on how to survive in the desert and steppe. They had to find food, build a temporary hut, and make a fire for cooking and warming up. They were given only two arrows and a bow for hunting, one dagger and a small lump of dried meat for emergency food.

Temujin was gazing at Burkan Mountain. What was on his mind? Nobody knew. The sun, which was already setting toward the west, was making the boys' silhouettes, with the dazzling, radiating background lights, appear to have halos.

They built a temporary hut and set the fire. They skinned and barbecued two rabbits they had caught that day, which were more than enough for dinner. After eating, Jamuka said, "Temujin, be careful. Just because your father died, the people around you won't treat you as the owner of the ordu of fifteen thousand households. Some people, who were polite to you so far, might be rude and some people who were smiling at you won't do that anymore. That is the nature of the human mind. My father was the chieftain of the Jadarats, who were twenty thousand households. I was the official heir of that ordu. However, since my father was missing, nobody would treat me as the heir. I had to get out of there with my mother to save our lives. That was what had fallen upon me. I hope the same thing does not happen to you. We are too young. We have to wait."

Jamuka was biting his lower lip. He continued, "My mother and I will leave your ordu soon. That is my mother's decision."

Temujin opened his eyes wide and asked, "If you and your mother leave my ordu, where are you going?"

"I don't know yet."

After these words, Jamuka continued with a grim smile on his lips, "My mother is still young and pretty, like your mother. She will surely find a way."

Jamuka saw his mother sleeping with Aman many times. It would have been impossible for Jamuka and his mother to stay in Yesugei's ordu such a long time without tacit approval of the shaman, who was the ruler of the spiritual world of the town's people.

There was a long silence between the two boys. It was becoming dark and the light from the campfire turned the two boys' cheeks red. The flames from the campfire were dancing gently in their eyes. Jamuka said to Temujin, after some silence, putting his hand on Temujin's and shaking gently, "Temujin, be my anda. I will be yours too. We have got to help each other. We have a long way to go."

"Anda" meant sworn brother among the steppe people. At that time, the anda relationship was stronger than that between real brothers and they helped each other, even risking their lives when in need.

Temujin looked into Jamuka's eyes. He could read the truth in his eyes, which was coming from deep inside his mind. The two boys began to smile at each other and then finally burst into laughter in great joy.

"Fine! Jamuka, let's be andas to each other. I like you too."

They hugged each other and shouted in excitement.

"If we become andas, who will be higher? You are one year older than me, so you will be my elder brother," Temujin said with sparkling eyes.

Jamuka replied, looking into Temujin's eyes, "There is no higher or lower between us. We are twin brothers."

The boys had a ritual for anda relationships. First, they exchanged their own arrows. Temujin gave an arrow made of juniper to Jamuka and Jamuka gave a "godori" to Temujin, an arrow that makes a whistling sound when shot. After that, they cut each of their little fingers with a knife and then touched their fingers together. Now, their blood had been mixed. They became andas. That was done under the holy Burkan Mountain, where their mutual ancestor, Batachigan, the first Mongol, had settled down.

CHAPTER TWELVE

Rebellion of the Taichut

*T*he deep water has dried up. The bright stone has broken into pieces. Those were the thoughts upon Yesugei's death. For a while, it was quiet and nothing happened. But people began to grow uneasy, because Yesugei's official heir was only a ten-year-old boy. The Mongols were a clan society. If one clan grew too big, as time went by, they would split up. This was inevitable for the nomadic people, who had to move around with their livestock upon every season. However, in many cases, their separation came from the disharmony among themselves or the pursuit of their own interests. About three hundred clans on the Mongolian Plateau were formed like this, and so, basically, they were neither enemies nor friends with each other. They valued only one thing, profit. If another clan's interests coincided with theirs, they were considered friends; if not, they were enemies. Their society was not a peaceful coexistence; rather it was a bitter feudal society. They had to kill their enemies, or be killed by them. Yesterday's enemy could be today's friend and today's friend could be tomorrow's enemy. The weaker clans were in constant danger from attack by the stronger ones and eventually they would become prey to them. The weaker clans or individuals who couldn't protect themselves had to find their own protectors. If one clan was conquered and combined with another one, through war, the losers became slaves. In that case, the losers were called "otogus bool." On the other hand, the individuals or groups who joined of their own will were called "nokhod." The nokhods were free men and they could leave any time they wanted.

After Yesugei's death, the people of fifteen thousand households began to split. They didn't feel safe. They were the people who'd been attracted by Yesugei, who showed great leadership. When Yesugei had gone, they could see no leader there. They were an endangered group. At any time, a neighboring, stronger clan could attack and enslave them. They left on an individual basis or as small groups. They sneaked out at nighttime or even during the day, while many others were watching them. Nobody knew where they were going. Mostly they went to neighboring strong clans, like the Jurkins or the Jalairs. Some of them crossed the Gobi Desert and went to the Shisha Kingdom. The Shisha Kingdom was the nation born and developed around the oasis cities on the southern side of the Gobi Desert. They amassed great wealth by taxing the caravans that passed through. And to protect their source of income they nurtured strong troops. The Mongol refugees faced discrimination there, but at least they could get food and necessities.

Within a year, the population of Yesugei's ordu had been reduced by half, but nobody could stop them. That was an example of a perishing clan.

One day, they were going to have the ancestors' memorial ceremony, which was the most important and largest event of the clan. It was held only once a year and the attendants were strictly limited. If someone was not allowed to attend, that meant he was expelled from the clan. While Yesugei was alive, he was the leader of the ceremony and he decided who would attend and who would not. The altar was set up at the Yekesun Hill, on the southern side of the ordu, where their ancestors' tombs were located.

Early in the morning, Ouluun cleaned her body and set out on a trip with her three sons. She left on time, but she couldn't speed up because she had to ride the horse with her four-year-old son, Temuge, on her bosom. She arrived at the site a little late. On top of the hill was the altar, which was a stack of a few rectangular stones, and around it were several wooden poles tied with many pieces of blue silk cloth.

In Mongolian culture, the first-born son of the family usually presided over the ceremony. They called the oldest son of the clan the "beki," which meant master of ceremonies. Usually, the beki started the ceremony by sprinkling the kumis around the altar and then reciting the prayer for the bliss of their ancestors. He burned the offerings, which were mutton and horsemeat, letting the smoke go up into the sky. The beki had the right to decide who could attend the ceremony or not, so his power among the clan members was enormous.

When Ouluun and her sons arrived at the site, the ceremony was already finished. Ouluun couldn't understand. The women who attended the ceremony were clad in long white costumes down to their ankles and wearing the bogtaqs on their heads. It seemed that they were cleaning and arranging things just after the ceremony. Some women were sharing the leftover offerings of mutton and horsemeat. When Ouluun and her sons showed up, nobody paid any attention to them. Some of women glanced at Ouluun with no greeting and turned back to the conversations among themselves, and some others even cast hostile looks at her.

"What? The ceremony has been finished already? How could you do it without my son, Temujin?"

When Ouluun heard that it was done already, she was shocked. She shrieked in protest. As Ouluun continued making a loud protest, two old women approached her. They were Orbay and Soqatay, the two widows of the late Ambakai Khan. Orbay said, "From now on, you and your children don't need to attend this ceremony. We will take care of all the ceremonies related to the ancestors from now on."

Ouluun was struck dumb with astonishment. She realized that she couldn't see anyone of the Kyat clan, which the late Yesugei and Temujin belonged to.

"How can you do this? You know that you were under protection of my husband, Yesugei, and that his son, Temujin, is the official heir of this ordu. How can you ignore him like this?"

As Ouluun's high-pitched complaint continued, Soqatay said, as she was casting a look of great contempt, "We recognize Yesugei, but we cannot accept you and your sons. Yesugei might have considered you his first wife, but we cannot approve your legitimacy. You didn't marry him in the official, traditional way. Yesugei has a son, Bektor, who is two years older than your Temujin."

Ouluun was stunned by her words. It was a greatly humiliating remark. If she had said that while Yesugei was alive, she might have lost her head on the spot. She was openly insulting Ouluun about being abducted by Yesugei. Ouluun hurried back to the ordu. Her sixth sense was telling her that very bad things might happen. She was right; the ordu was captured by the Taichuts. They rebelled.

The Kyats and the Taichuts had the same ancestors. The Kyats were the descendants of Kabul Khan and the Taichuts were the descendants of Ambakai Khan. After Ambakai Khan's death, the Taichuts were broken into smaller groups. They joined up with Yesugei, who showed great leadership at that time. They were a kind of nokhod to the Kyat clan.

But this time, after Yesugei's death, things had changed. The Kyats became weaker. The Taichuts took advantage of it. They took over all the properties Yesugei had amassed, including thousands of head of livestock, mountains of weaponry, silk and leather products, luxurious furnishings, decorative merchandise and jewelry. They didn't stop there. They snatched the legitimacy of their lineage, which the Mongols valued greatly. This was all masterminded and led by two brothers, Talgutai Kiriltuk and Todogen Girte. They deprived Yesugei's brothers and other important Kyat clan members of their weapons and horses and took them into custody. Talgutai put all the people of the ordu out on the open ground and began to provoke the crowd.

"Yesugei's time has gone! We couldn't leave all these problems untreated. If things go on like this, we will all be destroyed. We are going to have a new order and a new future. Join us, and follow me!"

It sounded quite reasonable. But the devil always comes wearing the angel's mask. He continued, "If you follow me, you will be accepted as brothers. If not, you are my enemies."

Next to him, Todogen Girte was on a horse, armed with a scimitar and spear, and hundreds of heavily armed horsemen were with them.

"From now on, we, the Taichut will take over the main lineage of Bodonchar and Kaidu. If there's anyone who is against this, step forward."

There was deep silence. The crowd was overwhelmed by the power of Talgutai Kiriltuk and Todogen Girte. At this time, one old man stepped forward and stood in front of them. It was the old man Charaka.

"Talgutai and Todogen, you cannot do this. You were under the protection of Yesugei and you are indebted to him. You are obliged to protect his family and his properties. Now you are going to take everything from them. It's not right! Drop your evil plan now!"

But before he finished speaking, Todogen spurred his horse and speared him deeply in his bosom.

From the wound, blood gushed. At that moment, Temujin rushed out from the crowd and tried to help the fallen old man by holding his head with one hand and trying to stop the bleeding by pressing the wound with the other. At this scene, Todogen whispered to Talgutai, "Let's get rid of him, too. I think that's the way we can prevent future trouble."

Talgutai stopped him.

"No. The time is not right. If we kill him right now, we might lose the support of the people. The time will come when we can get rid of him with good reason."

Talgutai and his Taichuts left there with all their property with them. Many families followed them. Now Temujin's family was left in complete ruin. Only several dozen families were with them. Nekun, Yesugei's elder brother, also left to find a group he could depend on. One day, Daritai, Yesugei's younger brother, came to see Ouluun.

"Let's get out of here. I think we'd better find some other clan that we can get help from for the time being."

Ouluun rejected his proposal.

"No. I will stay here with my children. This is the land my husband, Yesugei, breathes and his body heat remains. I am going to raise my children here."

Daritai also left there with his family. Nobody stayed with Temujin's family, except several handicapped and older people who didn't have their own families. Sochigel, the mother of Bektor and Belgutei, also left to find work to feed herself. She left her two sons to Ouluun, because she couldn't be sure that she could feed them.

Now Temujin's family fell into extreme poverty. First of all, they had nothing to eat. Ouluun had to go out to pick wild grapes and dig out wild taro, onions and garlic. Temujin and his brothers went out to the field to hunt marmots and to the Onon River to fish. Beef and mutton, staples of the Mongols' diet, was rarely available to them. They were always hungry and there were always disputes and disagreements at the dinner table over how much food each would get. Ouluun always told them a story or two to maintain her children's harmony.

"One or two arrows can be easily broken. But a pack of five can never be broken. You are like that. If you are together, you can beat even the most powerful enemy; if not, you will be broken one by one. The harmony should start at the dinner table."

They led a life of despair, hunger, fear and virtually no hope. It was a hard time for Temujin. Ouluun taught her children that the real value of an individual depends on how they overcome hardship.

"You need to have a dream. The one with the dream is the only one alive. If you've lost your property, you have lost a small thing. If you lose your people, you have lost a big thing. If you lose your hope, you have lost everything."

Ouluun encouraged their children like this. They managed, for some years.

CHAPTER THIRTEEN

Death of Bektor

There was not complete harmony in Temujin's family because Temujin could never get along with his half brother Bektor. Bektor was two years older than Temujin; however, he couldn't be the official heir of his father's ordu. He was very unhappy about that and he became a ruthless, violent boy. After their father's death, he openly insisted that he was the real successor to their father.

One day, two messengers from Talgutai of the Taichut visited Ouluun's yurt. That was the year Temujin was fourteen and Bektor was sixteen. The two messengers delivered Talgutai's message in front of Ouluun and all her children.

"If Ouluun, the widow of the late Yesugei, acknowledges and accepts the legitimacy of the lineage of the Taichuts, some part of her property will be returned. And it will be fine to live in the Taichuts' ordu."

Ouluun immediately rejected the proposal; that would be too great a submission. That meant that Ouluun and her children would become the Taichuts' otogus bool. Ouluun could never accept that. Talgutai took all the property and people that the late Yesugei had amassed, but he couldn't take the legitimacy. Now he was trying to buy legitimacy, not only for the lineage, but also for the property he had already taken. He tried to create the formal impression that everything was done by Ouluun's donation and free will, not by force.

The eyes of Bektor, who had heard everything from the beginning, began to shine. He stood with his arms folded.

This was because the Taichut acknowledged Bektor as the heir. If Temujin's family could get back some part of the lost property, it would be Bektor's. The property concept of the Mongols at that time included not only the weapons, livestock and material things, but also the people. So if they could get back the property, that meant they could have some power under Talgutai. However, the decision maker was Ouluun, the widow of the former leader of the ordu, and she refused.

"Anytime you change your mind, just let us know."

The two messengers left after these words. In the evening, at the dinner table, Bektor began to talk about the incident in a loud voice. "Let's get father's property back. I can no longer tolerate hunger."

Temujin was angry at Bektor's remarks. Temujin stared at him and said angrily, "Bektor, we cannot do that! They are our enemies. They took everything from us; once a traitor, always a traitor. We cannot submit to them now."

Even Belgutai, the brother of the same womb, was against it.

"We cannot trust them. Even if we got something back, it could be just a small amount and we will end up becoming their slaves."

But Bektor kept on insisting on it. The relationship between Temujin and Bektor went from bad to worse. Bektor claimed that he was the real successor of the late Yesugei and the head of the family. He even distrusted Ouluun. He thought Ouluun was trying to cover the truth for her own sons. He repeatedly mentioned the same thing, again and again, when he was in a dispute with Temujin:

"I am the real successor of my father. You are two years younger than me, so how can you become the successor?"

That was a serious challenge to Temujin, and a great humiliation for Ouluun, who was the official first wife of Yesugei, and a dishonor to their father's decision. Temujin was in agony. Who is the enemy? Anyone who is in the way is the enemy. It could be a close friend or it could even be a brother. It is much harder to get rid of the enemy close by. A great amount of courage and coolness is needed for that job.

One day, Temujin was fishing with his brother Kasar. It was around noon, in midsummer. They were fishing by the Onon River with a hook made of a sharpened, curved bird's bone attached to a thin string made from flax stem. It was a lucky day. Before long, they hooked two shiny, big silver trout out of the water. Kasar shouted in great joy. The trout, covered with shiny silver scales, was wriggling and flapping strongly in Kasar's hands. Kasar carefully tied the fish with the flax stem string through the mouth and the gills. He put the fish back into the water, holding the other end of the string. In this way, he could keep the fish alive and fresh until they finished fishing. Temujin clapped Kasar on the shoulder in pride. They were sitting side by side on the riverbank. They were so poor that they couldn't afford beef or mutton, and so fish was an important source of animal protein for them at that time. If they were unlucky at fishing or failed at hunting, they had to be satisfied with wild onion soup that Ouluun prepared.

At this moment, Bektor approached them from behind, silently. Temujin and Kasar did not notice him. Bektor snatched the string Kasar was holding. With the two trout, Bektor began to run away swiftly toward the hill. Kasar chased. However, big-bodied Bektor pushed Kasar down and kept on running. Temujin saw this and thought, "This is the time I have to get rid of him. Not long ago, he stole a big lark Kasar had caught. If I don't do it now, he will be my lifelong headache."

Temujin got to his feet, slowly, and called Kasar, who was swearing and shaking his fist in the direction Bektor disappeared.

"Fetch me a bow and an arrow. I will judge him."

With a bow and an arrow in his hand, Temujin slowly began to walk toward the hill Bektor had run to. Some time later, Temujin and Kasar found Bektor. He was taking a break on a small hill and Belgutei was with him. They had already eaten the two fish. Belgutei was holding a bow in his hand. Upon the sudden appearance of Temujin, Bektor seemed surprised and stood up with a tense look. Belgutei stood up, too. Temujin, staring at Bektor, slowly stepped toward him, ignoring Belgutei. Temujin stopped at a certain spot and, without saying a thing, just stared at Bektor for a while. Hot afternoon sunlight was pouring onto their heads and it was very quiet. The eerie silence and the air imbued with the coldness of death hovered over their heads. Temujin slowly raised his bow. He had only one arrow.

What was happening to Bektor? He didn't take any action to resist or protect himself. He was like the dog paralyzed with fear facing the tiger or the hypnotized rat that came across the snake.

Was it the truth? No. Humans tend to give up resistance when they accept their own faults. Bektor could fight back against Temujin with Belgutei's bow. But neither of them were taking any action.

"The successor of Yesugei, the chieftain of the Kyat Mongols, is Temujin. It's me. This is for you, under the name of the successor."

The arrow left Temujin's bow with a deadly whistling sound and at the same moment, its head lodged into the upper part of Bektor's belly. It penetrated and cut through internal organs and the liver artery. Bektor, holding the arrow with his two hands, stared at his front for a while, with unfocused eyes. On his forehead, beads of painful sweat stood and then flowed down his face like rain. Through the spaces between the fingers holding the arrow, came the blood and, at last, from each corner of his big mouth, the blood flowed. Finally, he knelt down on the ground and then fell over completely. It was a quiet afternoon and nobody moved. The sunlight was pouring on their heads like it had before.

Ouluun was enraged when she learned Bektor had been killed by the arrow shot by Temujin. She knew it was her responsibility to take care of not only her own children, but also Sochigel's. She lamented and rebuked Temujin severely.

"Did you forget the lesson of the five arrows? If you fight and kill each other, how can you accomplish revenge on the Taichuts, who took all of your father's property and still will not give up the plan to destroy our family completely, and on the Tartars who poisoned your father? Did you forget you have nothing but your own shadow?"

Ouluun shed tears. Temujin's heart was breaking to see his mother's agony. But he said to his mother, "Mother, the gangrenous finger should be cut off. If not, you will lose the whole hand later on."

Ouluun was still angry, even with this remark, because she was in a different situation. From Temujin's point of view, he removed his rival. However, from Ouluun's, she lost her husband's other son, who was under her care and responsibility even though he was not her own. And moreover, he was killed by her own son. That made her feel guilty and she would suffer a long, long time. Temujin knew this and he loved his mother, and so he was suffering too.

A dirty dog,
  Eats her own afterbirth.
A selfish camel,
  Bites his offspring's ankle for his own feed.

A hurried wild duck,
    Swallows her own chick in danger.
A hawk of poor judgment,
    Attacks his own shadow.
A foolish bear,
    Dashes against the cliff.
A furious lion,
    Cannot hold his anger.
A brutal tiger,
    Does not differentiate its prey.
A merciless serpent,
    Swallows its prey alive.

Temujin understood his mother's different world. He understood everyone had his, or her, own world. It is quite difficult, and sometimes impossible, to measure one world with another world's ruler. That is the weakness of mankind.

Temujin apologized to his mother. Temujin took out his dagger from his belt. It was a curved Turkish dagger given to him by his father, the handle of which was decorated with precious stones. Temujin said, as he was handing the dagger over to Belgutei, "Belgutei, you can judge me at this moment. Whatever will be your judgment, I will accept that. You have the right."

Belgutei looked from the dagger to Temujin's eyes, one after another, for a while. It was a tense moment. What action would Belgutei take? Temujin's eyes showed no fear or hesitance. Belgutei returned the dagger to Temujin and said,

"Temujin, I cannot do that. Bektor wasn't right. I advised him many times. I acknowledge you are the only official successor of our father. If I were in your position, I might have done the same thing."

Temujin could read the truth in his eyes. They understood each other very well. Temujin held Belgutei's hands and then finally they fell into each other's arms.

CHAPTER FOURTEEN

Attack of the Taichuts

Several months had passed and the new spring had arrived. The steppe had keen ears. The talk that Temujin had killed his half brother reached Talgutai. Talgutai thought it was the right time to get rid of Temujin. He summoned Todogen and discussed.

"I think the right moment has come. Now, we have a good reason to get rid of him. Nobody will reject the idea of punishment for someone who has killed his half brother. And he is bigger now."

Talgutai began to take action to carry out the plan, which he had been plotting for years.

Todogen, who was straightforward and ruthless, said with a light heart, as if going on a rabbit hunt, "Give me twenty men. I will bring him here within three days."

Lifting up his eyes, shaking his head, Talgutai answered with a negative.

"I know him. I have been watching him since he was a small boy. He is extremely smart and his wits are beyond imagination. A careless approach will give him a chance to run away forever. We'd better go together. Get two hundred men ready. We will start early tomorrow morning."

Talgutai and Todogen drove their horses northwest in the direction of Temujin and his family's yurts. They arrived there before noon, but they found nothing. Temujin had anticipated their attack, and he had already moved his family to a safer place. It was a place where three of its four sides were protected by cliffs that were impossible for men and horses to access, and only the northern side was open to the high mountains. Between the place they were now staying and the high mountains, a small stream was running, which was part of the upper branch of the Onon River. Temujin's family ordu, which was composed of three yurts, was protected by stacks of big logs to the north, where there was no protection from the cliffs. It was a perfect fortress.

After a thorough search, Talgutai finally located Temujin's ordu. He was struck with admiration by the toughness of the fortress.

"With all those features, even with only a few people, they might be able to protect themselves from several dozen attackers."

The log wall was built by Temujin and Belgutei. In case they were under attack, the logs could be released to stop or delay the advancement of enemy horses.

Talgutai ordered his men to shoot flaming arrows. The Taichuts' fiery arrows showered around the three yurts and some of them hit the walls and roofs of the yurts, which were made of well-dried felt. At last, thick dark-grey smoke was rising from two of the three yurts. A few horses, tied around the yurts, stood on their hind legs, neighing, surprised by the fire.

"Send us Temujin! We need only Temujin! If we get Temujin, we will go back!" Talgutai shouted to the hill. At this moment, a man on a horse jumped out from the yurt and swiftly galloped toward the mountain area. It was Temujin. Talgutai immediately ordered his men to chase him. Temujin's horse-riding skill well surpassed the pursuers'. Some time later, Temujin left his pursuers far behind and made it to the taiga area in Tergune Heights. The taiga was a densely forested area with sky-high tall trees, waist-deep accumulation of fallen leaves and thorny creepers twining around the tree trunks. If they didn't know the exact entrance, it was impossible to enter for both the men and the horses.

Talgutai, who was running after Temujin with other chasers, sighed in front of the taiga area, "Even a snake might not be able to get in there! We can do nothing but wait until he comes out by himself."

Talgutai took a long-term strategy. He surrounded the area with his men. Temujin held out for three days. At night, he slept on the ground and covered his body with fallen leaves, like a blanket. In the morning, he collected dewdrops on the leaves and used them for drinking water. From an early age, he had trained himself for survival in the forest and the desert. Even in the daytime, due to heavily forested trees, it was hard to get to the sunlight and due to the heavily piled-up, rotten leaves, the air was humid. All he could hear was the sound of the wind passing through the branches and leaves, the flapping of birds who were flying high up into the sky, shrieking like a baby's frightened cry, and the owls' hoots. He dug down in the piled-up, fallen leaves, which presented an unpleasant smell of decaying leaves, and a bunch of centipedes, as thick as an adult's middle finger, with a scary, dark red back, crept out and crawled up Temujin's back and shoulders.

On the fourth day, Temujin approached the borderline of the forest by crawling through the undergrowth to see the enemy's movements. He couldn't see any of them; however, he could smell the smoke coming with the wind. He noticed Talgutai didn't call off the encirclement. He again moved back deep into the forest. On the other hand, Talgutai tried to find different tactics, because even after three days, Temujin couldn't be found. He ordered his men to pick up Temujin's family members as hostages. He wanted to use the hostages to make Temujin come out. When Talgutai's men arrived at the location, they could find nothing but empty space and the half-burnt yurts.

"Alas! I have been outsmarted by Temujin!" Talgutai sighed. That was Temujin's original strategy. Temujin had made himself bait to lure the fish, which was Talgutai's attention. That was to give his family time to escape. Anguished, Talgutai reinforced the encirclement. He dispatched a messenger to bring an additional two hundred soldiers. With four hundred men, he completely encircled the area.

Another three days had passed. Temujin couldn't come out, knowing that the encirclement had been reinforced. He was exhausted. On the ninth day, Temujin began to think about what he had to do. He hadn't eaten anything over the past nine days.

If I stay here much longer, I will surely die. What would father do in this situation?

Exhausted, lying down on the ground, he recalled numerous conversations he shared with his father. He remembered that, one time, his father Yesugei told him this: "If you cannot find the way from the inside, try the outside."

Temujin had to find a way for survival based on this saying. He needed unimaginable courage to throw himself to the enemy who was waiting to kill him.

Talgutai, who needed four hundred men to capture fifteen-year-old Temujin, returned to his ordu. When he arrived at the entrance of his ordu, he put Temujin in a cangue, or yoke. The cangue was made with two parts of a split log, the length from fingertip to fingertip of an adult's outstretched arms. In the middle of the logs, a half-moon-shaped space was carved out, so when two parts were put together and tied, it created a round space for the captive's neck. Once it was tied, it was impossible to remove it from your own neck. They put the cangue on Temujin's neck, tied each end of the logs with the rope, and tied his two arms to the logs. That way they could limit the movement of the upper body of the captive.

"What are you going to do with him?" Todogen asked Talgutai as they were passing through the road between the lines of yurts, side by side.

"I will leave him be until the red circle day."

The red circle day was the day of their biggest festivities, and it was on April 16 of the lunar month. For the Taichut, it was considered to be a holy day and a good one as well. Talgutai wanted to hold off on killing until the holy day. It was April 10, so only six days were left until the red circle day. When Temujin, with the cangue on his neck, walked through the road, people stepped out of their yurts and watched him passing by with no expression on his face.

"Murderer!"

"Brother killer!"

Some of them showed enmity, shaking their fists in the air. Temujin felt miserable. Many of them used to be his father's men and were under his protection. By the custom, Temujin was put into detention in each household, one day each, in rotation. Structurally, they didn't have a prison system in their ordu or town, so the only possible, and the most effective, means of detention was to put the captive into each town member's home under the homeowner's responsibility. They didn't need a prison. Even if the captive escaped, it was next to suicide to run away from the tent town, which was like an island in the middle of an ocean.

As the red circle day approached, the Taichut became busier. They slaughtered well-fed, three-year-old sheep and horses a day before. On the holy day, they had the ancestor worship ceremony for their blessings and well-being. After the ceremony, they began a three-day feast at the Onon riverside. In the middle of the day, they began drinking kumis, and after building up campfires, they barbecued lamb and wild game. They danced all day long. In the evening, when the round, bright moon had risen, their feast reached its climax. The young ones of the Taichut, each of them, with a torch in his hand, prayed to the moon for their wishes. Most of their wishes were to meet a good mate or spouse in the future.

Temujin's guard, a youngster, similar in age to Temujin, was irritated, nervous and unhappy because he couldn't join the feast due to his duty. He kept on drinking kumis to relieve his unhappiness.

"Why don't you join the feast? Do you think I can run away with this cangue?" Temujin enticed the lad. The Taichut lad thought Temujin was right. He put a rope on Temujin's neck and stepped out toward the Onon riverside, where the main event was happening. When they had reached a certain spot, suddenly a big roar burst out from the riverside. It looked like daytime with the numerous torches and campfires. Unconsciously, the two stopped and looked at the site, their necks stretched out.

This is the chance!

Temujin thought it was the right moment and looked around. They were halfway between the faraway tent town and also from the Onon riverside. There was nobody around. It was just a few seconds of chance. Temujin leaned toward one end of the cangue, and then swung hard on the back of the lad's head. From the unexpected blow, the Taichut lad fell down on the ground with a short scream and didn't get up. Temujin ran away from that spot as fast as possible, toward the opposite side of the Onon River, away from the feast site. Because of the heavy cangue, he couldn't speed up and soon, he began to feel an unbearable pain in his neck and shoulders, like an ox was pressing on his neck with its hoof. He paused at the spot where the campfire became the size of the glow of a firefly. He stayed there. He knew it would be a foolish idea to try to escape with the cangue on his neck. He also knew that he needed help. He began to look around for a hiding place.

The Taichut lad regained his consciousness and woke up some time later. It was about the time when the people were coming back to town from the feast and beginning to rest in their own yurts. The lad rushed to the town and began to shout, "The captive has escaped! Temujin has run away!"

When Talgutai received the report that Temujin had escaped, he took it seriously and dispatched the searchers immediately.

"He can't be far away. Be sure to find him!"

By his order, the Taichut searchers, with torches in their hands, checked every corner. They tried to find a trace of a human being in the bushes, grass fields and on the Onon River bank. They were not successful.

They were tired and a bit drunk from the feast. Some of them began to complain.

"How can we find somebody in the dead darkness like this, when he ran away while the bright moonlight was still shinning?"

They continued searching till late in the night for nothing.

However, one person found Temujin.

He was Sokan Shira, who was of the Sudu, not the Taichut, but lived in Talgutai's ordu. Temujin had stayed in his yurt for one day as a prisoner. Sokan Shira was attracted to Temujin's character, toughness and courage. He had received many favors from Yesugei while he was alive, and he had sympathy for Temujin. But he was too fearful to help Temujin. Temujin was hiding his body in a stream covered with a lot of water plants, a branch of the Onon River, with only his head afloat. Sokan Shira approached Temujin when other searchers were far away, and whispered, "I won't tell the other searchers that you are here. Leave here before the daybreak. And never tell anybody that I saw you here, even at a later time."

The searchers knew that anybody in a cangue could not be far away, so they decided to discontinue the search for the night and restart early the following morning. They all went back to their own places.

Temujin, while he was in the water, pondered a lot. Icy-cold water from the mountain area of the upper stream of the Onon River paralyzed his body for a while. His superhuman mental and physical power saved him from the dangerous moments. After a fearful moment, just like a big serpent squeezing his neck, he came out from the water. He had only one place to go, Sokan Shira's yurt. That was the decision he came to after careful consideration.

Sokan Shira doesn't have enough courage to give me a helping hand, but his two sons do.

Temujin had met Sokan Shira's two sons, Chimbai and Chilaun, who were in the same age group as Temujin, when he was in their yurt as a prisoner. While Temujin was in their yurt, he caught a glimpse of their good spirits and their courage.

Temujin remembered the dialogue he shared with Chimbai when he was in their yurt.

"Isn't it heavy, the cangue you are wearing?" tall Chimbai asked Temujin jokingly, as he leaned one arm on a chest, chewing ardently at the jerked beef.

"Why? If I tell you it's heavy, then will you untie me?" Temujin responded, also half-jokingly.

Chimbai, shrugging his shoulders, asked, "If you can promise me you will not run away, I will untie it. Then, you are free while you are with us."

Temujin was struck with admiration for his courage. If Temujin tried to escape after he was untied, Chimbai and his family would never be forgiven and would be punished. If Temujin succeed in escaping, Sokan Shira and all his family members would be massacred. Temujin knew that.

"I, Temujin, solemnly swear on the names of my ancestors that I will never try to escape."

Temujin was free from the cangue for one full day.

Temujin began to look for Sokan Shira's yurt. But how? Which one was Sokan Shira's yurt among the countless lines of them? When they moved Temujin from one yurt to another, without exception, they always blindfolded him. It was midnight, dead silent and the people were in a deep sleep after the feast. When Temujin arrived at the town, he jumped from one yurt to another hiding himself behind each. Temujin knew that Sokan Shira's family was in charge of supplying the kumis for the feast. When Temujin was in their yurt, he saw they were making kumis all through the night. To make the kumis, first they poured the mare's milk into a leather bag, big enough to put a seven-year-old boy in, and then with the churn, a long wooden stick connected to a wheel, they stirred, agitated and beat it thousands of times. To make the fresh kumis out of the mare's milk, they had to beat it with the churn almost all night long. Temujin remembered the noise of beating the leather bag with the churn. That was how Temujin would find Sokan Shira's yurt.

Sokan Shira was astonished when he saw Temujin enter through the flap door. Sokan Shira was still making kumis.

"How did you find my yurt? Didn't I tell you to run away from the town as far as possible? Once you are discovered in here, not only you, but also all my family members, will be killed. Get out of here, right now!"

Sokan Shira, with his long, thin, wrinkled face, was in great embarrassment and fear.

"It is impossible for me to escape with this cangue on my neck. I need help." Temujin said this pointing to the cangue with his eyes.

At this moment, Chimbai and Chilaun were awoken by the noise. Chimbai recognized Temujin standing by the door. He sat on the corner of the bed. Once he found that his father was very reluctant to help Temujin, he stood up, stepped towards his father and said, "Father, he needs help. Even a small bird in danger comes to the trees for help, and the trees will hide him. Why are you hesitating to give him a helping hand?"

After these words, without waiting for his father's answer, he picked up a dagger, cut off the rope and removed the cangue from Temujin's neck. Chilaun helped his brother. From that moment, Sokan Shira became active in helping Temujin, encouraged by his two sons. Chimbai arranged a space inside their yurt for Temujin to rest and sleep. He burned the cangue right away. Temujin took a good rest for three days.

On the fourth day, Talgutai talked to Todogen. They had failed to find Temujin, even with hundreds of searchers.

"I am pretty sure that somebody in my ordu is hiding him. Check out each yurt thoroughly! Especially the non-Taichuts' yurts."

They began to search all the yurts in the ordu one by one, with a team of four members. First, they walked around the town shouting in a loud voice, "If any family is hiding and sheltering Temujin, give up and surrender! It's not too late! If we find him, the family who helped him won't be saved, even the toddlers. This order came from the chief, Talgutai himself."

They finally arrived at Sokan Shira's yurt. The four Taichut searchers checked underneath the beds and even inside the chests. They spent a long time in the yurt that Sokan Shira used as a storehouse. Nobody lived there; instead, stacks of hides and dried dung for fuel in winter filled the yurt.

They could find nobody there. They stepped toward the next family. At this moment, one of the searchers noticed a big cart stationed at the back of the yurt. In this cart was a mountain of newly sheared wool piled high. He began to dig into the pile, throwing the wool to the ground. Chimbai, at this sight, remarked in a complaining and mocking tone, "Who the hell would hide inside wool in this hot weather?"

The searcher glanced at Chimbai and nodded. Instead of continuing to search in the wool, he speared the pile a few times and left. Temujin was lying facedown on the floor of the cart.

That night, Temujin left Sokan Shira's yurt. The longer he stayed, the greater the chance of being discovered. Chilaun had surveyed the passes and told Temujin which way and direction would be safe.

Sokan Shira gave Temujin a brown mare with a black mane and a stripe down her back. He also handed over a big lump of boiled mutton, a bagful of milk, a bow and two arrows to Temujin.

"I really wish you good luck on your escape. Stay alive! And let's see each other again."

Chimbai said this as he was hugging Temujin. Temujin did the same thing with Chilaun. Temujin said good-bye to Sokan

Shira after he thanked him. Temujin also thanked Qadaan, Sokan Shira's nine-year-old daughter, with a smile for guarding the cart while Temujin was in there. Temujin mounted the horse, looked at them for a moment and then spurred the horse, swiftly fading into the darkness.

Temujin galloped almost half a day without rest. He wanted to leave behind any possible pursuers. He knew which way he had to go. He drove the horse in the northwest direction. At night, the North Star worked as a compass. He traced his mother and siblings along the way of the branch of the Onon River and crossed several rough mountains. After three days, he was reunited with his mother and siblings at a place called Qorchuki Hill. It was more than a hundred miles from the Taichut ordu, and yet Temujin didn't feel safe. They stayed there overnight and early the following morning, they left, southwest-bound.

They had to hunt for marmots and wild rats for survival. After four days, they arrived at the valley basin near the Kara Jirugen Mountain, which was a part of the Kurelku Mountains with its several dozen peaks. The Kara Jirugen Mountain was made of huge dark-brown rocks and near it was a small blue lake with crystal-clear water, called Koko Nuur. The basin was surrounded by mountains in three directions, with only the east and southeast side open to a low hill, which was connected by a gentle slope to the great plain. It was a good place for protection from enemy attacks and an escape from the heat and cold in different seasons. They built the yurts beside the lake, and planned to stay there for a while.

CHAPTER FIFTEEN

Meeting with Bogorchu

The power of the steppe aristocrats depended on the number of their followers and the degree of loyalty they had for their masters. The wealthiest of the steppe people could be measured by the number of livestock and the amount of war booty they possessed. They didn't hesitate to attack neighboring tribes, even if their chances were slim; if opportunity knocked, they took it. If they succeeded, they could add the plundered livestock and other properties to their own. If not, they would lose their own lives. Big or small, the head of the group was supposed to be able to protect his people and their property from the attackers. If not, his followers would lose confidence in him. The head of the group in that position would lose his followers and, in some cases, be killed by his own people.

A few months after Temujin's family settled down around the Koko Nuur Lake, something came up.

Temujin's family had nine horses and that was all the property they had. One afternoon, Temujin and Kasar were cutting trees

near the mountain. Suddenly, they heard a noise and horse neighing from the direction of their yurts. Kachun, Temujin's eleven-year-old younger brother, was rushing toward Temujin, shouting in distress.

"The horse rustlers, they are stealing our horses!"

Temujin and Kasar stopped their work and ran back to their yurts. Two men, after snatching off the reins, were running away with the eight horses that were stationed near the yurts. When Temujin arrived at the site, the two thieves were already crossing the hill. Kasar went into the yurt and brought a bow and arrows, but they were out of range. They could do nothing but watch in despair as the thieves and their horses disappeared from sight. Temujin had no horse to use to chase them; the only horse left was out with Belgutei hunting. In the evening, Belgutei returned home with many marmots and a hare. Belgutei and Kasar insisted on taking the job themselves of chasing and retrieving the horses. But that was a job for the head of the family. Temujin, armed with a bow and several arrows, left home with some dried meat and a bagful of water.

Temujin followed the east-bound tracks of the horses. The Mongolian Plateau was a vast land. It was not an easy job to trace the lost horses in an area where all four sides connected with only endless horizons. But his task was life or death for his family; they couldn't survive on the steppe without horses. The horse droppings were the only sign of their passing.

Temujin chased them for three days and three nights. On the fourth day, Temujin met a youngster who seemed to be of a similar age group, about fifteen. He had a good-looking face with bright eyes. Around him, numerous sheep and goats were grazing, and he was milking his mare into a wooden bucket. Temujin approached him and asked, "Hello, there! I am looking for my stolen horses. Did you happen to see two men driving eight horses with them?"

The youngster stopped working and looked at Temujin for a moment. He asked Temujin, "What colors are your horses? Male or female?"

"All are light-yellowish geldings."

The youngster pointed to the northeast and said, "This morning, just after daybreak, I saw two men driving eight light-yellow male horses, just like you described. If you keep following that direction you will probably see your horses."

Temujin thanked him and was about to leave, but the youngster stopped Temujin and said, "Friend, you might need help. I will go with you."

The youngster gave Temujin a light-grey horse with a black stripe down its back.

"Change your horse. Yours looks too tired."

The youngster poured the milk from the wooden bucket into two small leather bags and gave one to Temujin and put the other one on his horse's back. He moved and hid the wooden buckets and other bags in the grass. He mounted his horse and followed Temujin.

"My name is Bogorchu. My father's name is Naku Bayan and he is well-known around here," the youngster introduced himself.

"My name is Temujin. Is it all right for you to do such a big favor for me? Are you going to leave all your sheep and goats like that?"

"Don't worry. Soon my father will show up and take care of them. You look very worried. You need help. I want to help someone who is in trouble."

The two youngsters galloped all day, tracing the steps of the lost horses. They chased three days and three nights. On the fourth day, around evening time, they found a kuriyen, a tent town of more than a thousand yurts. They approached the kuriyen in silence. Temujin found the eight horses grazing near the town. Those were Temujin's light-yellow geldings, which he had been looking for for seven days and seven nights. The two youngsters lowered their bodies and looked around. Luckily, there was nobody around the horses. They approached the eight geldings, drove them, and galloped with them from the town swiftly. The big sound of ten horses galloping, rumbling and shaking the ground, reached the town. Several men came out from their yurts to investigate. Two of them began to go after Temujin and Bogorchu on horseback. One of them was holding a lasso and the other one had a bow. The man with the bow began to shoot arrows.

Bogorchu shouted at Temujin, panting, "Give me your bow and arrows! I will stop them."

"I don't want you to get hurt! I am the one who has to deal with them. I will handle them."

Temujin turned his torso around and shot an arrow. The arrow lodged in the center of the chest of the bowman's horse.

Shrieking, the animal stood on its hind legs, forcing its rider to fall to the ground. It was getting dark, so the man with the lasso gave up the chase.

They galloped all through the night. After three days, they arrived at the same spot they left.

Bogorchu found the wooden buckets and leather bags that he had hidden in the grass before they left. Temujin said to Bogorchu, "Friend, without you, how would I have gotten my horses back? I want to share these horses with you. Let me know how many you want."

Bogorchu glanced at Temujin as he was mounting the leather bags on his horse and said, "Reward was not my motivation. My father is rich. He has already put a lot of livestock aside for me. It is getting dark, so, how about staying in my yurt with me tonight?"

Temujin happily accepted his invitation. Temujin was deeply impressed with Bogorchu.

The two youngsters trotted their horses across the plain where the dusk had just began to fall. A thick purple curtain was falling on the western horizon and over it, feather-like clouds were changing colors from creamy white to orange-red. The dusk was covering the earth, and the dim light reflected from the clouds was shaping the two youngster's silhouettes.

Soon, they arrived at an ayil of two or three hundred yurts. Dim grey smoke was dancing out from the center openings of the domed roofs of the yurts. Around the town, large numbers of livestock, either within the wooden fences or out in the fields, were making a great noise, bleating and mooing.

As Temujin and Bogorchu dismounted and walked into the town, many people came out from their yurts to see them. From a yurt, a tall, thin middle-aged man came out and hugged Bogorchu.

"My son, you are my only son. I have been gravely worried about you since you disappeared."

Naku Bayan, Bogorchu's father, was the chieftain of this ordu and he was rich. Bayan was the title given to rich men. He rejoiced at his son's return as if a dead son had come back to life. Bogorchu introduced Temujin to his father and explained what had happened.

"Oh! You are Yesugei Bagatur's son! I knew him well. I had a very good relationship with him."

Naku Bayan slaughtered a big, fat sheep and fed his son and Temujin to their fill. People gathered in Naku Bayan's yurt and stayed, talking late into the evening. The two youngsters, lying on their stomachs in the same bed, watched the dancing flame of the sheep-oil lamp and kept on talking even after the people had left. Temujin was deeply impressed by Bogorchu's unselfish, sacrificing, helping spirit and Bogorchu was fascinated by Temujin's manly, dauntless, unyielding courage. However, the most attractive quality of Temujin, to Bogorchu, was indescribable, some kind charisma or inner power that could attract and lead many people.

"Bogorchu, let's help each other as comrades from now on. We have many things to do in front of us."

Temujin suggested this and Bogorchu responded with jubilation, "Good! I will accept that! I will be with you whenever and wherever you need me. I am happy to share the same destiny with you."

Temujin's meaning of comrade was more than a friend. Of course, Bogorchu knew that. They were communicating with each other through their own sixth senses.

Early the following morning, Temujin left Naku Bayan's ordu. Naku Bayan gave Temujin enough boiled mutton for his trip home and a bagful of mare's milk. Naku Bayan patted both Temujin's and Bogorchu's shoulders, and said, "Like I did with Yesugei Bagatur, you, too, should help each other and never give up your good friendship."

Besides Bogorchu and his father, many people came out to see Temujin off. After another three days and three nights, Temujin arrived at his home and was reunited with his mother and siblings.

CHAPTER SIXTEEN

Temujin's Wedding

By the time Temujin was seventeen, he was a manly, robust, high-spirited young man. His skin covering his broad forehead and well-developed cheekbones had been suntanned attractively. His two eyes, adequately sized and seated, were shining with wit and great insight and his straight, well-balanced nose and firmly closed mouth showed his dignity and decisiveness. He was tall and he had a well-shaped, strong body. He could run all morning long without a single rest and had tough hands and arms that could break off a rod the thickness of an adult's wrist in one breath.

Since his father's death, he and his family had had to live in seclusion in a remote area, and had to suffer extreme poverty. This adverse situation couldn't kill his spirit; it did the opposite. He became a much stronger, more ambitious young man. He had a fearless heart, strong willpower and tough endurance, the qualities he needed for self-control and self-mastering. He had powerful intuition, an insight and an ability to make the best judgments. He grew up to be a strong man in both mind and body, like an iron man, which was the meaning of his name, Temujin.

Is that all he had? No. He had faith in his own destiny. This unwavering faith in his own destiny was the compass and fuel for his soul. That was his greatest power.

Temujin began to think of getting married. There was not a single moment that Temujin forgot about Borte since he was betrothed to her eight years ago. Now, Temujin began to miss her as a woman. He always remembered her beautiful eyes and the warm smile on her lips.

One day, at the dinner table, Temujin brought up that issue. He talked about his plan and asked for Ouluun's permission. Upon hearing his plan, Ouluun became gloomy and remarked with a worried look, "Well, she is your fiancée, but I don't know that they still want you, since your family has been completely ruined."

Temujin looked at his mother for a moment. Temujin always listened to his mother. Besides the fact that, in the Mongolian custom, the mother was the head of the family when the father died, regardless of the ages of her children, there was another reason Temujin was quite obedient to her. Temujin knew his mother's life history. His mother was supposed to marry Daritai, Temujin's uncle, by Mongolian customs, when Yesugei died. If an elder brother had died, his younger brother was supposed to take care of the widow and their children by marrying her. What could be the origin of such a custom? Nobody knew. It was probably due to the nomadic lifestyle and social circumstances. War and conflict were part of their life. Nobody knew what would happen to them tomorrow. The Mongols highly valued their familial lineage and they preferred to leave their wives and children to their own siblings, instead of someone else that they couldn't trust, when something happened to them. If the widow refused to marry her late husband's brother, she had no choice but to live alone until she died. She couldn't marry another man. Ouluun had already made her choice.

After Yesugei died, his younger brother, Daritai, asked for Ouluun's hand and she refused. She had only one reason for refusal, the legitimacy of the lineage of her children. If she said yes, she would be the second wife of Daritai, after being the first wife of Yesugei. She preferred legitimacy for her children. Temujin knew this and he looked up to his mother.

Ouluun remarked again, still in a gloomy mood, "We have only nine horses and ten lambs. How can you feed her?"

Temujin's family's nine horses were all castrated geldings. They couldn't get any milk from them and they couldn't use them as studs either. They were low-valued property. As for the lambs, they traded for them with foxes and sables they caught hunting, as their hunting skills had improved.

"Will she eat marmots and rats?" Temujin's eleven-year-old younger brother, Temuge, asked in an excited but cynical tone. The main meal of the Mongols was beef and mutton. Horsemeat and camel were eaten on special occasions. Marmots and rats were temporary food for survival, for the very poor or families in difficult situations. Temujin's family had led this sort of life for the last seven years, since Yesugei had died.

"Why don't you wait a little bit more until we are better, socially and financially?"

Ouluun was pessimistic. Even the iron-strong woman, Ouluun, couldn't be sure on this issue. Temujin stretched his hand out and held hers, and said in a clear voice, "Mother, I have to get married to succeed."

Eventually, Temujin was successful in getting Ouluun's approval. Temujin busied himself getting ready for his departure, right away. Ouluun handed a small silver box containing two gold bangles over to Temujin. Ouluun had not sold those belongings, even at the toughest times.

"I got this from my mother. Give this to Borte."

From the Koko Nuur Lake, under the Kara Jirugen Mountains, Temujin's family's campsite, to Dey Sechen's ordu near the Mountain Chekcher, was well over five hundred miles.

Temujin left for Dey Sechen's ordu with Belgutei. Kasar remained to help their mother and take care of the other family members. Belgutei, already a big and muscular man of six feet five inches, was the Mongolian wrestling champion from an early age and strong enough to duel the giant Siberian black bear. He was silent, discreet, cautious and yet quick with good judgment. He was six months older than Temujin, but was always loyal to him. Unity, familial harmony and mutual support were absolutely required among family members for survival on the steppe. In this family, Ouluun was the head of the family and Temujin was the second. Temujin had already fought for this.

Seven days later, Temujin arrived near the entrance of Dey Sechen's ordu. Dey Sechen, while he was falconing with his men at a nearby mountain, had found Temujin's group and approached them. Dey Sechen recognized Temujin immediately after he saw him.

"Oh! Aren't you Temujin, the son of Yesugei Bagatur? You are alive! It is my great happiness to see you grown up to be a nice young man," Dey Sechen rejoiced.

Temujin dismounted his horse and greeted him by kneeling and bowing to him. Belgutei did the same. Dey Sechen also dismounted his horse and walked up to Temujin. He hugged Temujin, patting him on his back. Temujin introduced Belgutei to Dey Sechen and Dey Sechen asked Temujin how the rest of his family was doing. They headed for Dey Sechen's ordu side by side. Dey Sechen dispatched one of his men to inform his wife and daughter of Temujin's arrival.

"We were gravely worried about the safety of your family after your father had passed away. Especially when we heard that you and your family members had disappeared after being attacked by the Taichut."

When they arrived at the entrance of the ordu, Dey Sechen ordered his men to set up a temporary yurt for Temujin and Belgutei. Mongolian custom didn't allow the newly arrived bridegroom to enter the bride's ordu or hometown until the official ceremony started. Two big wooden bathtubs, filled with hot water, and new clothing were supplied to Temujin and Belgutei.

Later in the afternoon of the same day, Temujin was visited by Borte and her mother Chotan. She was eighteen years old, a fully-grown woman like a flower in full bloom. Her extraordinary beauty, which shocked Temujin years ago, had matured to a great extent and her two, big, thick-brown eyes were twinkling like before. Unlike most steppe women, she had milky-white skin and her fully developed breasts and hips showed their volume and curvature from under the silky, light-blue traditional Mongolian costume she was wearing, which covered her from her neck to her knees, with a tight belt at the waist. When Temujin's eyes met hers, she opened her eyes wider and put a big smile on her lips, sending the message of her surprise and happiness. The steppe women were never coy. They were much like men, emotionally and psychologically, and they also had almost equal rights with men from a social standpoint. Sometimes they even participated in battles. In these cases, picking up the weapons and taking the armor off dead bodies was their job.

When Temujin saw Chotan, he knelt and lowered his head like he had to Dey Sechen. Chotan was pleased to see Temujin grown up to be a strong, fine-looking young man.

"How was your trip? Is everything fine with you now?"

Chotan asked many things about Temujin and his family and left well-prepared food and beverages for them. Dey Sechen discussed the situation with the chief priest and officially declared that there would be a wedding for his daughter, Borte, and Temujin, three days later. Three days was the minimum time needed for preparation. They slaughtered sheep and camels and readied themselves with all the necessities of a wedding. To make the whole baked camel, first they had to remove the internal organs and then replace them with a sheep that had had its skin and internal organs removed also. Then they put the camel into a rectangular pit in the ground, filled with burning charcoal, with metal beams across it. It took three whole days to complete the baking.

On the eve of the wedding, Borte gave a tea party for her friends. It was a traditional custom to celebrate the wedding eve. Her friends brought gifts like clothes, ornaments or accessories and they congratulated Borte on her wedding. At the same time, they all shared the sorrow of separation, which would come to them in the very near future.

On the wedding day, Temujin got up early in the morning, took a bath and changed his clothes to the new ones Borte's mother had brought. Temujin readied himself for the wedding parade. A few town elders had stayed overnight with Temujin and explained all the procedures related to the ceremony, so he would not make any mistakes. The wedding ceremony started late in the morning. Temujin was clad in the traditional blue silk Mongolian costume and was wearing an almost cylindrical hat, of which the top was wider than the bottom. In the center of the hat was a cone-shaped elevation. Temujin was holding a bow in his left hand and two arrows in his right hand. It was a tradition related to the wedding ceremony. Temujin walked toward the wedding place. Belgutei followed Temujin, also in a clean silky Mongolian costume. From the town's entrance to its central open ground, the actual wedding place, numerous people had gathered in two lines and watched Temujin's wedding parade. When Temujin arrived at the entrance, a good-looking young man, in traditional costume, stopped Temujin's party, raising his two hands. He was Dey Sechen's son, Alchi, Borte's elder brother. In a loud voice, in a musical tone, he asked Temujin who he was and why he was there.

To these questions, Belgutei stepped out from the line, on behalf of Temujin, and answered, in a loud, singing tone:

> *In this wonderful season with ten thousand blessings,*
> *On this happy day filled with grace and peace,*
> *Attracted by the destiny which will bind us forever,*
> *From the eternal past to the eternal future,*
> *We are here from the faraway land.*
>
> *Representing the parents and relatives of the bridegroom,*
> *Followed by our splendid, never-ending traditions,*
> *Expecting the best weapon to be given in his hand,*
> *The toughest armor on his shoulders, for your new son,*
> *We are here to bow to the parents of the bride.*

Belgutei had to practice these phrases late into the night. Nonetheless, he was stammering, and had to pause frequently to recall the next phrase. He looked funny and at this, the girls giggled and the elders guffawed. Originally, that was the job for the bridegroom's father or uncle. But, at that time, Temujin didn't have a father and his uncle's whereabouts were unknown. In that situation, it was Belgutei's job.

When Temujin walked through the street between the lines of yurts and crowds of townspeople, girls and maids exclaimed and cheered, impressed by Temujin's tall, handsome, manly look.

At the wedding site was a white tent supported by four columns, of which three directions, east, west and south, were open, with only the northern side being closed with a white flap. In front of the southern side of the tent was a rectangular table on which numerous wedding ceremony items were arranged. Dey Sechen and his wife, Chotan, were sitting on chairs side by side inside the tent, facing the south.

When Temujin arrived in front of the tent, he kowtowed nine times. Next, Borte showed up, assisted by her two serving women. She was wearing a traditional wedding costume, which was made of a red and pink silk with luxurious floral patterns, covering her from her neck to her toe, and with wide sleeves. On her head, she was wearing a hemispherical red cap embedded with numerous pearls, from which silk strings with beads were hanging down to her forehead and shoulders. Temujin and Borte bowed to each other three times. Dey Sechen prayed to the holy spirits and the spirits of their ancestors for blessings. Then, he picked up the silver kettle and poured the kumis into a small silvery bowl, and sprinkled it around the ceremonial site. He then picked up a shining helmet from the table, blessed it, and then put it on Temujin's head. It was a Mongolian-style helmet, called a duulja, that looked like a half-dome at the top connected to a half-cylindrical shape at the bottom. He helped Temujin with the shiren hantaaz, a Mongolian-style armor made of lacquered leather, which was as tough as a turtle shell and designed to protect a warrior from spears and arrows.

For Borte, Chotan put a bogtaq, a tall, cylindrical headgear with a slender middle part, on her head.

Dey Sechen blessed the new couple:

> *With the name of heaven and the holy spirit,*
> *The helmet and the armor, they just had,*
> *Will protect them from their enemies.*

> *With the name of the earth and the spirits of the ancestors,*
> *The bogtaq, they just had,*
> *Will bring them prosperity and a fortunate future.*

Dey Sechen declared a three-day feast. The happy event for Dey Sechen, the head of ten thousand yurts, was a celebration for the whole town. A new yurt had been built for the new couple near Dey Sechen's yurt and Temujin and Borte stayed there for three sweet nights.

"I have been waiting for you," Borte whispered in Temujin's ear. At the tip of his nose, Temujin could sense the fragrance of the Arabian perfume and the Chinese noblewoman's shampoo. They were in Chinese silk pajamas, in the same bed, together. Inside the tent house, the air was infused with the sweet scent coming from the incense burner and the tent was filled with dim light coming from the Baghdad lamp.

"I wanted to come earlier, but I couldn't. Even the baby fawn hides in the grass until his legs become strong enough to run away. By any chance, did anyone in your family press you to marry someone else?"

Borte, getting closer to Temujin's bosom, answered, "Yes. My mother, one time, mentioned that when you and your family members had disappeared, after the Taichut attack. But, I and my elder brother were strongly opposed to that idea."

After these words, Borte chuckled.

The long night of the steppe, filled with the desert's heat, started like this. The flame of love of the teenaged couple added heat to the desert air. They were a stallion and a filly running on the endless open land, caressing and petting each other. Their manes were flowing and their smoothly curved, voluptuous waists and hips were all wet. They ran toward the infinite horizon, tirelessly. On their shoulders, beautifully shining silver wings had sprung up and they flew into the deep blue sky filled with mystery. They flew up into the space passing over the huge crystal-clear lake and pyramid-shaped mountains covered with snow. In the timeless, everlasting blue sky, covered with the purity of the crystal and silence of the ice, the sun and the moon were in one body, radiating enormously bright lights and around them, countless stars were twinkling. At last, together, they flew into the huge circle formed by flashing lights like an aurora.

Many visitors swarmed from neighboring tribes when the news went out that Dey Sechen's only daughter had been married. They congratulated the new couple and left their own gifts.

The highlight of the event was the wrestling tournament. The wrestling tournament and the archery contest were essential parts of any Mongolian feast. Belgutei was one of the contestants in the wrestling tournament. From an early age, he was the champion of almost all the official games. His power and technique were outstanding and nobody had beaten him so far. Belgutei was the final contestant on the third, and last, day of the feast. Thousands of spectators were gathered around their match. Before the game, Temujin called Belgutei and whispered in his ear, "Give away the win."

Belgutei could read Temujin's mind and nodded. The wrestling match was neck and neck. The excited duel lasted for quite a while. But the winner was one of the town's young men. The champion usually enjoyed a lot of benefits and became the hero among the town's girls. If the same man won the tournament repeatedly and nobody could match him, the chieftain of the ordu gave him the official title of boko. The title of boko was very honorable for the Mongols.

Temujin left Dey Sechen's ordu with Borte early in the morning of the fourth day of his marriage. On the journey back home, Borte's mother, Chotan, and the old servant woman, Koachin, accompanied them. Koachin had been the caretaker of Borte since she was a newborn baby. Dey Sechen put sixty heavily armed cavalrymen to guard Temujin's returning journey. He also sent out two oxen and two hundred sheep, in addition to the bountiful gifts. Among the gifts, the most valuable one was the cloak made of black sables. The Mongols considered clothing the best gift, and especially a cloak or coat made of black sable fur, which was the best of the best. It was worth two thousand bezants, or gold coins, at the international markets. Usually, in the Mongolian custom, the best one was the gift from the bride's father to the bridegroom's father.

Temujin and Borte left Dey Sechen's ordu. Dey Sechen and a large crowd gathered to see them off. Since it was taboo in their culture to show tears to the leaving bride, they were all smiling. Borte's friends threw small pieces of hard, dried cow dung to the new couple as a token of good luck and farewell. Temujin bowed toward them on his horse, and Borte, in her luxurious two-wheeled carriage, opened the flap door and waved to them in return.

After a fifteen-day journey, they arrived at the Koko Nuur Lake, Temujin's family campsite. Ouluun and Chotan exchanged bows with each other. Ouluun introduced the other children to Chotan.

"I really appreciate you allowing your daughter to marry my son, whose family fortune has been disrupted."

Ouluun showed her appreciation to Chotan and Chotan responded with comforting words. Chotan stayed for three days in Ouluun's yurt and then went back to her ordu with the guard soldiers. Temujin's marriage brought on many changes. The steppe had keen ears. The news of Temujin's marriage had spread through the steppe people like wind. One day, Sochigel, Belgutei's mother, whose whereabouts were unknown up until that time, returned. The woman who had left seven years ago, leaving her two sons with Ouluun, came back the same worn-out figure. She was moving around, working as a temporary serving woman here and there, for survival. No sooner had Ouluun seen Sochigel than she burst into tears. After Yesugei's death, these two women, Yesugei's first and second wives, who had suffered from extreme poverty and hardship, embraced each other and burst into tears, overcome by emotion. They were the ones who had enjoyed the glorious life while Yesugei was alive, but now they could find nothing but the exhausted, worn-out figures of each other. Belgutei was exhilarated at his mother's return.

CHAPTER SEVENTEEN

Temujin's Visit to Toghrul

Temujin began to take the very first steps of his ambitious plan; that was to find the comrades who could share the spirit and work together to reunite the scattered tribe members. Temujin tried Bogorchu first. Temujin sent Belgutei with these words:

> *The one with the will,*
> *Shall find the road.*
>
> *Heaven loves*
> *The self-seekers.*
>
> *Those are the wise*
> *Who can see the invisible.*
>
> *Those are the brave*
> *Who have no fear of changing.*

Only the challengers
Will achieve.

Only the self-hatchers from shells
Will fly.

Upon receiving Temujin's message, Bogorchu immediately followed Belgutei, without even bidding farewell to his father. He had already made up his mind, long ago, to share his destiny with Temujin's. He became Temujin's first comrade.

Next, Temujin searched for Jelme and Chaulqan, the brothers, by tracing rumors. Jelme responded to Temujin's call and showed up with his father. Jelme's father, Jarchuiday, who belonged to the Uriangkad tribes, had presented swaddling clothes made of precious sables to Yesugei when Temujin was born. He swore to Yesugei that his son Jelme would be Temujin's supporter when they grew up. In return, he received many things from Yesugei, including protection. That defined the relationship between Temujin and Jelme as master and retainer, whereas Temujin and Bogorchu were comrades.

"Thank you for coming, Jelme. How about Chaulqan? Why didn't you come together?"

Temujin hugged Jelme and patted his shoulders. Jelme also had become a strong, robust young man. Jelme had two brothers, Chaulqan and Subedei.

"Chaulqan will join us soon. He is helping his father now. After the work, he will be here."

The number of Temujin family's yurts went from two to five. Temujin decided to move, as a security consideration and to make it easier to move onto the next step of his plan. They traveled eighty miles north-northwest, crossing Kurelku Mountain, and arrived at the southern side of Burkan Mountain, where the upper stream of the Kerulen River began. Unlike the Onon River, which started at the upper side of Burkan Mountain, the Kerulen River had its upper stream at the lower side of the mountain. These two rivers travel several hundred miles individually and then join together to become one, the Amur River, which finally finds its way to the Pacific Ocean.

The place Temujin's group settled down in was called Burgi Ergi, which was twenty miles south of Burkan Mountain. It was covered by the very rugged Kurelku Mountains to the east, and the Khenty Mountains to the west, which served as protective walls, and only to the south were they connected to the plain, so it was a cozy place, like a mother's womb. Temujin's five yurts were near a stream of cool, crystal-clear water, which made a pleasant sound as it flowed. Its origin was in Burkan Mountain. Nearby hills and mountains were covered by thick forest with pine trees and fir trees, and if they walked down for a while, they could find a plain big enough to feed their two hundred sheep and two oxen.

Temujin made up his mind to visit Toghrul, the chieftain of the Keraits. That was the second step of his plan after getting married. At that time, the Keraits were one of the most powerful tribes on the Mongolian Plateau. Their territory was a large area neighboring the Naimans to the west, the Merkids to the north and the Gobi Desert and the Shisha Kingdom of the Tanguts to the south. They were a group of about 250 thousand people, with more than 50 thousand yurts, and the head of their group was called khan, the title which was given only to the head of a nation.

Originally, they were Mongols; however, influenced by the neighboring Turks, Naimans and Uighurs, their culture had become more Turkish and many of them were of mixed blood. They had accepted Nestorian Christianity about one century before Temujin was born, and at the time, when Temujin made his visit, almost all of them were Christians.

Temujin set out on his journey with his two brothers, Kasar and Belgutei. Their destination was Toghrul's summer resort by the Tula River, which was about 150 miles southwest of Temujin's place. While Temujin was gone, Bogorchu and Jelme were asked to take care of the rest of the family. Temujin took the sable cloak with him as a gift for Toghrul. Temujin's younger brother, Kasar, was now a good companion and an essential guard for Temujin. He was an excellent archer, whose skill was highly valued on the plain, where the bow and arrow was the main weapon.

He had thick eyebrows, sharp, sparkling eyes like an eagle and a straight nose and sharp angled jawbones. While Temujin and Belgutei were wearing the del, the Mongolian costume, Kasar only wore a vest made of animal skin, so his well-developed arms and chest muscles were nicely exposed. Belgutei was wearing harnesses on his arms and all three were wearing wide leather belts on which a scimitar and a short dagger were hanging on the left and right sides, respectively.

Temujin had never met Toghrul. He had only heard about him from his father or from other people around him when he was very young. Temujin knew that his father was in the anda relationship, or sworn brotherhood, with Toghrul. Temujin had tried to collect as much information as possible about him, including character and personality, before he left.

"When you arrive at his ordu, open your eyes and ears. You'd better watch your tongue and pay attention to the movements of people near you. You'd better not let them know that they are being watched." Temujin gave this advice as he was driving his horse, side by side with his two brothers. He continued after he eyed his two brothers, both left and right, as if he wanted to make sure they were listening, "Never forget the road you passed once. Never drink. If it's hard to refuse, just pretend. Be careful about what you are drinking and eating; if you feel different, stop drinking or eating."

After these words, Temujin turned his head again to both sides to see his brothers' reaction.

"How do you feel? If he doesn't like us, there might be a chance that we can never get out of there alive."

To these words, Belgutei and Kasar kept silent for a while and then guffawed at the same time.

"Only the risk takers are the real men. You told us this many times and we remember that," Kasar responded, and again gave a loud guffaw. Belgutei, who was laughing with Kasar until that time, suddenly stopped laughing and asked Temujin in a serious manner, "It won't be an easy job to make a deal with him. How are you going to do it? Is it worth it?"

Temujin kept silent for a moment, and then answered, "You need a ladder to get to a higher place. As long as we are successful in giving him the impression that we could be useful to him, instead of useless or even harmful, he will accept us."

After a three-day and three-night journey, they arrived at the hill and could see the deep purple Tula River winding like a big serpent. In a large area by the river, thousands of yurts were arranged in an orderly manner, and to the east and the north, there were high, rocky mountains with thick forests covering the area like protective walls. It was late in the morning and the Tula River was sparkling like silvery fish scales, reflecting the exploding morning sunlight, and the pine forests were dazzling like black pearls. The Mongols at that time called it the Black Forest because it looked black, rather than green.

When Temujin and his brothers were passing along the road through the thick pine forests toward the tent city, the thick, dull sound of a horn was coming from somewhere and it waved into the space filled with fresh morning air and the fragrance of the pine trees. They ignored it and kept on their way. Before long, five Kerait cavalry soldiers galloped up in front of Temujin and his brothers. They were wearing helmets and armor, even though it was in the middle of summer, and they were heavily armed with spears and scimitars. Three of them were holding round leather shields. As Temujin and his brothers reined in their horses, one of them stepped out, carefully eyed each one in Temujin's group, and then asked, "Who are you? What are you doing here?"

Temujin also stepped out a few steps and answered, "Tell Toghrul Khan his Kyat Mongol son, Temujin, is here for an audience."

With this answer, they seemed to be surprised and for a while they talked to each other. At last, one of them galloped his way back. Some time later, a mounted man, appearing to be in his early twenties, slowly approached Temujin's group. He was unarmed and wearing a fluttering white robe with wide sleeves. He halted his horse at a safe distance from Temujin and his brothers, and gave a sharp, searching glance at each one of them. A moment later, as if his judgment came to the conclusion that Temujin's group couldn't be dangerous, he opened his mouth and asked, "Who are you? Identify yourselves!"

Temujin answered in loud voice, "I am the son of Yesugei, who was the anda to your khan, Toghrul. And these two men are my brothers."

The man in the white robe cocked his head a little to one side and then talked to the soldiers next to him for a moment. He then turned his horse back and moved slowly forward. A soldier next to him gestured for Temujin to follow.

As Temujin began to follow them, two of the soldiers separated from them and tailed after Temujin and his brothers. They passed through the street lined by the yurts and finally arrived at the northern end, where they could see a huge rectangular tent near the forest. Unlike the other dome-shaped, ordinary yurts, this huge white tent structure was decorated with luxurious golden patterns in every corner, signaling that it belonged to the khan, and it gave an overpowering image to the viewers. Temujin's group was guided to a small tent next to the khan's, which seemed to be for visitors. Inside the tent, many long, luxurious, comfortable sofas were arranged and in the center of the room was a short, long, shiny, lacquered table. On the table was a big oval-shaped silver plate and on it were a stack of dried dates and numerous delicious-looking pomegranates, which were fully ripe with their skins opened.

The man in the white robe showed Temujin and his brothers their seats and said, "Wait here a moment. I will be right back."

He was Nilka Senggum, the only son of Toghrul Khan. He had a tall, slender body and also had thin eyebrows, a sharp-pointed, well-developed nose and clear, white facial skin, unlike the steppe and desert men. His two eyes on Temujin and his brothers were full of contempt and, at other times, they gleamed like a wolf's. After Nilka Senggum opened the flap door and went out, two serving women came in, one with a silver basin full of clean water for hand washing and some towels, and the other one with silver goblets and a carafe full of fresh goat milk. This was the common treatment for every visitor.

Nilka Senggum informed his father of Temujin and his brother's arrival and asked him whether he would see them or not.

"The Kyat Mongol beggars are here."

He said this with a displeased look, as if he was hinting to his father that it would not be a good idea to see them, as they looked unqualified for an audience.

"Oh! Yesugei's son Temujin and his brothers are here? Of course, I will see them."

Toghrul Khan granted an audience for Temujin and his brothers.

Years before Temujin was born, when the Kerait khan Kyriakus died, Toghrul killed his elder brother, an heir apparent, and took over the throne. But his rule didn't last long. His uncle, the gurkhan, mobilized troops and drove him out. Toghrul managed to escape death, and then came to Yesugei, who was well-known as an emerging power on the steppe at that time. Yesugei made an anda relation with him and moved his troops against the gurkhan. For this, Kutula Khan, who was Yesugei's uncle and the Kyat Mongol khan at that time, warned him, "Do not give a helping hand to Toghrul! We have found that he has an evil character. Cut off his head and send it to the gurkhan."

Yesugei ignored his instruction. He responded, "I don't stop anyone who is coming to me and I don't stop anyone who is leaving from me. This is my policy."

Yesugei helped him out, driving out the gurkhan, and restored Toghrul's khanship.

When Temujin arrived at the entrance of Khan's golden tent, guided by Nilka Senggum, the two guards, Kerait soldiers, disarmed him.

"No form of weapon is allowed in the khan's tent," Nilka Senggum explained. As Temujin stepped inside, the luxuriousness of the interior design struck his eyes. Thin white silk curtains were hanging around all four walls and rosy, soft Persian carpets covered the floor. This huge rectangular tent, big enough to hold at least two or three hundred people, stretched in the north-south direction. In the center of the northern wall, a huge silver-coated cross was hanging and, underneath it, was a big soft leather chair with a gorgeously decorated back. Along the east and west walls were lines of chairs stretching all the way to the southern end and, every five chairs, there was a marble statue of an animal, like elephants, leopards, oxen, wolves, lambs, tigers and lions. It seemed to be designed for multifunctionality, including Khan's daily, official duties.

Temujin walked all the way up to the northern end, close to the big leather chair underneath the cross. When he arrived at the spot marked as the stopping point for all visitors, he could see an extremely obese man, seemingly in his late forties, sitting in a chair. He had small, slanted eyes and possibly high cheek bones too, which were covered and hidden in his thick, fatty facial tissue. His mouth was relatively small compared to his body and just above it was a short, trimmed mustache. Generally, he gave the impression of a tough guy and his two eyes were glaring, giving an image of power and terror to the viewer. He was clad in a white silky robe with wide, long sleeves and a silk strip for belting, designed mainly for comfort. Hanging on his wrists were golden bangles and eight out of his ten fingers were adorned with rings. On his right side was a bald-headed Christian monk in his dark-brown wool robe and the rosary in his hand, and on his left side, his brothers, Jagambu and Buka Timur, were standing in leather vests with their arms exposed. As Temujin stood in front of them with his head highly raised, Toghrul Khan scanned him from head to toe with his sharp eyes for a while. Then, without taking his eyes off of Temujin, he gave a signal to the priest with his fingers. At this, the priest made a cross with his right hand and announced in a thick but clear voice, "In the name of the Holy Spirit I welcome you! May peace be with you!"

It seemed to be the same, the usual greeting phrases they give to every visitor. Temujin knelt down and kowtowed three times, touching the ground with his forehead. He raised his head and shouted in a loud voice, "Greetings from the son of Yesugei, Temujin. I am here to pledge my loyalty to the khan! I am very grateful for your generosity in allowing me your audience."

Toghrul stared at Temujin with his eyes half-closed. After carefully searching Temujin with his eyes for a while, at last a big smile arrived on Toghurl's lips and eyes. He opened his mouth and said, "Oh! You are the son of my anda Yesugei! Then, you are like my own son. This is a very happy day for me! The Holy Spirit has blessed me to send me such a nice son like you! Come over here and sit to my right side."

As Temujin sat down in the chair next to him, Toghrul Khan asked him how he and his family had been doing while putting his hand on Temujin's shoulder and even touching his hands affectionately. While he was listening to Temujin, sometimes, he showed a look of anger by clenching his fist, or clicking his tongue, or at other times he just shook his head. When he heard Temujin was married to the Onggirad maid not long ago, he smiled big, as if he were his own son. He was like a loving, considerate, attentive father. However, Temujin's sixth sense made it possible for him to read the other side of his mind. Like many other winners, he was wearing multiple masks on his face and he wouldn't let out his last, true self.

Temujin could sense that he was greedy, cold-blooded and indiscreet to achieve what he wanted, just like vultures, which feed on any kind of dead body. Though he was a Christian, he was giving the impression of someone who was far from the Bible's teaching. On the other hand, Temujin could also sense that he was suffering from loneliness, which was eating at him like leeches in his brain. It was partly caused by the fact that he had killed his brothers and uncle to attain his throne, and also partly because he was disappointed with his only son, Nilka Senggum. Unlike his father, who had experienced numerous difficulties and hardships, he was a man like a tender plant in the greenhouse. His main concerns were fair maidens and fine wine. He was a pleasure seeker.

Besides the fact that the most valuable property for the steppe rulers was their useful, trusted followers, he seemed to be in desperate need of something more than that.

"I brought a gift for my revered khan."

Temujin noticed Toghrul's reaction to the gift he brought and Toghrul showed great interest in it.

"Ho! A gift for me? What could that be?"

As Temujin told him that the guard soldiers were keeping his gift, Toghrul clapped his hands for the slaves who were standing by the entrance to bring Temujin's gift. After Temujin had taken the black sable cloak from the slave, he knelt down and presented it with his two hands.

"Oh! What a nice, beautiful cloak!"

Toghrul seemed to be appreciating it very much and exclaimed in happiness. He kept on with the exclamations as he touched and rubbed the soft furry animal skin, raising it high with his two hands, examining one side and the other. It was nothing to him, who was the khan of fifty thousand yurts and who possessed enormous wealth and power. However, this gift had some kind of meaning to him.

In the Mongolian custom, the best gift from the father of the bride was for the father of the bridegroom. Temujin told Toghrul that it was from the bride's father. Toghrul knew that. Toghrul happily accepted Temujin's gift. Toghrul ordered the slave to handle it carefully and treasure it. He gave a look of affection to Temujin and said, "My son, let me know what you want. Whatever you say, it is already given to you."

Temujin bowed again and answered, "I am here only for greetings and to show my respect to the khan, who is like my own father."

Toghrul showed a look of being touched by his words, and then said, "From this moment, you can call me father. You are my son."

Toghrul took off the big sapphire ring from the middle finger of his right hand and then personally put it on Temujin's same finger. Temujin again bowed deeply as a token of gratitude.

CHAPTER EIGHTEEN

Reunion with Jamuka

Late in the afternoon that day, a big banquet was held in the khan's golden tent and in attendance were Toghrul Khan and about a hundred of his generals. Before the banquet, Belgutei and Kasar had been introduced to Toghrul by Temujin.

"They are my brothers."

Toghrul gave an attentive look to Belgutei and Kasar. He might have been impressed with Belgutei's big body. He paid extra attention to him. After taking a careful look, Toghrul asked Belgutei, "Do you know how to wrestle?"

Belgutei knelt down on one knee, lowered his head and answered, "Yes."

Temujin offered additional information about Belgutei. "He already has established his own name. He has not been defeated so far."

Toghrul Khan gave a look of surprise, with his eyes wide open. He ordered Nilka Senggum, who was standing nearby him, "Go bring Checheg!"

Checeg was the wrestling champion of the Keraits. As the banquet started, several dozen male and female slaves began to serve the drinks and food on big silver plates. The khan's seat was in the center of the northern wall, and next to him, to the right, was Temujin's seat. Belgutei was sitting next to Temujin and then next to him was Kasar. About a hundred of the khan's generals were in the seats arranged in two lines, along the eastern and western walls, with long tables in front of them. At the southern corner, close to the entrance, seven or eight musicians were sitting with their musical instruments and they began to make smooth music, sending it into the banquet hall.

Temujin was asked by a woman slave in a Persian costume, with eyes of blue tint and red hair, what he wanted to drink.

"We have Persian honey wine, red wine from Samarqand, Chinese rice wine and simple mare's milk."

Temujin's choice was mare's milk. Temujin had strong self-control over alcoholic beverages. He knew that if he did not control it, it would control him. He whispered in Belgutei's ear, "The wrestling match will start soon. Get ready for it, emotionally. Whoever your opponent will be, you surely have to defeat him. If not, you might risk your life."

Even before Temujin's words ended, a big man showed up at the southern entrance and walked up to the khan's table, guided by Nilka Senggum. Upon his arrival, the Kerait warriors let out big shouts, shaking their fists in the air. He had a big body, like a giant, and the neck below his bald head was double or triple the size of a normal neck it was so fat.

He was wearing short leather pants and Mongolian-style long boots. He seemed to be ready. He walked up close to the khan's table, knelt down on one knee and bowed. Belgutei, dressed in the same leather pants and boots, also walked up to the table and did the same thing. He had readied himself as soon as Toghrul Khan ordered his son to bring his opponent.

"One of you will be the champion. If you are not sure, it's not too late to give up."

Checheg, the Kerait champion, who had eyes of a tiger, glared at Belgutei, who had a smaller body than himself, in contempt. Belgutei stared back at him for a while and accepted the match.

In the center of the banquet hall, in the specially arranged wrestling ring, the two big men began their duel, at the risk of their own lives. Before the match, Nilka Senggum whispered in Checheg's ear, "Break his spine and send him to his death!"

At that time, many wrestlers were killed during wrestling matches, and yet there were no rules to put any restriction on the killers. Rather, it was viewed as a crown or decoration for the winner. Therefore, the Mongols used the wrestling match as a legal way to remove their political enemies. By that time, Checheg had already killed nine of his opponents by breaking their necks or spines.

The two wrestlers, staring at each other, bent at their waists, moved their steps slowly, making a circle. The fight to grab the opponent's wrist in a favorable position lasted for a while.

Soon, Checheg's big right hand grabbed Belgutei's left wrist and at the same time Belgutei's right hand grabbed Checheg's left wrist. Their arm wrestling had begun. For a while, they tried to free their left hands while trying to break the opponent's left arm with their right hand. On their foreheads and backs, beads of sweat began to stand out and the lights from the numerous Baghdad lamps in the banquet hall were reflected from their bodies, making their skin shiny like fish scales. The Kerait warriors kept on shouting and shaking their fists in excitement. The two wrestlers stepped back, releasing their hands from their opponents.

In a Mongolian wrestling match, both muscular strength and technical skill were required, equally, to win. This time, it was Belgutei's turn. He attacked Checheg first by grabbing his right wrist with his right hand, twisting it, and then swiftly stepping to his back, holding his neck from behind with his left arm. He began to squeeze his neck. However, before long, Checheg freed himself from Belgutei's attack, and then successfully put himself in an attack position by knotting his two arms between Belgutei's two arms and the back of his neck from behind. He began to put enormous pressure on Belgutei's back to break his spine. Again and again, he put his knee into Belgutei's lower back to direct and increase his pressing force. That was his specialty. It was a dangerous moment for Belgutei. On Belgutei's forehead, countless beads of sweat stood out and then dropped down like rain. Suddenly, the banquet hall fell into complete silence. Belgutei seemed to be doomed. He could be Checheg's tenth victim. Everybody thought the game was over. Then, suddenly, Belgutei bent his upper body, powerfully stretching his two arms, and untied Checheg's two arms. It happened in the blink of an eye. It was so powerful and so fast that Checheg lost his balance temporarily and staggered. Belgutei did not lose his chance. He held Checheg's neck firmly with his left arm, adding more power by holding his left wrist with his right hand, and then strongly and swiftly rotated. A thick, dull breaking sound echoed into the banquet hall, breaking the deep silence. Checheg's big body was lying on the floor with his eyes rolled up and bubbles at the corners of his mouth. He never moved again. The game was over. When four men came into the banquet hall and moved the body of Checheg out, there was quite a stir in the audience.

At this time, Toghrul Khan stood up and gestured the audience to calm down. He declared Belgutei the official winner, and granted him a gold goblet, the symbol of victory.

The banquet continued. Fine wines and various cuisines were supplied on the big silver plates without interruption and the musicians filled the banquet hall with sweet, smooth music. They enjoyed and laughed. Toghrul Khan asked Temujin, "If I give you ten thousand men, what do you want to do first?"

Temujin gave a little thought to this question and answered, "A snake without the head cannot move. I am just a part of your body."

Toghrul Khan seemed to be happy with that answer. He continued to ask questions.

"My main income is coming from the taxes collected from the caravans passing through the southern desert. However, nowadays, the Tanguts invade my territory more than before. I am going to hit the Tanguts. What do you think?"

Toghrul was one of the most powerful men on the plateau, though Temujin did not think he was strong enough to attack the Tanguts, who had 150 thousand troops. Temujin gave his answer after he took a sip of mare's milk.

"If that is your plan, I think you would be better off being allied with the Juchids of the Chin first. And then, if you attack them from one side and the Juchids from the other, chances are good for you, my lord."

"How can I become allied with the Juchids?"

Toghrul seemed to be very anxious for the answer.

"That would be simple. If you hit the Tartars, who turned against the Juchids not long ago, the Chin emperor might agree with the alliance."

The Juchids of the Chin had used the Tartars to destroy the emerging power, the Mongols, years ago. However, after they had gotten what they wanted, they forgot about the promise to send tribute each year to the Tartars. Enraged, the Tartars attacked the Chin territory and looted them as many times as they could.

"The Tartars are my enemy, too. But how can I justify my attack?"

Toghrul Khan had bitter experience in his early years. When he was seven, he was kidnapped by the Merkids, and had to spin the millstone, like a donkey. When he was fourteen, he was captured in the battlefield and enslaved by the Tartars. That lasted for several years. Now, the Merkids and the Tartars were both sworn enemies to Toghrul Khan.

"You have to wait, my lord. Sooner or later, the Juchids will come to you asking for help. Before that time, you should not make a move."

Toghrul Khan's jaw dropped and he could not close it. How could it be possible for a young man who had been hiding in the plain, to have such international knowledge and views? It was shocking and mysterious for Toghrul Khan. Toghrul Khan's eyes were partly closed for a moment, as if he tried to see something better that was far away from him. Soon, a smile arrived on his lips and he looked bright and accepting. He firmly grabbed Temujin's left hand with his right and said, "I will help you regroup your scattered tribesmen. This is my promise on my kidney and the breath of life."

The Mongols believed that the kidney was the base of trust and telling a lie would lead to suffocation. Those were some of the expressions the Mongols used, based on their beliefs, when they gave strong promises.

Toghrul Khan continued, "Recently, I was lucky to find a wonderful young man. He is smarter than a snake and braver than a lion. He had the capability to lead tens of thousands of men and also had a great vision. I accepted him as my youngest brother. Now, I have you and him, which means two wings have sprung up on my shoulders. I want you to meet him."

This time Temujin asked with great interest and attention, "My father, lord, what is his name?"

Toghrul answered with smile on his lips, "He is a Jadarat. His name is Jamuka."

Temujin was stunned.

"Oh! Jamuka! I never forgot about you during the last seven years. How wonderful it is to hear about you after all these years!" Temujin thought.

"Do you know him?"

At this question, Temujin answered with a bright look, "My lord, he is my anda. I haven't seen him over the last seven years."

Toghrul Khan gave a look of surprise, with his eyes wide open.

"Is he your anda? What a coincidence! This clearly shows that the Holy Spirit is helping me now. I really want you to have a good relationship with him."

Toghrul Khan gave an order to his brother Jagambu, "Dispatch the express messenger! Tell Jamuka in Qorqonak Jubur to present himself within three days."

After these words, Toghrul Khan raised his big body from the seat and shouted to the audience, "Listen! The Kyat Mongol Temujin is my son now. His enemy will be my enemy and my enemy will be his enemy. Everybody stand up and celebrate it!"

Temujin stepped out from his seat and kowtowed to him three times, in gratitude.

Jamuka arrived at Toghrul Khan's ordu just three days after. They hugged and patted each other.

"Jamuka, this is a real blessing that we can see each other again."

Jamuka, putting his two hands lightly on Temujin's shoulders, responded with big smile, "Temujin, this is the happiest day of my life. I am really glad to see you and to find out that you are doing fine."

They had a long talk as they were walking side by side on the forest trail. Temujin and Jamuka were in similar situations. Temujin was the official heir of the ordu of fifteen thousand households, but lost everything to Talgutai, the Taichut, and Jamuka had to leave his ordu for his safety, even though he was the official heir of his ordu of twenty thousand households. They were both born leaders, and they had brilliance, vision, extraordinary valor, persistence, passion and unlimited ambition.

"Why don't you borrow the troops from Toghrul Khan? The newborn baby birds cannot build their own nests. They need support and protection." Jamuka gave his advice to Temujin and that was what Temujin was seeking.

"I borrowed ten thousand troops from Toghrul Khan to retrieve the khanship of the Jadarats, which I lost when I was very young. When I made a surprise attack, with ten thousand troops, most of my tribesmen recognized me and surrendered without fighting. I could get a bloodless occupation. However, I killed a former chieftain and his two hundred followers and then threw away their dead bodies in a field."

He had already retrieved his khanship and was given the title, the sechen, which meant smart leader. Jamuka Sechen, eighteen years old, was the new Jadarat tribal leader and emerging star of the Mongolian Plateau.

The two young men, as they did before, lay on their stomachs in the same bed, looking at the burning flame from a sheep-oil lamp, and talked the night away. They both were married and began to know women. They talked about women and giggled all through the night. Temujin stayed one more night with Jamuka and left Toghrul Khan's ordu. Jamuka said he would stay there a few more days.

It was a very successful, productive, meaningful journey for Temujin. He proved himself a talented diplomat. It was a giant step for him to win the confidence of Toghrul Khan, who was one of the most powerful men on the plateau.

CHAPTER NINETEEN

Revenge of the Merkids

The Selenga River, which originates at the Kangai Mountains, located at the west side of the Mongolian Plateau, runs northeast, and, after it merges with the Orkhon River coming from the south, changes its direction to due north. It finally finds its way to the great Lake Baikal. The large, densely forested area covering the northern part of the Selenga River valley, south of Lake Baikal, was called taiga. With many different kinds of giant, cold-resistant trees, it was also the home for the Siberian animals, big and small, like tigers, wolves, bears, deer, foxes, weasels and sables.

The people who lived there were hunters and fishermen, unlike the steppe or desert people. They built triangular-shaped tents with long poles and covered them with animal skins. They also used animal skins for their clothing. Among all the tribes on the Mongolian Plateau, they were the least civilized and, at the same time, the most wild and fierce. However, unlike other tribes, who had to import iron, they had their own iron manufacturing systems, thanks to the unlimited source of iron ore in their territory. Thanks to their superior quality iron weaponry, they became one of the most powerful tribes of the Mongolian Plateau.

One day, it was just before daybreak when the eastern hills and mountains began to show their silhouettes and the sky above them began to change its color from pitch black to purplish blue. It was still dark, quiet and peaceful. Even for the birds, it was too early to wake up for the worms. Temujin's family's five yurts, near the upper stream of Kerulen River, were still in a deep sleep.

Koachin, Borte's loyal old servant, was the first to rise on that day, as usual. It was about fifteen days after Temujin's return from Toghrul Khan's ordu. After she put on her coat, she opened the flap door and stepped out of the yurt. The cool morning air touched her wrinkled cheeks. The old servant Koachin walked toward the fold, where about two hundred sheep were being kept, with a wooden bucket in her hand. She had keen eyes in the darkness. It was her daily routine to collect goat and sheep's milk and put it on the Temujin family's morning table. When she collected enough milk to fill the bucket halfway, the sky began to change its color to bright orange and the day began to break.

She suddenly began to feel something unusual in her ear. It was a low but heavy and thunderous sound. Based on her experience, she quickly realized that it was the distant rumbling made by hundreds of horses galloping all together. She had keen ears, like her eyes, which were considered to be essential for survival on the steppe. To make sure, she knelt down and touched one ear to the ground. She confirmed that it was horses galloping. Now she began to feel the shaking of the earth on her feet and small wave lines began to appear in the milk in the bucket.

Koachin, an old woman who had spent her whole life on the steppe, where the big and small conflicts continued endlessly, realized that it was a major-scale attack from one tribe to another. She also confirmed that the direction of origin of the rumbling was due north. She threw away the bucket and rushed to Temujin and Borte's yurt. She began to shout in front of their yurt, "Borte! Borte! Wake up! Enemies attack!"

Temujin and Borte both woke up from Koachin's urgent cry. Temujin rushed out of the yurt, pulling on his clothes. He climbed to the top of a nearby hill on his horse to find out the direction and scale of the attack. They were approaching from due north and appeared to be more than three hundred horse soldiers. Their image and rumbling were fading in, making a long tail of grayish dust, which was scattering into the cool morning air. They would soon sweep away Temujin's five yurts like a storm.

Temujin confirmed they were the Merkids. Temujin pondered for a while. What did they want? What motivated them to travel over three hundred miles? Did they travel all the way to attack and pillage Temujin's five yurts with nine horses, two oxen and two hundred sheep? The answer was very clear to Temujin: it was Borte.

When Temujin's father Yesugei had kidnapped Ouluun, who was Temujin's mother, killing the Merkids, the relationship between the Kyat Mongols and the Merkids had been damaged and they automatically became sworn enemies. It happened twenty years ago, but the Merkids did not forget. It was the steppe tradition that they always had to get even with someone who had caused them trouble. If it was impossible in the same generation, it was automatically transferred to the next generation. They never forgot their humiliations.

Temujin came back to his yurt. He held Borte's shoulders with his two hands and said in a sad voice, "Borte, they are the Merkids."

Borte gave a look of surprise, yet she regained her calmness within a moment. Borte knew what that meant. Borte heard the story that Yesugei had kidnapped Ouluun from the Merkids many times from Ouluun herself and Temujin also. Of course, Borte knew that if the attackers were the Merkids, she was their target. Borte dropped her head for a moment, and then raised her head, her eyes filled with tears. "If they are the Merkids, their target is me. Leave here, please! I will stay here. Take care of yourself. If I go with you, they will come after us to the end of the world. You will surely risk your life."

It would be next to suicide for four or five men try to stop three hundred horse soldiers. As long as their target was Borte, they surely would not go back until they got what they wanted.

"Borte ..."

Temujin did not know what to say. He was just looking into her eyes. The rumbling became louder and louder, and at any moment, the soldiers would fall upon them.

"Hurry, leave right now! The women are born, but the men are made. It takes a very long time for a man to be made. Save your life, please!"

Temujin embraced her firmly. His heart was breaking. Borte's eyes were full of tears and they flew down her cheeks.

"Just one thing, though. If you can promise to come back to save me, it would be much easier for me."

Temujin embraced her more tightly and said, "Borte, I love you. I promise I will go to any place in the world to save you."

From outside, Temujin's brothers and comrades were urging him along after they had readied themselves. Temujin stepped out of his yurt and mounted his horse.

While Temujin and Borte were parting in tears, Belgutei and his mother, Sochigel, also were facing a sad, heartbreaking moment. They did not have enough horses for everybody. Sochigel knew that and, in addition, she was in fear that she might delay everybody. She gently refused to join them, regardless of Belgutei's urgent request.

"Don't worry about me. They might not kill me."

Sochigel tried to put her son at ease. Now, only three women would remain, Borte, Sochigel and the old servant Koachin. Temujin left there with his mother, Ouluun; half brother Belgutei; three of his brothers, Kasar, Kachun, Temuge; and his nine-year-old sister, Temulun. The comrades, Bogorchu and Jelme, accompanied them. They galloped at full speed along the Kerulen River bank in the northeast direction. Their destination was Burkan Mountain. It was the place that they could expect the highest chance of survival from the Merkids' raid, due to its rough terrain of thick forests.

When Temujin and the other members galloped away from sight, the old servant, Koachin, approached Borte and honestly suggested, "My lady, you'd better hide yourself, too."

Koachin forcefully pushed Borte into the oxcart of sheep's wool and covered her with piles of wool. Koachin and Sochigel tried to drive the cart to the nearby forest. Fortune was not on their side, because one of the wheels broke in the middle of the trip. At that moment, the Merkid raiders arrived like a tempest. They were Toktoa of the Uduyid Merkids, Dayir Usun of the Uuas Merkids, Qaatai Darmala of the Qaad Merkids and their three hundred heavily armed horse-soldiers.

When they arrived in front of Temujin's town of five yurts, it became very noisy, with sounds from the horses' hooves and panting, as they were soaked in sweat. Toktoa ordered his men to search Temujin's five yurts. Of course, they could find nothing. Toktoa drove his horse in front of the two women, Koachin and Sochigel, who were frozen in fear.

"What's in the cart?"

To his question, Koachin answered in a trembling voice, "Nothing, sir, only sheep's wool in there."

Toktoa ordered his men to search the cart. Two soldiers dug out the wool and easily found Borte. She was taken roughly out of the cart. The wool was all over her body. Toktoa gazed at her for a while and then asked, "Are you Temujin's woman?"

Borte, standing tall, staring at Toktoa, answered yes. Toktoa ordered his man to put her on the horse. One soldier put her on his horse and he mounted behind her. Toktoa, this time, asked Sochigel, "Who are you? Identify yourself."

As Sochigel did not give an answer, Qaatai Darmala, who was standing by him, answered instead, "I know who she is. She is Yesugei's widow. Her name is Sochigel and she was his second wife."

Toktoa exchanged a few words with Qaatai Darmala.

"If she is Sochigel, she is a Merkid. She is one of us!"

Qaatai Darmala agreed. Toktoa ordered to put her on the horse. After this, Toktoa asked Koachin, "Old woman! Tell me which way Temujin ran away. If you do, you will save your life."

Koachin kept on saying no.

"I really don't know. I left early in the morning to the fold for milking and I just came back."

Qaatai Darmala, looking at Toktoa, gave his comments, "This woman is telling a lie. We know that she lied a moment ago."

Toktoa gestured his hand. Two soldiers stepped out and shot arrows. Two arrows shot from a close distance lodged deeply in her chest. She dropped down and, holding the two arrows with her hands, fell on her back.

"Koachin! Koachin!"

Borte cried out on horseback, writhing. Toktoa gestured his hand again for his soldiers to move. They set fire to Temujin's five yurts. The five yurts were wrapped in flames in a short moment. The Merkids moved out in pursuit of Temujin. They followed the tracks of Temujin and his group. They found out that Temujin and his group were moving toward the northeast, to Burkan Mountain. They kept on following the tracks along the Kerulen River bank. However, when they arrived at a certain area of the mountainside, it became almost impossible to continue. It was ankle-deep mire, with footsteps of numerous big migratory animals, like elk. To make it worse, after the mire, the slopes of the huge Burkan Mountain were covered with a thick forest of trees high up in the sky. They moved up, further north, to find a stream coming down from the Burkan Mountain. They kept on chasing Temujin along the valley connected to the stream, but they were not successful.

Toktoa discussed this with Dayir Usun and Qaatai Darmala. "We already have their women. This might be enough to recover what we had lost in the past. How about going back at this point?"

Qaatai Darmala and Dayir Usun nodded at that suggestion. They went down the mountain and proceeded to their hometown.

Temujin remained on the mountain for three more days, even after they had left. He sent Belgutei, Bogorchu and Jelme each in a different direction to make sure they really went back.

"We have to make sure they really left for their home or if they are just trying to trick us to come out."

Three days later, all three of them reported that the Merkids really had gone home. Temujin, with his family and comrades, went down the mountain. They came back to their home site only to find the five yurts half-burnt and Koachin's dead body with two arrows in her chest. Koachin's clothes were stained with hard and dark blood clots and her dead body had already begun the decomposition process, spreading a foul odor in the air. Because of that, flies and ants were swarming on her dead body, making it look even more miserable. Temujin knelt down in front of her dead body and closed her eyes with his hand, which were wide open until that moment.

"Koachin, I am really grateful to you. Without you, how could my family and I survive?"

Temujin kept on kneeling and remained still for quite a while. He slowly got to his feet and stared into space for a while. His facial muscles were distorted from the emotional pain. He slowly walked up the nearby hill.

"Where is he going?"

Murmuring this, Bogorchu was about to follow him, but Belgutei stopped him.

"Leave him alone. He's better off alone at this moment."

At the top of the hill, Temujin took off his belt, putting it around his neck, knelt and kowtowed nine times toward the sky and the sun. Then, raising his two hands high above his head, he cried out:

The everlasting blue sky,
The owner of the universe.

The mighty sun,
The origin of power and energy.

Do not let disorder and disunion prevail.
Do not let hypocrisy and betrayal gain the power.
Do not accept the selfish, who are building up only their
own homes.
Discontinue conflicts and disharmony in this land.

Allow me to create the new order in this world.
Where everybody shares and lives in harmony,
Justice surpasses injustice,
And truth overpowers falsehood.

May the followers of the ways of heaven stand high,
While the others shall fall down.

Temujin's earnest, heartfelt prayer echoed into the space filled with the desert's hot, dry air. The mysterious sky, which has never lost its vibrant blue since the beginning of time, was covering his head, and the forever-young sun, which never ceases its own explosion, was pouring its brilliant sunlight onto his face, which was covered with numerous beads of sweat.

After his prayer, Temujin went down the hill and buried Koachin. Temujin looked in every corner of the half-burnt yurts and found the silk roll that Borte had brought as a wedding gift. He carefully wrapped Koachin's body with the silk and buried her in the middle of the hill, where the sunlight was abundant during the day and there was a southern side view. They all gathered around the grave. They listened to Temujin's words of condolence with their heads down.

"Now we are saying goodbye, in sadness and pain, to the woman who had a pure and beautiful mind. How could we have survived without your keen ears and eyes? How can we stand on this earth again without your devoted, loyal heart? Someone who has her master and keeps her loyalty is still beautiful, even after death."

They went down the hill in silence. Temujin started rebuilding the yurts. They cut and collected branches of the willow and elm trees for temporary yurts. They collected scattered sheep that were left after the Merkids' plundering and put them into the newly built fold.

CHAPTER TWENTY

Ordeals for Borte

Several days later, Temujin revisited Toghrul Khan with his brothers. At that time, he was the only one Temujin could ask for help. He must get Borte back. Toghrul Khan was still staying in the Black Forest. When Temujin and his brothers arrived at Toghrul Khan's golden ordu, they could see many other visitors waiting for the khan's audience. After a half-day's wait, Temujin was able to see the khan. Temujin proceeded toward Toghrul Khan, who was sitting with his generals on each side, and showed his respect like before, by getting down on one knee and lowering his head. Toghrul Khan, with his eyes wide open in surprise at Temujin's unexpected return, which was within a month of his departure, asked the purpose of his visit. Temujin told him the story about what happened to him, including Borte's abduction by the Merkids. Toghrul Khan seemed to be astonished by Temujin's report.

"What? The Merkids kidnapped Borte?"

He remained silent for a moment with his jaw wide open. He asked Temujin with an angry look, "Do they know that you are now my foster son?"

Temujin answered with his head down, "Probably not, my father, lord."

Toghrul Khan jumped up from his chair, punching the arm-rest of his chair with his fist.

"I have been humiliated and seriously challenged!"

After a while, when he regained his composure, he sat down and said in a low voice, "My son, listen! I will surely get your wife back for you. I will keep my word, even if I have to kill them all."

Temujin showed his appreciation by bowing deeply again.

After Temujin went out of the tent, Toghrul Khan discussed this with his brother, Jagambu, his son, Nilka Senggum, and his generals.

"What is the size of the Merkids' power, currently?"

To Toghrul Khan's question, his brother Jagambu answered, "They are believed to be furious and valorous, and yet unorganized and scattered over a wide area. So it is hard for them to summon their forces. The total number of their horse soldiers could be forty to fifty thousand."

At this answer, Toghrul Khan pondered a while with his eyes half closed.

"To hit them, we need at least forty thousand men and forty thousand horses, I guess."

To Toghrul Khan's comments, Jagambu agreed, "That is right."

Toghrul Khan asked, "How long will it take to get ready for the war?"

Jagambu answered, "We need at least six months."

Toghrul Khan pondered again. Then he glanced around with his slanted eyes and said, "Six months? Fine! We will advance next April. We will send twenty thousand men only."

To this remark, this time his brother Buka Timur questioned, "If we send only twenty thousand, how can we cover the other twenty thousand?"

Toghrul Khan answered without hesitation, "The other twenty thousand should be covered by Jamuka."

The followers of Toghrul Khan had full confidence in their leader. They believed in his leadership and the way he handled things, his craftiness. They knew he had been through numerous experiences of life and death, and had joined countless battles. He was a careful man and always made his movements after exact calculation. He proved himself to become one of the strongest men on the Mongolian Plateau. Nobody could deny him.

However, only one man, his son Nilka Senggum, raised an objection with a look that said he really could not understand such a decision.

"Are you going to send forty thousand men to save just one woman?"

Toghrul Khan was frowning at him for a while and clicked his tongue in disappointment.

"Don't you understand? This is a good chance to hit the Merkids. You should always be able to justify yourself when you raise a war."

He was right. To raise a war, you need to justify your motivation in a way that everyone can agree on. Without justification, you could move the troops by force, but not by heart. What was on in Toghrul Khan's mind? Nobody knew. He probably needed skilled blacksmiths who could make different kinds of weaponry, iron ore and all kinds of animal furs, valued highly in the international markets. It was no wonder that Nilka Senggum could not understand, for he spent most of his time in his harem with a wine goblet in his hand.

Toghrul Khan always lamented that. He could never relax. He could not trust his son or his brothers. At the time, that was all right since he could manage everything by himself. But he was not ready for when the time came that he had to leave everything to one or two of his trusted men, while he sat in his comfortable chair. Unlike the Chinese, the Mongols did not have any kind of moral or traditional bond that deemed blind devotion for their emperor to be the utmost in respectable human behavior. The nomads on the Mongolian Plateau followed the simple rule that they would support anything that coincided with their interests and benefit; otherwise, they would not.

Temujin saw Toghrul Khan again in his golden tent late that afternoon. To the khan's left and right sides were standing his brothers and high-ranking warriors. As Temujin went down on one knee and lowered his head, Toghrul Khan gestured with his hand for Temujin to stand up. He gave a look of kindness and caring, with even a smile of warm, fatherly affection on his lips.

"My son! I still remember the warm support that your father and my anda Yesugei showed me in the old days. The black cloak you brought me touched my heart. We will take the steps in April, next year. For the Merkids, we need that much time."

After these words, Toghrul Khan picked up the big silver goblet filled with fresh sheep's milk from the silver plate being held by the bald-headed slave in wide pants, with nothing on his upper body, who was kneeling near him. He took a sip of it and continued talking. "We need at least forty thousand men to hit them. I will send twenty thousand and the other twenty thousand will come from Jamuka. Ask Jamuka. I will immediately dispatch the messenger to him."

Toghrul Khan took another sip of milk and continued. "I will send two hundred warriors with you. They will stay with you until the battle starts, to guard you and your family members. Do your best to gather your scattered tribesmen. Food, weapons and all other necessities will be supplied. Talk more, in detail, with Jagambu."

Temujin got on his knees and kowtowed three times in appreciation.

"My father, lord, I will never forget your favor. I swear that I will be loyal to my lord until my last breath."

Toghrul Khan nodded and gave a satisfactory smile in return for Temujin's remarks.

After Temujin stepped out of the golden tent, he had a meeting with Jagambu. Unlike his elder brother, Toghrul Khan, Jagambu was the muscular type of man with a thick beard, big eyes and a deep voice. He said in a deep, husky voice, "The two hundred Kerait warriors accompanying you will be selected from volunteers. You will be the chief of the troop while they are with you. Once a month, all necessities will be supplied. You will have to tell the supply officer what you need for the following month."

Early the following morning, Temujin and his brothers left Toghrul Khan's ordu with two hundred Kerait soldiers. Most of the soldiers were between the ages of fourteen and seventeen and unmarried, so no family members were with them. After they came back to Burgi Elgi, Temujin's base campsite, they began to build fifty more yurts for the soldiers. After that, Temujin dispatched Belgutei and Kasar to Jamuka as messengers. At that time, Jamuka was in Qorqonak Jubur in the Onon River basin, which was about 150 miles east of Temujin's campsite. Temujin's message was delivered by Kasar:

Anda Jamuka,
I have been robbed,
Half of my chest.
I have been thrown into
The empty bed.
We are the children of
The same womb.

We are closer than
     The flesh brothers.
How can I soothe
     The pain in my heart?
How can I retrieve
     My stolen soul mate?

"What?" Jamuka sprang to his feet from his chair. That was his first reaction when he heard the news from Belgutei and Kasar. He really seemed to be shocked. He murmured to himself after gazing into space for a moment, "The Merkid bastards..."

Jamuka, leader of twenty thousand households, eighteen-year-old chieftain of the great Jadarats, was already a man of dignified appearance. The hundred thousand Jadarats of twenty thousand households had accepted his legitimacy, believed in his brilliance and valor and approved of him as their leader, even at his young age. He sat down again slowly, asking for more details. Inside his yurt, which was supported by two big columns, numerous dried skins of wild animals like snow leopards and the white snow fox of the Gobi Desert were hanging on the wall, and the floor was covered with a Siberian black bear skin. Jamuka offered Belgutei and Kasar green tea mixed with fresh sheep's milk, brought by two serving women.

"What has happened to my anda Temujin is exactly what had happened to me. I will make a plan for that immediately."

Belgutei and Kasar told Jamuka about Temujin's second visit to Toghrul Khan and all the decisions made there.

"I haven't received anything from Toghrul Khan yet. To hit the Merkids, you need careful evaluations, plans and ample time. They are big and strong. If Toghrul Khan asks twenty thousand troops of me, it would be too much for me. I think a better plan is to pick up ten thousand from the Kyat Mongols scattered around the Onon River and then, the other ten thousand could be covered by my Jadarats."

At that time, on the Mongolian Plateau, war meant opportunity. For the victors, the war booty and loot could be added to their property. The concept of war booty covered not only material things, like weapons and livestock, but also the women and children. Plus, if the captives could be made into slaves, that meant free labor. War meant more than self-protection, it was business. So, either groups or individuals were always waiting for a good opportunity. Jamuka's idea, ten thousand from the Kyat Mongols and the other ten thousand from his own people, was a fair and reasonable one.

"If I can send ten thousand troops from the Kyat Mongols, I will transfer the command to Temujin, if possible. The most difficult and important part of this operation is security. The operation will start in six months, so the success of this plan will be depend on keeping it secret from the public.

"Nobody should know we are recruiting soldiers to hit the Merkids. Except for a few people, that should be top secret. I think the better way is to spread out idle rumors and let them go around."

Belgutei and Kasar nodded. Jamuka continued, "We will discuss later the date and time of the beginning of the operation and where we can put the troops."

Just as Toghrul Khan had personal grudges against the Merkids, Jamuka also had bad relations with them. Before he went to Toghrul Khan for help to retrieve the khanship of the Jadarats, he met with Toktoa Beki of the Merkids first. He went to Toktoa Beki with his thirty followers, asking for help. But, instead, he took Jamuka captive. Toktoa took Jamuka's mother, who still had her beauty, as his concubine and in return, he did not kill Jamuka. Jamuka had to stage a fake surrender and had to swear his loyalty to Toktoa Beki before he was released. When the time came and the moment was right, Jamuka made a successful escape, after retrieving his mother and his thirty followers. He directly went to see Toghrul Khan.

Belgutei and Kasar left Jamuka's ordu. Jamuka sent his message for Temujin with them:

> *Anda Temujin,*
> *My heart is breaking,*
>   *In the midst of your agony.*
> *And my mind is wandering*
>   *In the darkness of grief.*
>
> *When the day arrives,*
>   *I will do the war dance,*

Sprinkling the kumis.
  I will beat the drum
Of the black ox hide,
  Loudly and strongly.

I will wear the leather armor,
  As tough as the turtle shell,
On my chest.
I will wear the sharpest sword,
  On my waist,
And hold the longest spear,
Firmly and high.

We will annihilate the Merkids,
On this land,
And we will save our lady,
Borte.
Until that moment comes,
We are not even allowed to die,
For both of us.

The Merkids returned to their home as victors. Their tents were spread throughout a large area around the southern side of Lake Baikal, the Selenga River, and its branch, the River Kilko. When they arrived at the entrance of their tent city, the residents, young and old, came out to see their soldiers marching in, making loud noises with their horses' footsteps. Borte was sitting on a horse with no saddle, and a Merkid soldier was sitting just behind her, holding the reins. The townspeople were watching expressionlessly, but soon they found out the strange woman was Temujin's new bride. They began to swear and shout abusive language toward Borte. Some of the old men were shaking their fists in the air, showing enmity.

It was evening time. The smoke from the tents, probably from cooking dinner, was rising all around. Above their heads, a group of migratory birds were passing through, high in the sky. It was a peaceful scene, regardless of Borte's mind. Their dwelling tents were shaped in a triangle, or dome type, each of them, half-and-half. Borte and Sochigel were kept in custody separately, in different yurts. Two guards were posted in front of each of their yurts. Some time later, a Merkid woman stepped into Borte's yurt carrying a wooden plate with a lump of boiled boar's meat and a wooden bowl of goat's milk. She put the provisions down in front of Borte and stepped out of the yurt without saying a word. Borte gazed at the food for a while. She asked herself, "What are they going to do to me?" The answer came late in the evening. Borte was dragged by two soldiers to a huge tent, of which the entrances were guarded by several heavily armed soldiers. A bright light was streaming out through the half-open flap door, and boisterous talking noises and occasional laughter came out through it also.

Borte was roughly pushed into the tent. Inside the tent, she saw thirty or forty Merkids, men and women, sitting on the chairs lined up along the tent wall, drinking and talking noisily. Due to numerous torches, it was bright like daylight inside the tent. In front of them were tables and on the tables were numerous drinking cups, dishes and food bowls scattered around in a disorderly manner. It showed that it had been a while since they had started their feast. By the entrance, two servants were standing still, waiting for orders, and several serving women were busying themselves cleaning up the tables and serving more food and drinks. Once they realized Borte was in the tent, all their eyes fell upon her and a deep silence ran through the tent. Most of the Merkid men were accompanied by their own women. Just to break the awkward silence, a drunken man shouted in a loud voice, "Let's make her strip off her clothes and dance!"

Suddenly, laughter burst out. Men giggled and women shot sidelong glances at the man who said that, and yet smiles still remained on their lips. They were watching Borte in expectation of something exciting and amusing happening. Borte was glaring at them, one by one, with her head highly raised. The man who shouted actually got on his feet and approached Borte slowly. He was fully drunk, so his steps were very unstable. However, nobody tried to stop him, due to his high rank in their society. He approached Borte and tried to grasp her hand while she was staring at him with anger and fear. Ignoring Borte's resistance, he held both of her shoulders, pulled her dress down to her waist and pushed her, roughly, into the center of the tent. Borte fell down on the ground with her milk-colored, full bosom and upper torso exposed. Men giggled, looking at each other, and the women shrieked. After she regained consciousness, she put her dress back on and shouted in anger, staring at each one of them, "You will pay for this! You will never be able to get away from Temujin's revenge!"

At this, one Merkid man replied in ridicule, "Who is Temujin now? He has two men and nine horses!"

A low tone of scoffing laughter filled the tent.

At this moment, Toktoa, the chieftain of the Merkids, who had been watching all of this, got on his feet, hitting the table with his horsewhip. "That's enough! I think we have already got revenge for Chiledu. Now, let's talk about what we should do with this woman. If you have any idea, tell me!"

Temporarily, there was silence. Then, one man shouted out while he was still in his chair, "Let's have a wrestling match tomorrow! The winner will have her!"

At this suggestion, they talked to each other for a while. At this moment, an elder stood up from his seat and said in a low, gentle voice, "In the past, Yesugei, the Kyat Mongol, kidnapped Chiledu's woman. This woman should be his, in return, but since Chiledu passed away a long time ago, his brother, Chilger, should be the right person to take this woman."

There was deep silence. Toktoa glanced around and asked if there were any other opinions. Nobody presented any other opinion, as the elder's suggestion was quite right. Toktoa declared to the group, "This woman is now Chilger's. She will be Chilger's concubine."

Chilger was a big man and was the wrestling champion. They called him Chilger Boko. Boko was the title given to the wrestling champion. Just after Toktoa's declaration, Chilger, who was there at that moment, stood up slowly with a smile on his lips and staggered toward Borte. He was also fully drunk. Borte, shrieking, ran to the door, but two servants blocked her way. At last, Chilger could snatch her and he lifted her up in his arms. He firmly held Borte in his arms, as she was shrieking, struggling and wriggling, and walked out from the tent in drunken, staggering steps. Again, a low tone of laughter filled the tent. They continued the feast, laughing and drinking as if nothing had happened.

CHAPTER TWENTY-ONE

Reunion with Borte

The new spring arrived on the Mongolian Plateau, which meant the long, harsh and painful winter for Temujin had passed. Temujin never forgot Borte, even for a day. Sometimes, he stood still for a long time just gazing at the faraway mountains. Each time, Ouluun approached him and said to him, rubbing his back, showing her affection, "My son, men should not be too emotional. That will only make your eyes unclear. Surely you will be able to save Borte. However, you should also be emotionally ready for the one out of ten thousand chance of losing her. That should be your mindset."

Temujin knelt down in front of Ouluun and touched his mother's hand to his cheek, "Thank you, mother. I will surely get Borte back."

Ouluun's advice was quite appropriate. However, it was torture for an eighteen-year-old man to lose his loving wife to somebody else. Ouluun, smoothing his cheek with her hand, said, "I have to remind you that your dream is much bigger than one woman."

Temujin busied himself going around trying to regroup his people. There were many difficulties in doing this. First of all, there were the security problems. Everything had to be done in secret. It could not be known to the public that he was trying to recruit soldiers to raise a war against the Merkids. And more, it could not be known that Toghrul Khan of the Keraits and Jamuka of the Jadarats would join him.

Each time he met anyone of the Kyat Mongols he tried to persuade them to join him, but they wouldn't trust and follow him easily, as he was a mysterious young man to them. That was the second difficulty. Nonetheless, he did manage to recruit two thousand men before the war. Many of them were previously his father's men and they reunited in the dream of reconstructing Yesugei's glory. The rest of them were wanderers who didn't belong to any clan or tribe, or were slave escapees. Many of them joined Temujin solely for food, clothing and basic necessities. All those things were supplied by Toghrul Khan's supply unit.

Temujin also contacted Borte's father, Dey Sechen, though he didn't ask for help. Dey Sechen and his elders didn't want full-scale war with the Merkids. However, Alchi, Borte's elder brother, declared that he and his five hundred volunteers would join the operation.

During this period of time, Temujin met many Kyat Mongols, descendants of Kabul Khan, who were dispersed and living along the Onon River basin. They didn't have their own leader, so voluntarily they became the nokhods of Jamuka, who was controlling and ruling those areas. They were under Jamuka's control and protection. Altan was one of those and Sacha Beki was another. Altan was the grandson of Kabul Khan, the first khan of the Mongols and the third son of Kutula Khan, who was the third khan. Altan was the official heir for the khanship of the Kyat Mongols. Sacha Beki was the great-grandson of Kabul Khan and the grandson of Okin Barak, who was the first son of Kabul Khan. He was the head of the Jurkins, which was a sub-clan of the Kyat Mongols. The Jurkins were the descendants of the first son of Kabul Khan and the name Jurkin was derived from Kutuktu Jurki, who was the eldest grandson by the firstborn son of Kabul Khan. They were the nominal central force of the Kyat Mongols, who were the descendants of Kabul Khan. They would join the operation, however, not by Temujin's asking, but by Jamuka's order. When Jamuka retrieved his khanship of the Jadarats, he marched to this area and subdued all the tribes around the Onon River basin. Jamuka was supposed to protect them; in return, they had to obey Jamuka's orders. Temujin also saw his uncle, Nekun Tashi, and his son, Quchar. They, too, were supposed to participate in the operation, also by Jamuka's order.

The day had been set. It was the first day of July of the lunar month, which was the official commencement day of the operation. That was more than a two-month delay from the original plan. Toghrul Khan, Temujin and Jamuka all agreed to meet with their troops at Botoqan Boorji, which was about 250 miles south of the Buura Plain, where Toktoa Beki's ordu and his main troops were stationed.

Toktoa Beki had received information that Temujin was organizing his troops and planning to attack them. But, he was underestimating and ignoring Temujin. He didn't know Toghrul Khan and Jamuka were joining the operation. All the plans had been underway in complete secrecy. Actually, Jamuka had to kill two or three small group chieftains who refused to join, for security reasons.

"The Kyat Mongols have been broken into pieces for many years. They will never stand again. Even though Temujin tried to regroup his people, surely he will end up next to nothing."

That was Toktoa's comment and conclusion. However, he put ten thousand troops around the Kilko River basin, just in case. In the meantime, Temujin's spies had successfully infiltrated to get information about Toktoa's troops and Borte's whereabouts.

One day before departure, Temujin performed a war ritual with his 2,000 well-trained warriors and Alchi's five hundred Olqunuud volunteers, who had arrived about fifteen days earlier. It was about evening time and was beginning to grow dark. Many huge campfires were burning, making the area as bright as daytime. The soldeirs were all clad in combat uniforms and leather armor, and in their hands, their well-polished spears were shining. Hanging from their waists, on both the left and right sides, were scimitars and daggers, and on their left arms, they were holding round leather shields. They slaughtered a white horse and put it on the altar as an offering. Temujin sprinkled the kumis around the altar and prayed to the heaven:

Oh! Tenggri!
  God of the heaven,
  And almighty!

  We gathered here
  With one mind and one belief.

  Give us the strength!
  Give us the victory!

  The man with only one mind is strong.
  The man with only one belief is invincible.

  Glory lies in front of the brave.
  Glory is the privilege of the brave.

  Tenggri, god of heaven!
  Allow us glory!

After this prayer, Temujin sprinkled kumis again and kowtowed nine times toward the altar. The warriors chanted as they were repeatedly pushing their spears into the air in one motion, "Tenggri! Tenggri! Tenggri!"

The orange flames of the huge campfires were dazzling, reflecting in the razor sharp, well-polished spear blades. Their chanting echoed through the dry, desert air and into the mysterious darkish-blue sky. They continued chanting, "Temujin! Temujin! Temujin!"

The thick gray smoke from the campfires was spiraling into the sky like snakes. They began the war dance to the drumbeats. The beads of sweat on their foreheads were sparkling like quicksilver, due to the reflected lights from the roaring campfires.

Early in the following morning, Temujin and his warriors left Burgi Ergi and marched northward. He organized and divided his troops into vanguard, center force, right wing, left wing and rear guard. The commander of the vanguard of 300 soldiers was Kasar, of the right wing of 300 was Bogorchu, of the left wing of 300 was Jelme and of the 500 rear guards, Alchi. Temujin took charge of the center force and at the same time, he was the commander-in-chief. Belgutei was with Temujin in the center force and he was the second in command.

Temujin considered each soldier's specialty and all 300 of the vanguard were archers. The soldiers skilled at swords and spears were put into the center force unit. Temujin subdivided the center force into the light cavalry and the heavy cavalry. The heavy cavalry was the main destructive power of Temujin's army and also was the largest group, at 800 soldiers. Temujin used smoke and flags as a communication tool among the units in the daytime and torches and godori at night. The godori was an arrow that made a whistling sound when it was shot. Temujin had a great gift for organizing and systematizing the troops and it showed clearly from his very first effort.

Temujin stayed one night at the Tana Koroqan stream and then moved farther north, and stayed another night at the Ayil Karaqana near the Kymulqa stream. From there, it was only a half-day marching distance to the Botoqan Boorji, the appointed location where the three leaders were supposed to meet. Temujin had decided to wait for Toghrul Khan there. Toghrul Khan arrived three days later than scheduled. Temujin didn't move out, but waited for him patiently. When Temujin and Toghrul Khan arrived at the Botoqan Boorji, three days later than scheduled, Jamuka was very unhappy. At that time, the Mongols had an exact concept of time, especially in military operations. Jamuka protested strongly, and Toghrul Khan tried to appease him by giving an apology.

"My brother! I am sorry for being three days late. I will take responsibility for anything that happens because of it."

Jamuka seemed to be appeased; nonetheless, he told Toghrul Khan and Temujin in clear words, "From this moment, I am on my own. That's what I want."

After these words, he turned around and walked back to his camp. That was the moment he declared his independence. Jamuka had already built up his own power. He could stand on his own feet. He didn't need to take orders from Toghrul Khan any more. Jamuka was unhappy because Temujin also made him wait, even though he could have been on time. An independent relationship meant that they remained friends only when it was beneficial to each other.

Toghrul Khan actually brought about 18,000 troops and Jamuka brought the same. Toghrul Khan was commanding 9,000 troops only and the other 9,000 were led by his brother Jagambu. They got together and discussed the operations and tactics.

"If anyone of you has any ideas for this operation, tell me."

Toghrul Khan asked this and his brother Jagambu responded, "I think the frontal attack could be better, because we are believed to have superior power."

At this, Temujin gave his opinion.

"I think it would be better to make a surprise attack. They put ten thousand men at the northern side of the Kilko River. We need rafts to cross the river. While we are crossing the river, we could be attacked. We might lose a great number of soldiers. And more, in the meantime, their reinforcements could arrive. I, and my 2,500 men, will go further upstream on the river, where I don't need rafts to cross, and then attack their 10,000 garrison from behind."

At this point, Jamuka, who was listening to Temujin with his arms folded, remarked, raising his eyebrows, "The upper side of the river is steep and rough mountain terrain where nobody can approach. Am I right?"

Temujin replied with a smile on his lips, "You are right. It would be impossible for 40,000 men and horses to pass through that route. However, it might be possible for 2,500 men and horses. Surprise attacks should be done in surprise, am I right?"

After saying this, Temujin laughed loudly.

Toghrul Khan asked, while sitting on a small wooden folding chair with his two hands on the handle of his sword, which was stuck into the ground in front of him, "How long will it take to make enough rafts?"

To this question, Jagambu replied, "Two days could be enough."

Toghrul Khan pondered a while and then said, "Fine, we will use Temujin's idea. However, if things don't go as well as we expected, you could be in danger. Is it still all right with you?"

Toghrul Khan looked straight at Temujin, as if he wanted to make sure.

Temujin, lowering his head, replied clearly, "Leave it to me, my father lord. Only one thing, though. At the time when I commence the attack, the main body of troops has to cross the river as soon as possible. If not, I, and my 2,500 troops, could be massacred."

They agreed to commence the attack at nighttime, and to communicate with the fire arrows and godori at the time Temujin started the attack.

They marched farther north, and when they arrived near the Kilko River, they paused to make the rafts. Temujin helped to complete the raft work. After that, Temujin and his 2,500 warriors began to march alone, toward the upper part of the river. Temujin encouraged them. They successfully passed the steep, rough, rocky pass and taiga area, which were believed to be impossible to pass. Temujin lost seven warriors whose horses misstepped and fell down the cliffs. Three days after Temujin had left the main force, he and his warriors arrived at a small hill on the southern side of the Kilko River, where the Merkid troops were stationed. Temujin and his warriors planned to wait until it was dark.

Before it became dark, two Merkid patrolmen on their horses were approaching. One of them had a big drum on the side of his horse and the other had a big horn on his waist. Hiding behind the top of the hill, Temujin watched them approaching and waited until they stepped into shooting range. They were talking and laughing with each other as they were slowly driving their horses toward Temujin's troops. The one with the horn suddenly stopped his horse and carefully looked around, as if he had a hunch that some kind of danger was lurking. He suddenly turned his horse around and began to gallop away. The other one followed him without knowing why.

Temujin sprang to his feet and shouted, "Shoot them!"

Kasar took aim and shot the first arrow. Without pause, he cocked and released the second one. He didn't make a mistake. The two Merkids fell dead before they could do their duty. Bogorchu and Jelme went out immediately and picked up the Merkids' two horses. Two of their horses roaming alone could be a signal to others in their camp.

When the night was falling, Temujin could see the smoke from dinner being cooked coming out of the faraway tents. Temujin ordered his troops to get ready for the attack and shot two arrows, one fire arrow and a godori, toward the forest across the river where his main force was presumed to be stationed. Temujin got a response immediately; one fire arrow and a godori arrived in return. Everything was ready. Temujin mounted his horse, took out his scimitar and shouted, "Attack! Forward!"

Temujin and his 2,500 surprise attackers galloped toward the Merkids' garrison field camp like a tempest. Even the strongest troops might not be able to stand against such a surprise attack. The Merkid's 10,000 troops collapsed like tents with the posts removed. Temujin's warriors cut down whatever was in their way. Their dried felt or animal-skin tents were wrapped in huge flames, making smoke and lighting the area like daylight. At the same time, Toghrul Khan and Jamuka's troops were dashing to join the attack, crossing the river on several hundred rafts.

It was complete victory for Temujin and the coalition army. The Merkid's garrison had been completely destroyed and only several dozen survivors were able to escape. Without pausing, Temujin and the coalition troops dashed toward the Buura plain, where the Merkids' main force was stationed. Temujin's troops were the vanguard and wherever they went, the dead bodies of the Merkids were strewn all across the fields.

Toktoa, the chief of the Merkids, was sleeping in his tent when he received the urgent report that his garrison had been attacked and destroyed. It was too late for him. All he could do was run away with his second in command, Dayir Usun, and several dozen guards toward the northbound Selenga River. The Buura plain soon became like hell. Hundreds, thousands of yurts and tents were in flames, making the area look like it was daytime, and the thick smoke was covering the sky, shading the moon and the starlight. Killing, plundering and looting continued. With the guidance of the spy Temujin had planted, who was fluent in the Merkid dialect, Temujin found a way to the yurt where Borte was being kept. However, it was already empty. Temujin turned around and drove his horse toward the Selenga River. There were thousands of Merkid refugees moving along the riverside. It was midnight, but the bright moonlight was helping them move. Temujin, moving around on his horse, shouted in a loud voice, "Borte! Borte!"

Unfortunately, Temujin's shouting was mixed with the noise of screams and other people shouting, trying to find their family members. For a while, Temujin kept on shouting, coming and going along the riverside. Suddenly, Temujin thought he heard a faint woman's voice coming from a nearby place. Temujin turned his head and carefully looked around. He could see a woman who had just gotten off her two-wheeled carriage approaching him. Temujin dismounted his horse and walked up to her. Thanks to the bright moonlight, Temujin could see her face and she was Borte. They recognized each other. Temujin hugged her tightly.

"Borte, I never forgot you for even a single moment."

Borte was weeping. Tears sprang from her eyes and flowed down her cheeks continuously.

"I have always been sure that you were coming to save me," she said through her tears. They continued to hug for a while with the bright moonlight pouring on their heads and shoulders.

CHAPTER TWENTY-TWO

A Pledge of Friendship

Temujin contacted Toghrul Khan and Jamuka.

"I already have what I wanted. Unnecessary killings and further chase might be inappropriate at this point. We'd be better off stopping the fighting right now."

Temujin's opinion was accepted. The fighting ceased and they began to reorganize. Temujin gave an order to Kasar to regroup the troops and bring him the reports of the losses and gains. Borte met her elder brother, Alchi, again.

"Thank you, my dear brother."

Alchi hugged Borte and replied, "You must have suffered so much. I am really glad to see you again, Borte."

They patted each other and rejoiced. While all of Temujin's men were buoyed by the victory, only one man, with the shadow of sadness on his face, was searching the remaining empty tents, one by one. He was Belgutei. He was looking for his mother. He asked about his mother of every Merkid woman he encountered. At that time, Sochigel was sitting in a half-burnt tent with several other Merkid women and heard the news from another woman that her son was looking for her. She wept for a while with her face down. She stood up slowly. The other Merkid women, with worried eyes, looked at her face wet with tears.

"I survived because I am a Merkid woman. How can I see my son again? That could be the cause of problems for my son for many years to come."

After these words, she stepped out of the tent, disappeared into the forest, and was never seen again.

After learning what happened to his mother, Belgutei fell into a deep sorrow. The next morning, Temujin sent out most of his troops on an extensive search that, nonetheless, failed to find Sochigel. Temujin shared the sorrow with Belgutei.

Kasar brought Temujin the report. Belgutei, Bogorchu, Jelme and Alchi were all present at the report meeting.

"Our loss is 9 deaths, 27 wounded. We have about 700 enemy prisoners, about 2,000 horses, about 10,000 sheep and goats, 500 cows and yaks, and we are protecting numerous women and children, though I didn't count them."

No sooner had Temujin received the report, than he sprang out of his chair, hitting the armrest with his fist.

"A great victory! What about the 3 men and 300 followers who attacked my yurts and kidnapped Borte?"

At that time, on the Mongolian Plateau, it was the rule that, in the case of multiple tribes joining the same war, each tribe would get the war booty that they themselves had plundered and looted. They did not share and their property concept included the people, too.

Kasar continued his report, "Toktoa and Dayir Usun have run away. However, Qaatai Darmala has been captured and is in Jamuka's custody."

Temujin contacted Jamuka and asked him to hand over Qaatai Darmala. He also gave an order to search and pick up the 300 attackers. This job was given to Jelme. Jamuka put a cangue on Qaatai Darmala's neck and sent him to Temujin. Jelme questioned all the prisoners, including Toghrul Khan's and Jamuka's, and within a half day, he had picked up 112 of the attackers. The rest of the 300 were presumed to be dead or to have run away. When Jelme brought the 112 prisoners, Belgutei came to Temujin and asked, "Would you hand those 112 men over to me? I want to handle them in my own way."

Temujin regarded him seriously for a while, and then slowly nodded without taking his eyes off Belgutei. Belgutei took them to the field. Without any help, he cut the 112 men's heads into two pieces with the axes for slaughtering the cows and horses. His face and body were covered with blood. In the sky of the Buura plain, hundreds and thousands of crows, which had picked up their own taste for human flesh, swarmed. Temujin also gave an order to find Chilger, who took Borte. However, he could not be found and was believed to have run away.

Toghrul Khan, Jamuka and Temujin took over all the Merkid properties. They selectively picked up men for slaves, blacksmiths and skilled leather workers. For the women and children, they chose as many as they needed and left the rest of them there. However, anyone who was rebellious or considered a future enemy was slaughtered. The Merkids collapsed. This was the utmost disaster, which would leave them permanently damaged, or, at least, years away from rebuilding their power.

After regrouping their troops, they left for their home. They were with the Merkid captives and women, countless livestock and mountains of war booty. They slowly marched along the Selenga River toward the south. They took the easier route, not the route they took to get there. When they arrived at the diverging point of the Selenga River and its branch, the Orkhon River, each decided to take his own way back home. Toghrul Khan picked up the route to his home base, the Black Forest, passing through the Hokortu basin and the western, rear side of the Burkan Mountain. On the other hand, Temujin and Jamuka both took the way through the Ayil Karaqana to the eastern, front side of the Burkan Mountain.

They had a celebration there together, before their farewell. They erected huge tents and, early in the evening time, they got together. Toghrul Khan was with his brother Jagambu, his half brothers, Elke Kara and Buka Timur, and about 20 of his high-ranking warriors. Jamuka was also with about 20 of his high-ranking warriors, and among them were the Kyat Mongol chieftains like Altan, Sacha Beki and his brother, Taichu, and also Temujin's uncle Nekun's son, Quchar. Temujin was with Belgutei, Kasar, Bogorchu, Jelme and Borte's brother, Alchi.

They began to enjoy the wine and food, listening to soft music played by the captive Merkid musicians. In addition, the captive Merkid women were serving the wine and food, passing through the tables. Some time after the beginning of the feast, Toghrul Khan lifted his heavy body from his chair, which was at the northernmost side. Toghrul Khan gestured to stop the music and called everybody's attention. After he made sure that everybody's attention was on him, he opened his mouth and began to talk in a loud, husky voice.

"Today's victory is everybody's victory. I am giving you big applause for your valor. All the hardship has gone. This is the time for enjoyment. Let's have a drink for our victory!"

At Toghrul Khan's proposal for a toast, everybody stood up and had a drink. After they sat down in their chairs, Temujin got to his feet and said, "A man couldn't find a way to get his revenge, until he had the help of his revered foster father, Toghrul Khan, and also his friend, anda Jamuka. Victory is for these two honorable ones, and I am giving them my warmest appreciation. I sincerely propose a toast to these two victors!"

At Temujin's proposal, they all stood up again and had a second drink. This time, Jamuka stood up and remarked, "The most distinguished warrior in this battle is my anda, Temujin. Without his remarkable tactics and valor, the victory would not have been an easy one. I praise highly his superior tactics and valor and for this, I propose a toast."

At Jamuka's proposal, they had the third celebratory drink. The music continued and the wine and food were served without interruption. The night on the Mongolian Plateau grew deeper and the noise, laughter, and the Merkid women's sharp shrieks from being held by the waist by warriors grew louder.

Temujin and Jamuka left side by side on their horses, southeast-bound, after they bade a farewell to Toghrul Khan. They moved at a slow pace because they were with slow-moving sheep, cows and prisoners, who were walking. They made a long trail, possibly up to several miles.

Temujin and Jamuka both were pleased with the outcome of the war. Temujin had organized his troops for the first time, and even though it was a small scale, he successfully carried out his task as the wartime commander-in-chief. Jamuka had been a victor in war with other major tribes since he had become the official leader for the Jadarats clan. It was meaningful for them and was the turning point of their careers as warlords. The name Temujin began to be known to the people of the Mongolian Plateau and his strategy and valor was highly valued. Jamuka was given the name "the victor" by his clan people and amassed strong support from them as well.

Several days later, when they arrived at the foot of the Burkan Mountain, Temujin took the prisoner Qaatai Darmala to the top of the mountain. Belgutei, Kasar, Bogorchu and Jelme accompanied him. It was late afternoon, when the sun was hanging in the western sky. Temujin took off his belt and helmet, and kowtowed nine times toward the sun. He raised his two arms and began to shout, looking up at the blue sky:

> *The great everlasting blue sky,*
> *I thank thee for listening to my prayer.*
> *I have my revenge under your permission.*

The heaven's will is beyond human understanding.
Only the beloved by the heaven could be the final victor.
That is the only thing I know.

The enemy of the heaven is my enemy.
And my enemy will be thy enemy.
That is the only thing I hope.

After this prayer, Temujin picked up the razor-sharp scimitar from his belt and, in one breath, cut off the prisoner's head while he was kneeling with his two hands tied back. The body without the head thudded to the ground and dark-red blood spurted from the neck. Lured by the smell of blood carried by the wind, crows began to swarm and were circling in the sky. Jelme picked up Qaatai Darmala's head, in which the eyes were fixed and wide open, by grasping its long hair. Belgutei and Bogorchu, each holding one leg of the dead body, dragged it down to the foot of the mountain. The dead body and the head were thrown away in the field. The waiting hungry vultures and crows swarmed and began to compete to feed on the dead body.

They stayed there overnight and early the following morning set out again. Jamuka said to Temujin, "Temujin, how about staying with me for a while? Let's go to the Qorqonak Jubur. Let's take a break and have fun, like the old days."

They needed a rest, not only for themselves, but also for the soldiers and horses. Temujin knew that. Temujin answered with a smile on his lips, "Fine! I can stay there forever, as long as you are with me. Let's go back to the old days, enjoying horse racing and archery contests."

They both were filled with nostalgic sweetness of their childhood. They wanted to go back to that time, which was clean, pure and free from greed, conflict, agony, pain, scheme and conspiracy.

Temujin, with Jamuka, headed for Qorqonak Jubur, Jamuka's home base. Temujin sent Jelme to Burgi Ergi to bring his mother Ouluun and the other family members.

Borte's belly was swollen like a mountain. Borte was pregnant. Temujin noticed it when he saw her again. Her belly was covered by the wide and long Mongolian costume and because of that, she couldn't walk fast. Temujin really didn't know whose baby it was. Even Borte might not know. One night, when Temujin was with Borte in the same bed, Borte told Temujin in tears, "I am not sure. When I was raped by the Merkid, it was only three days after I slept with you. It was around that time that I became pregnant."

Temujin consoled her by smoothing her cheek and hair.

"Borte, I love you. I am the one who has taken responsibility for your kidnapping. Whoever is the father, this one will be my first child. This is my baby."

Temujin relaxed her with this. The following day, Borte began to have labor pains. Temujin and Jamuka's travels were temporarily halted. An interim yurt was built hurriedly for Borte, and ten Merkid women were picked to help her. The ten Merkid women busied themselves to get ready for the birth and one of them put a skein of thread in Borte's mouth. On Borte's forehead, numerous beads of sweat began to stand out. Two Merkid women were holding Borte's hands on each side.

At last, the baby was born. It was a boy. The Merkid women shouted in joy for the healthy and handsome baby. When Temujin was handed the baby, wrapped in the swaddling clothes, he was all smiles with joy and kissed the baby on his forehead. As is customary, Temujin put a bow and arrow on each side of the flap door of the interim yurt, and put guards to limit the visitors. Due to Borte's childbirth, the journey was delayed for seven days.

Temujin was congratulated by Jamuka first.

"Congratulation on your son! What will be the baby's name?"

"His name will be Juchi."

"Any special meaning in there?"

"Not at all. I like that name, that's it. However, if you are asking, it could have the meaning of noble man."

But the name Juchi had another meaning besides "noble man," and that was "a guest." Temujin declared a three-day feast. Jamuka stayed and joined the feast. Some of the Merkid women who helped Borte's childbirth told others that the baby looked like Temujin. On the other hand, some others whispered that the baby resembled the Merkid, Chilger. Temujin heard of the rumor, and so, on the last day of the feast, he gathered his people all together and declared Juchi was his firstborn son.

"Juchi is my firstborn son. There's no doubt about it. This is my official declaration. From this moment on, if anybody talks about this, he or she will be beheaded."

They set out again and soon arrived at the Qorqonak Jubur. By that time, Temujin's mother, Ouluun, had also arrived there with the other family members, so they rejoiced at their re-union. Temujin picked up many high-quality valuables for his mother as gifts from the mountains of war booty and selected and gave her twenty Merkid women for her servants. Temujin also gave his mother a five-year-old boy who lost his parents during the war. The boy's name was Kuchu and at the time he was found by Temujin's soldiers, he was clad in water sable, leather coat, an ermine fur cap and was wearing boots made of doe's inside, hind-leg skin. All these items were extremely expensive, so he was presumed to be a descendant of the Merkid aristocrats. Ouluun happily accepted the boy, who had sparkling eyes. From then on, she kept him close and took good care of him.

Temujin and Jamuka had combined their ordus. It was very unusual and exceptional on the steppe, where two individual, independent groups never got together, and, instead, chose be apart.

Several weeks after they had been together, Jamuka said to Temujin, "There is an old saying that two andas have only one life, even though they have two bodies. I like that say-ing. I think that not only can we help each other, but also share dreams and destiny all the years to come. What do you think?"

Temujin shook Jamuka's hand firmly and replied, "Fine, Jamuka. You can say that again. I am still keeping the godori you gave me."

They laughed and patted each other on the backs. They agreed to have a second anda ceremony. They headed for the Qurdakal area, which was not far from their ordus. Their first anda ceremony was done in the temporary hut under the Burkan Mountain, all by themselves, but this time, hundreds of their warriors followed them.

In the late afternoon, they arrived at a place where one side of the earth had erupted, forming a cliff-like rampart covering a certain area. The earth rampart was shiny with a shade of gold, reflecting the late afternoon sunlight, and. as time went by, it became bloody red. There, a several-hundred-year-old pine tree was standing alone and the earth rampart was encircling it as if protecting it.

That was the Qurdakal. In the old days, the third Mongol khan, Kutula, had his inauguration there.

They made camp there. Temujin and Jamuka exchanged their gifts. Temujin's gifts for Jamuka were Toktoa Beki's golden belt and yellowish-white horse with a black mane and tail. Temujin had picked out those items from his war booty. In return, Jamuka gave Temujin Dayir Usun's golden belt and a white horse that had a protuberance, like a horn, in the center of its head. They exchanged wine goblets.

"Our friendship comes first before any other things."

Temujin and Jamuka exchanged these words while they were exchanging the wine goblets. They had a feast. They set up a huge campfire and barbecued sheep. They drank and danced to drumbeats. The sun had already set and the earth rampart was now the shade of ruby from the light of the campfire. That was their second anda ceremony and they slept together under the same blanket.

CHAPTER TWENTY-THREE

The Dream of Unification

There were the Huns. The Chinese called them Hung-nu and the people west of the Caucasus called them the Huns. Their original hometown was Kerulen and the Orkhon River basin, on the northern side of the Gobi Desert. Like other nomads, rather than settle down, they migrated from one place to another with each season, in search of water and fresh grass. Occasionally, they would gather, making a huge group, and then attack the sedentary people.

From the third century B.C., they began to be known as a fearful and threatening power to the neighboring sedentary people. Consequently, this fear forced the Chinese to build the Great Wall. At a certain time, some part of them moved to the west, and settled down in the large steppe area between the Aral Sea and Lake Balkhash. History recognizes them as the West Huns. For several centuries, they were quiet. But at the beginning of the fifth century A.D., they moved again, further west. They crossed the Volga and Don Rivers. They destroyed every tribe they encountered on their way and, finally, took over the

Hungarian steppe across the Carpathian Mountains, expelling the Alans and the Goths.

As the Goth refugees surged into the Roman territory, the rulers of Europe, the Romans, sent troops to stop the power from the east, though it was not successful. At last, the Romans had to give up the territory above the Danube River to the Huns. They also had to promise to give 350 pounds of gold as tribute to the Huns each year, to keep the peace.

At that time, the Romans were divided in two, the East Roman Empire and the West Roman Empire, and their capital cities were Constantinople and Rome, respectively. When the Romans made the peace treaty with the Huns, they had to leave Aetius, the son of one of the powerful men in the empire, as a hostage. Then, the chieftain of the Huns, Rugas, arranged for his beloved nephew, Attila, to stay with Aetius. The two boys, of similar age, spent time together for some years. They galloped together side by side on the Hungarian steppe and became close friends. During that time, Aetius learned the Huns' language, culture, customs and military tactics. Some years later, when Aetius returned to Rome, Attila had to go with him as their hostage. Attila stayed in Rome for several years, learning and experiencing Rome. He had much contempt for the Romans. The Roman aristocrats abandoned themselves to luxuriousness and pleasure and the officials were corrupt. Everything was done by the slaves and even the army was mostly mercenaries.

In the year when Attila turned twenty, he returned home to the Hungarian steppe after saying goodbye to Aetius. By

that time, he had made up his mind to become a world conqueror. First, to secure his position in the Huns, he had to kill
his brother, Bleda. The year he turned thirty-two, he attacked
Rome twice. He justified it to himself as helping his boyhood
friend, Aetius, who was involved in a political war. Attila's
attack paid off. Aetius won the political war and became the
commander-in-chief of the West Roman Empire. This was
the beginning of Attila's involvement in the Roman Empire.
He conquered the nearby places one by one. He never lost
a battle and he leveled cities and towns. The Romans called
him the Scourge of God and his name was a symbol for terror. He also attacked the East Roman Empire and marched on
Constantinople. The emperor of the East Roman Empire had
to give up much of his territory to save his empire and had to
sign a treaty stating he would pay a tribute of 700 pounds of
gold each year.

Next, Attila set out to conquer his father's sworn enemy, the
Visigoths. He advanced toward the west, crossing the Rhine
River with a coalition army of Germans, who were barbarians then. He conquered Orleans; however, he was counterattacked by the King of the Visigoths and his Roman coalition
army. That was the only failure he faced out of numerous
victories. The commander-in-chief of the Roman army was his
boyhood friend, Aetius. His close boyhood friend was now
an enemy.

The next year, Attila reorganized his army and marched
toward Rome. Every city and town on his way was burned,
destroyed and leveled. Soon, he conquered half of the Italian

peninsula and arrived at the outskirts of Rome. Aetius, the Roman commander-in-chief, strongly suggested the transfer of the capital city to the West Roman emperor, Valentinian III.

Valentinian III left Rome. He asked the Pope, Saint Leo, to become a mediator. The Pope offered one payment of 6,000 pounds of gold, plus 1,000 pounds of gold each year thereafter. Furthermore, he also offered Honoria, the sister of Valentinian III, as a concubine for Attila. Attila accepted the offer. Actually, Attila had to accept the offer, because some kind of epidemic was prevalent among his soldiers, which was previously unknown to the steppe people. He put off his plan until the following year and went back to the Hungarian steppe.

However, in the spring of the following year, he fell in love with a beautiful woman he had met on the steppe and was getting married to her. Her name was Erika. Shockingly, the morning after the luxurious wedding ceremony and banquet, he was found dead. The cause of death was asphyxiation.

He drank too much, which made his nose bleed and the blood clot blocked his trachea. It was spring 453 and he was 53 years old.

After his death, the West Huns faded away from the stage of history. As time went by, they harmonized and amalgamated with neighboring tribes and lost their specific character. At last, they disappeared. Attila was a Mongol.

One year had passed. Friendship was beautiful. Temujin and Jamuka sang together of the ecstasy of life, decorating one chapter of their lives that could never be brought back.

They hunted together, enjoyed the polo games and had many feasts. Like in the early days, they had horse races and archery contests, too. Sometimes, they ran their horses side by side, toward the infinite horizon. Once they got on their horses, they felt like they could run to the end of the world. That was characteristic of a nomad. They were full of pride, passion and dreams.

One day, they were running slowly on the endless plain. The sun in the cobalt-blue sky was pouring bright sunlight onto the brown earth, where short, thick green shrubs were sparsely spread around. The air was as fresh as the water flowing through the mountain rocks, and yet still warm. The space between the heaven and the earth was filled with dead silence, and only the beating sound of horse hooves was ringing in their ears pleasantly. Occasionally, the flapping sound from the wings of small birds, rising high in the sky, surprised by their approach, were heard, and the scene of small lizards scuttling away from the hoofbeats of their horses were seen. The dim images of the small and big hills, hanging on the horizon, never seemed to change size and even though they were running for quite a while, they felt like they were making no progress at all.

As if to relieve the boredom of no progress, Temujin grinned at Jamuka once and suddenly whipped his horse's haunches strongly with a loud shout of "Yeeyat!" The surprised animal, neighing, stood on his hind legs and then started to gallop at full speed. Jamuka did the same and followed him. Their horses were swift ones. Temujin's white stud, with a horn in the center of his head, was flying as if he truly had wings.

Now they could see their movement. They kept on whipping their horses.

When the sun began to decline into the western sky, they arrived at a familiar place. It was the place where the big, muddy earth elevation, or the great red stiff wall, was standing magnificently. It was like the end of the world. The Great Wall was ruby-red, reflecting the afternoon sunlight, and was covering, with a slight curvature, a big, old pine tree shaped like a Y, which was standing like the earth god. It was the Qurdakal, where they had their second anda ceremony about a year ago. Temujin and Jamuka both pulled the reins and stopped their horses. Their horses were panting with foam in their mouths and were wet with sweat. Temujin and Jamuka were both fascinated by the awe-inspiring scenery, which was beautiful and yet quite unearthly or even holy. They stayed there for a while without any movements. They slowly approached the old pine tree. They both knew the history of the tree. In the past, Qutula Khan paid respect to the tree and prayed for victory before the final, decisive battle with the Merkids. He won. He had his enthronement ceremony there, as the third Mongol khan.

They dismounted their horses, walked up and stood in front of the pine tree. The huge pine tree covered with thick bark, split, distorted and twisted, like the skin of a hundred-year-old man, seemed to be looking down at the two young men like the earth god. Jamuka, after taking off his hood and holding it in his one hand, knelt down on one of his knees and paid respect to the tree. He stayed there without any movements for a while. Temujin watched him in silence.

Temujin pondered and tried to figure out why Jamuka was doing this. The answer came to Temujin through his sixth sense. It surely seemed to be true that Jamuka wanted to be the ruler of the Mongolian Plateau following Qutula Khan. That was exactly the same thing that Temujin was planning on! For a brief moment, Temujin's mind was complicated with mixed feelings. After a while, Jamuka got on his feet, put his hood back on and said to Temujin with a smiling face, "Aren't you going to pay respect to this tree?"

Temujin shrugged his shoulders and gently shook his head. Temujin said to Jamuka, sending him a smile, "I kneel down and bow only to heaven, nothing else."

They headed for the nearby forest, not far from the old pine tree. They found a nice place for an overnight stay, which had a brook flowing over the gravel, making a pleasant sound. They cut the branches of the nearby trees to set up the base for the temporary hut. Then they completed the hut by covering it with hides they had brought with them. They made a campfire with gathered tree branches and dried leaves. The air was fresh and it was quiet. They could smell the fragrance of the pine trees coming with the gentle breeze and could hear the wind passing through the spiny leaves of the pine trees like the waves. They chewed jerked beef and drank kumis. They giggled while they were talking about women and at another time, sang together at the top of their voices. A few does approached the brook to drink water and then ran away, startled by the loud noises they were making.

The moon rose. The silvery moonlight was pouring over the ground like a waterfall. They talked about many things.

Jamuka asked Temujin, as he was adding a few small branches to the campfire, "There is a rumor going around that you accepted the Merkid prisoners. Is it true?"

Jamuka asked this in serious manner. It was true that Temujin accepted more than half of his 700 Merkid prisoners and allowed them into his troops. On the other hand, Jamuka didn't allow anyone to join his regular troops out of his 1,000 Merkid prisoners, using them only as slaves, like blacksmiths, leather laborers and sheep and goat herders.

For a moment, without saying anything, Temujin poked the campfire with a small stick to make it brighter and bigger. He then answered clearly, "Well, anyway, they are all Mongols, like us. At this moment, temporarily, they are our enemies. However, one day, we will all stand in front of the same banner, that's what I think."

Seeing Jamuka's look of astonishment, Temujin gave him a smile and continued, "I interviewed them one by one before I accepted them. I only accepted the ones who are truly willing to follow me."

Temujin's policy was hard to understand and unacceptable at that time. It could even be dangerous. Jamuka asked Temujin again, with a look saying that he really didn't understand, "How can you trust them? Did you ever think about the disastrous result of putting weapons in their hands?"

Temujin answered clearly again, "I am going to give them what they want. When they have what they want, they won't have a second thought."

Temujin distributed all of the war booty evenly among his soldiers, and that included the converted prisoners. In return, Temujin asked only one thing from them, loyalty.

Jamuka asked again, looking straight into Temujin's eyes, "What they want? The women? The property? The livestock? The grazing land? Or, what else?"

Temujin also looked straight in Jamuka's eyes and answered, "All of it, and more."

At this moment, Jamuka gave a look of curiosity.

"What is more?"

Temujin regarded him in a serious manner for a moment and answered, "Freedom."

Jamuka raised his head and stared into space for a while, as if he were shocked. The dark silhouette of the mud cliff was revealing its curvature in the midst of the bright moonlight. This time, Jamuka gave a look of pity and said to Temujin, "Temujin, freedom is the privilege of the winners. Real freedom doesn't exist at all. It is like a mirage in the desert or a rainbow hanging on the horizon. What is your meaning of freedom?"

One time, Temujin gathered all his warriors, including the converted prisoners, and said to them, "Have only one mind! Have only one faith. This is the only way you can conquer your enemies and survive. I will treat you equally. Everybody is the same under my rule. Everybody includes me, too. You will get exactly what you have earned, and you will be judged by your loyalty. I will keep my word and I won't be the one who breaks his word."

Temujin's promise had been carried out without disruption. Temujin had begun to be known as a fair and just man among his warriors. He made right and fair judgments for his men's merits and demerits. His praises, rewards and punishments were very accurate. Criminals had to face the draconian law and punishments. Death penalties were given to the murderers, the adulterers and adulteresses, the sodomites, the spies, the over-the-limit thieves, the dealers in stolen goods, the perjurers, and the warriors who refused to follow official orders.

He was not only a gifted soldier, but also a gifted administrator. His food and clothes were exactly the same as those of the lowest-ranking warriors. And more, for anyone who wanted to try his horses, permission had never been denied. However, Jamuka was different; he enjoyed his aristocratic lifestyle. He used silver plates and golden cups. His clothes were expensive and luxurious. He had two horse keepers for his horses and nobody was allowed near them. One time, a man was beheaded after he had startled his horse.

Jamuka continued his comments, without changing his look of pity and disagreement, "Temujin, we have traditions. In many cases, the tradition is stronger than the law. Once the tradition is violated, the potential problems are not controllable by the law. Each tribe has its own traditions and each person has a different lifestyle based on their social status. We have to honor their traditions."

At that time, there were hundreds of different tribes on the Mongolian Plateau, even though, basically, they were the same people. The Mongols had strong affiliations to blood and lineage. Jamuka's comment represented what the chieftains of each tribe would think.

Temujin said to Jamuka strongly, looking straight at him, "If everything goes as you have said, the unification of the Mongols will never be achieved."

Temujin began to talk about the unification of the Mongols. That was another surprise for Jamuka. It surely seemed to be clear that Temujin was thinking of unifying the Mongolian Plateau, and that was exactly what Jamuka was planning to do in the future. The two men had the same goal. It seemed that a new era had arrived on the Mongolian Plateau, the unification era. Jamuka asked Temujin carefully, "Unification? What do you think about unification? How can the Mongols achieve unification after having split into hundreds of different clans and tribes?"

Jamuka was serious and Temujin knew that.

Temujin gave his honest answer. "By force; that is the only way."

"By force? You mean through war?"

"Right."

"Many people will die, right?"

"That is right. We don't have a choice."

"We can make a union or a committee of representatives of each tribe and then elect the ka-khan, or the khan of khans. Am I right?"

Temujin gave the answer without pause, still looking straight at Jamuka, "Theoretically, it sounds beautiful. However, practically, it won't work that way. Human beings are too selfish and greedy to become like that. Even if we create such a nation, we will never be able to keep it going."

Jamuka picked up the sheepskin bag beside him and had a little drink of kumis. Then he handed it over to Temujin. Temujin put the bag on his shoulder and took a sip. Temujin usually didn't drink. Jamuka asked carefully again, "Where do you think you can get such a force to make it happen?"

Temujin answered without hesitation, "Starting from the bottom to the top."

"Starting from the bottom to the top?"

"Yes. First, you conquer the people at the bottom and then going on up to the top."

"How do you conquer the people at the bottom?"

"By giving them freedom, like I said."

Jamuka sighed, making a short "um" noise, and then fell into deep thought. What Jamuka heard was quite revolutionary. It could turn the present society of the Mongolian Plateau upside down.

The nomads on the Mongolian Plateau had divided into hundreds of different clans and tribes for thousands of years and each tribe had its own strong tradition and social structure. The chieftain and his family members were on the top and below them were the nokhod, who were the free men who, nevertheless, still had to obey the orders coming from the top. The lowest class was the otogus bool, who didn't have freedom, and they were slaves. The Mongols wanted unification; however, the long inherited traditions, the social structures and the enmity among the tribes were their biggest obstacles. Most of all, the ruling class, the petty chieftains and their families who were enjoying their privileges, didn't want unification at all. The beautiful women, the sweet meat and the most freedoms were guaranteed for them.

Jamuka asked Temujin again, "Suppose you unified the Mongolian Plateau. Then there will be no more noble men and slaves, right?"

"Exactly, they will be evaluated by what they can do, not by which class or tribe they belong to. A new order and a new tradition will begin."

Jamuka kept silent for a while. He added more small dried branches to the campfire. At last, he turned his head toward Temujin and said, "Temujin, I cannot agree with you. With your idea and plan, I don't think the Mongols can unify themselves. Even if they do, there will be more unrest and conflict than there is now. How can the noble men accept that their former servants or slaves have a higher position than them and how can they break the stone walls that have been built among the tribes for such a long time? They have different lifestyles and different religions. How can they become one?"

Temujin answered without hesitation, again, "By force."

At this answer, Jamuka exclaimed with a raised and somewhat angry voice, "Those are not things that can be handled by force!"

Unlike Jamuka, Temujin said in a quiet voice, "The ones who accept the new order will be accepted. If not, they will be removed. That is the only way to put an end to the unrest on this land and open a new era."

Jamuka kept silent again. He was watching the orange-colored flames dancing out from the campfire, which sometimes made dull breaking noises. Temujin looked at Jamuka's profile, the line formed by his straight nose, closed lips and his chin, flickering in the light of the campfire. The image that Temujin saw was exactly the same one he remembered from his early childhood.

Temujin put a smile on his lips and patted Jamuka on his back.

"Jamuka, don't think too much. Too much thinking could lead you into a maze. Once you get in there, sometimes it is very hard to come out. I simply told you what I am thinking."

As he was saying this, Temujin wondered to himself if Jamuka really didn't understand the fundamental truth of the force or power. Even the greatest theory and idea cannot be put into reality without the vehicle of force. Temujin knew Jamuka was an extremely smart man. He didn't think Jamuka didn't know the principle of force, but he thought Jamuka's understanding or interpretation of force was different from his.

Temujin asked Jamuka, "To get to your final destination, there could be many different routes. Suppose you succeeded in the unification of the Mongolian Plateau, what would you do first?"

Jamuka squinted for a brief moment, as if he were trying to see something far away.

"That job belongs to the future. I haven't thought about that yet. What would you do first?"

Jamuka's answer was disappointing to Temujin. Temujin thought that if someone were planning on the unification of the Plateau, he should have a plan for after the unification as well. Nonetheless, Temujin told him all his plans and ideas without concealing anything.

"I think the first thing we have to do after the unification is to conquer China. If not, they will dispatch large numbers of troops to break the Mongols into pieces again. They don't want the Mongols unified."

Surprise filled Jamuka's eyes, and yet Jamuka's response sounded like he was not in agreement with Temujin.

"Temujin, even though China is divided into three now, just the northernmost Chin have 600,000 troops. That is a really big number. It wouldn't be an easy job to defeat them. There would be the possibility that the Chin and the neighboring country, Shisha, would form an alliance and attack the Mongols from two different directions. If that happened, it would be even more difficult to defeat them. Nothing would be left for the Mongols. It should be handled diplomatically."

Temujin continued his remarks.

"It should be done by force! In that case, we conquer the Shisha first, and then the Chin next. The only difference is the sequence, which one is first?"

Jamuka still disagreed with Temujin.

"Even the Shisha have 150,000 troops. That number is still big!"

Staring at Jamuka, Temujin gave his reply immediately.

"None of the nations around us want the unification of the Mongols. Unless we conquer them all, the Mongols won't be able to continue our unification and independence. The Mongols have to conquer the Chin for unification and the Shisha for continuing independence. We need to take over the Silk Road from the Shisha. The newly born Mongol nation will need money. Without financial support, the independence won't last long!"

Jamuka kept silent. A while later, he said, without looking at Temujin, "If so, there will be never-ending wars. For the Silk Road, you not only have to deal with the Tanguts of the Shisha, but also the Uighurs and the Khitans too. What are you going to do with them?"

Temujin's answer was short.

"Same thing! We have to deal with them by force."

This time, Jamuka turned his head, looking straight at Temujin, and then said in a raised voice, as if he couldn't tolerate any more, "You keep on talking about force, but where do you think you can get such a force?"

Temujin's voice was still calm and low.

"I told you, from the bottom to the top. Equality and fairness are the key weapons to conquer them. Even the Uighurs and the Khitans will follow, once they know they are being treated the same as the Mongols."

Jamuka raised his voice again, "You are going too far! There are many people on this earth. They have different languages, different religions and even different appearances. How can they live together under the same government?"

With the same low tone, Temujin said in a persuasive way, "Jamuka, I am telling you again, this is only my thinking. You can have a different opinion. I am not pushing my view on you. You may be right, too. Like you said, the Mongols can achieve their unification after all the tribal chieftains get together and elect their ka-khan, or solve all the problems diplomatically. It depends on the situation and the will of heaven. If I can add one more thing, the real meaning of the Mongol unification is to retrieve the Hungarian steppe, where one stream of our ancestors settled down 700 years ago."

After these words, Temujin got on his feet. Jamuka did too. They took a walk together on the sandy ground with sparsely grown grass. Jamuka put one of his arms around Temujin's shoulder affectionately and then said, "Temujin, you are excellent! Your imagination is going far beyond my limitation. But, I wouldn't change my mind. I still believe that my idea has more possibilities. Let's have a competition in good faith. Whatever route we take, we must achieve unification. The Mongols have been waiting too long."

The two steppe heroes walked together lazily around the temporary hut, putting each of their arms around each other's shoulders. The silvery moonlight was pouring over their heads and shoulders and the chirping of crickets echoed into the space filled with desert air.

They slept together under the same blanket that night. No sooner had Temujin lay on the bedding than he fell asleep. On the other hand, Jamuka couldn't sleep at all. Actually, he had brought Temujin there to take the chance to persuade him to join him in his master plan of Mongol unification. Now Jamuka realized that he had failed. He didn't know Temujin already had his own plan, actually a far more advanced one. The two outstanding men already knew that they were no longer friends, but had just turned into rivals. Like there are not two suns in the sky, there could not be two leaders of the same nation.

Jamuka sat up. He looked at Temujin, who was sleeping soundly beside him. Jamuka put his right hand on his Chinese dagger, which he had put on the floor next to him. He pondered a while, and then took his hand from the dagger with a deep sigh.

Jamuka was much more powerful than Temujin at that moment. He was the chieftain of a huge group; the Jadarats and most of the Kyat Mongols were with him. If he had to get rid of Temujin, that was the right moment.

Temujin knew Jamuka very well. He was a born leader, brilliant and with extraordinary valor. Above all, he was a gifted diplomat. However, he was cold-blooded and, at the same time, emotional.

Those were the characteristics of loners. He was a lonely man. He didn't have any siblings, in contrast to Temujin, who had many brothers and sisters. In his early years, he had had to move around with his mother, from town to town, for survival. He didn't even have a soul mate, like Temujin who had Borte, though he had many women. His loneliness was the main motivation for the anda relationship with Temujin and the combination of their two groups, which was very unusual on the steppe. Temujin knew that Jamuka couldn't remove him easily.

The next morning, after they pulled down the temporary hut and picked up their belongings, they headed for their ordu in Qorqonak Jubur. As usual, they exchanged jokes about women, giggled and raced their horses. The endless plain was laid out in front of them.

CHAPTER TWENTY-FOUR

Farewell to Jamuka

The new spring had arrived on the Mongolian Plateau. The buds hiding under the frozen ground during the winter frost began to sprout, energized by the strong spring sunlight. The Qorqonak Jubur basin, Temujin and Jamuka's joint campsite, was no exception. Tens of thousands of livestock were grazing peacefully on the nearby plain. The open space near the tent city was crowded with people, some taking out bundles of sheepskin or other animal hides for sun drying, some were repairing horse equipment, some warriors were sharpening their spears and scimitars and many children were hopping around. Occasional loud cheers came from the boys' archery contest site nearby, and the husky shouts of the sheep and cow herders were mixed together and echoed into the purple sky. This was a typical peaceful scene of the nomadic life in springtime.

Temujin and Jamuka had been together for about a year and a half now. They both enjoyed the spring of togetherness, which might never come back. On the red circle day, April 16 of the lunar month, they began their move to the summer pasture. They were moving to the north, making a never-ending trail. The line made by tens of thousands of people and their countless livestock went on for several miles. Temujin and Jamuka marched together in front of the line for half a day. Late in the afternoon, they had to look for a campsite.

Soon they came to the hilly district. Numerous big and small hills were lined up on both sides of a valley and a medium-sized stream was running in between them. The water was fresh and clean and the basin was large enough to accommodate a large number of people. It was the right place for an overnight stay. Jamuka asked Temujin, while pointing to the hilly district with his horse whip, "What do you think? I think this is the place we have been looking for."

As Temujin nodded, Jamuka continued, "Let the horse breeders camp on the hillsides and the sheep and cow herders in the basin area."

After these words, Jamuka turned back his horse and galloped away from Temujin toward his groups in the rear of the line. Temujin tried to figure out what he really meant.

Let the horse breeders camp on the hillsides and the sheep and cow herders in the basin area. The answer came to Temujin without delay. At that time in Mongol society, the herders were divided into two groups. One group was for horses and the other was for cattle, sheep and other livestock. The horses were the most important and valuable livestock for the nomads. The Mongols considered the horse their weapon and their second life, rather than just an animal. The horse herders were the steppe aristocrats, or at least the nokhods, the freemen. On the other hand, the cattle or sheep herders were the lowest class or the otogus bools, the slaves. Temujin's 3,000 men and their families were mostly otogus bools.

In military tactics, positioning the troops high on the hillside is the best strategy. Positioning the troops in a narrow valley is an open invitation for disaster. Temujin turned his horse around and slowly approached a two-wheeled wagon. In the wagon, Temujin's mother, Ouluun, and his wife, Borte, were sharing a seat. Opening the flap door, Temujin asked his mother, as his mother was still the head of the family, "Mother, Jamuka said the horse herders should put up the tents on the hillside and the cattle and sheep herders in the valley. What do you think?"

As Ouluun hesitated, Borte answered instead, "My lord, if he said so, we better not stay here. I want you to be careful. I think he is becoming wary of you."

Borte had been displeased that Temujin was always with Jamuka and she was also disagreeable about the joint community of the two different groups. Borte could never get along with Ssima, Jamuka's wife. Ssima was an arrogant, sly, lavish woman. Ssima treated Borte as one of her subordinates, not as a friend. That was probably because Ssima regarded Temujin as nothing more than one of her husband's subordinate chieftains.

Temujin thought to himself for a while. Then he turned around and galloped toward the front of the line, which had paused to wait for further instruction. He ordered the line to continue to march. That meant they would separate from Jamuka. Temujin, his families and warriors continued to march all through the night in the northward direction. The bright moonlight was helping them. They went over the big and small hills and crossed the plain, making long moon shadows. They chewed beef jerky and drank kumis in sheepskin bags kept on their horse's backs.

At daybreak, Temujin stopped for a moment and looked back. Temujin could see not only his 3,000 warriors and their family members, but also countless other groups of people following the line. The news that Temujin was separating from Jamuka had spread through the groups of people and many of them decided to leave Jamuka and follow Temujin. People had begun to have confidence in Temujin, not only as a warrior, but also as a distinguished administrator. Temujin had gained the confidence of the nomads by showing them his ability to manage the war, his valor, generosity, fairness in distributing the war booty and his way of valuing each individual for his or her ability, rather than his or her origin.

Temujin welcomed them. He shook hands and patted the shoulders of each one of them. They rejoiced together. Among them were Bogorchu's brother, Ogolen, who was with the Arulad clan at that time; Jelme's two brothers, Chaulqan and Subedei; Qubilai and Qudus, brothers of the Barulas tribes; Qachiun Tokuraun and his two brothers of the Jalair tribes; Qadaan Daldurkan and his four brothers of the Tarkud tribes; three brothers of Ongul, Chansiud and Bayauud of the Munggetu Kiyan clan; and two brothers of Jetei and Dokolku of the Mangkud tribes. There were also many people from the Besut tribes, the Suldus tribes, the Qongqotan tribes, the Dorben tribes, the Ikires tribes, the Noyakin tribes, the Oronar tribes and the Baarin tribes who joined Temujin. Among them were Temujin's uncle Daritai and even some of the Jadarats.

What they said about Temujin was this, "He eats the same foods that the sheep herders eat and he wears almost the same clothing as they do. Anyone can try his horse, if they want. This is the man we have been waiting for; he is the one who can unite the plateau and build a nation."

However, not all of them followed Temujin because of his philosophy or ideology. Some of them were unhappy with Jamuka, the way he treated them, or were simply motivated by greed. Temujin also accepted them. Temujin understood the deepest nature of the human mind. He acknowledged that the most basic motivations of human behavior were profit and fear. Temujin made contracts with them instead of refusing them. One of the examples was Qorchi. Qorchi was a kinsman of Jamuka and had been a very loyal follower. He came to Temujin and opened his mind.

"I devoted myself to Jamuka. Nevertheless, nothing has changed for me. If I support you to build a nation, what can I expect?"

Temujin put a smile on his lips, and, while holding Qorchi's hands, said, "You will be a commander of ten thousand men and the owner of thirty concubines."

Qorchi was satisfied. He began to shout in front of other people, "Folks! You know who I am. I am the Baarin, just like Jamuka. Jamuka and I are descendants of the same womb. I am the one who really shouldn't have left Jamuka. I devoted myself to him completely. Nobody can deny that. What did I get in return? Nothing! All I have now is a few shabby horses. I had a dream last night. I saw a huge golden ox and a cow and they were destroying Jamuka's yurt from two different directions. My sixth sense tells me that Temujin is the one who will bring us the unification of the plateau and a new nation."

Qorchi was talking about the dream he had had the previous night. Temujin heard him, from far off, with his arms folded and a gentle smile on his lips.

Temujin proceeded farther north, and temporarily settled down at Ayil Karaqana. They came to the Kimurka stream, a branch of the Selenga River, and around it was a large space, big enough to accommodate thousands of yurts, and so, it was the right place for the time being.

Several days after Temujin arrived at the Ayil Karaqana, thousands of people with their countless livestock, consisting of cattle, sheep and camels, were approaching Temujin's ordu. Temujin sent Kasar out to find out who they were. They were the Jurkins. Sacha Beki, the chieftain of the Jurkins, and his brother, Taichu, left Jamuka to join Temujin. Temujin welcomed them. Temujin showed his hospitality by a cheek-to-cheek greeting, touching his cheeks to theirs, one side to another, three times. It was a nomadic way of greeting between two parties who share complete confidence between them.

Temujin said to Sacha Beki, "It is a great pleasure to see you again. Let's work together to revive the glory of the Bodunchars."

Bodunchar was their common, distant ancestor. They were the Kyat Mongols, who were the descendants of Kabul Khan, the first Mongol khan. Sacha Beki and Temujin were both the fourth generation from Kabul Khan, but Sacha Beki was born earlier than Temujin.

Kabul Khan gave the best of his warriors to his firstborn grandson, Jurki. Since then, they were called the Jurkins, after the name of their chieftain, Jurki. They were the core and elite group of the Kyat Mongols. Until they left, they had been with Jamuka, who grabbed a part of the central Mongolian Plateau.

Sacha Beki told Temujin, "Altan and Quchar will soon join us, too."

As he had said, a few days later, Altan and Quchar joined Temujin with their thousands of people. Altan was the third-generation descendant of Kabul Khan and was the official heir of the khanship. Quchar was the son of Nekun, Temujin's uncle, so he was Temujin's cousin.

They stayed there through summer and autumn and moved toward the south again in early winter. They settled down at the Kara Jirugen, with the Koko Nuur Lake near the Kurelku Mountains, where Temujin stayed for some time to protect himself and his family from the Taichuts' attacks.

CHAPTER TWENTY-FIVE

Birth of Temujin Khan

They remained there for several years. In the meantime, their numbers had increased to fifty thousand yurts. With that number, it was possible to elect a new khan. Altan, as the man on top of the lineage of the Kyat Mongols, called a council. They gathered in a big, temporarily built, rectangular-shaped tent. There were about forty members and each one of them was representing a tribe or clan. The Kyat Mongols were the majority, and so one of them was expected to be the new khan. Among them were Altan, Sacha Beki and Quchar, who were considered the key members and the decision makers. Altan was a middle-aged man, with no particular ambition for the khanship. Sacha Beki was different; he was full of passion. Sacha Beki was not only the firstborn grandson of Kabul Khan, but was also the chieftain of the Jurkins, the elite clan of the Kyat Mongols. He was one of the eighty-one strongmen on the plateau, even though he was for a while under the control of Jamuka, who was the strongest emerging power at that time.

Altan, knowing that every attendant had been served a cup of green tea with a touch of fresh sheep's milk, stood up from his seat and said, "Today, we are here together to discuss future plans and to make decisions for the issues we are facing right now. We are now a big group of fifty thousand yurts. So far, we have made it without any big troubles. However, it could be dangerous, for a big group like this, to continue on without a leader. I know now is the time that we need a khan. If you have any opinions, please let us know."

After these words, Quchar, Temujin's cousin, got on his feet and said, "I think Temujin is the right person for our khan. He has already showed us his ability as an excellent administrator and outstanding warlord. And more, he is a real Kyat Mongol with direct lineage from Bodunchar and Kabul Khan. He will bring us the glory of the descendants of Bodunchar and also bring us unity on the Mongolian Plateau, which was the long-cherished desire of Kabul Khan. I recommend him."

After Quchar, Qorchi got permission to speak and said, "I also would like to recommend Temujin as our khan. However, I want to remind you of this. As you know, I am the Baarin. Our khan should be able to represent all the tribes and clans, not just one specific group of people. Our khan should cover everybody. So, I officially recommend Temujin, who values people not by which clan they belong to, but by what they can do."

As Qorchi sat down, they gave him a big round of applause.

After that, Taichu, the younger brother of Sacha Beki, got permission and spoke. "I hear very well the opinion of the

two respected and honored representatives. But, I think the leader of a big group of fifty thousand yurts should be a well-experienced one. A leader without enough experience could bring us disaster and chaos. We would be better off to choose the safer way."

Taichu's remarks spoke against the recommendation of Temujin as the khan, but he sat down without recommending anyone else. For a while, there was a deep silence with feelings of embarrassment and strain.

This time, Sacha Beki stood up and began to speak, after he got permission, as if he were trying to ease the tension.

"I agree with my brother Taichu's opinion. The bigger the group, the more experienced the leader should be. So, I recommend Altan as our new khan. He has been to many battlefields and is the number one and official heir of the Kyat Mongols."

As Sacha Beki took his seat after his remarks, there was a little stir among the attendants. This time, Altan got on his feet with a smile on his lips, and said, "I thank Sacha Beki for recommending me for the khanship. However, I am telling you now that I really don't have even the slightest inclination to become the khan. Many of us left Jamuka. Someday, he will surely wage a war against us. The new khan should be the one who can stand against him, whose power has exploded in recent years. I cannot be sure of myself to compete with him. In my personal opinion, Temujin is the only one who can take that job. I officially recommend him for our new khan. We will take a little break and then continue."

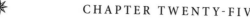

After this, Altan asked Sacha Beki, and his brother, Taichu, to come out from the tent and he began to persuade them. Election of the khan could only be possible with unanimous consent.

After a long break, Altan continued the meeting.

"So far, Temujin is the only one has a nomination. Let's take a vote on this. If you accept him as your new khan, stand up please. If you don't, remain seated."

The attendants stood up one by one from their seats, making a little noise. Sacha Beki and his brother, Taichu, also stood up, reluctantly. Now only one man was left. It was Temujin himself, who was sitting at one side of the southern corner. All eyes fell upon Temujin. If he didn't stand up, he would lose the khanship, because it would not be unanimous. Temujin, with a smile on his lips, slowly stood up from his seat. A thunderous applause filled the tent. Altan officially declared that Temujin had been elected as their new khan. Temujin made his first speech as the new khan in the council meeting, mainly supported by the Kyat Mongols.

"I sincerely appreciate you choosing me as the new khan. I will do my best not to disappoint you all. I won't be a sole decision maker, so I will always respect your opinions. I thank all of you, once again."

A thunderous applause filled the tent one more time. They decided to have an inauguration ceremony seven days later, along with a three-day feast following that. Temujin became the khan of the Kyat Mongols, and, with a larger range than that, the khan of the Borjigids, who were the descendants of the Bodunchar. He was in his mid-twenties.

The Mongols, at that time, elected their khan democratically. Yet the position or power of the khan was comparatively weak and far from those of the emperor of China or kings of other countries, who were absolute monarchs. The Mongols' social system was a clan-centered society. Each clan or tribe had its own strong independence, and so each clan or tribal member was loyal to their chieftain more than anyone else. The chieftains easily broke away from their khan if he made decisions that were against his clan's demands or interests. Their khan couldn't control them very efficiently in many cases. They could form a big group overnight to elect their khan, and yet they could collapse overnight, too, like a sand castle. It was their long-lasting tradition and because of that, it was hard for them to exert a combined force.

Temujin knew very well that that was their problem and weak point as well. He thought he had to change their social system into an absolute monarchy. That was another revolution he had to accomplish.

It was autumn when the dry, hot air from the south was gradually being replaced with the cool air from the northern Lake Baikal area. On the large, open ground, close to Koko Lake, where they could see the high peaks of the Kurelku Mountains, the altar was built and they had the inauguration ceremony there for their new khan. The sky was a deep cobalt blue, imbued with mysteriousness, and the rising sun was pouring its strong sunlight over the field. On the open ground, thousands of soldiers in their helmets and leather armor were standing in a line, holding spears or banners in their hands. The well-polished spears were flashing in the sunlight.

They slaughtered a white stud and put it on the altar, which was covered with a white curtain. They began the ceremony. The priest, Usun of the Baarin, clad in a white robe, sprinkled mare's milk ninety-nine times around the altar. After that, he lit a huge incense burner and began to pray to the heaven and earth. Temujin, after taking off his helmet and putting the belt on his neck, kowtowed nine times toward the heaven. The heads of the thirteen tribes and clans followed him. Usun, the priest, put a golden helmet, the symbol of the khan, on Temujin's head. The heads of the thirteen tribes and clans made a pledge of allegiance to their new khan.

> *Oh! Temujin Khan,*
> *We give you our pledge.*
>
> *On the battlefields,*
> *We are your eyes and ears,*
> *And will be your lance and scimitar.*
> *Their most beautiful women,*
> *Finest horses,*
> *Golden tents,*
> *And their land and slaves*
> *Will be brought to you.*

On the hunting grounds,
We are your guides and chasers.
When driving the beasts on the plain,
Or chasing the wild animals on the mountains,
We will go first,
Driving and chasing,
Put them together,
And send them in front of you.

In wartime,
If we fail to follow your orders,
Take away our women and wives,
Seize our properties,
Cut off our heads,
And throw them away in a field.

In peacetime,
If we break your rules and regulations,
Keep us away from our families,
Take our property and belongings,
Drive us into the land without the lord.

Temujin proceeded in front of thousands of soldiers, raised his two arms and shouted in a loud voice:

Glory shall be yours,
Who get heaven's love.
Dispersed shall be those
Who fail to follow heaven's will.

CHAPTER TWENTY-FIVE

Heaven bestowed enormous power upon me.
And those who will follow me,
Shall be given
Countless victories and shining glory.
Follow me!
And let's enjoy together
The sweet fruits of victory!

The soldiers began to give shouts of joy. The spearmen repeatedly thrust their spears into the air and the swordsmen also rhythmically pounded their round leather shields with their swords.

"Temujin Khan! Temujin Khan! Temujin Khan!"

Their chanting lasted for a while and echoed into the mysterious blue sky, the depth of which nobody knows. They began their three-day feast.

Temujin began to organize his governing system as the khan. First, he created two posts with the main function of guarding the khan. One of them was called the Quiver Bearers, whose main weaponry was the bow and arrow. The heads of this post were Ogolei, who was Bogorchu's younger brother, Kachun, Jetei and Dokolku. The other post was called the Sword Bearers and Kasar, Temujin's younger brother, Kubilai, Chilgudei and Kalkai were appointed as the heads. They were empowered to cut off the head of anyone who tried to enter the khan's yurt without permission and anyone who disturbed the peace.

Another important position was the Cup Bearers, whose main job was to handle and keep an eye on the khan's food and beverages. They were in charge of the khan's kitchen and the closest and most trusted men were appointed. They were Ongul, Soyketu and Qadaan Dalqulkan.

Other important positions were the horse breeders and keepers, Belgutei and Qaraldai; the sheep keeper, Dekei; the cow, yak and camel keepers, Kutu, Morichi and Muqalku; the manager of the khan's mobile yurt, Guchugul; the superintendent of male and female servants, Dodai; and the messengers and communicators, Araki, Taqai, Sukegei and Chaulqan.

Temujin appointed Subedei, Jelme's younger brother, as the spy and police chief, whose job was not only collecting information, but also controlling and protecting the people. Temujin also appointed Bogorchu and Jelme as the top administrators, whose positions were next to the khan.

After completing the organization, Temujin dispatched two messengers, Taqai and Sukegei, to Toghrul Khan for approval. Toghrul Khan approved Temujin's khanship.

"It is quite right that my foster son, Temujin, has become the khan. How can the Kyat Mongols go without a leader? Never break your own decision, which binds you together."

Temujin also sent Araki and Chaulqan to Jamuka. When Jamuka received the message, he was enraged. Jamuka helped Temujin get his kidnapped Borte back, but what he got in return was losing his people to Temujin. And more, Temujin declared himself as the khan supported mainly by the people who had left Jamuka. That aggravated his anger. He jumped up from his seat and burst out, "Altan! Quchar! You two bastards!

If you need a khan, you should have done this while you were here with me. What's the reason you left me and made someone else the khan? This is piercing my loins and pricking my ribs!"

Jamuka did not approve Temujin as the khan. Even though Jamuka lost many people to Temujin, he was still much more powerful than Temujin. Until that time, Jamuka had never declared himself as the khan.

After the two messengers left, Jamuka's men gathered around him. One of them said to Jamuka, "My lord, I think we must get rid of Temujin. We have to do it now before he becomes even bigger."

Jamuka's men were as furious as Jamuka. Nonetheless, Jamuka tried to persuade them, "The time will come. To raise a war, you need a justifiable cause. If we do it right now, Toghrul Khan might be on his side."

CHAPTER TWENTY-SIX

The Battle at Dalan Baljut

One year had passed and then another. The new spring had arrived on the Mongolian Plateau again.

The springtime is vibrant with life. The people take all the livestock out to the fields and feed them until they are full, as they had become weak during the winter months. That was the first job of the new spring for the steppe people.

On the large plain, at the upper part of the Orkhon River, about 300 miles from Temujin's ordu, near the Koko Lake and the Kurelku Mountains, a branch of the Jalairs had lived there since further back than anyone can remember. They called it the great Saari Plain. The Jalairs, a small group of 200 yurts, had maintained a good relationship with Yesugei, and once Temujin became the khan, their chief, Jochi Darmala, established a new relationship with him and came under Temujin's protection.

One day, three unknown men on horseback stepped onto this plain. They were covered with sweat and dust from their long journey. It was about midday and the sun was high above.

When their eyes fell upon the hundreds of horses grazing on the nearby plain, their eyes began to glare. They approached the herds as a team and began to drive them on. About twenty horses fell into their circle. Driving twenty horses with them, they began to run away in the direction they came from at full speed. The Jalair herd boy saw all this happen, but he couldn't do anything about it. He just stood there, watching them fade away, making thick dust, disappearing from sight. He reported this to Jochi Darmala immediately. A group of chasers was quickly formed and in no time, they set out. The chasers, totaling six including Jochi Darmala, followed the footsteps of their lost horses until it was close to evening.

When the team rode to the top of a hill, a scene of three rustlers driving their twenty stolen horses came into their view. The six chasers approached them from behind, with their bodies lowered onto their horse's backs. The three were talking, giggling with each other, and did not notice the chasers approaching. Jochi Darmala picked up one of his arrows and shot at a man who came into shooting range. His arrow lodged into the back of one of the rustlers, breaking his spine, and killed him on the spot. The other two began to run away at full speed. When the five other chasers began to pursue the two remaining men, Jochi Darmala stopped them.

"We already have our horses back. We should avoid any unnecessary killings."

Jochi Darmala dismounted his horse and tried to identify the dead man, but he couldn't.

"Who the hell is this man? Which clan?"

The dead man was completely unknown to them. They returned home, leaving the dead body in the same spot.

"What? Taicha has been killed?"

Jamuka jumped up from his seat when he heard the news from the two survivors. The dead man was Jamuka's cousin from his mother's side. His name was Taicha and he was seventeen years old, and he lived near Jamala Mountain. He wasn't living with Jamuka, but Jamuka had been thinking about him a lot because he didn't have many siblings.

Jamuka dispatched his soldiers to pick up the dead body, along with officers to find the facts. Jochi Darmala was nervous when he met them. Horse rustling was not uncommon on the steppe at that time, and often it developed into reciprocal killings. However, Jamuka's questioners made a big deal about the fact that the dead man was unarmed at the time.

"Did you know he was unarmed?"

Jochi Darmala tried to give an excuse to defend himself to the browbeating question.

"How would I know he was unarmed?"

Jamuka was given his cousin's dead body, which was almost unidentifiable because his face had been eaten by the crows. When he received the report from the officers that his cousin was unarmed at that time, he immediately gave an order to arrest Jochi Darmala. Jochi Darmala, who sensed that things were going unfavorably for him, sought refuge at Temujin's ordu with his family. After learning of Jochi Darmala's escape to Temujin, Jamuka dispatched a group of messengers to Temujin, asking for him to turn him over to them.

"Jochi Darmala is a murderer! Turn him over to us."

Temujin refused. If he turned him over to Jamuka, nobody would follow him. It was Temujin's obligation to protect his followers, even if he had to face a full-scale war with Jamuka. Obliging was out of the question.

Jamuka's prediction had come true. Now he had a justifiable cause to raise war against Temujin. That was exactly what he had been waiting for. Jamuka had a staff meeting with his generals and declared war against Temujin. Jamuka was much more powerful than Temujin and almost all the powerful men on the plateau were on his side. Jamuka mustered 30,000 horse soldiers from his clan and thirteen other tribes that were allied with him.

Temujin, after he received the information about Jamuka's movement from Mulke Todak and Boroldai of the Ikires, with whom he had good relations, began to gather troops against Jamuka. He amassed 30,000 troops, an equal number to Jamuka, from thirteen other tribes and groups.

Jamuka's troops advanced south, crossing the Alauud Mountain and the Turkaud Mountain toward the Kurelku Mountains where Temujin's ordu was located. Two friends, very close from their early years and even bound to each other as andas, became enemies and were going to meet on the battlefield.

Temujin and Jamuka's troops collided at Dalan Baljut, which was surrounded by high hills and mountains and located at the center of the Mongolian Plateau. First, they showered arrows on each other as they were approaching and then commenced hand-to-hand combat. The battle started in the morning and lasted until the late afternoon. The field and the hills were covered with countless dead bodies. In the early evening, the images of the victor and loser became clear. Temujin's sixth sense told him that he had lost. Temujin gave orders to Belgutei, Kasar and Jelme to find an escape route. Some time later, Kasar brought bad news: "The southern route has been blocked by Jamuka's troops."

The southern route was the one to their base at Koko Lake at Kara Jirugen.

Soon, Belgutei and Jelme also brought the same news.

"The western and northern routes have been blocked."

Only one route was left, the eastern one. Temujin realized that he was surrounded by Jamuka's troops. The eastern route consisted of many steep, rough cliffs and was considered next to impossible to pass. It could be suicidal and a real danger even without enemy attacks. Temujin didn't have choice. He encouraged his troops and took the course to the Jarene Gorge, which was the starting point of the Onon River. Jamuka stopped chasing, because he could lose many of his troops.

It was a great victory for Jamuka. He conducted a mass funeral ceremony for his fallen men after he picked them up from among the dead bodies scattered widely on the field, and buried them. As for the dead bodies from Temujin's side, he just left them there. The sky above the Dalan Baljut was covered with hundreds of thousands of crows and condors and it was quite noisy because of them.

Jamuka made a triumphant return with mountains of war booty. He didn't take prisoners. They killed almost everyone left there. Jamuka cut off the head of the Chino tribal chief, Neudei Chakaunua, himself. He ordered his soldiers to tie the cut-off head, with the eyes wide open, to his horse's tail.

Seventy-one high-ranking soldiers, who had been saved temporarily, were executed on their way back to Jamuka's ordu. One of his men came to Jamuka and asked, "My lord, what shall we do with them?"

"Put them into cauldrons and boil them to death!"

Under Jamuka's strict order, his soldiers set up 70 large cauldrons, which were mainly for big animals, like horses and cows, filled them with water and set fire underneath them. Next, they took off the prisoner's clothing, tied their hands and feet, and put them into the cauldrons.

Jamuka, on his horse, circling around the cauldrons, encouraged his soldiers. Each time his horse took a step, the human head tied to its tail rolled over and over. As the water temperature was going up, the screaming of the prisoners in burning pain filled the plain and the valley.

The Mongols believed that a man's spirit was in his blood. If they were killed by bleeding to death or by beheading, their spirit would be scattered into space. So, the "friendly" way of killing was suffocation. In that case, the spirit would remain intact. However, if they were killed by boiling, even their spirits would be dead, with their bodies. That was the cruelest way to kill.

Temujin was defeated in the battle. That was the beginning of another time of hardship. The people on the Mongolian Plateau believed Temujin's revival was impossible. Temujin did not let himself fall into utmost despair. He had to prove himself as the iron man on the Mongolian Plateau, where only the toughest survived.

CHAPTER TWENTY-SEVEN

Toghrul Khan's Exile

As Temujin, who was the most loyal and strongest follower of Toghrul Khan, disappeared into the plain, seeking safety after losing the battle at Dalan Baljut, the secondary effect fell upon Toghrul Khan. One day, early in the morning, Toghrul Khan was drinking fresh sheep's milk on his soft sofa in his golden tent. He was planning and designing a hunting expedition, which was scheduled to start three days later.

At this time, a Turkish serving woman opened the flap door and said that he had a visitor.

"I don't allow any early-morning visitors, you know that! Who the hell is he?"

As Toghrul Khan responded in an annoyed tone, the Turkish slave woman bowed politely and answered, "My lord, he is one of your generals, Altun Usuk. He said it's very urgent."

Toghrul Khan's eyes were wide open and he asked, putting his milk goblet back on the table, "Very urgent? What in the world could be very urgent at this hour? Let him in!"

Toghrul Khan straightened his upper body and gazed at the entrance. Altun Usuk was the commander of 1,000 soldiers. Wearing his combat costume without helmet, he walked up to Toghrul Khan and knelt down in front of him, showing his respect to the khan. He looked around a moment, as if to make sure nobody else was there. Altun Usuk was not a Kerait, and yet he was one of the most trusted of Toghrul Khan's men.

He had been one of the abandoned babies on the battlefield, and Toghrul Khan picked him up and raised him.

"What is so urgent? Speak up!"

As Toghrul Khan was pressing him for an immediate answer, Altun Usuk turned his eyes on to the two big men standing behind him. The two bald-headed men, with mountainous upper bodies exposed, were standing with their arms folded.

Toghrul Khan noticed what the general was looking at and said him in low voice, "Don't worry. You can say whatever you want. They don't have tongues."

Altun Usuk seemed quite relieved and opened his mouth.

"My lord, I want you to be careful. Some kind of plot is being developed to assassinate you."

Toghrul Khan jumped up from his sofa.

"What? A plot to kill me? Who is it? Who is the leader?"

Originally, Toghrul Khan had forty brothers. That meant his father, Kyriakus, had many wives. When his father died, he removed his rival brothers one by one and took over the khanship. However, since then, there had been numerous attempts on his life.

"The leader of this plot is unknown, my lord. I don't know, but I was in a secret meeting last night. I really couldn't betray you."

Toghrul Khan took his seat slowly, letting out a short sigh. For a while, they put their heads together for further discussion about the matter.

On that day, in the early evening, there was an unscheduled banquet in the khan's golden tent. About 200 of Toghrul Khan's brothers and generals gathered in the huge tent. Toghrul Khan noticed that his brother Elke Kara and about ten of his generals were absent. The banquet started. On each attendant's table, a silver goblet was placed for wine, but for ten people, smaller, gold goblets were placed. The women slaves in gorgeous costumes, with silver carafes in their hands, began to serve the wine.

After Toghrul Khan made sure everyone had his own wine goblet, he got on his feet with his goblet in his hand and began to speak.

"The purpose of today's banquet is to enjoy the high-quality wine together, which arrived from Samarqand yesterday. Let's have a toast for glory of the Keraits."

They toasted together. Toghrul Khan sipped a little bit of wine while he was still standing and continued his talking.

"This morning, I heard bad news. I heard a rumor that some kind of assassination plot was being devised and is aimed toward me. I am going to uncover the truth, so if you are loyal to me, remain seated and don't move, whatever happens."

Just after these words, thirty of Toghrul Khan's guards stepped inside the tent and made those with gold goblets in front of them stand, one by one. There were ten in total. The guards, without giving them a chance to move, tied their hands from behind and shackled their feet. It caused quite a stir among the diners. Toghrul Khan ordered his guards to take them out from the tent and said, "I am going to interrogate them myself. Continue to enjoy the banquet."

Toghrul Khan told his brother, Jagambu, to handle the banquet and drove the captives with his armed guards to a place far from the tent. Among them were top ranking generals like El Qutur, Qulbari and Arin Tasi.

"Who is your leader?"

Toghrul Khan pressed hard for the answer. At last, he got the answer that the leader was his half brother, Elke Kara. Elke Kara, realizing his plan had been disclosed, escaped with ten of his close followers before the banquet. The ten arrested were the ones who didn't know their plan had been disclosed.

"You swore allegiance to me, so how could you betray me like this?"

Toghrul Khan took a mace, which had numerous metal spikes on its head, from a nearby guard and hammered hard on El Qutur's head. With short screams, El Qutur fell down on the ground. For a moment, his body trembled roughly and then became quiet. The other nine were beheaded on the spot and were thrown onto the field to feed the wolves. Their families and property were seized. Their male offspring were all killed and the females were distributed among the soldiers.

Elke Kara, who successfully managed to escape with his family members and ten of his followers, proceeded west, crossed the border and stepped into the Naimans' territory. The Naimans were pure Turkish and had a relatively more civilized society on the Mongolian Plateau. They were using the Uighurs' writing system and had adopted the Chinese administrative system and, hence, had a primitive government.

Elke Kara was asking Inanch Khan, the head of the Naimans, for help, claiming that his mother was a Naiman.

"Let me borrow 20,000 troops. I will remove Toghrul and after that, I will be your loyal follower. I promise."

Inanch Khan, with his long white beard, who was already in his later years, regarded him silently with his eyes narrowed, as he was kneeling in front of him, begging for help. He seemed to be calculating which would be more beneficial to him, to take him into custody and sent him back to Toghrul Khan, or to mobilize the troops as he had asked, remove Toghrul Khan and extend his power over to the Keraits.

Inanch Khan summoned Sabrak, one of his best generals. Sabrak, with big, bright eyes, was an outstanding man with valor and intelligence. He whispered to Inanch Khan, "My lord, I think this is the right time to remove Toghrul, who has been our enemy for years, and extend your power over to them. Recently, Toghrul lost his two most powerful subjects. Jamuka left him declaring his independence and Temujin has disappeared after losing the battle to Jamuka. Now, Toghrul is like an eagle with his two wings broken. It would be quite reasonable to remove him at this time."

Inanch Khan accepted Sabrak's suggestion. He immediately mobilized 20,000 horse soldiers.

Twenty thousand Naiman troops led by Sabrak dashed toward the east and surrounded the Black Forest, the base camp for Toghrul Khan. Toghrul Khan, taken by surprise, was forced to flee. He managed to escape with about 200 of his family members and followers, and headed south. He crossed the Gobi Desert and stepped into the territory of the Kara Khitai. His brother, Jagambu, also escaped and sought safety in the Chin territory.

Sabrak, the victorious general who successfully subdued the Keraits, named Elke Kara a puppet khan and made a triumphant return to his Naiman base with mountains of war booty along with hundreds of thousands of livestock and countless gold and silver treasures.

Toghrul Khan, after setting up something similar to an exiled regime in the Kara Khitai territory, tried to make a deal with the king of the Kara Khitai, Guru Khan.

Kara Khitai was founded by the Khitans, who migrated from their original eastern land, the Lio, which had fallen and was taken over by the Juchids of the Chin. The Mongols called it Kara Khitai, which meant the land of the black Khitans, and the Chinese call it the West Lio. They took over some parts of the Silk Road and accumulated enormous riches. To protect it, they nurtured strong troops. They built walls, lived in Chinese-style buildings and accepted Islam as their religion.

Guru Khan, the king of the Kara Khitai, didn't like Toghrul Khan. From his point of view, Toghrul Khan was an infidel who was a Christian and his request for mobilization of troops didn't make any sense to him. At last, Guru Khan issued an ultimatum, "Within three days, you must leave Kara Khitai. If not, you will be arrested and handed over to Elke Kara."

Frustrated, Toghrul Khan left Kara Khitai with his group and stepped back into the Gobi Desert. The toughest time for Toghrul Khan had now begun. He roamed the Uighur's territory and the Shisha Kingdom.

He managed to survive on wild camels in the Gobi Desert and on a lucky day, when he came across a caravan, he could swap his or his family members' jewelry for daily necessities and food. He roamed the desert for a year.

On the other hand, Jagambu, with his small party, went into the Chin's territory after he successfully dodged the border patrol, and became like a bandit. He hunted for food and pillaged the nearby villages. His situation was worse than his brother's. Toghrul Khan was with his family, but Jagambu had left his family in Elke Kara's hands. He continually tried to contact his brother, but failed.

CHAPTER TWENTY-EIGHT

The Struggle for Resurrection

Most of the people and groups under Temujin's rule left him after the defeat at Dalan Baljut. Only a fraction of his followers remained. It might not have been a misfortune for him though, because if he had a noticeable number of followers, Jamuka may have tried a second attack. It was not unusual, at that time on the Mongolian Plateau, for the head of a group who lost a war to be killed at the hands of his own followers. He remained inactive and silent, biding his time. He was the master of self-control. He knew that one misstep could mean suicide. He was like the grass on the plain, which hides itself deep inside the ground at the time of the harshest conditions, but never perishes.

Two years had passed. The greatness of his character depended not on how he made his victory but how he overcame his loss. Again, groups of people began to gather around Temujin. He valued the people not by their origin, but by their loyalty and ability. Even when he was the khan, he ate the same food as sheep herders, and he used wooden dishes and bowls, while other chieftains or khans used only silver or gold dishes. He took care of the orphaned children of his fallen followers like they were his own. In the meantime, he was given his own two new sons, Chagatai and Ogodei. Temujin used to say, "It is more valuable to have one good friend or comrade than a chest full of gold."

Now people were coming to Temujin because they were attracted by his character. Munglik was one of those. Originally, Munglik was the loyal follower of Yesugei; however, when Yesugei had died, he left, like others. He had been under Jamuka's protection, but changed his mind and rejoined Temujin with his seven sons. The same thing happened with Jurchedei of the Uruud and Quyuldar of the Mangkud; they joined Temujin with their clan members. They were outstanding warriors under Jamuka, but left him in disappointment.

One day, Temujin gave a feast. It was with the Jurkins. Temujin wanted good relations with the Jurkins and eagerly hoped for their support, like before. The Jurkins were the main branch of the Borjigids, the descendants of Bodunchar and one of the strongest clans among the minor groups. However, they ignored Temujin and never showed any respect to him, a vanquished general, and humiliated Temujin's people openly. They didn't accept Temujin as their khan any longer.

Upon Temujin's request, they made a friendship agreement and were about to celebrate it.

It was early summertime and the place was a forest area near the Onon River. They made several campfires, barbecued meat and sat in groups, making circles based on their status and social rank. The northernmost circles were for the highest-ranking groups, like royal seats. In those, Temujin's family members and the families of the head of the Jurkins, Sacha Beki, were together. The musicians began to play their musical instruments and the servants began to serve beverages and food. Nobody was allowed in and around the royal seats except a few select persons. Sikiur was Temujin's family's butler and he was given the waiter's job for the royal seats. With a big silver kettle in his hand, he began to serve wine, one by one. First, he appeared in front of Temujin, bowed down, and poured wine in his big silver cup. The next was Ouluun, Temujin's mother, Kasar and then Sacha Beki. For the Mongols, the sequence of wine serving was important, because, by their custom, it meant the order of their rank. The higher the rank, the earlier they should be served.

When Sikiur arrived at the seats for the Jurkins' women, since he didn't know who was who, he just served as he saw, not in any particular order. That was a mistake. He served wine for Ebegei first, who was the third wife of Jurkin, the late father of Sacha Beki, before Qorigin and Qoulchin, who were the first and second wives. They complained, looking at each other, "How come this guy served Ebegei before us?"

The next moment, Qorigin got on her feet and slapped Sikiur's cheek. "You bastard! You don't even know the right order?"

This incident added some tension to the feast. Because of this, Kasar was about to stand up, but Temujin, who was sitting next to him, stopped him. "This is Sikiur's fault. Remain seated."

The feast continued, but enraged Sikiur, having been slapped on the cheek by a Jurkin woman, couldn't control his anger and cried out, repeatedly hitting a nearby pine tree with his fists, "This would have never happened while Yesugei and Nekun Tashi were alive!"

He left there. It was one poignant illustration of how the Jurkins treated Temujin's people. However, a second incident happened in the middle of the feast, because it was no longer a gathering of two groups of people in mutual respect and friendship. Somebody had stolen the snaffle off Temujin's horse. This wasn't a small thing. It was a big crime to steal the snaffle from the khan's horse. If the thief was captured, he would be beheaded on the spot.

The Mongols always posted a superintendent when they had a feast or a festival to keep everything in order and to minimize troubles. In many cases, they were appointed by the khan or the chieftain, and were given a lot of authority. They were the only ones allowed to keep their weapons in the feast site and usually were picked from among the tough guys with strong muscles, who could handle the drunken troublemakers. Belgutei was the feast superintendent appointed by Temujin. However, there was another superintendent appointed by Sacha Beki, whose name was Buri Boko. Buri Boko was the wrestling champion of the Jurkins and was a giant.

At last, Belgutei captured the thief. He was a Qadagin tribesman who belonged to Sacha Beki and was under his protection. Belgutei grabbed him by his collar, dragged him to Temujin and asked what his punishment should be. But at that moment, Buri Boko, dragging his big body, approached Belgutei and said, "Let him go!"

Belgutei stared at him in response to this outrageous remark and replied, "What? Let him go? He stole the khan's possession. How can you say that?"

Buri Boko, ignoring Belgutei's protest, took one more step towards Belgutei and said again, "I said let him go! Can you not hear me?"

Belgutei's jaw dropped at his shocking demand. He grabbed the thief more roughly and faced Buri Boko with a look of disapproval. The next moment, Buri Boko drew his dagger from his waist and brandished it, cutting Belgutei's right shoulder. Blood from the wound soaked his right sleeve. In Mongolian customs, there was only one solution for this kind of situation: a wrestling match. The loser had to yield to the winner's demand, and the same thing went for someone who refused or gave up.

The wrestling match began. People from the two parties gathered around with great concern for the unexpected duel and cheered for their side, shouting and waving their fists. Some time later, the wrestling match ended. Belgutei lost. He couldn't use his right arm, due to the cut Buri Boko had made with his dagger. The thief had been set free. The people of Temujin's side became enraged because they didn't think it was fair for Belgutei. They began a group fight. Since they didn't have any weapons with them, they used their fists and feet. Someone picked up the churning rod with the wheel from the kumis bag, and used it. The fight continued for a while.

Belgutei, flushed with anger came to Temujin, who had been watching from the beginning, and said, "Temujin, let's kill them all. This is our chance! Can you tolerate their humiliation? Is this a friendship agreement?"

Temujin persuaded him to stop.

"No. This is not the right time."

At that moment, Sacha Beki presented himself for a truce and reconciliation. They stopped fighting, picked up their belongings and went back to their ordus. The friendship agreement between Temujin's people and the Jurkins ended in failure. Actually, their relationship became even more strained. Temujin never forgot the humiliation of that day.

CHAPTER TWENTY-NINE

Truth of Human Nature

A man needs a woman when he is disturbed. A woman is the last resting place for a man. Borte was good at her role in this regard. Temujin's future was uncertain. During this hard time, Borte was always by his side.

One day, Temujin was with Borte. Borte was now the mother of five children, three sons and two daughters. Though she was still in her twenties, her face had begun to show crow's feet. She was expecting another baby; her belly was swollen like a mountain.

"I feel like it's a daughter again."

Borte said this as she was gently touching her belly with one hand and putting the other on Temujin's hand.

The Mongol women were tough. Like the Mongol horses, they had strong endurance and viability.

The main job for the Mongol men was going to battle and almost all the other jobs were left for the women. Setting up the tents, tending to the livestock, milking the horses, sheep and cows, weaving and making clothes and felt were their jobs.

Sometimes, they even joined the battle. Under those circumstances, they handled the confirmatory killings of the fallen enemy soldiers and retrieved the weapons, armor and helmets from the dead bodies. The Mongols moved with their family members when they went to war, especially for a long-term or long-range battle.

The Mongol women had equal rights and social status equal to the Mongol men. They had much higher social recognition than any other women in the civilized world such as China, Persia or Europe. If the father died, the mother became the head of the house, not the firstborn son. The women participated in all occasions, official ceremonies and celebrations. Women's opinions were never ignored simply because they were the women's.

"Borte, I heard a weird rumor recently," Temujin began. Only Temujin and Borte were in the yurt and the light from the Arabian lamp on the chest was casting long shadows of the two of them on the other side of the wall. It was late in the evening and was silent except for the occasional wolf howling from the distance. The dancing flame of the lamp reflected in Borte's eyes and was reflected back into Temujin's. Temujin did not miss the sign of surprise passing through Borte's eyes like a flash.

"My lord, what do you mean by weird rumor?" Borte asked in a low, soft tone.

Temujin hesitated for a while and at last opened his mouth. "I heard that Munglik is seeing Mother on a regular basis. Is that true?"

Borte looked into Temujin's eyes for a while and then dropped her gaze, remaining silent.

Munglik was the loyal servant of Temujin's father, Yesugei. Before he died, Yesugei asked Munglik to take care of Ouluun and his children. Yet he had left Temujin's family when everything was going against them, forsaking Yesugei's request. He rejoined Temujin's family after all; however, he already had two wives and seven sons. After the long silence, Borte raised her head slowly, looking into Temujin's eyes, and said in a low, quiet voice, "My lord, you didn't know? I guess it is true."

A thunderbolt of surprise fell on Temujin's eyes and then it caused him to blink. Borte watched Temujin's reaction to the shocking news with eyes full of sorrow and anxiety. Temujin sighed as he was dropping his head.

Temujin loved and revered his mother very much, who had refused Daritai's hand and happily accepted all the hardships to raise her children in the correct way.

Adulterers shall be put to death.

This was one of Temujin's promises, as well as a warning to his people, after he became the khan. The Mongols, at that time, were allowed to have as many wives as they could afford, regardless of the number. However, it was strictly prohibited to have relations with other women who did not belong to them. Adulterers were put to death regardless of their sex, age or excuses. It may have been a necessary policy to keep the peace and protect the society's polygamist system.

Temujin pondered a while, wondering if his mother could officially marry Munglik. No, it was impossible. It was not socially or customarily acceptable that the khan's mother marry one of the khan's subjects and become a third wife. Even though it was not hot inside the yurt, beads of sweat began to appear on Temujin's forehead. Borte, who had been watching Temujin with eyes of worry, held his hand and said, "My lord, I think you'd better ignore what's happening with your mother. That would be best."

Temujin carefully thought about what she had said. However, he could not accept it either, as the khan. Just in case it was already known by many people, it could not be ignored.

"How many people know about this?"

To Temujin's question, loaded with deep uneasiness, Borte gave an honest, sincere answer, "Not many people know about this. Only a fraction of the people who are very close to her, so you don't need to worry about that part."

A deep silence hung over the yurt for a while. The emotional pain of tough decision-making emerged on Temujin's face. *How can I judge my own mother?* That was another impossibility for Temujin. The basic human unit is not a single, but a couple. How lonely had she been for so long! Temujin's thinking reached that point.

"My lord, a man and a woman's relationship should be left to their own hands, as long as it doesn't cause any problems," Borte said with a look of entreaty.

As the night advanced, the wind began to blow. The flap of the yurt was drumming the wall, forced by the strong wind. Temujin could not sleep at all that night, but not because of the drumming. He woke up very late the following morning. He felt great. He had slept on that issue and woke up with his decision. He decided to follow Borte's advice. Temujin's new policy came about: *A man and a woman's relationship is a personal thing, unless it causes social problems.*

Just as Temujin announced the new policy, which considered a man and woman's relationship a personal matter, he also decided that religion is a personal choice. He gave the freedom of religion to his people. The people under his rule could believe in any religion they chose.

At that time on the Mongolian Plateau, many different forms of religious beliefs were coexisting, among them Christianity, Islam, Buddhism, Zoroastrianism and many others. The Keraits and the Onggirads, Borte's original clan, were Nestorian Christians and Temujin himself believed in the original Mongol belief, the God of Heaven, or the Everlasting Blue Sky. The Mongols at that time believed that the God of Heaven ruled the universe and it had ninety-nine different forms, acknowledging "Tab Tenggri" as the highest one.

There was a young man named Kokochu. He was the middle child of seven, or the fourth son, of Munglik. At age twenty, he was six feet seven inches tall. From an early age, he drew public attention because of his weird behavior, and when he turned twenty, he began an unexplainable series of strange acts. One time, he walked around in the field all day long, naked and barefoot, on a cold winter day, cold enough to freeze the horses and cows to death. Amazingly, he was completely unharmed. Another time, he astonished the people by telling them the exact number of newborn pups, even before their pregnant dog gave birth. People believed he was possessed by evil spirits and began to fear him.

One day, he retreated to a cave in the nearby high mountain to fast and pray, and then three days later, he came back. In the beginning, he muttered to himself in some kind of language nobody could understand and then he began to shout in the Mongolian language, "I have been to heaven! God told me this, 'I gave all the land to Temujin and his descendants. His followers shall prosper on this land, and shall not perish.'"

The Mongols accepted shamanism, and they had many shamans in their society. They made predictions, performed rituals to soothe mental and physical pains, cured illnesses and picked dates for travelers. The shamans representing the tribes performed the rituals for their ancestral memorial ceremonies and sometimes, at wartime, they even picked and suggested the direction of the troop's movements. They were so powerful, it was not unusual that the shamans themselves became the chieftain of their tribe. They were the rulers of the spiritual world of the Mongols.

On the other hand, there were a lot of fake shamans and sorcerers roving on the steppe. They were luring, cheating and scaring the people for dishonest rewards.

One day, Temujin called in Kokochu, in the name of the head of the group. Temujin's brothers, comrades and all the town elders were present for this meeting. The man of six feet seven inches had a light-skinned, long face with little slanted eyes that shone with unaccountable charisma. Someone might fall into the illusion of being hypnotized just by looking into his eyes, which gave him the image of possessing mysterious power.

He was presenting himself in front of Temujin, clad in a white robe, which covered him from neck to ankles. Temujin said to him, looking up at him, like a human pole, "Do you know how I treat the evil-minded, dishonest shamans or sorcerers who cheat the people and disturb the public order?"

To this question, Kokochu answered clearly, peacefully and even with a smile on his lips, without any sign of unrest, "I know. The punishment is death. However, I possess many supernatural powers, which even I do not understand. I do not know where it is coming from. Sometimes, I see clear visions of the future or hear the shouts of someone from somewhere. Sometimes I talk with them, and yet I don't know who they are. If I concentrate on my mind, I can stay in the icy water for half a day, and I won't get burned even if I touch a flame. This is true."

After hearing this, Temujin looked around. Belgutei, Kasar, Bogorchu and Jelme were all gazing at him with a look of disbelief. Kasar, who was standing by Temujin sitting in his chair, bent his body and whispered in Temujin's ear, "Do you believe what he has said?"

Temujin said to Kokochu, "Fine! We will find out if you are telling the truth. We don't care if you can talk to somebody in heaven or can hear strange voices from another world. However, if you can prove what you have said, that you can touch a flame and stay in the icy water for half a day, then you will be accepted. I will consider you as the chief priest of my ordu. If not, what are you going to do?"

To Temujin's straightforward words, he replied with a slight smile on his lips, "It will be easy for me. I can show you right now. If not, I promise I will give you my neck."

Temujin ordered his men to put down a carpet and make a fire on the open ground in front of him. They placed a carpet in front of Temujin, as well as a metal burner with three legs in which a well-dried log fire was built. People gathered around in great curiosity for this very unusual trial and, soon, the site was surrounded. Kasar approached the burner and put his hand into the flame, as if he wanted to make sure it was very hot. Strong laughter burst out from the spectators when he immediately removed his hand from the flame, making the comic gesture of a surprised buffoon.

Temujin asked Kokochu, "How will you do it?"

"I will put my hand into the flame while someone counts from one to ten."

Temujin picked up a small boy from the front line of the spectators and let him count. The boy, maybe in consideration of Kokochu, counted from one to ten in a speedy way. Temujin asked Kokochu again, "With this speed, will you be fine?"

Kokochu answered with a smile on his face, "It will be fine, even at a much slower speed."

Kokochu knelt down on the carpet in front of the burner and began to control his breathing and meditate. Some time later, he opened his eyes and put his right hand on the orange-colored flame, under the eyes of the spectators. The boy began to count slowly in a scared voice. People watched him in deep silence, without any movements. At last, when the boy was done counting, Kokochu slowly took his hand from the flame and got to his feet. His right hand was darkly stained and still had some smoke around it. People kept on watching his right hand with astonishment. With a smile on his lips, he opened and closed his fist a few times, as if to prove that his hand was unharmed. Then, he walked up to Temujin and showed it to him up close. People began to talk to each other, making quite a noise for a while and then, at last, they applauded loudly and shouted.

The following morning, by the order of Temujin, Kasar took Kokochu to a nearby lake. This time, it was for his second supernatural power test. Temujin told Kasar, as he was handing the bronze sundial over to him, "If he comes out of the water, without proving his claim that he could stay in the icy water from sunrise until noon, cut off his head."

Though it was March, numerous blocks of ice were floating on the surface of the water. When the sun began to rise, Kokochu took off his robe, and only in short pants, he jumped into the water. Many people gathered to see this miracle, just as they had watched the night before. Around noontime, Temujin made a visit to the site with his men. Kokochu was still in the water at that time. As Kasar notified him that noon had passed, Kokochu slowly walked out of the water. He was fine. Ordinary men would have been dead hours before from hypothermia.

Temujin confirmed his supernatural powers. As he had promised, he appointed him the official chief priest of his ordu. Kasar intervened and told Temujin his opinion, "Though he showed his supernatural powers, there is no guarantee that he can communicate with the spirits, right?"

Temujin regarded Kasar a moment and said, "As long as people believe that he can, there is nothing else to prove."

Since that trial, people believed he could communicate with the spirits and gave him the nickname Tab Tenggri.

CHAPTER THIRTY

The Warriors on the Steppe

The Mongols started horseback riding at age three and when they grew up to be big enough to handle weapons, they were already warriors. From a very early age, they joined the hunting expeditions to learn how to chase after game, how to camouflage themselves, how to get over the fear of facing wild beasts, like tigers, bears and boars, and then how to strike a fatal blow to minimize their counterattack. They learned by themselves through team hunting the importance and efficiency of the group effort. Their skins were hardened by the hot desert air and the bitter cold Siberian winds, their muscles and nerve tissue were naturally trained to exert the maximum strength and speed, and their souls and spirits were tough, like sinew, toughened by the extremely unfavorable environment.

Their stamina and endurance were extraordinary, for they could run horses for days without a rest, with a minimum food supply. In extreme cases, they could stay on horseback for weeks. They did everything on horseback, like eating, resting and sleeping; the only exception was when they had to relieve themselves. Their combat food was dried beef and sheep's milk; however, when they were in an emergency situation, such as running out of food, they would suck their horse's blood. In that case, they carefully opened the neck vein with a tiny blade, took the amount they needed and then closed and pressed the wound for a while to stop the bleeding.

Unlike that of townspeople, warriors' visual, auditory and olfactory senses were exceptionally highly developed, and, so, in clear weather, they could recognize people's, or horses', movements from fifteen miles away, sensing horses galloping and smoke from a great distance. Their well-developed sixth sense allowed them to differentiate empty tents from tents with enemy soldiers hiding inside, and in the combat zone, they could differentiate the dead bodies from live enemy soldiers playing dead.

When they joined full-scale war, they used iron helmets with leather neck-covers and leather armor as tough as a turtle's shell to protect their chests, abdomen and back, and they wore leather protective covers on their arms. Their major weapons were bows, scimitars, spears with hooks that could pull down enemies from their horses, maces with metal spines and hand axes.

On a balmy spring day, a small number of people and horses were drawing near Temujin's ordu from the eastern end of the horizon. This group, which looked like a tiny moving point on the horizon at first, became larger and larger as time went by, and finally became clearly visible.

After receiving a report from the sentry covering the area between the north and the east, Temujin went up the nearby hill with Bogorchu and Jelme. Temujin's eyes focused on an image of two men, each on horseback, galloping at full speed toward Temujin, making a long tail of grayish dust. Temujin sent Bogorchu and Jelme out to find out who they were.

Bogorchu and Jelme met them midway and stopped their proceeding.

"Who are you? Identify yourselves!"

The two men were clad only in animal skin vests on their torsos and were wearing summer fur caps without brims. They seemed to have no weapons with them. They seemed to be decent men, with suntanned skin and well-developed bodies.

One of them opened his mouth and said in a loud voice, "We are the Suldus. My name is Chimbai and his is Chilaun. We came to join Temujin. Let him know that Sokan Shira's two sons are here. Then he will understand everything."

At this answer, Bogorchu and Jelme looked at each other and then Jelme turned back to Temujin to report.

"Oh! Chimbai and Chilaun are here?"

Temujin never forgot Chimbai and Chilaun, the two sons of Sokan Shira, who helped him to escape when he was a captive in the Taichuts' camp. Temujin galloped to them, and found two high-spirited, robust, fully-grown men. Temujin recognized them easily, "Chimbai, Chilaun! What a pleasant surprise!"

They dismounted their horses and hugged each other. They continued to embrace and pat each other for a while. Temujin looked at them one after the other with a face filled with smiles and great happiness.

"How is your father? How about Qadaan?"

Qadaan was their sister, who also helped Temujin, and she was nine at the time. Chimbai said to Temujin, "Temujin, we are here to join you. We planned this a long time ago. However, we couldn't take the chance until now. We have been talking to each other about you being the only one who could unite the Mongols. We want to support you, with what we have, only the two of us, though. Our father is doing fine and so is Qadaan."

Temujin hugged and patted their backs one more time.

"I really welcome you. Let's join our efforts and forces together. However, I am a little bit worried about your father and Qadaan. I hope your joining me will not be harmful to them."

Temujin couldn't hide his concern, because they were still in the Taichut's hands, Temujin's sworn enemy.

This time Chilaun answered, "Qadaan married a Taichut. She already has two children. As long as Qadaan is with the Taichut, they can do nothing to her and Father."

Temujin nodded. He asked with a smile on his lips, "How are your own families? Of course you have already married, both of you, right?"

Chimbai answered, "Of course we did. I have three kids and Chilaun has two. They are not far from here. We will bring them right away."

Chimbai and Chilaun turned their horses and galloped back to their families. Temujin gazed at the two valiant men galloping away for a long time, his eyes showing mixed emotions. It had been years since Temujin bade farewell to them, possibly fifteen or twenty, and yet, Temujin felt like he was seeing them again after only a few months. That was probably because they had been in Temujin's mind all the time. Temujin had deep appreciation for the two brothers and their family members for helping him escape from death, risking their own lives.

Temujin gave them a three-day feast. That was very exceptional. Temujin never forgot someone who did him a favor, and always rewarded them accordingly, without failure. Chimbai was the man with a sense of justice and an open mind. His brother, Chilaun, had outstanding valor, a superior physique and great skills in weaponry. Later, he proved himself to become one of Temujin's four kulugs (heroes) with the title of the bagatur.

Just as Belgutei was a man with incredible physical strength and muscle power, Kasar was a gifted archer. To survive in an extreme feudal society, like that of the Mongolian Plateau, people needed physical and mental superiority over others, as well as skills in handling weapons. Kasar was a man with thick eyebrows, an eagle eye, a prominent nose and narrow chin. His height was just a little more than average, though he had exceptionally well-developed chest, arms and shoulders. Undressed, he was shaped like a triangle pointing toward the ground. He used to show off his well-developed muscles by wearing only a leather vest on his torso when it was not so cold. He could hit a man on a galloping horse from 400 yards away 99 times out of 100.

Temujin's number-one comrade, Bogorchu, number-two man and most loyal follower, Jelme, and his brother, Subedai, all had valor, resourcefulness, physical and mental power and the required qualities of a warrior. They were the core members of Temujin's power. Temujin, who had the exceptional talent of finding the right men, had done his job right yet again. He found Kubilai, the Barulas. He had the valor of a mountain lion and the tenacity of a snake. As he was a good swordsman, Temujin made him chief of the cavalry specializing in hand-to-hand combat.

Now Temujin had Chimbai and Chilaun, which made him exultant, not only because he would have the chance to repay them, but also because he sensed that Chilaun had the strong possibility of becoming a talented warrior.

Temujin began to organize his troops systematically. His troops, in regular marching formation, were composed of five units, which were the advance guards or vanguards, the main body, the rear guards, and the left and right wings. However, once they were engaged in battle, they reformed the structure quickly to form the archery unit, the light cavalry and heavy cavalry. At the beginning of the battle, the archery unit advanced first and attacked the enemy with their arrows, and then there would be an open road for the light cavalry. They attacked the enemy troops with their main weapon, lances, destroying half of them. After them, the heavy cavalry advanced.

They were the main destructive power. They were heavily armed with spears, scimitars, axes and maces, and wore armor not just on themselves, but also on their horses.

This systematic organization was completed at later time, but Temujin started with this concept from the beginning. Temujin considered organization and the speed of the troops the key elements to win a battle, especially when he had to face a large number of enemies with a comparatively much smaller number of his own. Temujin was a gifted warrior, especially in the area of surprise attacks, psychological warfare, espionage, and camouflage tactics. Temujin always emphasized the importance of the spiritual power of each individual or soldier. An individual or a soldier without spiritual power had already lost half the battle, he stressed.

CHAPTER THIRTY-ONE

Return of Toghrul Khan

Around a small oasis at the northwestern corner of the Gobi Desert, about thirty yurts had gathered, forming a dense, tiny village. It was early fall, when the hot, dry desert winds were replaced with the cold northern winds at nighttime. It was late afternoon, and the sun, hanging in the western sky, began to make long shadows. An obese man in his mature years was sitting on his chair, alone, in front of a yurt, seemingly enjoying the afternoon sunlight. His head was covered with grey hair and his body was swollen with fatty tissue, and yet his eyes were glaring like the eagle's. He was Toghrul Khan, roving in and around the Gobi Desert with only his family members and intimate followers.

He caught sight of a long line of camels, moving slowly from one corner of his vision to another. As he could clearly see stacks of luggage on the camels' backs, he determined that it was surely a caravan. His eyes began to sparkle. He shouted behind him, with a husky, yet strong voice, "Senggum! Where are you, Senggum? Come here, right now!"

In response to his shouting, three men opened the flap door and stepped out of the yurt. They were wearing leather vests, wide pants with boots, and had Turkish curved daggers hanging from their waists. Among them was a tall, light-skinned man, who walked up to Toghrul Khan and bowed, "Father, Senggum is here."

Toghrul Khan, without looking at him, pointed to the southern side of the horizon with his finger. The eyes of the three men fell on the southern horizon. After a long, careful look, Nilka Senggum looked at his father, trying to figure out what was on his mind. Toghrul Khan, without taking his eyes off the caravan, gave an order, "Go find out who the owner of the caravan is and who is the sponsor."

Before Toghrul Khan had been pushed out of power, all the caravans passing through his territory had to get his permission and had to pay the appropriate taxes.

Nilka Senggum thought to himself, and then, raising his eyebrows, told Toghrul Khan, "Father, let's attack them and take their luggage!"

With a frown on his face, Toghrul Khan glanced at his son's face once and spat out his words, "With that long a line of camels, they probably have more than 400 escort soldiers. With our thirty men, what can we do?"

Toghrul Khan was right. Behind the long line of camels, another long line was following, a cavalry of 400 to 500 soldiers fully armed and armored. As time went by, the image became clearer.

Nilka Senggum was a man who spent more time with musical instruments, good wine and beautiful women than with bows or scimitars. It is no wonder he had suggested such a foolish idea.

Toghrul Khan decided to gamble. There was a chance the escort troops were Elke Kara's men. If they were Elke Kara's men, he could be in trouble. He could be chased down by Elke Kara if he exposed his whereabouts. If they weren't Elke Kara's men, he could swap his jewelry and precious metals, like gold or silver, with them for what he needed desperately for daily life. Toghrul Khan dispatched his son Nilka Senggum and three other men to the caravan. He waited for the result of the mission anxiously.

Some time later, he could see about ten horsemen galloping toward him, raising a big cloud of dust. Toghrul Khan got on his feet and ordered his men to bring him his scimitar. The ten men approaching on horseback caused the earth to shake and rumble, and as time went by, their outline became clearer. It was his son, Nilka Senggum, his three other men and six of the caravan's escort soldiers. Toghrul Khan felt relieved. Toghrul Khan noticed that one of the six soldiers looked very familiar and later found that he was a young Muslim merchant named Jafar. He was the owner of that caravan. Jafar, in a white robe and a white turban on his head, dismounted his horse when he saw Toghrul Khan. He walked up to him and gave him an Islamic greeting, lowering his head as he was touching his forehead with his right hand.

"My greetings to the khan! I never expected your audience in such a place like this."

Toghrul Khan welcomed him. Toghrul Khan's eyes turned to the five escort soldiers, who had dismounted their horses and were standing at attention nearby. They were heavily armed with bows, spears and scimitars, and wearing armor and helmets on their upper bodies and heads. Toghrul Khan's eyes fell on one of them, a handsome young man with large round eyes and a good physique. He looked quite young, and yet he was dignified. After handing his horse's reins to another soldier, he walked up to Toghrul Khan, kneeling on one of his knees and bowed. He opened his mouth and spoke in a clear, strong voice, "My greetings to the khan! My name is Subedai and I am with Temujin Khan. I have met you a couple of times before."

Toghrul Khan gave a look of surprise by raising his eyebrows.

"Oh! Subedai! Aren't you the younger brother of Jelme, Temujin's outstanding comrade? Of course, I remember you. Today is a really happy day!"

Toghrul Khan invited them into his yurt and served tea. Toghrul Khan asked, "How is Temujin doing? It has been more than two years already since I have seen him."

Jafar answered his question, "Temujin Khan has almost recovered his strength. Now he is at the upper part of the Kerulen River. I know he has been looking all over for you."

Toghrul Khan was glad to hear that. He knew that Temujin was his last hope.

Temujin had established a good relationship with Jafar since he had met him in Toghrul Khan's golden tent. Temujin met him first at the visitors' quarter. The visitors' quarter of Toghrul Khan's court was always busy with a continuous line of visitors, especially the caravans who wanted to get permission from the ruler whose territory covered a large area of the Silk Road.

"Salem! My greetings!"

Jafar had approached Temujin and lowered his head to show his respect and goodwill toward Temujin when they had met for the first time. The young caravanner, Jafar, was speaking perfect Mongolian. From a very early age, he traveled regularly with his father, who also caravanned, from Samarqand to China, as an apprentice. Jafar, whose parents were Persian, spoke not only Persian, but also Mongolian, Chinese and a few other languages. Since he had been to China so many times, he knew every corner there and was familiar with their politics. He was the so-called China specialist. Temujin had a favorable impression of him, someone who could speak many different languages and was familiar with international politics. Likewise, Jafar was attracted by Temujin's character. When he saw Temujin the first time, he quickly realized that he was not an ordinary man and after a few conversations with him, he envisioned Temujin as the future ruler of the Mongolian Plateau. This is how their relationship had started.

Temujin used to have close relations with caravans crossing the Gobi Desert on a regular basis.

In his early years, he sold them game, like foxes and sables, that he had hunted with his brothers. From them, he could learn and get a lot of information about international movements and politics, and so he valued them highly as informants. Jafar entrusted his escort business to Temujin, not to Elke Kara.

After receiving the report about Toghrul Khan, Temujin immediately dispatched two of his messengers, Taqai and Sukegei, to make sure the report was true. After confirmation, Temujin set out with his warriors to see Toghrul Khan. Temujin met Toghrul Khan and his shabby group near Guseul Lake, which was at the northeastern corner of the Gobi Desert. Temujin dismounted his horse, knelt on one of his knees and bowed to him, showing his unchanged loyalty toward him.

"My lord, I have been worrying about your safety and well-being. You have suffered long enough. I am with you now and I am ready to serve you again."

Temujin did his best to comfort him.

Toghrul Khan was exultant.

"Oh! Temujin, you are like my own son. I am glad to see you and feel grateful for your coming."

They marched together. They drove their horses slowly, side by side, swapping their stories.

"Elke Kara is the one to be blamed. I will surely annihilate him!" Toghrul Khan remarked in great fury when the topic of conversation came to Elke Kara.

"My lord, I think you'd be better stay with me until the right time comes."

Toghrul Khan stayed with Temujin through the winter. Temujin moved from the upper part of the Kerulen River to

Quba Qaya, a remote area, for the winter. It was the right place to defend themselves from a possible attack from Elke Kara.

The new spring had arrived. Spring had two different meanings for the steppe people; one was new life and another death. It was time for war. The nomads hesitated to take their weakened horses on to the battlefield during winter.

One spring day, early in the morning, two men on the top of the hill at the northern part of the Black Forest, near the Kerulen River, the place of the Keraits' stronghold, were looking down at the tent city of hundreds of thousands of yurts, spread out on the enormous plain. They were wearing toughened black leather armor and helmets, and were heavily armed with all different kinds of weaponry. They were grinning with satisfaction, looking down at the peaceful tent city. They knew their surprise attack had already half won. They were the Merkids, Toktoa Beki and Dayir Usun. After their defeat by the three-group coalition army of Toghrul Khan, Jamuka and Temujin, they gathered themselves, regrouped, reorganized and tried hard to recover their strength. They came down south with 20,000 well-trained horse soldiers to punish and retaliate against the Keraits, who were the leader of the previous attack. They knew the Keraits had been weakened by the absence of their strong leader, Toghrul Khan.

One of the two men raised his spear high into the air and shouted in a loud voice as he brought it down pointing to the tent city, "Charge! Forward!"

Then, the 20,000 horse soldiers hiding underneath the hill spurred their horses and dashed to the target area, raising the terrifying battle cry. They began mass destruction and massacre. The Keraits, hit by a surprise attack, couldn't resist. They were killed or fled in any direction they could. The Keraits' stronghold became the location of their own bloodbath.

The surprise attack of the Merkids on the Keraits had been reported to Temujin immediately. Temujin planted his men in the Black Forest area to watch the Keraits' movements. Temujin called out the troops without delay. Temujin told Toghrul Khan, "My lord, this is the time to retrieve the khanship and recover your lost people and property. Wear your armor and helmet and pick up the scimitar, please."

Temujin and Toghrul Khan set out together. Three thousand of Temujin's cavalry, with the vanguard of Bogorchu, Qubilai and Chilaun, advanced at maximum speed. Before they arrived at the Black Forest area, numerous defeated Kerait soldiers and stragglers gathered around Temujin and Toghrul Khan. Temujin regrouped and reorganized the defeated troops and handed them over to Toghrul Khan.

When they arrived at the Black Forest, they saw a completely destroyed and ruined ordu. Dead bodies were everywhere and the dark smoke from burning yurts and furniture was covering the sky. The cries of the children who lost their parents were deafening and it wasn't easy to move the troops due to the stacked dead bodies and broken battle or transport carts on the road.

Temujin chased the Merkids, who were running to the north with mountains of war booty and livestock. Temujin's troops stood face to face with the Merkids on a large field about 100 miles north of the Black Forest. Temujin went up to the top of the nearby hill and looked around. The Merkids were waiting for Temujin, with a one-mile-long defensive line, showing off their superiority in numbers. Temujin decided to try the wedge tactic. The wedge tactic was designed to break the strong enemy defense line with a small number of attackers. It was like splitting a log in half; drive the wedge into the middle, and then hit the head of the wedge. Leading the vanguard of Temujin's troops was Bogorchu.

At this time, a man on a horse ran out from the Merkids' line and stopped halfway between the two sides. He began to shout in a loud voice to ridicule Temujin and Toghrul Khan and then cursed and swore. He was Togus, the firstborn son of Toktoa Beki. The archery unit of Temujin's troops sent arrows to rain down on him, but he was out of range.

At this, Temujin nudged Kasar, who was standing next to him, and gave an eye signal. Kasar picked one of his arrows from his quiver and aimed at Togus with the bow, which was custom-made for him. He stared at the target, took a deep breath and let go. The arrow left Kasar's hand, flew away with amazing speed and hit the target, right in the center of Togus's forehead. Togus fell down from his horse and never moved again. There was a big stir on the Merkids' side, and without delay, several Merkid soldiers galloped out to save him. Temujin didn't lose his chance. By Temujin's order, the signal flags were raised high and the drummers began to beat their drums. Temujin's vanguards, led by Bogorchu, Qubilai and Chilaun, dashed at full speed towards the Merkids' defense line. They penetrated the Merkids' first, second and third defense lines. Temujin, without pausing, pushed his second and third group of troops into the Merkids' main body. It was a complete victory for Temujin. The Merkids collapsed like the fallen leaves hit by a gale or sheep chased and attacked by hunting dogs or wolves. Temujin continued chasing down Toktoa Beki and his Merkid troops, destroying them one by one. Temujin successfully retrieved almost all the Merkids' lost property and livestock and, in addition, he captured ten Merkid generals and a huge amount of grain.

Toktoa Beki, Dayir Usun and their defeated Merkid troops escaped to the Barkujin Gorge.

Temujin helped Toghrul Khan rebuild the Keraits. They gathered around Toghrul Khan again. Toghrul Khan retrieved his khanship. It took more than three months for reconstruction. Temujin handed all the war booty over to Toghrul Khan.

One day, a messenger from Toktoa Beki arrived. Toktoa suggested swapping his captive, Elke Kara, for his ten generals.

Temujin asked Toghrul Khan's opinion.

"My lord, Toktoa wants to swap Elke Kara for ten of his men. What do you think?"

Toghrul Khan gave it some thought, and then approved gladly.

"Fine! Let me have Elke Kara."

Five days later, Elke Kara was handed over to Toghrul Khan. Toghrul Khan chastised him openly in front of his subjects and followers. He denounced Elke Kara, who was kneeling in front of him with his two hands tied back.

"I had been good to you. How could you betray me?"

Toghrul Khan spit on his face. Elke Kara was his half brother. When he took over the Keraits' throne, he killed his own uncle and Elke Kara's real brother. After Toghrul Khan, all of his men who were there also spit on Elke Kara's face, one after another.

"Cut off his head and his four limbs, and give them to the wolves in the field."

Toghrul Khan handled and finished up Elke Kara's rebellion like this. Later, Jagambu, Toghrul Khan's younger brother, who was roving in the Chin territory, rejoined his brother. Toghrul Khan had completely restored his power.

CHAPTER THIRTY-TWO

War with
the Tartars

The steppe people were like water. If water accumulates and builds up a heavy stream, nothing can stand against it. On the other hand, if the water disperses and permeates into the soil, it disappears and is hard to bring back. Likewise, if the steppe people came together, making a huge stream, and attacked the sedentary people, it was like a flood. Their opponents couldn't stop them. However, if the sedentary people, after regrouping, struck back and pushed them back home, they dispersed into the steppe and disappeared. Trying to find the enemies who had already dispersed into the enormous steppe in all different directions was just like trying to bring back the water that had already permeated the soil. This was why the sedentary people couldn't root out the steppe people, even after they had been attacked and pillaged.

Opportunity knocks for everybody at some time. The only difference between the lucky and the unlucky is who is there to open that door. Though Temujin was still confining himself to a limited area, he was fully aware of what was going on in the world. Most of the information could be obtained through the caravans. In the meantime, Temujin paid visits to Toghrul Khan on a regular basis, so as to maintain close relations with him. Temujin's loyalty toward Toghrul Khan had not changed.

One day, at Toghrul Khan's banquet, Temujin was talking with Jafar, who was sitting next to him.

"What is your speculation of the political movement in China?"

At this question, Jafar sipped his Samarqand wine in a silver goblet, moistening his throat, and answered in a serious tone, "The northern Chin already control the southern Sung. Before long, the Chin Empire might launch a big assault on the northern people. When I was in Yenking, I saw numerous troops gathering and getting ready to move north. I asked the soldiers which direction they were moving to, and they said they didn't know yet."

The caravans needed be well informed about war zones and battle areas for their safety. It was quite natural to avoid the dangerous areas, and so, to get the information, sometimes they had to bribe high-ranking soldiers or government officials. Even after the banquet, Temujin stayed with Jafar in the same quarters and they shared their opinions about international political movements.

At the same moment that Temujin was in deep conversation with Jafar, in Yenkin, the Chin's capital, a meeting was being held with the Chin emperor, Wie-zong, and high-ranking officials and generals. The Chin emperor, Wie-zong, opened his mouth and said, "We have taken control of the problems with the southern Sung. However, I have had numerous, urgent requests from the northern border garrisons. From now on we have to concentrate on the northern side. If you have any suggestions, don't hesitate to tell me."

Just after Wie-zong finished his words, Wanyen-Xiang, the highest ranking official and general as well, got to his feet and said, "Your Majesty, I dare to suggest a few things. Historically, we used the tactic 'barbarians for barbarians' when it came to the northern people. This tactic has worked. One time, the Mongols disturbed peace in the border area. We put the Tartars on the front line to defeat them. Now the Tartars have grown too big. They are the ones who are making trouble now. It is time to weaken their power."

Wie-zong answered with a question for Wanyen-Xiang, "How can we weaken their power?"

Wanyen-Xiang answered, "If we try to handle them with our own troops, it might not be best. The best way would be to win other tribes over to our side and attack them from two different directions."

Wie-zong asked, "Who could be the other rival for the Tartars?"

"Your Majesty, I think the Keraits, who control the south-western part of the Mongolian Plateau now, could be the rival for the Tartars. Their chieftain, Toghrul, acknowledges the Tartars as his sworn enemy."

The Chin emperor, Wie-zong, asked, "How many Tartars are there?"

"Their population is believed to be about 400,000, and, among them, about 100,000 could be the number of male adults. They are divided into nine big groups or thirty small groups, and the ones who are making trouble now, killing the garrison chief, are just a fraction of them."

"How can we win over the Keraits to get them on our side?"

To his emperor's question, Wanyen-Xiang answered, lowering his head, "Your Majesty, allow their chieftain, Toghrul, to have the title Wang [king], and then if you approve him as the official ruler of the Mongolian Plateau, he might accept it and come to us."

The Chin emperor pondered a while. Since they believed the Mongolian Plateau belonged to the Chin Empire, it was possible for the Chin emperor to appoint anybody he chose king of the Mongolian Plateau. Emperor Wie-zong said in conclusion, "For this operation, send 50,000 troops. The commander-in-chief will be Wanyen-Xiang. Try to win the Keraits over to our side. If they respond to my call and the operation is successful, let their chief have the title of king. The commander-in-chief, Wanyen-Xiang, shall have all the power to do this on behalf of myself."

Wanyen-Xiang began to mobilize his 50,000 troops to the north, and at the same time, he dispatched two messengers to Toghrul Khan. The two Chin messengers, with their forty escort soldiers, arrived at Toghrul Khan's golden ordu five days later. Toghrul Khan, after receiving and having read the royal letter from the Chin emperor through the interpreter, held his reply. He didn't give an answer right away. He gave an order to Jagambu, "Send somebody out to the Hariltu Lake and tell Temujin to come here immediately."

Jagambu sent out an emergency messenger. One day later, Temujin sat down with Toghrul Khan face to face.

"The Chin troops, 50,000 of them, are on their way to attack the Tartars. The Chin emperor has asked me to help them. What shall I do?"

Temujin answered, "My lord, I think this is a good chance to enhance your power. Answer their call. However, I think it would be better to move your troops about ten days after the battle has commenced."

"Why is that?"

"The Chin troops will surely be defeated by the Tartars. It would be better to move your troops after that has happened."

Temujin returned to his ordu at Hariltu Lake. Temujin mustered his troops immediately. The tent city of 3,000 yurts at Hariltu Lake was suddenly shaken by loud drumbeats and the white banner in front of the khan's yurt had been replaced with a black one, which meant war. Temujin devised many different types of military equipment and devices for communication to control the troops and for stronger mobile power. Flag signaling, flaming arrows and torch signaling were examples. They used many different colors of flags and, to communicate, they used each of them in a specific sequence or specific grouping to compose special meanings. At nighttime, they used flaming arrows or torches in a similar way. The Mongol army was the first to use smokescreen tactics.

Temujin ordered Kasar to make a unique banner. The basic structure of the banner was two parts. One was a cedar tree post and the other was a round silver plate on top of it that had ninety-nine small holes of exactly the same size and distance between each other around the edge. In each of the ninety-nine holes white or black horse mane was knotted, and on top of the pole was a spear blade, making the whole thing nine feet tall. The number ninety-nine referred to the ninety-nine different levels of heaven that the Mongols believed in, and the banner as a whole meant that, with the power and spirit of heaven, Temujin's warriors would defeat the enemy anytime and anywhere. They called it "Sulde" and they had two: one white, for peacetime, and one black, for war.

Temujin's warriors began to gather the horses and the weapons, and the messenger soldiers kept on blowing their horns toward the herders and herd boys to bring their livestock back to the fields.

Temujin could amass at most 3,000 horse soldiers. Temujin called in Kasar and gave an order to take a message to Sacha Beki, the Jurkins' chief.

"The time has come to destroy our common enemy, the Tartars, who humiliated and put an end to our fathers and ancestors. I am officially giving you an order in the name of the khan, to bring your troops, with the maximum number you can mobilize, and join me at Hariltu Lake within three days."

With this order, Kasar, giving a look of doubt and confusion, remarked, "Big brother! It has been a long time since they disapproved of you as the khan. Do you think they will follow?"

Temujin gave a meaningful eye signal and said in a persuasive tone, "Just do as I said."

Three days later, Toghrul Khan joined Temujin with his 10,000 Kerait cavalry. After that, Temujin and Toghrul Khan waited six more days for Sacha Beki, but he never showed up. The next day, Temujin advanced toward the east as the vanguard of the Temujin–Toghrul Khan coalition army.

The Chin troops crossed over the Great Wall and moved along the Ulja River and clashed with the Tartars, who were waiting after building two strong fortresses at the Qusutu and Naratu highlands. The Chin troops, composed of 10,000 cavalry and 40,000 foot soldiers, were losing battle after battle to the Tartars, who had 20,000 cavalry. Megujin Seultu, the commander-in-chief of the Tartars, could see all the movements of the Chin troops from his postion on top of the highlands. The Tartars used the hit-and-run tactic. They opened the gates of the fortresses and attacked the Chin troops at night, when they got tired, or in the evening, when they were cooking their evening meal, and then retreated back into the fortresses when the Chin troops regrouped and began to counterattack.

Wanyen-Xiang, the commander-in-chief of the Chin troops, was very nervous after losing battle after battle and losing a large number of soldiers, including one of his generals. He was stuck there. He couldn't move forward or backward, and could only wait for help from Toghrul Khan, as agreed. Temujin, who was marching forward with his black banner, stopped at the point ten miles from the battleground. He sent out Kasar and Jelme as scouts. Kasar and Jelme returned about half a day later, reporting the situation of the enemy fortresses and geographical characteristics.

"They built up two strong fortresses on the hills at the southern side of the Ulja River. They enclosed the fortresses with ramparts made of big logs. It is impossible to cross over the ramparts with horses. The northern side of the hill is less steep than the southern side, but is protected by the Ulja River. It is not quite appropriate to approach that side with a large number of troops."

After this report, Temujin discussed the situation with Toghrul Khan. Temujin and Toghrul Khan agreed on a night-time surprise attack, because a routine face-to-face attack was presumed to have a very low success rate and a high number of casualties. After this, Toghrul Khan sent Jagambu to the Chin camp to inform Wanyen-Xiang that Toghrul Khan had arrived and asking them to surround the fortresses from the east and southern sides.

After an early evening meal, Temujin's 3,000 surprise attackers began their movement. They searched routes and advanced with the help of the moonlight, leading their horses. Toghrul Khan's main bodies of troops were supposed to start movement later, between two and four o'clock in the morning, and approach the western side of the fortresses.

Temujin's surprise attackers successfully approached the hill underneath the rampart without being noticed. They remained there, motionless, until Toghrul Khan's main body arrived nearby. Temujin looked around the rampart. The Tartars had built up the rampart with tied-up logs up to six feet high, and it stretched out endlessly in two different directions. They were guarding the rampart with seven or eight soldiers, as a team, with a big campfire, and other similar-sized teams were lined up endlessly, every 100 steps. They also lit many torches, lighting it up like daytime, where they believed their weak areas to be, to make it hard to approach. Temujin saw that the enemy chief was an outstanding general who knew how to protect his campaign.

Wind delivered the noises from the Tartar soldiers, talking and occasional laughter, to Temujin's ears. Temujin looked at the sky. The moon hanging in the southwestern sky began to be covered by floating clouds. Temujin sent out an advance force of 500, a special unit. The advance force, led by Kasar, crawled up to the hill, with only minimal weapons, leaving their horses behind. When they got on the rampart, they began to shoot. While some of the commandos were fighting hand-to-hand combat, the others began to destroy the locking system of the gate to open it. Kasar also sent out several dozen soldiers to free the Tartars' horses. They destroyed the fences and set the horses free.

The fortress turned into hell. The sharp sounds of horns blowing from the Tartar guards announcing the urgent situation, horses' neighing, and the clattering noise of horses' hooves were all mixed together and then carried into the air covered by the dark curtain of the night. After confirming the two flaming arrows rising high in the sky, Temujin sent his 2,500 raiders into the southern gate. It was like daytime inside the fortress from the big flames coming from the burning tents. Even the strongest troops cannot stand long when they are hit by a surprise attack. The Tartar soldiers fell like autumn leaves.

When Temujin arrived at a certain point with his troops, he could see a man on his horse, directing the Tartar troops with his sword, protected by several layers of horse soldiers. He had a thick beard and a mustache and was wearing a helmet with two big horns on it. Temujin's sixth sense told him that he was the one he had been looking for, the Tartar chief, Megujin Seultu.

Temujin dashed toward him like a gale, with his spear blade pointing at him. Bogorchu and Jelme escorted him on both sides. The protective layers of horse soldiers covering their chief were crushed like an egg thrown onto a rock. Megujin swung his sword toward the approaching Temujin, but Temujin dodged it by swiftly lowering his head. Megujin's body swayed because of his unsuccessful swing. He turned his horse and began to run away. Temujin ran after him. Temujin's horse soon caught up with Megujin's horse. Temujin caught him with the hooked portion of his spear. Megujin fell to the ground with a short moan and rolled over.

Carefully watching his movements, Temujin slowly got off his horse. Megujin got on his feet and drew out his wide-blade

Chinese sword from his waist. Temujin threw away his spear and took out his scimitar. Temujin slowly approached him and asked him with a voice, low, but filled with dignity, "Are you Megujin?"

The man, who had lost his helmet, just stared at Temujin without saying anything. He raised his sword with his two hands and slowly stepped toward Temujin. His eyes were glaring like a tiger's, even in the darkness. Temujin stepped toward him with his scimitar firmly gripped in his hands. One of them must die. The shadow of death flew down from the dark-blue sky like oil and covered the two men's heads.

The Tartar chief raised his sword high and then swung from above to hit Temujin's head. However, that didn't happen. Instead, Temujin's scimitar cut the artery in his neck. Temujin ducked from Megujin's blade. The opponent fell down on the ground and rolled over a few times. The color of the spurting blood from his neck eerily harmonized with the color of the flames coming from the burning tents. He was still alive. The fallen opponent glared at Temujin, silently, panting.

"In the name of my father and my ancestors, I am giving you this!" And with that, Temujin cut off his head. The head, detached from its body, rolled a few times and then stopped. The blood gushed out of his body for a while. Jelme put the fallen Megujin's head onto his spear tip and marched forward with it raised high in the sky.

At last, the day was breaking. Inside the fortress, it was hard to move around on horseback due to the stacks of dead Tartar bodies all around. The thick smoke from the still-burning tents stained the morning sky dark grey. The surviving Tartars tried to escape toward the west and north, avoiding the southern and eastern sides, which were blocked by the Chin troops; however, they were massacred by the Keraits' troops who arrived there before dawn. Only the escapees to the north made it, and they scattered far away into the steppe.

CHAPTER THIRTY-THREE

Toghrul Gets
the Title of King

Wanyen-Xiang immediately dispatched messengers to Yenking, reporting the victory to the Chin emperor. He also sent Megujin's head, after salting it and putting it in a box. Wanyen-Xiang celebrated the victory the most. His position in the Chin court would surely be solidified. He was the victorious general in the war with the Southern Sung and had been enjoying the power next to the emperor.

Toghrul Khan, Temujin and Wanyen-Xiang got together in the Chin camp. Wanyen-Xiang, the old general with a long grey beard, welcomed them with a big smile on his face, and, as customary in the Chinese culture, he poured Chinese rice wine into big silver cups to the brim and offered it to the guests. He said to Toghrul Khan, "You have rendered distinguished services for the Chin emperor. The title of king will be bestowed upon you as promised."

At that time on the Mongolian Plateau, there was no well-organized government like China's, and many parts of the plateau belonged to the Chin Empire (at least according to them), so it was possible for them to bestow such a title. Toghrul Khan had a very practical reason for accepting. The title of king from the Chin Empire wouldn't bring him any direct profit, but he could remove the Chin's interferences from the area, in particular, a certain part of the Silk Road he had been controlling. In addition, he could improve his image and political status.

Toghrul Khan introduced Temujin to Wanyen-Xiang.

"He is my foster son, Temujin, and he is the most meritorious man in this battle. Without him, the battle would not have been an easy one."

Wanyen-Xiang, after listening to Temujin's distinguished accomplishments through the interpreter, took a close look at Temujin and said, with a smile on his face, "I praise you highly. If you have provided such a distinguished service, I am glad to give you the title 'jaud quri.' That is the highest title I can give you with my power. I will ask his Majesty if you can have the title 'jautau.'"

Jaud quri was the chief of 100 men whose main job was guarding the border, which meant, in case of any urgency, he could draft a hundred men from the nearby village dwellers. Jautau was a slightly higher position, like a garrison chief, who commanded 400 soldiers. These titles or positions meant that, in case of a revolt or riot, they could subdue the troublemakers in the name of the Chin emperor.

These positions had nothing to do with Temujin and he found them meaningless nonsense; however, he didn't refuse.

He just nodded with a smile on his lips. Wanyen-Xiang considered Temujin no higher than one of the many generals under Toghrul Khan and to the eyes of the second man of the mighty Chin Empire, Temujin was just a young man in a remote area. The Chin court, and even Wanyen-Xiang himself, must have been ignorant of the real picture of the Mongolian Plateau and what was going on there. The next morning, Wanyen-Xiang bestowed the title of king upon Toghrul Khan on behalf of the Chin emperor. A huge, temporary, golden tent, the symbol of the Chin court, had been built, and in there, all the Chin generals and the Kerait and Temujin's high-ranking warriors gathered. Wanyen-Xiang performed all the rituals of the Chin court, and then opened the ivory box wrapped with golden silk cloth. He took out the rolled letter from the Chin emperor, and read through the messages. The letter was written in Juchid, so the interpreter reread it in Mongolian. Through the messages, the Chin emperor highly praised Toghrul Khan's distinguished service and entrusted him as the ruler of the northern area.

It looked like it had been already written when Wanyen-Xiang left Yenking.

Next, Wanyen-Xiang gave the royal gift to Toghrul Khan, a golden sword with an ivory handle embedded with precious stones and jewels. Toghrul Khan bowed to the south, twice, where the Chin emperor was, and then received it. Now Toghrul Khan had two titles: one was the Chinese king, which was pronounced "wang" and the other, the nomadic ruler, khan. From that point forward he was called Wang-Khan and that became his official name.

They celebrated their victory together for several days and, at Wanyen-Xiang's suggestion, they erected a memorial stone there. It was 1196 and the year of the dragon. After that, they began their long journey back home. Temujin and Wang-Khan, with mountains of war booty and thousands of livestock that the Tartars had left, were returning to their ordus, forming a long line reaching several miles. Temujin's physical trophies were enormous. Among them were a luxurious bed embedded with hundreds of pearls on its edges and a silver cradle for a baby that used to belong to Megujin Seultu.

While Temujin's soldiers were going around searching and destroying the empty yurts, they found a boy about four or five years old, left alone in a half-burnt yurt. They didn't know who he was, but he was presumed to be a descendant of one of the Tartar's aristocrats, because he was wearing a gold nose ring and a luxurious vest made of golden silk, decorated with expensive sable fur around the edges. The soldiers brought him to Temujin. Temujin liked him because he looked very smart. He put the boy on his horse and they rode together.

Temujin used to pick up orphaned babies and children on the battlefield and bring them into his ordu. His mother, Ouluun, was the one who took care of them. Even though children were descendants of the enemy, it didn't matter to him at all. It was not only from a humanitarian standpoint, but also from a political one. It was Temujin's policy to unify all the tribes on the Mongolian Plateau. Among them were many of the Merkids' and the Taichuts' children. At a later time, many of them grew up to be Temujin's close men and made great contributions to building up the Great Empire. Temujin gave the Tartar boy to his mother, and she favored him very much. She fostered him as her sixth son.

"This boy must be a descendant of a good family and good blood."

As she was saying this, she gave him the name Sigi Qutuku.

CHAPTER THIRTY-FOUR

Surrender of
the Jurkins

Temujin triumphantly marched toward his ordu near Hariltu Lake. He and his 3,000 warriors approached his ordu with several dozen carts stacked with war booty and thousands of cows, horses, camels and sheep. Temujin sensed something weird when he arrived at the point where he could see the lake and numerous mushroom-like domed tents where his ordu was based. Temujin was expecting all the town's children, elders and women to come out to see their family members returning, like they did before. Temujin could see nobody and moreover, he could see no livestock around. Under normal circumstances, livestock would be freely grazing. Temujin's sixth sense told him that his ordu had been raided and looted by other tribes.

Temujin urgently dispatched Kasar and Jelme to find out what had happened. Kasar and Jelme dashed to the ordu, making a long tail of grey dust. Some time later, they came back with an astonishing report.

"We have been raided! It's the Jurkins!"

Temujin was struck dumb by this report. The Jurkins were a group who had pledged loyalty to Temujin as their khan. Temujin had asked Sacha Beki, the Jurkins' chief, to join the war with the Tartars, but the order had been ignored. Temujin had waited for six days. Instead, the Jurkins took advantage of Temujin's absence and raided Temujin's ordu and looted it. That was the reality of the Mongolian Plateau at that time. Yesterday's friend was today's enemy. They were pursuing only two things, power and profit. Sacha Beki must have thought that Temujin could never win the battle with the Tartars.

As Temujin stepped into the ordu, one or two children or women began to emerge from their hiding places, and the refugees, scattered into the plain, came back under Kasar's lead after they confirmed Temujin's return.

"We found our guards." Bogorchu and Jelme reported this after they rushed back from checking around the tent town.

When Temujin arrived at the west side of the lake, he could see about fifty of his guard soldiers tied to the trees, stripped. Temujin left sixty guard soldiers when he departed, and among them, ten were slain, while the remaining fifty were tied to the trees in humiliation.

"How many of them were here?"

"They were surely more than 400. We were outnumbered and couldn't defeat them. They stripped us like this in humiliation. They took all the cows and sheep with them."

Temujin's anger rose to the extreme. He shouted to his warriors, "Now it is very clear! They are our real enemies! Follow me!"

Temujin marched against the Jurkins with his 3,000 warriors. The Jurkins' base camp was on Doloan Hill, near the
Kerulen River, about fifty miles northeast of Temujin's ordu.
Temujin divided his troops in three groups, and appointed
Kasar as the leader of the first group, Bogorchu of the second
and Jelme of the third. He ordered them to surround the Jurkins' base camp. Temujin's troops closed in the circle, killing
all the rebellious Jurkins. In about two hours, they had a firm
grip on the Jurkins.

Temujin chased down Sacha Beki and his younger brother,
Taichu. They were on the run with only four or five close
supporters, and, at last, they fell into the hands of Temujin's
soldiers at the Teletu River mouth. After being tied up, they
were brought in front of Temujin and were forced to kneel
down. Temujin dismounted his horse and slowly stepped toward them. Temujin asked, looking down at them, "In the
past, what did you pledge to me?"

With their mouths closed, Sacha Beki and Taichu, the two
brothers, were just looking forward, their eyes focused on the
distance.

"Answer the question! The khan is asking you!"

Rebuking them, Jelme whipped the two men's cheeks with
his short horsewhip mercilessly. Soon, on their cheeks, the
marks of his whip erupted like red snakes.

Stopping Jelme, Temujin made one more step closer to them
and asked again, "I am reminding you that you two gave me
a pledge to cut off your heads and throw them away in the

field if you failed to follow the khan's order in wartime. Is that right?"

Sacha Beki glanced at Temujin once and said, staring forward again, "I know what I have done. Go ahead. Cut off my head."

Temujin drew his scimitar.

"In the name of the Borjigid Khan, this is for you!"

Temujin raised his scimitar and cut off Sacha Beki's head. The head fell onto the ground, making a short, low, dull sound and rolled over a few times as the body without the head thudded to the ground. Temujin also cut off Taichu's head. That was the way Temujin recovered his lost prestige and injured dignity from the Jurkins. They left there with the dead bodies still in the field.

Most of the Jurkins surrendered themselves to Temujin. They pledged allegiance to Temujin as their khan. The Jurkins were the elite group among the Kyat Mongols. Individually, they were outstanding in many ways and peerless warriors. Nonetheless, they were no match for the well-organized troops led by Temujin. Temujin assembled them on the open ground and addressed them in a loud voice, "I will rule my people not by the law, but by the heart and blood. The only way we can survive this world is in unity. Selfishness won't be tolerated and individualism won't be accepted. The selfish individuals are more dangerous than the enemies. I will be fair to everybody and treat you with discretion. Let's get together under one banner and march for glory!"

Thus, about 20,000 people of 4,000 households came under Temujin's rule. While Temujin was heading for his ordu, or base camp, with the newly joined Jurkins, an elderly man drew near Temujin with two young men, seemingly in their mid-twenties. He knelt down in front of Temujin and said, "These are my two sons, Mukali and Buqa. I am giving you my two sons as your personal servants."

The man's name was Guun Ua. His two sons, Mukali and Buqa, had good physiques and looked very intelligent and handsome. Temujin was very much drawn to them. Temujin thanked their father and accepted them on the spot. At that time, in the Mongolian culture, the concept of property included people, too, making it possible to give or receive people as gifts.

Let them be your doorkeeper.
If they neglect,
Cut their ligaments and make them cripples.

Let them be your gatekeeper.
If they desert,
Cut their livers out and throw them away in the field.

Guun Ua pledged allegiance to Temujin in this way. In the same way, Chilagun Qauchi's two sons, Tungge and Qasi, were given to Temujin also. A young man named Jebke was given to Kasar. Jebke brought a boy in his early teens named Boroqul, who was an orphan. Boroqul was sent to Temujin's mother, Ouluun, and for some years, he was under her care.

People kept gathering around Temujin, making his group a huge one. Altan and Quchar, who had been away from Temujin for some years, and even Temujin's uncle Daritai, rejoined him with their kuriyens, groups of more than 1,000 households.

Basically, Temujin didn't like the people who came to him when he was strong and left when he was weak. Temujin just followed his father's policy: "I don't stop anyone who comes to me; at the same time, I don't stop anyone who is leaving." Temujin began to purge the unacceptable Jurkins. Most of the Jurkins wanted to follow and support Temujin from their heart, but not all of them. Some of them were rejecting Temujin's leadership, in spite of the fact that they had surrendered. They were the ones who could turn into enemies at any moment. One of them was Buri Boko. Buri Boko was a big man who was the Jurkins' champion wrestler. By that time, nobody had beat him. Several dozen of his opponents had been killed by him breaking their necks or spines during a wrestling match.

One day, Temujin had a banquet for his high-ranking warriors. A huge rectangular tent was erected and red Persian carpets were spread on the floor. At the Chinese tables, which were placed in front of about 200 attendees, wine and food were served continuously by women who were clad in thin, luxurious silk garments. The musicians played their musical instruments, filling the tent with smooth music. Some time later, a female singer, in fine pink and purple silk garments and a half-domed cap, with numerous beaded decorations on her head, showed up and began to sing a song.

CHAPTER THIRTY-FOUR

The two main posts
Of the pagoda of life,
Are love and passion.
The two main wheels
Of the cart of life,
Are love and passion.

Inextinguishable flame of desire
That is love.
Inexhaustible fountain of desire
That is passion.

Have you had a drink
Of the wine of love?
Have you emptied
The goblet of passion?

Where the joyous angel spreads its wings,
And a sweet melody of a flute echoes through,
It is in the crystal palace of love.

Please, don't blame me,
Because those are the only truth of life.
Are you willing to come with me
To burn this night out, together?

When spirits at the banquet were high, Temujin gestured to Bogorchu, who was sitting near him. Bogorchu stood up from his seat, drew everybody's attention, opened his mouth and said,

"Folks, we are all enjoying this banquet and everything is fine except one thing. We are missing something. That is a wrestling match. As you all know, our champion is Buri Boko. He has the official record of sixty wins out of sixty fights. He is still undefeated. We all admire his extraordinary performance. Folks, let's give him a big hand."

A thunderous clapping of hands burst out and lasted for a while. Bogorchu waited patiently until it became quiet, and continued his talking.

"But, now, we have one man who is going to challenge him, to break his record. His name is Belgutei. In the past, he was defeated once. He said this will be his return match to redeem himself. He said he is well-prepared. Folks, let's give him a big hand, too."

Thunderous applause burst out again. No sooner had Bogorchu finished speaking than Buri Boko showed up through the southern entrance. He was only wearing triangular-shaped leather pants and long boots. He stepped into the ring, which was specially arranged in the center of the hall, and began warming himself up, rotating and swinging his neck and arms. At this moment, Belgutei stepped in, also only in leather pants and boots. As the two giants stood facing each other, thunderous cheers filled the inside of the tent.

At last, the wrestling match between the two giants began. For a while, the duel was neck-and-neck. The excited audience shouted and shook their fists in the air. However, Buri Boko seemed to be lacking one crucial element of winning, spiritual power. He seemed to know that he was destined to die. As he was twisting his right hand, Belgutei stuck out a leg and tripped him up. Buri Boko fell down like timber. Belgutei sat on his back with his two hands on Buri Boko's chin. Belgutei quickly looked at Temujin. Temujin bit his lower lip firmly.

Losing no time, Belgutei pulled in his two hands swiftly and strongly. A dull, low, breaking sound reached even the ears of some of the servants who were standing and watching the duel at the southern entrance. That sound was Buri Boko's neck breaking. The banquet hall became absolutely silent. Belgutei grabbed his hair and lifted his head. His eyes had rolled up and bubbles were flowing from the corners of his mouth. He was already dead. Four men came in and moved him out, holding each one of his four limbs. There was a stir among the audience.

Temujin's grandfather was Bartan Bagatur and his younger brother was Qukuktu Munggur. The son of Qukuktu Munggur was Buri Boko. So, even though Temujin was in the same age group as Buri Boko, he was an uncle to Temujin in the family lineage.

Bogorchu got on his feet again and spoke as if he were trying to change the mood, "Folks, now we have a new champion, Belgutei! Let's congratulate him and give him a real big hand."

Applause and cheers filled the tent. The banquet continued. The musicians went back to their musical instruments, making smooth music, and wine and food were served again without interruption. Their banquet continued until midnight with noise and laughter.

CHAPTER THIRTY-FIVE

Battle with the Taichuts

Two years had passed. The vast Mongolian Plateau was once again covered with spring buds. Temujin was now in his early thirties. He began to show his dignity and greatness. His facial skin, covering his broad forehead and balanced cheekbones, was suntanned due to the desert's hot air and the strong sunlight that poured onto the plateau. His sparkling eyes were imbued with the reverence of the Everlasting Blue Sky, the spirit of the Burkan Mountain, the greatness of the steppe and the unyielding, resilient life force of the desert. His straight and well-balanced nose and firmly closed lips showed his strong will and decisiveness and projected an image of trustworthiness and reliability. He was tall and strong, with a backbone as hard as stone and muscles as tough as those of the Siberian black bear.

He always kept in his mind what he had learned from his father.

Leadership is to make others help you accomplish what you want.

*Be fair to everybody. People cannot tolerate unfairness
any more than hunger.*

*While they are with you, inspire them to believe they will
be winners. Then they will follow you to the end of the
world.*

*Everybody has a weakness and something they need.
Make up for it and supply them. They will become one
with you.*

*There are two sides of human nature, one that will push
them and one that will pull. One is fear, and the other
is greed.*

*People are constantly seeking two things: safety for their
bodies and satisfaction of their souls.*

Temujin decided to make the very first step toward the unification of the Mongolian Plateau. This was a long-cherished
dream of his and his ancestors. His first target was the Taichuts.
The Tartars were the enemy of his father and ancestors; the
Taichuts were his enemy.

Temujin had very good reasons to make the Taichuts his
number-one target. They took away all the property, seen or
unseen, that his father had left, and drove him and his family
into utter poverty. After that, they still continued to try to take
his life.

Temujin had numerous outstanding friends, supporters and warriors: the master archer, his brother Kasar; the
wrestling champion, his brother Belgutei; his right-hand man
and number-one supporter with good sense and judgment,

Bogorchu; a man with supreme loyalty and courage, Jelme; a man with a mountain lion's heart and a fox's wits, Subedei; a man with courage, wits and decisiveness, Chimbai; a gallant soldier with good swordsmanship, Chilaun; a man who dared to stand in front of 1,000 enemies, Mukali; a man with a leopard's swiftness and a skillful spearman, Kubilai; a man with the valor to gallop into 10,000 enemy soldiers, Quylda; the best axman, with extreme cruelty, Julchedai; and a teenage soldier with high expectations, Boroqul. About 13,000 soldiers were under Temujin's rule, but Temujin had no more than 7,000 troops of his own. The other 6,000 belonged to Altan, Quchar and his uncle Daritai and they didn't receive direct orders from Temujin. Temujin trained his own troops to be the best.

At the upper part of the Onon River, in a large basin area where they could see the foggy image of the grandeur and mysteriousness of the Burkan Mountain, was a tent city, densely populated with about 20,000 yurts. That was the place where Temujin's father, Yesugei, used to camp. Now it became the base campsite for the Taichuts, led by Talgutai Kiriltuk.

One day, Talgutai was conversing with his brother and his generals, Todogen Girte, Achu Bagatur, Qodun Orchang and Quduguldar, over wine goblets. Talgutai, now middle-aged, had become a very obese man of over 300 pounds. His fatty face, with a short moustache and his slanted two eyes with swollen eyelids gave him an appearance of cruelty and arrogance. Sitting on a big sofa, custom-made for him, he opened his mouth and said in husky voice, after taking a sip of kumis from his large silver cup, "Lately, I have noticed that Temujin has been making very unusual movements. The odds are that he will attack us. What shall we do? Tell me, if you have any ideas."

Todogen, with his untidy thick beard and moustache, spat as if it were a matter of no seriousness, "Big brother, what are you worrying about? Their manpower is not even half of ours. They are just a disorganized rabble. We can destroy them any time we want!" Todogen uttered this without hesitation, probably in a belief of their 30,000 troops backing them.

With a grimacing face, Talgutai remarked in admonishment, "You tend to underrate Temujin. That's your problem. I know him. He should not be underrated. In the old days, he slipped from our hands."

With a displeased look, Todogen remarked, "That was your fault, big brother. We should have killed him right after we captured him."

As the two brothers were arguing with each other, Achu, who was sitting next to them, cut in on their conversation. He was the best general among the Taichuts, and had won numerous battles, so was given the title Bagatur, which meant the brave.

"Lord, what is the exact number of Temujin's troops?"

Talgutai gave an answer in an unpleasant mood, "Based on the information I have, he has about 13,000 men."

Achu gave that a little thought, staring into space, and then said, "Thirteen thousand? Don't you think we can handle that with our power?"

This time, Qodun Orchang cut in on the conversation, "In this case, the real point is Wang-Khan's reaction. If Wang-Khan joins Temujin, it would be a tough job. He is 40,000 strong and is controlling the western region."

At Qodun Orchang's short remark, Talgutai responded with a wry grin on his lips, "The old weasel is very crafty. If there's nothing in it for him, he will never join him. Even if he joins him, if things don't go well with Temujin, he will easily turn his back on him."

This time, Todogen said, "Big brother, let's hit them before they attack us. We'd better do it before they become stronger."

They were all silent at Todogen's suggestion. All eyes fell upon Talgutai. After slowly putting his silver cup on the table, Talgutai spat out his words, "Fine! We hit them first. We will start on the last day of April, just one month from now."

Temujin was learning every detail of the Taichuts' movements. Temujin was well aware of the importance of espionage. He had already established his own spy system in every major group or tribe on the Mongolian Plateau. He appointed his brother Kasar as spy chief and received reports from him on a regular basis.

Before dawn, on the last day of April, Talgutai moved his troops of 30,000 cavalry toward the Quba Qaya, the place of Temujin's base camp. The Quba Qaya was located 250 miles southwest of the Taichuts' camp. The Taichuts' advancement was reported to Temujin immediately.

The sound of the horns declaring a state of emergency resounded through the wide area of Quba Qaya. Temujin's warriors gathered quickly in the open space with their helmets and armor on. Temujin's 7,000 elite troops had practiced this numerous times before. In their right hands were well-polished, shining spears, and in their left hands and arms were round leather shields. On the left and right sides of their waists were scimitars and Turkish daggers, respectively. Each of them was carrying his own bow on his shoulder and a quiver, a battle-ax and a mace on his horse's waist and hip. It took only moments for them to assemble themselves fully armed on their horses. Temujin saw the importance of the speed of the troops' movements in operation, and so, much of the time, his drills were invested in increasing the mobile power.

The reflected rays of the rising sun from the well-polished spears of Temujin's neatly lined cavalry were dazzling. Temujin began the ritual. After he kowtowed nine times, he prayed to the heaven in a loud voice, with his two hands raised high.

> *Oh! The almighty,*
> *Everlasting blue heaven!*
> *You allowed me unlimited power.*
> *Let me destroy the Taichuts!*
> *And so, let me place the foundation,*
> *For the unification of this land.*

Only the glorious victory is waiting,
In front of your followers,
While all the others shall be blown away
Like the ashes in the wind.
Your enemy is my enemy,
And my enemy is your enemy.

Let your will be done!

He picked up a ladle made of cedar and scooped kumis from a wooden bucket, also made of cedar, and sprinkled it on the ground nine times. The warriors began to chant in a loud voice, as they pushed their spears into the air repeatedly, "Temujin Khan! Temujin Khan! Temujin Khan!"

The thunderous shouts of the warriors echoed into the vault of the sky, like the voice of the earth shaking the ground. Next, Kokochu, the official chief priest of the ordu, stepped out and blessed the troops.

The supreme god, Tab Tenggri,
Allow victory for Temujin!
The Taichuts will be blown away,
Like leaves in a gale,
And will cease to exist on this land,
Forever.
This is the will of God.

Kokochu, wearing a white, cone-shaped headgear with a flapping rim covering his neck and a white robe, waved the ritual fan three times over the heads of the warriors. The fan had a handle as tall as him and numerous thin willow branches on its head to expel the evil spirits and ensure the good fortune of the battle. The warriors again began to chant.

"Tenggri! Tenggri! Tenggri!"

The war drums began to beat. Two huge cowhide drums were secured on both the left and right sides of each of nine camels' backs, and the drummers, sitting behind them, beat the drums rhythmically. Temujin's 7,000-strong cavalry marched forward in an orderly manner, with their banner in front of them. The vanguards were Bogorchu, Mukali and Kubilai. The leader of the left wing, with its 1,000 cavalry, was Subedei; Kasar was on the right wing leading 1,000; Julchedai was with the 1,000 rear guards; and Temujin himself led the central troops of 3,000. Jelme, the second-in-command of the central troops, asked Temujin, riding side by side with him, "Lord, where are we going to meet the Taichuts?"

Temujin gave an answer without turning his head, "We will see them at the entrance of the Sira Tala Plain, on the north-eastern side of Jalaman Mountain. They will be slow."

Temujin was right. Talgutai was riding a two-wheeled war wagon instead of a horse due to his extreme weight.

They couldn't speed up.

Temujin stepped onto the Sira Tala Plain after passing Jalaman Mountain. On the left-hand side of the entrance, they could see the foggy images of the faraway Kurelku Mountains, while on the right, they faced a vast reed forest, which was taller than a man on a horse. Just after detouring around the reed forest, Temujin stopped because numerous small, hazy images of men and horses emerged on the northeastern horizon. As time went by, the images became clearer. They were the Taichut troops with thousands of banners in front of them. They were approaching, shaking the ground and making clouds of dust. The sun was hanging in the vault of the sky and the air was cold, as if it were foretelling the massacre that would happen in a moment. The reeds were waving, dancing, in the dry desert wind from the south. Temujin ordered his troops to get ready for battle. The vanguards for the Taichuts, Achu, Qodun Orchang and Quduguldar, found Temujin's troops. Achu sent out the signal by raising his hand high to stop his troops. The 30,000 Taichut horse soldiers stopped marching right away. Achu took several steps forward to take a careful look at Temujin's troops and the surrounding geography. After that, he turned around and galloped to his main troops to report to Talgutai.

"Temujin seems to have only seven or eight thousand troops. The other five or six thousand must be hiding somewhere. To the left of Temujin's troops, I saw a reed forest, which I do not know the size of. There is a chance that the rest of them are hiding there. I think it would be better to fall back three miles and meet them there."

At this suggestion, Todogen, who was standing on his horse next to Talgutai's wagon, gave an unpleasant look and disagreed in a loud voice, "What? Fall back? What nonsense!

We've never done that before. They are just a rabble. Destroy them in one blow! That's the best way!"

Talgutai stopped Todogen's harsh words with his golden commander's baton and thought for a moment. He then opened his mouth and spoke slowly, "There are some good points in Achu's comments. However, we will advance as planned, but detour the reed forest. Destroy everything in front of you."

Achu couldn't continue to object. He went back to his position and drew out his scimitar, raising it high.

He shouted to his 10,000 vanguard troops, "We, the vanguards of 10,000, will break through their defense line. Soon, 10,000 of our main troops will arrive at the battle area. The moment they arrive, we will turn around and hit the enemy on both sides with our main troops. Don't get close to the reed forest! Detour around it!"

That was the strategy the Taichuts made before they left. They divided the attacking troops into three groups, the vanguards, the first main body and the second main body. The vanguards would break through the defense line without fighting, and, when the first main body arrived, they would turn around and attack Temujin's troops from both directions. When Temujin's troops were halfway destroyed, the second main body would be sent into the battlefield for complete annihilation. This plan was made on the assumption that Temujin's 13,000 troops would move in one mass because of their inferiority in numbers.

Achu Bagatur, pointing at Temujin's troops with his scimitar, shouted, "Charge! Forward!"

The Taichuts' vanguards dashed toward Temujin's troops, like a tidal wave. It would be a scary scene to see 10,000 soldiers on horseback approaching, making a thunderous sound and shaking the ground. Temujin's soldiers were waiting for the order from their commander in complete silence and stillness. Temujin, watching every movement of the Taichuts from a small hill, told Jelme, who was standing next to him, "They won't fight. They will just pass through. Let them through! Try not to touch them."

Jelme, by the order of the commander, gave the instruction to the banners unit. Next, three of the blue banners were raised high by the unit soldiers, and then Temujin's main troops split into two parts without delay. The arriving Taichuts' vanguards passed through Temujin's defense line without major fighting.

Next, Temujin gave an order to shoot three godoris, the arrows that whistled when shot, toward the peak of Jalaman Mountain. The three godoris flew to the mountain peak one by one, making an earsplitting, high-pitched sound. Just then, on the round mountaintop, the image of thousands of horses with soldiers appeared. They were the 6,000 cavalries of Altan, Quchar and Daritai, who had been waiting at the same spot for three full days by the order of Temujin. Temujin ambushed his enemies behind the top of Jalaman Mountain, not in the reed forest. Achu's vanguards were crushed like eggs hit by rolling rocks and swept away by Temujin's 6,000 ambushing cavalry.

The red banners were raised high in Temujin's headquarters, because the movement of the second group of Taichuts had come into view. The leader of the Taichuts' second group was Todogen. Todogen, at the front of his group, with his spear pointing forward, was drawing near like a gale. Temujin's archers, all together, began shooting toward the approaching enemies. The Taichuts kept on dashing, jumping over their fallen comrades and horses.

From out of Temujin's headquarters, the war drums began to beat all at once, and just then, Temujin's vanguard, 1,000 cavalry led by Bogorchu, Mukali and Kubilai, counterattacked. Kubilai, who was at the front of the group, dashed toward Todogen. The two warriors ran toward each other at full speed, with their spears pointing at each other's hearts. One of them fell from his horse and thudded on the ground, making a short moan. It was Todogen, who was speared through his waist by Kubilai. Todogen's spear blade made only a minor scratch on Kubilai's cheek. Temujin put his right and left wings into the battlefield. The Sira Tala Plain changed into a fierce battlefield and the place of a massacre.

Temujin's main troops were still not moving. Temujin was waiting for the third group of Taichuts. Soon, the third group came into sight. According to their plan, the Taichuts' third group was supposed to be the final blow to Temujin's troops; nonetheless, they became merely the rescue group for their first and second groups.

Temujin slowly began to move. He was escorted by two warriors, one on each side, Jelme on the left, and on the right was Boroqul, a teenaged warrior who joined in battle for the first time.

Temujin sent in all his troops. So did the Taichuts. They both knew that the Kyat Mongols and the Taichuts could not coexist under the same sky. This was the decisive battle for both of them, for their very existence. One of them must be gone forever. Temujin cut down numerous enemy soldiers approaching him, again and again, like waves. Temujin's helmet and armor were stained with blood. Temujin faced several dangerous moments, but with the help of Jelme and Boroqul, he managed.

The battle lasted until early evening. The purple-hued veil began to cover the western sky and long, thinly stretched clouds hanging on the horizon were reflecting orange and pomegranate red as they crossed each other.

The Sira Tala Plain was covered with countless dead bodies, some without heads, some of which had been cut in half, some bodies with crushed skulls, bodies with exposed internal organs and heads, hands and arms without bodies. Some of the Taichuts hid in the reed forest because that was the only escape route. Temujin had already told his men not to go in there. Temujin's soldiers set fire to the reed forest. The reeds, which were dried out during the winter season, caught fire quickly and the flames and smoke soon flared up. In a moment, the whole reed forest was enveloped in flames. The Taichuts' horses inside the forest neighed and bolted out of it.

Temujin's soldiers cut off the Taichuts who were coming out of the forest one by one.

Talgutai began to run away toward the north under the escort of Achu and Qodun Orchang, with only a couple thousand of his defeated troops. Talgutai lost a total of 22,000 men, of which 20,000 were dead and 2,000 held captive. Temujin lost 2,000 men. Todogen and Quduguldar were dragged and brought in front of Temujin. They were wounded, but were still alive.

Temujin gazed at Todogen for a while and asked him in a low, quiet voice, "Do you remember my face?"

Kneeling with his hands tied behind his back, Todogen raised his chin and looked at Temujin's face, with the eyes of a dead man, a man who has lost everything. He was just panting, with no response. Temujin left there, leaving him to Julchedai. Temujin also left the 2,000 captives to Bogorchu.

Bogorchu gave an order to his soldiers, "Among the captives, anyone who is not Taichut and is willing to convert, leave him alive until further instruction. However, anyone who has Taichut blood or bone should be cut into pieces!"

Many of the Taichuts' soldiers were not Taichuts, but subordinated tribesmen.

Julchedai took Todogen and Quduguldar out to the field and cut their feet off with his ax. The two men shrieked for a while and then became quiet. Temujin set out to chase down Talgutai, with only his 3,000 center troops.

CHAPTER THIRTY-SIX

Fall of the Taichuts

I t was getting dark and Temujin was with Jelme, Boroqul and Chilaun. Temujin was tracking the footsteps of the defeated Taichuts' remaining troops. After about fifty miles of chasing, Temujin faced a huge mountain covered with thick forest. It was already dark, so only dim light from the waning crescent moon showed the image of the mountain, standing like a demon. Temujin felt displeased. He stopped the movement of his troops. The mountain was enveloped in total silence and death was in the air; the occasional sound of wind passing through the needles of the pine trees passed by the edge of total silence.

No sooner had the short, whistling sound hit Temujin's eardrum than he felt sharp, piercing pain around his neck, along with a breeze on his facial skin. In the following moments, Temujin could hear the sounds of some soldiers behind him falling off their horses with short screams and thudding on the ground. Hundreds of enemy arrows were showering over the heads of Temujin's soldiers. As Temujin jumped down from his horse, he shouted towards his soldiers, "Get off your horses! Hide yourselves in the forest!"

Temujin and his soldiers spread out into the forest. Temujin lay on the ground on his face, with his dagger drawn, in case of an enemy attack. Total darkness made it impossible for them to recognize someone who was just a few steps away. Temujin never neglected to train his troops on every occasion, and in that kind of situation, they were told that they should never make a fire, not expose themselves, never talk to each other in loud voices, minimize their body movements, spread out instead of grouping and should never fall asleep, among other tactics. The forest was again enveloped with deep silence, with the exception of periodic waves of cold wind sounds. Temujin lay on the ground in complete stillness. The humidity from the thick layers of fallen leaves infiltrated into his body through the leather armor. At this moment, Temujin could sense and hear a dark figure approaching, making its way through the fallen leaves. Temujin paid complete attention to that side, tightly holding his dagger. The unknown moving figure stopped at a certain point and whispered, "Lord, I am Jelme. Are you all right?"

He was Jelme. Temujin felt relieved. Suddenly, Temujin began to feel a sharp pain in his neck. The Taichut's arrow had scratched his neck, making an open wound on his neck. Temujin hadn't noticed that the blood from his neck vein was wetting his neck and shoulder. On the right side of his neck, a thick blood clot was forming even while the bleeding continued. Temujin said to Jelme in a low voice, "I think I was hit with an arrow in my neck."

Under the dim crescent moonlight, Jelme took a careful look at Temujin's wound. Jelme tried to stop the bleeding by pressing the wound with a cotton cloth he was carrying. Jelme told Temujin in great worry, "Lord, the poison should be sucked out. If not, it could be dangerous."

Some of the tribes on the Mongolian Plateau were using poisoned arrows. The Taichuts were one of those. They used either Chinese- or Persian-made poison arrows and the Chinese were more powerful. The Chinese merchants sold the poison at a high price, but the ingredients and manufacturing process were secret. The Chinese poison paralyzed the nervous system. The victims usually lost their eyesight first and then died of suffocation because they were unable to breathe. Usually they died within four hours of being poisoned.

Jelme began to suck out the poison with his mouth. He repeatedly sucked out a mouthful of blood with poison and spit it out. The corners of his mouth were stained with blood. Temujin lost consciousness for a while. This time, Jelme had to stop the bleeding. He tended and nursed Temujin all through the night. He had to take off his clothes to cover Temujin, to keep his body temperature from falling.

The dawn was near. Misty images of trees and rocks began to reveal themselves. Numerous drops of sweat were sitting on Temujin's forehead, even though the morning was cold.

It was a critical moment for Temujin, a matter of life and death. Temujin muttered, moaning, in his consciousness or unconsciousness, "Water! Let me have water!"

Jelme knew he needed water because of the blood loss. However, he realized that he left his sheepskin bag with sheep's milk on his horse. He couldn't call out to his men because numerous Taichut soldiers were hiding in the same place. He took off all his remaining clothing, except his short pants. He began to look around nearby for water. Before long, he could see three soldiers under a huge larch tree and, around them, three horses with leather bags on their backs, which looked like they were holding some sheep or mare's milk. Jelme approached them at a slow pace. They were in the Taichuts' uniforms. Because of the indication of someone approaching, one of them woke up from his short sleep and leapt to his feet, drawing his scimitar. Because of this, the other two got on their feet simultaneously.

"Halt! Who are you? Identify yourself!"

As he approached, Jelme gestured for them to be quiet. The Taichut soldiers felt relieved because the stranger was all by himself, with no weapons. Yet they gave him a dubious look, putting their heads a little to one side, because the stranger was almost naked.

"Be quiet! Temujin's soldiers are around here. I am Talgutai Khan's secret guard. Did you know that Talgutai Khan was wounded last night? All through the night I nursed him, covering his body with my clothes. He needs something to drink, immediately. Give me your sheep or mare's milk, if you have any. Hurry up!"

Jelme knew they were calling Talgutai khan. One of them untied the bag from the horse and handed it over to Jelme.

"Thanks! What's your name? You will get rewarded from the khan later on."

The soldier who handed over the bag answered in a low voice, hesitantly, "My name is Gonba."

"Oh! Gonba! I will never forget that name."

Jelme bade farewell to them. He even waved his hand to them. The three Taichut soldiers were just standing there, gazing at him blankly.

Jelme let the milk flow into Temujin's mouth. Temujin began to regain his consciousness. The bleeding had also completely stopped. The morning had dawned bright, and yet it was quite foggy. The birds were chirping everywhere. Temujin opened his eyes and looked around.

"Oh! I can see again!' Temujin's eyes turned upon Jelme, who was standing by him, almost naked. "Why are you standing there almost naked?"

Temujin had his eyes wide open in surprise. Jelme had to explain the things that happened while he was unconscious.

"Lord, I had to look around for water or milk. If I went around in my uniform, it would be trouble if I encountered the Taichuts. That's why I had to take it off."

After all the stories, Temujin laughed without making a sound. Temujin held his hand tightly and then said, "Jelme, you are my shade and a real comrade. From the very early days, you have helped me a lot and now I owe you another one. I will never forget your devoted support."

After that, Temujin's trust in Jelme doubled.

Temujin regrouped his troops and praised his soldiers. It was clear that the Taichuts had escaped completely before Temujin regained consciousness. Temujin gave up the immediate chase of the Taichuts because of his neck wound. He remained there and rested until noon.

On the same day, in the late afternoon, Temujin and his 3,000 troops arrived at the top of a hill, where they had a complete view of the upper part of the Onon River, the place of the Taichuts' base camp. Temujin looked at the tent city of countless mushroom-shaped domed tents and the winding Onon River, whose surface was sparkling like precious stones, reflecting the afternoon's sharp angled sunlight. Temujin's mind was filled with thousands of emotions. It was the place he was born, and the place he spent most of his early days. It was the place his father, Yesugei, built a foundation for him and his children. However, the Taichuts took over the place and had been living there for twenty years.

Temujin gave 2,500 troops to Jelme to destroy the remaining Taichuts' power and take over the city. Temujin himself set up the tents on the hill and stayed there with his 500 troops. Chilaun also stayed there, supporting Temujin.

Jelme, with his 2,500 troops, attacked the tent city at dusk. The last resisting powers of the remaining Taichuts, who hurriedly built a defense line at the entrance of the city, were annihilated. Jelme jumped over the piles of bodies of dead Taichuts and entered the city. Jelme's soldiers set fire to the yurts, and the flames lit the town like daytime. The Taichuts' tent city turned into hell. Shrieks and screams, the beating sound

Sokan Shira answered in a depressed voice, "I wanted to. ...t my daughter, Qadaan, married a Taichut, so I just stayed ...re."

Temujin called for Chilaun. Chilaun was not far from there, ...they had a family reunion. Temujin said to Chilaun, "This ...my fault. But why didn't you tell me that you had to go to ...ve your family members?"

Chilaun answered, lowering his head, "Saving my family ...mbers is a personal thing. When the khan's official order ...s not been carried out completely, I didn't think it was the ...ht time to ask for personal things. So, I didn't."

Temujin nodded. Temujin invited them into his interim ...an's tent and consoled them. Temujin treated them like his ...n family members ever after that.

Talgutai was on his way north with only his family members ...d close followers. He was heading for the Merkids' territory ...surrender to them because they were enemies of Temujin. ...ong the followers accompanying him was an old man named ...guetu who had two sons, Alak and Nayaga, both in their ...enties. He wasn't a Taichut; he was a Baarin of the Nichugud ...nch, which was a subordinated tribe to the Taichuts. He was ...no mood to be loyal to the completely destroyed Taichuts ...more. He was worrying about his two sons' futures. He ...de up his mind to surrender to Temujin with his two sons. ...Talgutai and his followers had been running all through the ...ht and arrived at a small hill with a forest around daybreak.

of the horses' hooves, the collapsing sounds of burning yurts, all these mixed together and echoed through the dark space.

Jelme faithfully carried out Temujin's proclamation: "The ones with Taichut bone, even the young ones, any taller than the center wheel of a wagon, shall be cut into two pieces."

At that time, the height of the center wheel of a wagon was about four feet, and so, usually boys older than seven or eight years old were in this category. However, Taichut women, girls, slaves and other tribesmen and tribeswomen were saved. Temujin's policy was not to accept the Taichuts as prisoners. Talgutai escaped to the north, with only his family members and several dozen of his close servants and aides. Achu Bagatur and Qodun Orchang, left alone, escaped to the east.

CHAPTER THIRTY-SEVEN

✳

The Last of Talgutai

The night was far advanced, yet the flames from the burning yurts in the Taichuts' tent city continued to flare up and the dark smoke was soaring into the dark-blue night sky endlessly. In the nearby open space, thousands of Taichut women and their babies were put together with their former slaves, and Temujin's soldiers, on their horses, were guarding them. In the burning tent city, Temujin's soldiers were controlling and guiding the people who were moving around in confusion. Some soldiers were taking the belongings from the yurts that had not burned, and some others were gathering the livestock, which had scattered in all directions.

Temujin was discussing the control and management plan for the aftermath of the war with his men. Just then, a woman's sharp screaming in despair came from a distant place. Everybody could hear it. Temujin called his meeting off and paid attention to the screaming. Soon, the woman's screaming turned into wailing, and then she repeatedly shouted something. Temujin gestured his men to be quiet and bent his ear to the woman shouting.

"Temujin! Temujin!"

She was calling Temujin. Who dared to call Temujin Temujin opened the flap door and stepped outside followed him. Temujin mounted his horse and ro direction of the woman shouting. A moment later arrived at the spot where the woman was sitting on th wailing and screaming, and beside her, a man lay dea her were several of Temujin's soldiers and an elderly was holding the hands of two small children who be his grandchildren.

Temujin dismounted his horse and, after taking a one of his soldiers, he flashed it in the woman's fac was very familiar to Temujin. Temujin quickly reali was Qadaan. When Temujin was captive in the Taic a nine-year-old girl hid him in a wool cart and w him. Temujin never forgot her face. Now, she wa with children. Temujin, looking at her, asked her voice, "Qadaan, I am Temujin. Do you recognize

The woman looked at Temujin in surprise. Tem her, and patted her back. Qadaan said to Temu "The soldiers tried to kill my husband, so I calle to save him."

Temujin carefully checked the fallen man. His n cut in half and he was already dead. This unlu Qadaan's husband. Temujin's soldiers cut his ne him as a Taichut escapee. Temujin looked at the standing by them. He was Sokan Shira. Temujin hands hastily, said to him in regret, "Why didn't a little earlier?"

They hid themselves in the forest and were about to fall asleep out of exhaustion. Sirguetu called his two sons quietly. They approached Talgutai, who was in deep sleep, subdued him and tied his two hands while covering his mouth with cloth to muffle the noise. They put Talgutai into the cart and were about to leave. At this moment, Talgutai's three sons and his brother, who were awoken by the disturbance, were approaching the cart to save him. Sirguetu put a dagger on Talgutai's neck and shouted, "Stay where you are! One more step, I will cut his neck! Lie flat on the ground, on your face! Touch your foreheads on the ground!"

As Talgutai's three sons and brother didn't know what to do and were hesitant, Talgutai shouted to them, "Do as you were told to do! How would it benefit you for me to die? Temujin might not kill me, either! At this moment, listen to him!"

Talgutai repeated the same thing. Talgutai's three sons talked to each other.

"Father is right. If we don't listen to him, he surely will cut our father. At this moment, we'd better listen."

Talgutai's three sons and brother lay down, touching their foreheads to the ground. Sirguetu and his two sons, pushing the cart carrying Talgutai, slipped out of the spot undisturbed. They were headed for Temujin's base camp. A while later, Sirguetu's second son, Nayaga, who was running in front of them, turned back his horse and came to his father.

"Father, Temujin doesn't accept anyone who betrayed his master. Even if we surrender to him, presenting Talgutai, he will treat us no better than someone who betrayed their master. We'd be better going without him. Let's leave him here."

The old man, Sirguetu, thought his second son, Nayaga, was right. It was true that Temujin never accepted anyone who betrayed his master. Even if the master were an enemy, someone who brought his master's neck would surely be beheaded. They continued on their way, leaving Talgutai right at that spot.

Sirguetu and his two sons surrendered to Temujin. They were guided to the khan's tent by soldiers. The old man, Sirguetu, told the full story, from start to finish, to Temujin.

"We were successful in taking Talgutai into our hands, and yet, we couldn't betray our old master. So, we let him free and came here empty-handed. Please, accept my two sons as your slaves, and let them have the chance to support you, though they don't have much to say."

After these words, Sirguetu begged while kneeling and touching his forehead on the ground. His two sons did the same thing. Temujin said, as he was hammering the arm of his chair with his fist, "It is quite right not to betray your master! If you had brought his head, you all might have lost your heads, too."

Temujin accepted the old man, Sirguetu, and his two sons. And then, Temujin eyed his high-ranking warriors standing in two lines near the walls and asked, "The route to the north is rough. He might not have gone too far. Who will go there and bring back his head?"

To these words, Chilaun stepped forward and said without hesitation, "I will surely bring his head."

of the horses' hooves, the collapsing sounds of burning yurts, all these mixed together and echoed through the dark space.

Jelme faithfully carried out Temujin's proclamation: "The ones with Taichut bone, even the young ones, any taller than the center wheel of a wagon, shall be cut into two pieces."

At that time, the height of the center wheel of a wagon was about four feet, and so, usually boys older than seven or eight years old were in this category. However, Taichut women, girls, slaves and other tribesmen and tribeswomen were saved. Temujin's policy was not to accept the Taichuts as prisoners. Talgutai escaped to the north, with only his family members and several dozen of his close servants and aides. Achu Bagatur and Qodun Orchang, left alone, escaped to the east.

CHAPTER THIRTY-SEVEN

The Last of Talgutai

The night was far advanced, yet the flames from the burning yurts in the Taichuts' tent city continued to flare up and the dark smoke was soaring into the dark-blue night sky endlessly. In the nearby open space, thousands of Taichut women and their babies were put together with their former slaves, and Temujin's soldiers, on their horses, were guarding them. In the burning tent city, Temujin's soldiers were controlling and guiding the people who were moving around in confusion. Some soldiers were taking the belongings from the yurts that had not burned, and some others were gathering the livestock, which had scattered in all directions.

Temujin was discussing the control and management plan for the aftermath of the war with his men. Just then, a woman's sharp screaming in despair came from a distant place. Everybody could hear it. Temujin called his meeting off and paid attention to the screaming. Soon, the woman's screaming turned into wailing, and then she repeatedly shouted something. Temujin gestured his men to be quiet and bent his ear to the woman shouting.

"Temujin! Temujin!"

She was calling Temujin. Who dared to call Temujin's name? Temujin opened the flap door and stepped outside. His men followed him. Temujin mounted his horse and rode in the direction of the woman shouting. A moment later, Temujin arrived at the spot where the woman was sitting on the ground, wailing and screaming, and beside her, a man lay dead. Around her were several of Temujin's soldiers and an elderly man who was holding the hands of two small children who seemed to be his grandchildren.

Temujin dismounted his horse and, after taking a torch from one of his soldiers, he flashed it in the woman's face. Her face was very familiar to Temujin. Temujin quickly realized that she was Qadaan. When Temujin was captive in the Taichuts' camp, a nine-year-old girl hid him in a wool cart and watched over him. Temujin never forgot her face. Now, she was a woman with children. Temujin, looking at her, asked her with a soft voice, "Qadaan, I am Temujin. Do you recognize me?"

The woman looked at Temujin in surprise. Temujin hugged her, and patted her back. Qadaan said to Temujin, sobbing, "The soldiers tried to kill my husband, so I called your name to save him."

Temujin carefully checked the fallen man. His neck had been cut in half and he was already dead. This unlucky man was Qadaan's husband. Temujin's soldiers cut his neck, regarding him as a Taichut escapee. Temujin looked at the elderly man standing by them. He was Sokan Shira. Temujin, grasping his hands hastily, said to him in regret, "Why didn't you show up a little earlier?"

Sokan Shira answered in a depressed voice, "I wanted to. But my daughter, Qadaan, married a Taichut, so I just stayed there."

Temujin called for Chilaun. Chilaun was not far from there, so they had a family reunion. Temujin said to Chilaun, "This is my fault. But why didn't you tell me that you had to go to save your family members?"

Chilaun answered, lowering his head, "Saving my family members is a personal thing. When the khan's official order has not been carried out completely, I didn't think it was the right time to ask for personal things. So, I didn't."

Temujin nodded. Temujin invited them into his interim khan's tent and consoled them. Temujin treated them like his own family members ever after that.

Talgutai was on his way north with only his family members and close followers. He was heading for the Merkids' territory to surrender to them because they were enemies of Temujin. Among the followers accompanying him was an old man named Sirguetu who had two sons, Alak and Nayaga, both in their twenties. He wasn't a Taichut; he was a Baarin of the Nichugud branch, which was a subordinated tribe to the Taichuts. He was in no mood to be loyal to the completely destroyed Taichuts anymore. He was worrying about his two sons' futures. He made up his mind to surrender to Temujin with his two sons.

Talgutai and his followers had been running all through the night and arrived at a small hill with a forest around daybreak.

They hid themselves in the forest and were about to fall asleep out of exhaustion. Sirguetu called his two sons quietly. They approached Talgutai, who was in deep sleep, subdued him and tied his two hands while covering his mouth with cloth to muffle the noise. They put Talgutai into the cart and were about to leave. At this moment, Talgutai's three sons and his brother, who were awoken by the disturbance, were approaching the cart to save him. Sirguetu put a dagger on Talgutai's neck and shouted, "Stay where you are! One more step, I will cut his neck! Lie flat on the ground, on your face! Touch your foreheads on the ground!"

As Talgutai's three sons and brother didn't know what to do and were hesitant, Talgutai shouted to them, "Do as you were told to do! How would it benefit you for me to die? Temujin might not kill me, either! At this moment, listen to him!"

Talgutai repeated the same thing. Talgutai's three sons talked to each other.

"Father is right. If we don't listen to him, he surely will cut our father. At this moment, we'd better listen."

Talgutai's three sons and brother lay down, touching their foreheads to the ground. Sirguetu and his two sons, pushing the cart carrying Talgutai, slipped out of the spot undisturbed. They were headed for Temujin's base camp. A while later, Sirguetu's second son, Nayaga, who was running in front of them, turned back his horse and came to his father.

"Father, Temujin doesn't accept anyone who betrayed his master. Even if we surrender to him, presenting Talgutai, he will treat us no better than someone who betrayed their master. We'd be better going without him. Let's leave him here."

The old man, Sirguetu, thought his second son, Nayaga, was right. It was true that Temujin never accepted anyone who betrayed his master. Even if the master were an enemy, someone who brought his master's neck would surely be beheaded. They continued on their way, leaving Talgutai right at that spot.

Sirguetu and his two sons surrendered to Temujin. They were guided to the khan's tent by soldiers. The old man, Sirguetu, told the full story, from start to finish, to Temujin.

"We were successful in taking Talgutai into our hands, and yet, we couldn't betray our old master. So, we let him free and came here empty-handed. Please, accept my two sons as your slaves, and let them have the chance to support you, though they don't have much to say."

After these words, Sirguetu begged while kneeling and touching his forehead on the ground. His two sons did the same thing. Temujin said, as he was hammering the arm of his chair with his fist, "It is quite right not to betray your master! If you had brought his head, you all might have lost your heads, too."

Temujin accepted the old man, Sirguetu, and his two sons. And then, Temujin eyed his high-ranking warriors standing in two lines near the walls and asked, "The route to the north is rough. He might not have gone too far. Who will go there and bring back his head?"

To these words, Chilaun stepped forward and said without hesitation, "I will surely bring his head."

Temujin gave him fifty warriors to chase down Talgutai. Nayaga, Sirguetu's second son, had been picked as the guide.

Chilaun and his fifty warriors set out to chase down Talgutai. They galloped all the way without a single pause, and then finally caught up with Talgutai and his group at a place close to the Merkid's border. Chilaun cut off the heads of Talgutai, his three sons, his brother and his grandchildren, ten in all, and put them into three leather bags. He returned to Temujin's base camp with the three bags, along with three of Talgutai's wives, ten concubines and his sons' wives, a total of twenty-five young and old women.

That was the way Temujin annihilated the Taichuts. But Achu Bagatur and Qodun Orchang escaped to the east and surrendered to Jamuka.

CHAPTER THIRTY-EIGHT

Split of the Naimans

On the Mongolian Plateau, which was bordered by Lake Baikal to the north, the Gobi Desert to the south, the Altai Mountains to the west and the Manchu Plain to the east, many different people and tribes had been holding their ground and had lived there as far back as anyone could remember. They were divided into three major groups, the Turks, the Mongols and the Tungus. There were many similarities among them, including their languages, which had come from the same origin, and later were collectively known as the Altaic languages.

The Mongoloid Turks lived in an area on the western side of the Mongolian Plateau bordered by the Altai Mountains. The neighboring tribes were the Kirghiz to the north and the Uighurs to the south, who were of the same Turkic origin, and to the southwest were the Kara Khitans, of Mongol origin. They were called the Naimans. They were holding both advanced and traditional customs. They had a primitive administrative system modeled after the Chinese and were using the Uighur writing system, but at the same time they were still following 1,000-year-old nomadic customs. Much of their population was Nestorian Christian, and yet the traditional shamans were ruling their spiritual world. They had both Christian priests and shamans.

One day, Inanch Khan, the Naiman ruler, was enjoying his usual nap on a sofa in his huge, luxuriously decorated tent. From noon to about three o'clock in the afternoon, nobody could come into his tent. At around three o'clock, as usual, a young woman with light skin and extreme beauty, in pink, thin silk garments, opened the flap door and entered, after getting permission from the guard soldiers. She was carrying a big shining silver plate, on which was a covered silver goblet containing green tea mixed with fresh sheep's milk. She walked up to the tea table near the khan's sofa and gently put the plate on the brown lacquered teakwood table. She had brown eyes with a bluish tint, thin eyebrows and a nicely shaped nose and lips, and they were all well-proportioned to create an unusual beauty. Her nicely shaped body was visible under her silk garments. Sarazad was her name, a beauty from Samarqand, and she was in full bloom at twenty years old. She was the most beloved concubine of the khan among the sixty of them.

She sat down beside the khan, which was her daily routine. By this time, the khan was supposed to wake up and drink the tea, his first job of the afternoon. Sarazad was suddenly struck by a feeling that was very unusual, weird and frightening. Sarazad carefully examined the khan's face. It was not the face

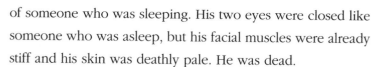

of someone who was sleeping. His two eyes were closed like someone who was asleep, but his facial muscles were already stiff and his skin was deathly pale. He was dead.

She jumped to her feet. She began to shout in shock and horror as she was running toward the door.

"Help! Help the khan!"

She continued to shout as she was coming out of the khan's tent. The two astonished guard soldiers went into the tent, carefully approached the sofa and confirmed the khan's death. The two guard soldiers began to blow their horns, proclaiming a very urgent situation. Soon the open space in front of the khan's tent was swarming with people. Gurbesu, the khan's official first wife, and the khan's two sons, Buyiruk and Tabuka, hurried to the site once they heard the news. They all mourned after they confirmed the khan's death.

All the Naimans' aristocracy, high-ranking officers and generals gathered in the khan's tent.

Gurbesu was a beautiful woman in her thirties. At the same time, she was a woman with a hot temper, extreme jealousy, greed and arrogance. She became the khan's first wife after the former first wife, Asada, the mother of Buyiruk and Tabuka, died. She had been chosen from the group of concubines.

Gurbesu summoned Sarazad. She said to Sarazad, after she picked up the goblet and handed it over to her, "Drink!"

She was suspicious that the khan had been poisoned. Sarazad received the goblet with her soft white hands and then drank the still warm tea in one breath. Nothing happened.

Inanch Khan, in his old age, had died of natural causes. They moved the khan's dead body to his usual luxurious, gold-decorated bed and put a curtain screen around it. They also posted 100 guard soldiers around the khan's tent to control the traffic. Three Nestorian Christian monks in brown robes, with crosses on their necks, prayed and gave a recitation, counting their rosary beads. After this, a shaman in his five-colored silk garment with decorative long birds' feathers on his head, showed up and gave a ritual for the bliss of the dead, beating a small hand drum. That showed a specific feature of the Naiman society, that Christianity and shamanism coexisted.

In the late afternoon, they got together and discussed the details of the funeral procession and ceremony. Those attending were Gurbesu, Inanch Khan's two sons, Buyiruk and Tabuka, and about twenty of the Naimans' high-ranking officials and generals. Inanch Khan was an excellent leader of the Naimans; nonetheless, he made one mistake. He died without making it clear who would be his successor. If they went by the tradition, Gurbesu, the widow of the deceased khan, was supposed to rule as a regent until the enthronement of the new khan. Gurbesu, who had a lust for power greater than a man's, did not waste her chance.

"From this moment, please call me regent. For the time being, I will make the final decisions on every important issue. I am just following our old tradition. Anyone who is against my decision, let me know right now."

Gurbesu said this in front of Buyiruk, Tabuka and other high-ranking officials and generals. Nobody was against her, not only

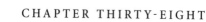

because she was the official first wife of the deceased khan, but also because their tradition was just as she had said.

She looked around at the people present, and continued, "The funeral ceremony will be in three months. Three months should be enough time for the construction of the khan's tomb. Seven messengers have already been dispatched to invite the Uighur morticians and embalmers. I am expecting them late in the evening today."

The Uighurs had the most advanced skills and techniques in tomb construction and embalming at that time.

At this moment, Qori Subechi, the chieftain of one of the Naiman clans, said in his seat, "Why does it take three months to construct a tomb?"

Gurbesu answered, "Three months is just my rough estimate. As soon as the Uighur specialists arrive, I will talk to them and decide. I will let you know all the details of the schedule later on. It is our ardent wish for our beloved khan to rest in peace in the next world. In that regard, I plan to arrange everything, articles and people he loved, for him to take with him to the next world."

Suddenly, there was a deep silence among the audience. Putting the daily articles of the deceased in the tomb with the dead body was quite common. However, for the deceased khan to take people he loved with him, they would have to bury someone alive with him. The first and second sons of Inanch Khan, Buyiruk and Tabuka, were in their forties and when their father was alive, they had to call Gurbesu "mother," although she was only in her early thirties.

This time Buyiruk asked, "What do you mean by letting my father take loved ones with him?" He regarded her dubiously.

Gurbesu answered with a low, quiet voice, "That means let him take his sixty concubines, whom he favored, with him."

The eyes of the other twenty-two people in the room fell upon her in astonishment. She seemed to be undisturbed at all and answered calmly, "That is our tradition, am I right?"

They all looked around and started talking to one another, as this had caused quite a stir. Kokseu Sabrak, the brilliant and best general of the Naimans, got on his feet and calmed the people, then opened his mouth and said, "It is quite true that in the past, we had a custom to bury someone alive with the dead. But nowadays, most of the tribes have given up that belief and they do not do that anymore. Why should we go back to the old barbaric custom? That is not the right thing to do, so we want you to reconsider your plan."

Upon facing tough opposition, she gave a little thought and then said, "Fine. I will respect your opinions. So, instead of sixty, I will put only one. This is my final decision and I do not want to hear any other objections. It would be humiliation for the khan if I have further opposition."

This time Tabuka asked, "Who would be the one?"

Gurbesu answered calmly, "The most beloved woman of the khan, Sarazad."

Some of them groaned and some others sighed. Sarazad was the biggest rival of Gurbesu. There was constant veiled enmity between them and, while the khan was alive, the two were in a private struggle to remove each other.

The steppe people at that time were under the levirate law. If a father died, his brother or one of his sons was supposed to marry his widow, as long as he was not her biological son. Nobody knew when such a custom had started and why. Because of the never-ending conflicts and wars between the tribes that led to extreme social unrest, this law must have arisen. By this law, it was quite certain that Gurbesu would marry one of the deceased khan's two sons, Buyiruk or Tabuka. It was clear that Gurbesu tried to remove Sarazad, who had been her rival in the past, and at the same time, could be her future rival too. Gurbesu knew that both Buyiruk and Tabuka were keeping their eyes on Sarazad and her extreme beauty. They agreed to have the funeral ceremony one month later and adjourned the meeting.

One month later, they had the funeral ceremony. Inanch Khan's tomb was a large rectangular room, built twenty feet underground. Tiles covered the floor and on the plastered walls and ceiling, murals were painted. They arranged the coffin at the northern side of the room, along with many articles he used when he was alive. They slaughtered two stallions and, after embalming them, placed them to the left and right sides of the coffin.

All the royal family members and descendants, his concubines, and about forty of the Naiman clan chieftains and top-ranking generals attended the ceremony. They minimized funeral attendants so the tomb's location would remain secret. The steppe people never erected tombstones, never built any structures or mounds on their burial sites. Once they closed the tomb and covered it with soil, it became part of the leveled ground. With the lapse of time, nobody would be able to tell where the khan's tomb was, and that was what they wanted.

To both the east and west sides of the huge ceremonial altar that was arranged in front of the tomb, were two big bronze incense burners in which aromatic tree bark was burning. After a group of Nestorian Christian monks performed their religious ceremony, the shamans' traditional rituals followed. After the religious ceremonies, Sarazad, beautifully dressed and nicely made up, was pulled out. She was weeping. Two slaves, each holding one arm, ushered her to the entrance into the underground tomb.

At this moment, Sarazad began to resist and tried to shake off the slaves' hands holding her arms. She screamed and yelled at Gurbesu, cursing and yelling, "Gurbesu! You cannot do this! You are the one who should be in here! You will meet the living hell soon!"

Without a big disturbance, Gurbesu shouted back in response, "I am the regent. That is why I cannot be in there! Put her into the tomb, quick!"

Embarrassed and ashamed in the presence of all the attendants, Gurbesu ordered the servants to bring a dagger, a small table and a jewelry box. Gurbesu put her left hand on the table and with a dagger in her right hand, pushed down and cut off two of her fingers, the little and ring fingers. She took her silk cloth from her neck, wrapped the fingers in it and put the bundle into the jewelry box. She ordered the servants to put the jewelry box on the table in front of the khan's coffin.

"This will replace me."

This was the way Gurbesu handled the situation. The funeral ended. A huge square stone cover was placed to close the entrance and after that, they completely covered it with soil. No more screaming and cursing could be heard from Sarazad, who was trapped inside the tomb. Later, all forty slaves and servants, brought for labor and work, were killed to protect the secrecy of the tomb.

Gurbesu had the right to appoint the new khan. She appointed Inanch Khan's second son, Tabuka, as the new khan, instead of the first, Buyiruk. Gurbesu preferred Tabuka, a man of weak character and easy to handle, rather than Buyiruk, a tough one. Gurbesu even declared that she was going to marry Tabuka.

Buyiruk was upset with her decision. He warned Tabuka, "She is a bitch! Don't listen to her!"

Tabuka ignored his brother's warning. He not only accepted the khanship but also married her. Defiant Buyiruk left them and moved to a place close to the Altai Mountains with his followers, clan chieftains and many of the generals, and declared the birth of a new Naiman nation and his khanship. In opposition to his brother, Tabuka declared his legitimacy and titled himself the Tayang Khan, which meant great khan. Thus, the Naimans were split into two nations.

CHAPTER THIRTY-NINE

Temujin and Wang-Khan's Attack on Buyiruk Khan

Temujin became more powerful after he had rooted out the Taichuts and united the Borjigids' clan. Victory over the Taichuts was quite meaningful for him, because he, alone, in a major battle, did it. He portrayed himself as a young bird that had just learned to fly. The very first step of his plan had been a success. What was the next?

One day, Temujin made a visit to Wang-Khan, at Wang-Khan's request. After the banquet, Temujin and Wang-Khan sat down, face to face, in his golden tent, alone. Wang-Khan offered Temujin a goblet of Persian honey wine, which was delivered by a woman slave. Due to his obesity, his voice sounded like he was somewhat out of breath. "I am going to hit the Naimans."

After these words, he again took a sip of the honey wine. Temujin was just looking at his face quietly. As if trying to smooth his husky voice, Wang-Khan kept on sipping his wine, and then continued, "You know that the Naimans have split into two factions. I think this is the right time. I reckon I need your help. That is why I have invited you here, to talk about this."

Wang-Khan sipped his wine again and sat back on his comfortable sofa. He regarded Temujin as if trying to read Temujin's response. Temujin thought for a moment and then asked Wang-Khan, "Which one are you going to hit first? Buyiruk or Tabuka?"

Wang-Khan gave a hesitant response, "Well...which one would you hit first, if you were in my place?"

The Naimans were the sworn enemy of Wang-Khan. It was like the Taichuts were to Temujin. They could never coexist under the same sky. It was definitely necessary that Wang-Khan remove the Naimans for his safety and the future well-being of his people. Temujin knew that. Temujin answered in a careful manner, "Well, my lord, if I were in your situation, I would hit Buyiruk first."

"Any particular reason why?"

"If Tabuka is attacked first, there is a nine out of ten chance Buyiruk would join him. However, in the opposite situation, Tabuka might not care at all."

Wang-Khan gave a look of uncertainty, as if he could not follow. Temujin had to continue with further explanation, "Tabuka's territory is the original Naimans' homeland, where their power and wealth originated. It is rich grazing land. On the other hand, Buyiruk's territory is a remote mountain area, which is no good for nomadic people like us. If Tabuka is attacked first, Buyiruk will join him to save his nation, regardless of the disharmony with his brother. Temporarily he is being pushed away by his brother; however, he might think he is the real owner of the Naiman nation, because he is the firstborn son. If you hit Buyiruk first, Tabuka might not budge, because that's what he wants."

Wang-Khan nestled further into the sofa and pondered a while. Wang-Khan's motivation was not their land. The Keraits and the Naimans had been sworn enemies for a long time and someday, surely, one would conquer the other and enslave them. Wang-Khan wanted to remove the present and future danger in a proactive manner, while he had the muscle. Wang-Khan, sitting up in a straight position, opened his mouth and made his final decision.

"Fine! Buyiruk will be the first one!"

Temujin welcomed his decision. Temujin did not forget to give him additional advice.

"My lord, the Naimans' best generals are with Buyiruk. Be especially aware of Sabrak; it should be a surprise attack, otherwise, you might face a big loss of soldiers."

Wang-Khan asked Temujin calmly, giving him a friendly look, "Will you be with me?"

Temujin responded without hesitation, "Of course, my father lord; I am just one of your vassals. I will be with you, but only on one condition."

Wang-Khan's eyes were wide open. "What could that be?"

Temujin answered again without hesitation, "The operational directorship should be on me, my father lord."

Wang-Khan fell back into his sofa, groaning. What Temujin asked for was the commandership of the whole operation.

Temujin began to persuade Wang-Khan carefully, so as not to hurt his feelings.

"The war with the Naimans could be a tough one. The operations should be controlled in perfect order by one commander. If not, it could mean self-destruction. Please take this into consideration."

Wang-Khan sank into deep thought. Transferring the commandership was not a simple thing; however, Wang-Khan did not want to lose his chance. What he wanted was to remove the Naimans. It did not matter to him who would be the commander-in-chief of this operation, as long as he achieved his objective. Wang-Khan accepted Temujin's condition, "Fine! You are the commander-in-chief of this operation."

Temujin and Wang-Khan discussed the details of the operation until late in the evening. Both agreed to commence the operation one month later, in the form of a surprise attack and agreed to use 7,000 horse soldiers from Temujin's side and 20,000 from Wang-Khan's.

Exactly one month later, Temujin and Wang-Khan marched toward the west, side by side on their horses. Their destination was Soqok Lake close to the Uruk Tak Mountains, a branch of the Altai Mountains. For security purposes, they killed all the individual families and small, migrating groups they encountered on their way. Mainly, they marched at night, resting and hiding themselves in the forests or behind the hills during the day. They arrived at a point thirty miles southwest of Soqok Lake after marching 700 miles in four days and nights. Temujin set out searching, accompanied by Mukali and Boroqul. About twenty warriors followed them. Temujin took the mountain forest route, for safety, to the northwest, to avoid the eyes of possible enemy sentries. When they arrived at the spot close to the lake, they dismounted, hid their horses and walked up to the mountaintop. The image of a military tent at the top, which seemed to be used for the Naiman sentry soldiers, came into Temujin's eyesight. Temujin and his group approached silently. When they reached a point about twenty steps away from the tent, Temujin could hear the sound of the enemy soldiers chatting away. Temujin checked the numbers. They were about four or five. Hiding himself behind a tree, Temujin gestured to Mukali and Boroqul, showing his five fingers. Temujin's warriors crawled up to the top of the hill and fell upon the enemy sentries. They were cut into pieces before they even had a chance to blow the huge horn hanging on the tree.

Temujin stepped onto the mountaintop. The high peaks of the Altai Mountains, with the background of the cobalt-blue sky, were reflecting a mysterious blue hue in the late afternoon sunlight, with a few thin lines of clouds hanging around them. The eastern end of the mountains was connected with low hills that gently sloped toward the lakeshore. The mid-sized lake, which seemed to be created by numerous streams from the mountains, was sparkling like sapphires. In the wide area around the lake, countless dome-shaped felt tents were spread out neatly in a radial pattern. Thin lines of smoke were emerging through the ventilation holes of some of the yurts, possibly a result of cooking the evening meals, since it was close to evening time. It was a quiet and peaceful scene. Temujin engraved the map of the tent city on his memory.

Early in the morning of the following day, the coalition troops of Temujin and Wang-Khan launched an attack on the Naimans' tent city. Temujin divided his attacking force into three groups. The leader of the first group was Bogorchu. The second and third groups were led by Kasar and Jelme, respectively. Wang-Khan divided his troops into three groups, the left wing, center force and right wing. The leaders of his left and right wings were Nilka Senggum and Jagambu, respectively, and he was in charge of the center force. Temujin gave 2,000 horse soldiers to each of the group leaders and he retained the remaining 1,000 troops. Temujin joined Wang-Khan's center force to control the whole operation, since he was the commander-in-chief. After they successfully approached the entrance to the tent city, the attacking forces waited for Temujin's order. Temujin gave an order to raise the banners of five different colors, black, white, yellow, blue and red. Upon the signal, the attacking force of five groups, led by Bogorchu, Kasar, Jelme, Nilka Senggum and Jagambu, spread out and surrounded the city from the north, east and south directions. The next moment, upon the signal of loud drumbeats, the attackers spurred their horses and dashed to the city, shouting their battle cry. Temujin orchestrated the operation just as a superb conductor makes beautiful music.

The Naimans fell down everywhere. They did not have a chance to organize themselves for a counterattack, so they scattered in all directions on an individual basis, if they were still alive. Thousands of the Naimans' yurts were in flames and the streets were covered with dead bodies. Since the north, east and south sides of the city were blocked by Temujin and Wang-Khan's coalition troops, most of the Naimans escaped into the western Altai Mountains. Buyiruk Khan of the Naimans crossed the Alay Mountains with only 2,000 of his defeated troops. Knowing this, Temujin set out to chase down Buyiruk Khan.

Victory is not a victory until it is complete.

That was Temujin's policy. After leaving Bogorchu and Jelme to handle the aftermath of the battle, Temujin began to follow Buyiruk Khan's footsteps. Kasar, Belgutai, Mukali and Boroqul were with him, along with 3,000 horse soldiers. Temujin crossed the Altai Mountains, which were filled with rough rock walls, steep hills, giant larches and fir trees, but were connected with gently sloped hills to the endless plain. Temujin could see a mid-sized, winding river that seemed to be originating from the Altai Mountains on his left side, flowing into the western horizon. The name of the river was Urunggu. Temujin noticed Buyiruk and his troops had passed along the riverside. Temujin followed their tracks for one day and one night. When Temujin and his troops had advanced about 350 miles from the Altai Mountains, two blue lakes, one big, one small, filled with lapping water appeared. They were the Kishil

Bashi Lakes, and Buyiruk and his 2,000 troops were camping there.

Temujin fell upon them immediately. Buyiruk's remaining troops were completely destroyed. Buyiruk would have never imagined Temujin would chase him so far. Now, he was running away, all by himself, toward the west. Temujin looked around and asked, "Who will chase him and bring me his head?"

Kasar stepped forward and said, "We don't need to chase him."

Kasar picked one of his arrows from his quiver and put it on his bow. After a deep breath, he drew his bow to its full extent and then let it go. The arrow flew in surprising speed toward the target, making a horrible sound, and lodged in Buyiruk's back. Temujin heard his dead body thud on the ground after he fell from his horse. Belgutai galloped to the site and cut his neck. Kasar's arrow was strong enough to make the arrowhead stick out two inches from his chest, even after piercing the leather armor. Belgutai, holding it by its hair, brought Buyiruk's head, which was still shedding blood. This was the last of Buyiruk Khan; he was an unlucky man.

CHAPTER FORTY

Sabrak, the Naimans' Best

One day, in Tayang Khan's huge golden tent, a banquet was being held in the presence of the khan and his official wife. The tent, which had a 400-person capacity, was often used for official conventions or large banquets. It was just one of the khan's many exclusive tents. On that day, they were enjoying a special performance of the women's dancing troupe and dwarves' circus team from Bukhara. At the northernmost part of the tent, the royal seats were arranged with two teakwood chairs luxuriously decorated with golden ornaments. Seated there was Tayang Khan and his official wife Gurbesu, who used to be his stepmother, and they were watching the show. All the khan's family members, chieftains of the clans and generals were watching the show in the seats neatly arranged in two rows along the east and west sides of the tent walls. There was a constant flow through the four doors of male and female slaves carrying silver plates stacked with the Naimans' rare cuisine and silver carafes filled with high-quality wine.

The audience kept on shouting in admiration of the dwarves' circus game and the tent was filled with shrieks of laughter. With a triangular crown decorated with pearls resting on her head and a purple silk manteau on her shoulder, Gurbesu, wearing heavy makeup on her face, was sitting on her chair with a tame leopard gently lying on the ground in front of her feet. The leopard occasionally raised its head, surprised by the roar of laughter, and looked around.

At this moment, a uniformed officer entered through the northeastern entrance and informed Tayang Khan of an urgent message that had just arrived. With a frown on his face, Tayang Khan received the letter on a sheepskin scroll. The letter, written in Uighur, was from the Naiman general Sabrak, who successfully escaped from the Temujin-Wang Khan coalition troops' attack. The key point of the message was to mobilize the troops immediately to save his brother, who was in danger. When the letter was written, Buyiruk was still alive. Tayang Khan's hands, holding the letter, were shaking and he had a look of extreme anxiety. He handed the letter over to Gurbesu, sitting next to him. Gurbesu glanced over it and handed it back to the uniformed officer, with no sign of concern.

"It would be a good thing for us if someone removed him. He should have been gone a long time ago."

When Gurbesu said this, the audience was bursting into laughter over and over again while watching the dwarves' group wrestling match. The performance lasted until late into the night without interruption.

Tayang Khan didn't take any action. At that time, his biggest enemy was his own elder brother, Buyiruk Khan, who was a threat to his khanship. Tayang Khan was not a man of the battlefield. He rather enjoyed entertainment and light hunting. He was a man with narrow mental vision and not much courage. Most of the important decisions were made by Gurbesu. Tayang Khan began to think that it would be just his luck if someone could remove his brother, just like Gurbesu said. Yet he wasn't sure of himself, so he shared his thoughts with Gurbesu, "I hope Temujin and Wang-Khan don't come for us."

Gurbesu glanced at him and spat, "Our 50,000 Naiman troops are invincible. Neither Temujin nor Wang-Khan can be our rival."

Since there was no response or help offered from Tayang Khan, Sabrak lamented and worried about the future of the Naimans. He belonged to Buyiruk, yet he was the Naimans' best general.

At the time of Inanch Khan, he had helped him and played a major role in building up the Naimans to become one of the most powerful nations on the plateau. He had everything a good general is supposed to have: leadership, good judgment, decisiveness, strategic power, valor, driving force, caring mind for his soldiers and self-defense skills like physical strength and good hands for handling weapons. However, he was an older soldier, one generation older than Temujin's.

He came out from the Altai Mountains, where he had been hiding, and gathered and regrouped the defeated Naiman troops.

Temujin and Wang-Khan left Soqok Lake side by side, with mountains of war booty. They were moving at a slow pace because of the numerous livestock they had taken, like cows, sheep and camels. After several days of marching, about 350 miles, they arrived at the western end of the Kangai Range, which lay to the east side of the Altai Mountains. It was an area called the Bayidarak Junction, where two small rivers originating from the Kangai Range, joined together: the Qachir Stream coming from due north and the Qara Seul River from the northeastern direction. The combined river of the two ran due south about fifty miles farther and then found its way into a medium-sized lake.

Temujin and Wang-Khan's coalition troops crossed the river. It was shallow, so the cavalry could cross without trouble, as could the cows and camels. However, it was too deep for sheep, so they had to build a temporary floating bridge. Each of the Mongol soldiers were carrying two sheepskin bags that they could use as life buoys, inflating them with air and tying the ends tightly. They used them to cross the river. They made a bridge by tying tens of thousands of them together and on top of them they built rafts made from logs the thickness of an adult's wrist.

After crossing the river, Temujin looked around and checked all the specific features of the land and the surroundings. That was an important job of the commander before he chose the camping ground.

Temujin could see the Kangai range, stretching from the northwest to the southeast, surrounding the potential campsite like a folding screen. Many mountain peaks of the Kangai range took on a scarlet hue from the late afternoon sunlight, and halfway up the mountains were thick forests of pine and fir trees. Temujin realized it was not a suitable area for troops to camp. In case of an enemy troop ambush from the forest, the Temujin-Wang Khan coalition troops would have to fight with the river to their back, which could be dangerous. Temujin gave an order to his troops to not dismount their horses or unload the packages.

Subedai and Chilaun were sent out scouting. They passed through a field of reeds that was covering a wide area between the mountain forests and the location where the coalition troops were waiting, and made an approach to the forests. When they reached a certain point, they dismounted their horses, hid them, and crawled up to where they had a better view. They could see, in the forests, numerous hidden horses and soldiers in Naiman uniforms moving around. Subedai and Chilaun looked at each other and nodded.

Temujin's sixth sense told him that they were Sabrak's troops. Temujin knew Sabrak had escaped, and he also knew that Sabrak was the only one who could ambush his troops in this particular spot, taking advantage of the natural environment.

Actually, Sabrak had gathered the defeated and scattered Naiman soldiers to form a new troop of 4,000 suicide commandos and was waiting at a point where the Temujin-Wang Khan coalition troops would surely pass by. He encouraged his soldiers, "The destiny of the Naimans depends on us. Let's fight to the last drop of our blood to defeat Temujin and Wang-Khan."

Temujin talked with Wang-Khan.

"My father lord, it is quite certain that Sabrak's troops are waiting to ambush us in the mountain forests. We should get ready for their attack."

Wang-Khan, sitting on a battlefield folding chair and putting his hands on the handle of his scimitar stuck in the ground, opened his eyes in wide surprise and said, "Sabrak is in the forest? How many of them? Don't you think we'd better hit them first?"

"No. They are hiding in the forests and we are exposed. Moreover, to attack them, we have to pass through the field of reeds, and it could be dangerous. If things don't go well for them, they can escape to the mountain. In addition, nobody knows what is in there. And, we'd have to fight with our back to the river. It could be very dangerous if we need to retreat."

This time, Jagambu, who was standing beside Wang-Khan, remarked, "Then how about crossing the river back before it gets dark?"

Temujin glanced at him and said, "That wouldn't be a good idea either. When half of our troops cross the river, Sabrak will attack us. It would also be dangerous."

At Temujin's remarks, everybody kept silent, just looking at each other. Temujin, Wang-Khan, Jagambu, Kasar and Nilka Senggum were the only ones in the meeting. Wang-Khan asked Temujin nervously, giving a bitter, perplexed look, "What would be the best choice at this point?"

Temujin explained his opinion clearly.

"Sabrak will surely attack us at daybreak tomorrow. We should not be here together. I will move my troops three miles to the north and wait there. When the battle starts, I will swiftly come down and attack Sabrak from the side. That will be the only way we can subdue him."

Wang-Khan, correcting his posture, as if his folding chair were too small for him, asked Temujin in a tricky manner, "Then, how about you stay here and I move to the north?"

Temujin answered without pause, "No, my lord, their target is you."

The sun had already set. Above the western horizon, the purple curtains were dropping down and the riverside was being hidden by the veil of gray darkness. Wang-Khan accepted Temujin's tactic. After leaving his firm request for Wang-Khan to build up many campfires, Temujin moved to the north with his troops. Arriving at a place about three miles from the original starting point, Temujin stationed his troops and let them take a break until daybreak, on their horses.

After Temujin left, Wang-Khan built up several dozen campfires in a row between his campsite and the forest area, making it as bright as daytime, as a warning. At this moment, Jagambu and Nilka Senggum entered Wang-Khan's tent. Senggum told his father, Wang-Khan, "Father, do you trust Temujin's words? How can he read an enemy general's mind like his own? He is surely tricking you. He will run away, instead of helping us. He is trying to weaken us. We'd better make a plan now, before it is too late."

With a frown on his face, Wang-Khan reproached his son, Nilka Senggum, "Why can't you trust Temujin? Without him, we might not be successful in this operation. We had better follow his advice."

Nevertheless, Nilka Senggum kept on insisting, and Jagambu joined in. Wang-Khan was a second-rate leader. He didn't have firm self-confidence. He would always look back on his decisions, second-guess himself and think he needed to reevaluate, then choose a different solution and confuse himself and his troops throughout the process.

At last, Wang-Khan pulled his troops out of there and headed for the Black Forest, his home base. The next morning, before daybreak, when the eastern sky above the Kangai Range began to change into a purplish blue, he gave the marching order to his troops. All the mountaintops of the Kangai Range began to stand out in silhouettes in the brightening light. All Temujin's soldiers slept on their horses.

Temujin headed for Wang-Khan's campsite. When Temujin arrived at a spot where he could see the campfires, which were still burning, he sent Jelme out as a scout. Some time later, Jelme came back and gave a report with a frustrated look, "There's nobody there! They all left! Wang-Khan's troops are not there!"

Temujin shook his head. Kasar, who was standing next to Temujin, remarked, "Wang-Khan is an unreliable man."

Temujin was enraged. Chewing his lips, Temujin murmured to himself, "They treated me like burnt offerings."

The Mongols used to handle their offerings very carefully when they were going to have their ancestors' memorial ceremonies, and yet, after the whole process, they tossed it away or stamped on it after covering it with soil. Temujin compared himself to these offerings.

Temujin turned his troops back immediately. It would be dangerous to stay there without Wang-Khan and there was no reason to, either. Temujin passed through the Etel Valley in the middle of the Kangai Range and stepped onto the Great Saari Plain.

Meanwhile, Sabrak was watching every move of the Temujin–Wang Khan coalition troops. He was very careful because he had to deal with 27,000 coalition troops against his 4,000. The night before, when Temujin's troops were on the move toward the north, parting from Wang Khan's troops, one of his men suggested, "Temujin is going north, leaving Wang-Khan. Let's hit Wang-Khan tonight."

Sabrak, smoothing his white, long beard, narrowed his eyes and remarked, "It could be a trick. They surely know that we are here."

He waited and his decision paid off. He confirmed that Wang-Khan and Temujin's troops had definitely split. Sabrak chased down Wang-Khan, because he knew he was the key figure of the invasion. Sabrak kept chasing Wang-Khan, and at last caught up with him in the Keraits' territory, near the Black Forest. Sabrak and his 4,000 commandos completely broke down Wang-Khan's defense line and pushed on. The Naimans killed numerous Keraits. It was genocidal. They even killed the babies, but not the women. They wanted to remove the Keraits from the earth completely. Over a period of two days, tens of thousands of dead bodies of the Keraits were strewn across the field.

CHAPTER FORTY-ONE

Wang-Khan Declares Temujin as His Successor

Wang-Khan was continuously pushed by the Naimans. As he was retreating, thousands of the Keraits who had fallen behind were killed by the Naiman soldiers each day. If things were to go on like that, the Keraits would surely be annihilated. Ten of Wang-Khan's veteran fighters had already lost their heads by Sabrak's scimitar. Wang-Khan had been pushed to the Telegetu River mouth, which was the source of the Kerulen River, and built up his last defense line there. Wang-Khan gave 5,000 cavalry to Katu, who was believed to be the best fighter in all of Wang-Khan's troops. The big-bodied Katu was a furious fighter and a master of the Mongol spear as well, which had both a long blade and a hook. Up until that time, nobody had survived an attack from his Mongol spear.

He drove his horse slowly to the middle point of the field, where two troops were facing each other. He was wearing a helmet and leather armor for protection and had a Mongol spear in his right hand and a round leather shield in his left. The Naiman soldiers were stunned and became tense, because one man from the Kerait side was drawing near with no sign of fear. When Katu reached the middle point, he shouted in a loud voice, "Sabrak! Come out! I know you are a veteran fighter. If you can beat me, you are the real one!"

Katu was challenging Sabrak to a duel. At these words, all the Naiman archers raised their bows in one motion and aimed at him. Sabrak raised his hand to stop his archers and stepped forward.

"That man wants to gamble. He is going to put 5,000 lives on his spear tip! What an idiot!"

After smoothing his long white beard, he drew his scimitar and approached him slowly. The two men stood facing each other, keeping sufficient distance between them. The air on the field was desert hot, yet it was infused with the coldness of death. Who will win this kind of duel? Will the one with physical strength and technical superiority in handling weapons win? Maybe, but the real indicator was spiritual power.

Katu shouted briefly as he spurred his horse and dashed toward Sabrak at full speed, with his spear tip pointing at Sabrak's heart. Sabrak also galloped toward Katu with his scimitar in his hand. On the plain, two horses were approaching each other at a horrible speed, with their golden tails on their backs.

The soldiers on both sides were watching this breathlessly. The tip of Katu's spear was aimed exactly at Sabrak's heart. Until that time, there was no known mistake in Katu's career.

What happened after the two horses had passed by each other, so closely they almost touched, was that one man's head was cut off his body and thudded to the ground, making a short, dull sound. The body without the head stayed on the horse for a while and then, finally, fell off.

From the Naiman side, thunderous cheers burst out. Sabrak, after cleaning the blood off his scimitar with a cloth he was keeping, sheathed his scimitar and returned leisurely. It was crystal clear that the Keraits were completely destroyed, for they had lost their commander. Five thousand dead bodies were scattered around on the field. Sabrak pushed on. Half the Kerait people and Nilka Senggum's four wives and nine children had fallen into Sabrak's hands. Wang-Khan was pushed into a corner. He began to regret that he had separated from Temujin. He also realized that Temujin was the only one who could save him. Wang-Khan dispatched urgent messengers to Temujin, who was stationed at the Saari Plain.

> *I lost half of my people and property to Sabrak.*
> *The fate of me and my people hang by a thread.*
> *I am begging my foster son, Temujin, for help.*
> *Please, send me the four kulugs,*
> *Since they are the only ones who can reverse the situation.*
> *I am giving my pledge to my foster son, Temujin,*
> *That you will be my first son.*
> *This is my truth,*
> *And if I don't keep my word,*
> *I shall be bled like this.*

Wang-Khan ordered his man to bring a small wooden container. He drew his dagger from his waist, cut his little finger and collected the blood in the container. He put the lid on it, wrapped it tight and gave it to the messengers. What Wang-Khan meant through the message was that if Temujin gave a helping hand to him and his people, he would entrust the khanship of the Keraits to Temujin one day. Wang-Khan used to say to himself, "My siblings are wicked. My only son is a useless incompetent. I am a man of mature years now. Someday, just like all the others, I have to go onto the high hill. Who will take care of my children and my people when I am gone?"

The four kulugs Wang-Khan asked for were Bogorchu, Mukali, Boroqul and Chilaun. When the coalition troops attacked Buyiruk Khan's ordu, Wang-Khan had a chance to see the four men's outstanding valor. He was very impressed with them. Later, he bestowed the title of kulug, which meant war hero, upon them.

Wang-Khan's messengers arrived at Temujin's camp on the Saari Plain the following morning. The two messengers galloped all through the night. After receiving Wang-Khan's message, Temujin pondered a while in front of the wooden container. Then, he ordered all his troops to move. Temujin immediately dispatched the four kulugs with 4,000 troops. Bogorchu was the commander of the vanguard. Temujin followed them slowly with Kasar and the rest of the 3,000 troops. When Bogorchu and his vanguard of 4,000 arrived at the Ulaan Qusu, which was the last mountain pass connected to Wang-Khan's base campsite, a fierce battle was going on between the Naimans and the remaining eraits. Wang-Khan seemed to be doomed. Nilka Senggum fell down from his horse after his horse had been shot by Naiman arrows, and was about to be captured by the Naiman soldiers. Temujin's troops saved him.

Temujin stood face to face with the Naimans. Temujin took a look around the enemy front line and carefully examined the situation.

"I wouldn't allow my soldiers to have man-to-man combat with them. We will lose too many. They are afraid of nothing. They are suicidal."

Temujin launched an attack called "Operation Porcupine." How do you catch a porcupine? You need a long stick. If you try to pick it up with your own hand, you will get hurt. Temujin and Wang-Khan's combined troops surrounded Sabrak's troops on three sides. Then their archers showered arrows on the Naimans. If they were attacked, they retreated, always leaving some distance between them. Temujin used only archery units. Half a day later, the Naimans showed signs of exhaustion. At that time Temujin launched a full-scale attack. All of the Naimans were dead. Among them, seven or eight survivors tried to escape, but they didn't make it. They became the targets of Temujin's archery unit. The field was strewn with 4,000 dead Naiman soldiers. Temujin's soldiers checked the dead Naimans one by one to confirm they were dead and to pick up the weapons. They found a body of a man with a long white beard who had several arrows in his body. He was Sabrak.

Temujin gave an order to take good care of his dead body. Temujin removed all the arrows lodged in his body, cleaned up his face, put a little makeup on him and buried him on the high hill.

> *Even though he was an enemy general,*
> *He was an outstanding warrior,*
> *And a man of strong will and firm conviction.*
> *His good name and legacy shall remain.*

Those were Temujin's words at the burial site. Temujin and Wang-Khan returned to the Black Forest, side by side. Wang-Khan had retrieved most of his lost people and livestock. Nilka Senggum was reunited with his wives and children. Several days later, Wang-Khan gave a banquet. In his golden tent, all of Temujin's and Wang-Khan's high-ranking officers and warriors got together.

At the beginning of the banquet, Wang-Khan, sitting next to Temujin, raised his heavy body and said, after looking around the whole assembly of those present, "In the past, my anda, Yesugei Bagatur, gave me a warm helping hand and saved me and my people. Now, his son Temujin has done the same thing and saved me and my people again. So, for two generations, we have received their kindness and favor. Who in the world gives warm helping hands to save our Kerait people, risking their lives, for the period of two generations? I have already reached a mature age. Someday, I will have to go onto the high hill like all the others. When that moment comes, my soul will be happy to see our Keraits and the Kyat Mongols together, enjoying common prosperity and glory. Now I am declaring that Temujin will be my first son. Now I am very happy and feel very comfortable to have two sons, Temujin and Nilka. May the heaven and the earth remember my words."

What Wang-Khan meant by going onto the high hill was to die and to be buried on the high hill. At that time, the Mongols had a custom to bury noble men on a high hill.

After these words, Wang-Khan picked up his golden goblet and proposed a toast. All those present, the Kyat Mongols and the Keraits, got to their feet and raised their goblets high, celebrating the new formal relations between them. By Wang-Khan's declaration, Temujin was now the first successor in line to the Kerait throne.

However, there was a man with a gloomy look, who stood up unwillingly and raised his goblet hesitantly. He was Nilka Senggum. He couldn't be happy because he was relegated to the second in line, when he had been the first. Temujin and Wang-Khan, together, made a written agreement. The main points were to help each other and move together in wartime and, most importantly, they should never make any decision related to moving troops until they faced each other and talked.

The latter part was requested by Temujin. After this, Temujin and Wang-Khan's relationship was strongly reinforced and their combined power began to shake the power balance on the Mongolian Plateau.

Sam Djang

His epic novel, *Genghis Khan, the World Conqueror*, was written after eight years of intensive research. During those eight years, he made a number of trips to Mongolia, Russia, China and related countries. He interviewed numerous people in those countries and read hundreds of articles and rare books in the libraries of Mongolia and beyond. Sam Djang testifies that his book, *Genghis Khan, the World Conqueror*, was written in the form of a historical novel, and yet 90 percent of its contents are based on the true story. Also, he believes that his book covers many facts that the majority of past historians failed to see due to their lack of understanding of the unique cultural, social, political, historical and geographical background of the people of Genghis Khan.